Keeping Score

Keeping Score

EMMA O'DEA

Keeping Score

Copyright © 2026 by Emma O'Dea

This is a work of fiction. Names, characters, places, and incidents are either the product of the author's imagination or are used fictitiously. Any resemblance to actual persons, living or dead, events, or locales is entirely coincidental.

Cover design by Megan Jayne Designs
Interior design by Alt 19 Creative

When she turned to go home,
She heard the echoes of new words
"May your heart remain breakable
But never by the same hand twice"
And even louder:
"without your past,
you could never have arrived-
so wondrously and brutally,
By design or some violent, exquisite happenstance
…here."

TAYLOR SWIFT

CHAPTER ONE

Maggie

There was something different about him. I could tell from the moment I met him that he wasn't going to be like the others. So many of them didn't care, not really+. They sought me out because of some suspected obligation, or maybe to avoid being thought of as a 'bad guy' if they didn't make some attempt.

But hey, if they showed up for a few meetings, put in some type of effort for a couple of weeks before realizing it was going to be a longer, more time-consuming process than they thought, then they could walk away with a guilt-free conscience, telling themselves, at least they tried.

If you could call it that.

But this man?

It was clear from the darkness beneath his eyes and the hollowness to his very presence that he lived and breathed for his children.

That the past few weeks without them had haunted him more than any words could express. The same could not be said for so many of the ones who came to me before him.

"Mr. Reilly?" I asked, staring at the man in the chair outside my office, whose face was cradled in his hands.

His head popped up, back straightening, as if he were ashamed to be caught in a moment of human vulnerability.

I couldn't say I didn't know the feeling.

"Ms. Brynn." He stood to his feet immediately, straightening himself out.

I could tell that he'd tried his best to look presentable for our meeting, with his button-up shirt that was in dire need of an iron, and the trousers that might've fit him a few years ago, but were now past the point of being considered 'snug.'

And to top the whole look off, a worn-out, raggedy scrap of a Red Sox cap sat atop his head, as if it were such a staple to who he was he might've forgotten to take it off.

Yes, he was different. I could tell.

"Hi," I held my hand out to him, "it's nice to officially meet you after all the emails."

"Thank you for meeting with me." He stood, grasping my hand in a firm shake.

He was thanking me—and he meant it. That alone was a good sign. So many men who came through here carried a quiet resentment toward me, as if I were the one keeping them captive for these custody meetings, rather than them choosing to give up a few hours of their week to fight for their children.

"Come into my office, we can talk about your case there."

I held the glass door open, gesturing for him to go first. He hesitated, as if he might have some notion that a lady should enter first, before heading inside.

"I know we've discussed the basics of your case during our phone call, but I'd like to go over it again, if that's okay."

I smiled, trying to convey to him that he could relax, ease the tension set in his shoulders. I was here to be his ally, after all. I was fighting for his side.

"Is that your daughter?" he asked, knee bouncing as he nodded towards a photo on my desk.

I looked down, smiling at the picture of the little blonde clutching a piece of watermelon with a wide grin.

"My niece," I corrected. "Lily."

"She's cute."

"She takes after her aunt." I laughed.

It was a lie. She didn't look like me at all—except for those green eyes. The Brynn eyes.

Besides that, she'd managed to come out as the perfect combination of both her parents, though I still had hope she'd inherit my sparkling personality, at the very least.

Mr. Reilly ran a hand over his baseball cap, and by the faraway look in his eyes, I wondered if he was thinking of his own children.

I cleared my throat.

"So, just to recap our prior conversation, could you tell me a little bit about your situation?"

"Sure," he nodded, "uh, well, my wife—shit, I mean my ex—well, the divorce isn't finalized yet, in fact, it's not even started, but—" He let out an exhale. "I'm sorry, a lot has changed really fast. I'm still trying to wrap my head around it all."

"That's fine," I assured him, "but you're anticipating this separation between the two of you to be… permanent?"

He swallowed. "Looks like it."

"Tell me about the kids," I said, typing a few lines onto the document I'd opened for his case. "What's the custody arrangement now?"

"There isn't one." He stared at me with pain in his eyes. "She's not letting me anywhere near them."

I nodded, having heard it all before.

"Is there a history of drug use? Criminal charges?"

"Jesus, no," his eyes widened. "We were fine. We were just a normal family until—" He paused, lowering his eyes to the floor, "until I screwed up."

"Can you elaborate on that?" I furrowed my brows.

"I'm not proud of it," he stated, "in fact, it's probably the worst thing I've ever done in my life, but I cheated. Just once. But it was enough to get me sitting here in your office."

I kept my face neutral. I wasn't here to judge. I was a professional.

"Anyway, my wife—ex-wife- kicked me out as soon as she found out. "Hasn't let me back home or near the kids since then. That was about three weeks ago, now."

I typed.

"I know—" He started with a faltering voice, "I know that what I did was unforgivable. But I'm not a bad man. I deserve to lose my wife, I know that. But not my children." He choked up. "Not my babies."

He looked away, scratching at his eye as if there were a speck of dirt irritating it, rather than emotion.

I paused, fighting the urge to assure this man that everything would be okay. I knew better than to make promises like that to people.

But I was going to try.

"I understand," I told him, meeting his tear-filled eyes. "Right now, it's about showing the court that you're capable of providing a good life for your children. You're employed, I assume?"

He nodded. "I work in construction. I've been with the Local 223 since I got started working."

Good job. Consistent pay. Great benefits.

I could tell by the calloused hands he kept wringing that this man was a hard worker. The courts liked that. It was all too easy for them to deny custody to someone on account of being unable to provide for their children.

Besides, this guy seemed like a fighter. Five minutes with him and I could already tell he would go to ends of the earth for his kids.

It caused something in my heart to ache. I wanted to help him. Needed to, even.

Kids shouldn't have to grow up without their father. No matter what type of relationship their parents might have.

"Okay," I told him, adding a few more lines to the document before turning my focus back to him. "Here's what we're going to do. We're going to file a petition for temporary visitation rights, and in the meantime, I suggest you sign up for parenting classes or enroll in therapy, maybe? The court loves to see that stuff. It proves you're willing to go above and beyond."

"I am." He assured me, "I'll do whatever it takes."

"In regards to the mother," I said, not wanting to step on his toes by referring to her as his ex, when clearly he hadn't reconciled himself to that fact yet. "I would keep contact limited. Nothing that could escalate the situation further. You don't want to give her any ammunition to use against you."

He nodded, face furrowing as if the enormity of the situation overwhelmed him.

"It wouldn't do me much good anyway. Not like she's answering my calls." His knee bobbed as he spoke. "I never thought I'd be sitting in an office for this reason."

I could tell that he meant it.

Most people went into marriage with the best of intentions, never imagining that they'd end up part of that horrible statistic that haunted the back of my mind.

I understood what so many people didn't. Parents were human. They made mistakes. They screwed up like any other person. It didn't mean they didn't deserve forgiveness or second chances.

"Don't worry," I went against my better judgment by saying. "It's going to be okay."

I said it because I wanted it to be. Because I had faith that I was capable of making that happen for him. Not only because I had a gut feeling about it—I did, and was seldom wrong when it came to those—but there was more to it than that.

Because any man who put the time into fighting for his children? That was a man who deserved to be in their lives.

When his eyes met mine, I knew without him even having to say it: He was putting his faith in me.

And I didn't plan on screwing up.

CHAPTER TWO

Brody

"There's my pretty girl," I called out, watching as Maggie bounded out the door of her law office.

I was perched across the street, in my usual spot. Lately, I'd taken up residency on the steps of a brownstone I had recently learned belonged to an old man.

Mr. Waterman, as it turned out, was less than pleased that I'd chosen his steps to spend my evenings while waiting for my lovely girlfriend to get off work.

Loitering, I believe he called it.

Well, lucky for me, my girlfriend's a hotshot lawyer who would save my ass if the old man decided to take it to court, so *ha*.

Maggie rolled her eyes when she saw me—or at least, I imagined she did based on the shadowy glimpse I got of her as she passed under the streetlamp.

It was late, and this bourgeois area of the city had almost certainly settled in for the night. Us, though?

We had a whole night ahead of us.

"Hi," I grinned, looking her up and down. "You look hot."

She scrunched her nose at me.

"I'm in work clothes. I shouldn't look hot. I should look professional."

"Well, I have a thing for corporate girls, so I'm biased," I said, settling an arm around her shoulders.

"*Girls?*" She narrowed her eyes at me. "Plural?"

I flicked her nose.

"How long is it going to take for you to remember you're my one and only?"

She let out a laugh, but even if she wouldn't say it, I knew the assurance settled something inside her.

"Where are we going?" she asked, letting me lead her down the street.

"Oh, I know a place," I smirked.

"That never ends well."

"Come on," I scoffed, affronted. "Have a little faith in me."

"Last time you planned date night, it was bowling on senior night." She shot me a glare.

Maggie wouldn't let me live that down anytime soon.

"Hey, I like a quiet atmosphere!" I held my hands up. "Sue me!"

"I could," she teased.

"On account of?" I asked, directing us toward the corner where my car was parked.

"On account of you not letting your beautiful girlfriend pick where she wants to go on her very special night." She frowned at me, but let me hold the car door open for her anyway.

"Special night?" I whipped my head back dramatically. "What's tonight?"

Her face paled, mouth opening and shutting in disbelief.

I threw my head back and laughed.

"You have major trust issues, babe," I told her, leaning in to kiss her beautifully pouty lips. "I'm not going to let you down. I promise."

She relaxed, breathing out in relief, before her hand shot out to lightly smack my arm.

"Don't do that," she ordered. "It's not funny."

"It's a little funny," I told her before shutting her door and making my way to the driver's seat.

"I knew you were lying. *You're* dressed up, so we must be going somewhere."

We were, but she'd just have to wait and see.

Even though the thought of waiting for anything made Maggie practically combust on the spot, I was willing to risk it tonight. The payoff would be worth it.

As soon as I turned the keys in the ignition, the audiobook I'd been listening to started playing. I turned it off in mortification, looking at her sheepishly.

"Are you listening to *Fourth Wing*?" Maggie giggled, sending me deeper into the depths of humiliation.

"I just wanted to see what all the hype was about!" I defended.

"And the verdict is?"

"It's pretty good," I admitted under my breath, eyes focused on the road ahead of me.

She laughed, scrolling down my Spotify until she found the playlist she'd created titled "Maggie," while I drove us to the destination that I hoped would be the backdrop for her perfect night.

I parked a little ways down the street from our destination, just to throw her off my tracks until the last possible minute.

I opened the door, lending her my hand so she could climb onto the sidewalk before grabbing the bag I'd packed in the backseat.

"Newbury Street," Maggie noted, eyes taking in our surroundings. "Are we going on a shopping spree?"

"Not tonight," I told her, feeling my palms start to sweat a bit with anticipation.

Maggie was so smart. She saw every move coming. It was hard to ever *really* surprise her.

But tonight, I think I had her.

"Then, what are we—" She paused when she saw the restaurant I stopped in front of. "You *didn't!*"

I shot her a sly grin.

"Are we finally eating at Contessa?" she gaped at the Newbury Hotel, housing one of the city's most prestigious restaurants—one Maggie had been dying to eat at as long as I've known her.

"It's impossible to get reservations here!" she squealed, jumping up and down as she stared between me and the entrance.

Yeah, it was. Which is why I had to book the damn place a year in advance—not to mention the time spent coordinating everything else. But the pure bliss on her face told me it had all been worth it.

"You want to go in?" I asked.

"I'm not dressed for Contessa!" she said, face paling in realization. "I can't go in dressed like a *lawyer!*"

"I packed the essentials." I held up the bag I'd packed for her. "Change of clothes. Perfume. Makeup."

"Ah!" she squealed again, reaching out to grab it. "But did you remember—"

"Your facial wipes? Yep, babe. I did."

"You perfect man!" She leaped into my arms, letting me spin her around as people maneuvered around us.

"Come on," I laughed, setting her back down. "If we're late, it'll be another year before we get the chance to eat there."

We went in, Maggie taking off to change in the hotel lobby bathroom while I shot off a text to Liam.

BRODY: About to come up!!!!

Liam's response appeared before my eyes.

LIAM:

I shook my head at his lackluster response. He was a man of few words. That translated to text as well.

But hey, at least he was using emojis now. That was major progress as far as I was concerned. I much preferred being thumbed-up by Liam than the ominous "Ok." I was used to getting.

Which was a total scam, because last time I peeked over his shoulder at practice while he was texting, I saw his thread with Cassie filled with not only dozens of hearts, but kissy faces and heart-eyes galore.

Maggie's reappearance had my head snapping up, and I pocketed my phone before she could look at the message.

"Damn, Mags." I looked her up and down, admiring every curve emphasized by that tight black dress. "You're stunning."

"And you're incredibly handsome." Her hands fisted my tie. "And I'm incredibly hungry, so how about we go try the food that every big name in Boston has been bragging about for years."

I nodded, leading us toward the elevator that would bring us up to the rooftop restaurant. Lacing her hand in mine, I felt her energy vibrating through the air.

The doors started to open, and I felt it happen in slow motion. Would she be disappointed? Should I have done something bigger? Damn, I probably should've seen if I could book Ariana Grande or something to make an appearance.

But it was too late now.

The elevator doors opened, fully revealing the rooftop restaurant and every single one of our friends and family screaming in unison,

"Surprise!"

Maggie dropped the bag she'd been holding and screamed back—a scream of joy, I realized with relief.

She looked at me with wide, awestruck eyes.

"You did this?"

I pulled her in, pressing a kiss against her temple.

"Happy birthday, Mags."

CHAPTER THREE

Maggie

irthdays had always been special to me.

It was the one day a year where I could bask in my slightly self-absorbed tendencies and force everyone around me to celebrate my existence.

But usually, if I wanted something really special, I had to plan it out myself. My mom tried. But her idea of a good time was a supermarket birthday cake and a few balloons.

My idea of a good time? Well, it looked something like the scene in front of me. And since Brody had come into the picture, I'd never had to worry about planning my own birthday.

He just *got* me in a way I didn't think a person could. Hence, the perfect party.

"I don't even know how you did this, but I love you for it," I told him, staring out at Boston's hottest restaurant now reserved solely for the occasion of my birthday party.

"Did I surprise you?" Brody leaned over to ask, wide, eager eyes pinned on me.

I stared into the dimly lit room filled with all the people I loved as the lights of the city glittered behind them. The looming arched windows set the backdrop of the city I loved so much, filling me with more emotion than I knew what to do with.

There was a table in the corner stacked with gift bags, a banner that read *Happy Birthday, Maggie!*, and balloons shaped like the number thirty floating all around the room.

"You did," I confirmed with a laugh. "An impossible feat, might I add."

"Go on," he gestured toward the crowd. "Go be the birthday princess."

He didn't have to tell me twice. I bounded into the crowd, ready to throw myself into a night of dancing and socializing while a DJ filled the room with my favorite songs.

I had my obligatory conversations with all the guests I passed by before rushing over to the pair lingering at a candlelit table.

Even in a room full of friends, I couldn't help but have my favorites I wanted to spend the night with.

"I can't even believe you're awake right now!" I wrapped my arms around Cassie when she stood up from her chair.

"Do you think I'd sleep through your birthday?" She laughed, swaying side to side as we hugged.

I saw her regularly—probably more than any normal person saw their sister-in-law—but before she was my brother's wife, she was my best friend. And the thing about best friends? You never get tired of seeing them.

She let me go, letting me turn my sights on my older brother, ready to reward him with a dramatic squeeze of his own.

He still wasn't much of a hugger—his wife and daughter being the only exceptions to that sentiment—making it all the more hilarious to force him into one.

"Happy birthday, Mags," he said, giving me a sideways hug that he tried to make last longer than half a second.

"Did Lily not want to celebrate her aunt's birthday?" I teased, wondering who had my niece, considering both her parents and grandmother were here.

"She's with a babysitter," Liam said through gritted teeth, taking a peek over at Cassie's strained face. "Let's not talk about it."

"I told you, I'm fine," Cassie attempted breezily. "People get babysitters all the time! I'm not freaking out about it!"

I knew Cassie well enough to say with confidence: she was totally freaking out.

"She'll be fine, Cass," I assured her, watching Brody approach us.

The crowd parted for him, and I swear, everyone in the room was probably halfway in love with him at first sight. It wasn't just that he was handsome—he was, with his dimples and puppy-dog eyes—but more than that, he embodied an easiness that few possessed. He was the type of person to make you smile, even when it was the last thing you felt like doing.

Maybe that's why Liam kept him around as a best friend. Brody was capable of balancing out my brother's grumpiness like no one else I'd ever met.

"Who will be fine?" Brody slipped an arm around me, making my stomach feel like champagne bubbles from his proximity.

"Lily," I told him at the same time Liam said, "New topic."

Cassie exhaled and stepped closer against Liam's side.

"Oh, yeah," Brody nodded. "That kid's a trooper, just like Uncle Brody. Last week, she ate an acorn. It was hilarious."

"She *what?*"

"Shut up, Brody," Liam growled, "before you give my wife a heart attack."

"Don't stress, Cassie," Brody said. "It was just the little hat on top. Not the whole thing."

Liam exhaled the weariest sigh while Cassie let out a whimper.

I pinched Brody's arm, trying to convey that if he kept talking, we'd be revoked of our babysitting privileges.

And as much as kids freaked me out, I genuinely enjoyed spending time with Lily. I imagined it would be different, being stuck with a kid for twenty-four hours a day. Being an aunt was definitely more my speed.

Way less opportunity for me to screw her up that way.

"Let's go sit down," I suggested. "I might have to order one of every-thing on the menu if this is the only time in my life we'll get to eat here."

Liam and Cassie looked grateful for the suggestion, while Brody looked at me with an expression that asked, *What did I say?*

It wasn't him. Liam and Cassie had just gotten neurotic since having a kid. Don't get me wrong, they were fantastic parents—they just took that position *very* seriously.

Given each of their individual personalities, I couldn't say I was entirely surprised by the development.

Brody and I, though? We didn't have that type of lifestyle in us. We liked to have fun. Date nights and vacations. Staying up till the sun rose on days we didn't have work. Spending Sunday afternoons drinking on the beach.

We were as far removed from the life Cassie and Liam were living as two people could possibly get, but that's how we liked it.

I had enough responsibility in my work life without the added pressure of having to be a parent on top of it all.

"How's your birthday been so far, Mags?" Cassie asked, sitting across from me at the table.

"You know," I shrugged. "Work. Coffee. More work."

"I can't believe you didn't take the day off!" Cassie exclaimed. "Turning thirty is a big deal!"

"How would you know?" I teased. "You're still a baby."

"Hey, I'm only six months younger than you," Cassie protested with a laugh. "And anyway, I have wisdom beyond my years," she said, batting her eyes dramatically.

Liam snorted.

"You're right, Cass," Brody nodded. "You give the best advice. Thanks for reminding me about renewing my registration, by the way. Apparently, it was like six months overdue."

I rolled my eyes while Liam asked,

"How did you not already know that, man?"

This was the way we always were.

The four of us had become a unit over the last few years, in a way I'd never had before, and I couldn't imagine ever living without it.

It was funny. You'd think setting my best friend up with my brother would make them both more distant, but actually, it sort of jump-started my relationship with my brother again.

I saw him more now than I had since we were kids. I don't know what miracle Cassie had worked on him, but I wasn't complaining.

And with Liam's help, Cassie had made some insane progress of her own, though she still carried a few scars from childhood. There were some conditionings that took longer to escape from.

I saw it now, in the way her back went rigid every time her phone buzzed. She was always expecting it to be some emergency text from the babysitter saying—I don't know—that the house burned down? That Lily, in all her three-year-old capability, ran away? That an earthquake affecting only the area surrounding Liam and Cassie's house destroyed their home?

If you could dream it, Cassie could worst-case-scenario catastrophize it. I couldn't say I didn't understand where it was coming from. She was still always waiting for the other shoe to drop. But Liam was helping her through it. And luckily, things had been calm for them the last few years. They were happy.

But old habits die hard, I guess.

"I should call the babysitter." Cassie bit her lip, looking over to my brother.

"Nope," he said, laying his hand on top of hers as she reached for her phone. "Everything's fine, baby."

"Okay." She nodded. "You're right."

While they talked, I checked my phone again, the way I'd done all day.

It was stupid, waiting for a birthday text from my dad. He probably didn't know it was today. It wasn't his fault—dads were notorious for having bad memories. They forgot things all the time—birthdays, anniversaries, holidays. It didn't mean they didn't care.

Besides, he'd been gone for most of my birthdays, so the date wouldn't really have stuck out in his brain. It was only the last few years we'd been back in contact, so it was too much to expect him to remember some random date.

Still, I felt that familiar pang of disappointment when I didn't have any notification from him.

"Maggie!" my mother's voice appeared right behind me.

I let out a shriek of surprise, shoving my phone away before she could see whose text thread I'd been in.

I'd made a point over the last few years that I'd been seeing him to *never* reference him in front of my mother. Liam barely tolerated the subject, but my mother would absolutely blow a gasket over it. She'd always been fragile when it came to him.

"Hi, Mom," I said, standing up to give her the hug I knew she was coming over for.

"Look at my big girl," she said, shaking me side to side. "Thirty years old! I can't believe how fast time goes."

"Mom—" I tried to pull away.

"Just you wait," she pointed at Liam and Cassie, "one day they're babies, the next they're a fully grown woman. And no one warns you how fast it goes by."

Cassie's lip quivered, and I couldn't help but laugh. My mom knew better than to pull on Cassie's heartstrings in public.

"Look at everything you accomplished for yourself. A successful career, a loving partner. I'm so proud of you, Maggie."

I wanted to ask her why. It wasn't like she had anything to do with those things.

She hadn't wanted me to be a lawyer. *She* cautioned me against dating one of Liam's teammates. Everything I had, I'd done on my own.

But I wasn't about to get into it with her. Not on my birthday.

Before I had to fumble for a way to interact with my mother in a way that didn't make me lose my mind, Brody stepped in.

"You and me both, Diane," he joked, slinging an arm around my shoulders. "This girl's a gift to society."

"And you," my mom turned her attention on him, just like he must've known she would, "arranging all this? All the time it must've taken you—"

I mouthed a thank you at him for the escape he'd given me while my mom continued to talk his ear off. He winked, giving me the go-ahead to make a break for it before turning his full attention to her.

He was good that way. Always willing to take one for the team.

"I need you," I said, pulling Cassie up from her chair.

"For what?"

"Don't question the birthday girl, Cass," I instructed. "Just do as she says."

Cassie laughed, relenting as I pulled her toward the dance floor where the chorus of Pink's *Raise Your Glass* was booming.

I laughed as Cassie tried and failed to dance like a normal person, but God help her, she tried.

"Just relax," I said, grabbing her arms and moving her to the rhythm. "It's supposed to be fun."

"It is fun," she lied badly. "I'm vibing."

Friends from all of my different circles surrounded us, forming one big messy group of girls with nothing in common, but somehow we made it work.

I couldn't believe Brody had done this. Gotten everyone here together like this, for me.

There were people here I hadn't even thought he would think to invite, but not for the first time, he had gone above and beyond for *me*.

After a while, I heard his voice behind us saying to Cassie,

"Mind if I steal my girl?"

Cassie smiled at him, gesturing for him to go ahead, before slipping off into the crowd—no doubt to go find her husband, who was probably hiding in a corner somewhere.

"Having fun?" he murmured into my hair, joining in a dance with me as if it were as natural as breathing.

Cassie was my best friend, and always would be.

But Brody? We fit like puzzle pieces together, in a way I never thought I could with someone.

He understood me. Could predict what I wanted, needed—before I even knew it myself.

He was so much more than just my boyfriend.

He was my best friend.

"Any special birthday wishes?" His voice was low in my ear.

I smirked at him, shaking my head.

"Uh-uh," I tsked. "You know the rule. If you say it out loud, it won't come true."

"Then think about it as hard as you can, because it's time to blow out the candles."

I spun in the direction he was staring, seeing a group of waiters carrying over the most elaborate cake I'd ever seen in my life.

The crowd gathered around me, filling the room with the chorus of "Happy Birthday" as I took in every detail of the night around me.

Friends. Family. Food. Love.

There was nothing more I could've asked for.

And when it was time to make that birthday wish, I had one thought echoing in my head:

I wish that everything could stay like this forever.

And then I blew the candles out.

Five Years Ago

I hadn't even seen him at first.

There had been one thing on my mind when I burst into the locker room that night: a mission to complete. And I knew it wouldn't be an easy one, considering how much I was asking of someone who gave so little.

I wasn't blaming Liam for that. I never could. Not after I'd seen the way the world had treated him since he entered the public eye.

They'd dehumanized him, sexualized him, made him into some caricature of himself that was far less appealing than my real, flesh-and-blood brother.

He did his job and played damn well for our city, and all he asked for in return was privacy.

And here I was, coming in to ask him to give that up.

Only temporarily, I justified.

I wouldn't have asked if it were anyone else. But I loved Cassie as much as I loved Liam, and I didn't trust her in anyone's care but his.

20

For all his flaws, he was good. In his heart and mind, he was good.

And once he set his eyes on Cassie, he'd be as softened by her as everyone was. She had that effect on people, and the funny thing was—I didn't even think she knew it.

And even though my brother had higher defenses than a national-security prison, if anyone had a shot at breaking through them, it would be Cassie.

He would take care of her, I was sure of it.

It was just getting him to agree to it that was going to be the problem.

So, I launched into the story, preying on the sympathy factor that most humans with a heart would experience after hearing the way my best friend had been treated by her long-term boyfriend.

Liam, seemingly unimpressed, apparently wasn't the only one listening to me air Cassie's dirty laundry.

"Oh, that blows," a voice called from the background, alerting me to the fact that my brother and I weren't the only ones in the locker room.

I turned, and there he was.

I fought the urge to widen my eyes at the sight of him, standing there with freshly showered hair and puppy-dog brown eyes.

He was attractive, but so many of the hockey boys were. It didn't mean anything. I was immune to a pretty face. Because I knew that it never really meant anything. In fact, the more beautiful the boys were, the bigger the asshole they usually turned out to be.

Still, I couldn't resist a good banter.

"Right?" I grinned at him, taking the opportunity to give him the quickest of look-overs.

He was tall. Not as tall as Liam, but taller than most guys. And he was handsome. In that department, he was definitely above average.

I turned, determined to refocus my attention back to the task at hand. I opened my mouth to speak when Liam's teammate's voice beat me to the punch.

"Like I said, girls love dickheads."

"What?" I spun to face him again.

Did he say that because he was a dickhead and knew from experience? God, I hoped not.

Why do I hope not? It doesn't matter if he is or isn't. I'm never going to see him again.

But when he blushed—really and genuinely blushed—I knew with a profound certainty that this boy I didn't know might be many things, but a dickhead was not one of them.

"Nothing," he responded quickly, seemingly shy that I even noticed him at all. "Forget I said anything."

Yeah, that won't be happening.

I went through the motions with Liam, finishing the conversation until he finally relented, and I left without sparing the beautiful boy so much as a second glance.

But that didn't mean I forgot him.

Not even close.

CHAPTER FOUR

Brody

"**D**raw four, asshole!" Maggie cackled, slamming down a card against the floor between us.

I stared down open-mouthed at the cursed image in front of me. Those four little colorful rectangles that Maggie *somehow* never seemed to have a shortage of during every round of Uno.

If I loved her less, I might've called her out for mixing the deck in her favor, which I *knew* she did on occasion.

She really hated to lose.

"Margaret Brynn, you take that back right now," I protested, trying to balance my already full hand of cards. "Using a draw four card right now is evil. Even for you."

"Nope." She shook her head, leaning forward to hand me the next four cards from the deck.

If normal Maggie was competitive, drunk Maggie was a demon training for the Olympics of Hell.

"I don't know why I agreed to play Uno with you," I said, throwing my cards down in forfeit. "It never ends well for me."

"Because it's my birthday," she reminded me *again*. "And you have to do what I say."

It was a good thing I'd grown up with three sisters, because a lesser-trained man might've crumbled when encountering the drunk, diva energy of a birthday girl.

"Your birthday ended three hours ago," I said, looking out the window at the pitch-black sky. "But nice try."

"If we haven't gone to sleep yet," she reasoned, "then it still counts."

"Then maybe we should go to sleep." I leaned across the floor to pluck the cards from her hands.

"Sore loser," she said through a yawn.

I pulled her to her feet, planting a kiss on the top of her head to ease the blow of her bedtime punishment.

The apartment was trashed, but I figured that was a problem for Morning Us. Or, I guess, Afternoon Us—since judging by the way Maggie stumbled to the bedroom, I figured there was no way she'd be getting up before noon.

"Can you set the alarm for seven thirty?" she mumbled, throwing the duvet back to crawl into bed.

I laughed at the request, earning a scowl from Maggie.

"What, are you serious?"

"Why would I joke about alarm clocks?" Maggie groaned, slinking down beneath the covers.

"What would you possibly need to get up that early for? You know that's like four hours from now?"

She winced.

"We're meeting my dad for breakfast."

That surprised me.

And irritated me.

I hated that guy. I'd gone with Maggie to see him whenever she asked, but every time I did, he seemed to spend more time talking to me about hockey than he did talking to Maggie about any of the numerous, more interesting things she had going on in her life.

"When did that happen?" I asked, sliding into bed beside her.

"I texted him during the party and asked if I could see him. He said yes."

I frowned.

"What?" Her head turned in my direction, but her sleep mask was already covering her eyes.

I laughed, shaking my head.

"Nothing."

Maggie still got defensive at any hint of a negative comment aimed toward her dad, and I wasn't going to get into that with her when she was already drunk and exhausted.

"I wish you got along with him better," she mumbled, cozying up against her pillow.

It was a hard position to be in. Hating the guy of my own accord, while my girlfriend wanted me to be his best buddy, all while my best friend could barely hold back his irritation that we were still seeing this guy he wished would just go away for good.

Yeah, well, I wish he was easier to get along with.

"He's my dad, you know?" Her words slurred with exhaustion.

"Yeah, Mags," I told her heavily. "I know."

I didn't say anything else.

I wasn't going to lie to Maggie. But I also wasn't going to piss her off either.

So, I stared at the ceiling above me, listening to the sound of her snores fill the room.

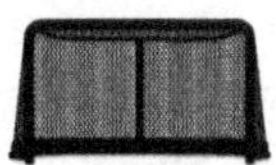

Timothy Brynn kind of gave me the creeps.

Not because *he* was creepy. He was more of an asshole, if anything.

But looking at him and seeing Liam's face had a remarkably eerie effect on a person. The expressions, the build, the facial features—they were so similar it was as if I were looking at my best friend twenty years in the future.

Not to mention those same green eyes that seemed to be everywhere I looked. Damn, the Brynn genes were strong.

As he walked over to where we were waiting in the lobby of the restaurant, Maggie leaned up to whisper in my ear.

"*Be nice.*"

I gave her a smile of silent reassurance that I would.

I was never rude, exactly, but it was hard to pretend to care about conversations that revolved around only three things: her father's career, Liam's career, and my career.

It was like the topic of Maggie being one of Boston's best family lawyers slipped his mind every time he saw her.

Infuriating, really. Though apparently, Maggie didn't care.

"Hi, Dad," she said, grinning as he approached.

"Hello, Margaret," he responded with the formal manner you might greet a colleague.

I let out a snort. *No one* called Maggie *Margaret*—except me as a joke. But this guy? He did it earnestly and with his full chest.

What shocked me more was how Maggie never corrected him. The same way she never said anything when he suggested restaurants that I had on good authority she would rather drop dead than eat at.

I loved the girl, but the term picky didn't even begin to describe her.

But today, she happily agreed to meet at the place of her dad's choosing—the same place I'd personally heard her refer to as a *breeding ground for old bachelors* every time we'd passed it.

And why the hell did Timothy Brynn get to pick the place anyway? It wasn't like yesterday was his daughter's birthday or anything.

"Brody," he said, approaching me with a level of familiarity I personally didn't feel we were at yet, but I shook his hand anyway.

"Nice to see you again, sir."

"Oh, call me Tim," he laughed. "We're practically family."

I almost choked on the snort threatening to spill out but was saved by the appearance of a host asking how many were in our party.

Maggie rewarded me with a pinch for my slip-up, and I shot her a wink as we followed the waiter to a table.

"After you, Margaret," I said with a smug look, gesturing for her to go ahead of me.

We had barely sat down and ordered our drinks before Tim had already mentioned something about how the hockey game I'd played a few nights before had been a strong game overall.

I didn't know what to say, because it hadn't really been a question, but still I nodded.

"We're lucky to be having a great season," I said, shifting in my seat.

"I wouldn't call it luck," he countered. "It's pure talent. It's a hell of a lineup the Harbor Wolves have got there. And Liam? He's somehow playing better than men ten years younger than him. Incredible."

"Yup," I said. "He's something."

I couldn't believe the first thing he wanted to talk about was *hockey*. Actually, I could believe it. But it didn't piss me off any less that he proved me right in my assumption about him.

Maggie sat silently beside me, her leg twitching under the table. I could feel her dejection like a punch to my chest.

"So, what have you been up to, son?" Tim asked, and I had to fight my brows from furrowing at the nickname.

"Oh, you know," I shrugged, "same old. Nothing as exciting as what your daughter's been up to."

I rested an arm around her shoulder, trying to signal her into the conversation.

His eyes scanned to her briefly, as if waiting for her to produce whatever information she found relevant to share.

"Um," she faltered, "I—I—"

I frowned.

Maggie never struggled to find something to say. Maggie never shrank away from any opportunity to talk about herself. She was proud of her life and everything she had accomplished.

So why did she look like the last thing she wanted to do was talk about it with him?

A moment passed. Tim cleared his throat. I squeezed her knee under the table, and she looked up at me with a grateful smile.

You got this, babe, I tried to convey. *Go brag about what a superstar you are.*

But when she finally spoke, it wasn't about her career, or her feature in Boston's *30 Under 30* a few months ago, or even the fact that she'd convinced her law firm to start taking on pro bono clients.

No—what she said came from the deepest parts of herself, where she was still a little girl trying to be recognized by her father.

"My birthday was yesterday."

"Oh, was it?" he asked, eyes widening slightly.

"You didn't know?" I raised my brows, unable to keep the irritation from my tone.

"Must've slipped my mind," he said. "Happy birthday, Margaret. We'll have to order a slice of cake to celebrate."

Then his eyes traveled to a TV in the corner of the restaurant, and just like that, Maggie was brushed under the rug again.

I watched as Maggie panicked at the loss of his attention, watched as her brain whirled trying to take back control of the situation, and then I watched her mouth open, stunning me again by what she said next.

"Lily's birthday is soon, too. She'll be four in June."

Forgetting the fact that it was still currently January—so technically Lily wouldn't be four *soon*—I froze because I knew Liam would be pissed beyond all hell that we were talking about his daughter with his estranged father.

I elbowed Maggie slightly, aiming to make it look as accidental as I could, but the damage was done.

"Really?" Tim looked to Maggie with interest.

Maggie beamed. She'd gotten what she wanted. Her father and his attention were back on her.

"Yeah," Maggie nodded, her usual vibrancy bleeding through. "She's in a total princess phase right now. She's got the tiaras and fairy wings and puffy dresses."

I inhaled sharply through my nose, tensing at the turn of the conversation.

"I'll bet Liam has his hands full with her," Tim chuckled.

"She's an easy kid," Maggie shrugged, "or maybe Liam and Cassie just make it look that way. They're a great team."

"Do you have pictures of them?" Tim leaned forward eagerly. "I can't believe the only time I get to see my son is on a television screen. Have you talked to him again about that? About coming to lunch with us?"

"I tried," Maggie said dejectedly, "but I can ask again. I'm sure he'll come around to it eventually."

"You do that," Tim nodded his approval. "In the meantime, I'd love to see a picture of the girl."

Maggie reached into her purse to pull out her phone, and I panicked. With an elaborate swing of my elbow, I knocked over both mine and Maggie's water until it spilled all over the table, dripping down onto Tim's lap.

He cursed, standing up from his seat in a hurry.

"Shit," I muttered. "I'm so clumsy. Sorry about that, sir."

"Don't worry about it, son," Tim said, dabbing the napkin against his pants. "I'm just going to head to the men's room to dry off."

I nodded as he left, turning my attention toward a furious Maggie.

"What the hell was that for?"

"I think you're about to cross a line, Mags," I told her, a warning edge to my tone.

"What line?" she scoffed.

"You can't bring up Lily. You know how Liam gets about that stuff."

Some guys on the team plastered their kids all over their social media, even doing interviews with their families by their side.

But Liam?

He kept Lily and Cassie as far away as possible from that type of stuff. Sure, he mentioned them in practically every public interview he gave—crediting his family for just about everything—but he didn't want their faces circulating the internet for the public to comment on.

And honestly, I didn't blame him.

"What's the big deal?" Her green eyes narrowed on me oppositionally. "I wasn't telling him their home address or anything."

"I just don't think it's our place," I said. "Your relationship with him is one thing, but you know how Liam feels about him."

"She's my niece!" Maggie exclaimed. "He's her grandfather!"

"And he's never met her for a reason," I countered. "Mags, come on. You have to respect Liam a little here. It's his choice, and he doesn't want that guy in his daughter's life."

"I hardly think showing him a picture is going to do anything."

I exhaled heavily, cursing the stubbornness that ran bone-deep in the girl beside me.

"You're right, maybe it would be nothing," I said. "But do you really want to risk ruining your relationship with your brother because you want validation from your father?"

Maggie flinched at my words.

"Maggie," I started, reaching out to try to take it back—rephrase it in a way that didn't sound so harsh—but her dad was already coming back to the table.

Her smile snapped back into place, all signs of irritation gone as he made his return, but it wasn't her real smile. It wasn't the one that overtook her face and made the corners of her eyes crinkle. This one was tighter. Practiced. The kind she might wear in court while trying not to show her cards.

One thing was clear though:

Tim Brynn couldn't tell the difference.

Brody

Five Years Ago

Fuck, I'd forgotten how beautiful she was.

When Maggie Brynn walked into the bar that night, I felt the air sucked out of me as if someone had taken a vacuum to my lungs.

As if I had summoned her from my sick, depraved fantasies, Maggie Brynn walked into the bar that night looking like every man's wet dream.

Now, I understood why the fangirls were always gushing about Liam's eyes. I had just needed a different easel to see them clearly.

His sister served as the perfect example.

God, she was perfect. Long, midnight-dark hair framing a face that made every expression look like a dare.

I wanted to blind every man in the bar to make sure no one else could look at her but me.

I hadn't spoken more than two sentences to her, but I felt the possessiveness growing in my chest in ways I'd never felt before.

But she didn't even notice the way they all watched her. Or maybe she didn't care.

Hell, it worked for me.

I didn't know what the hell was happening to me, because despite only being two beers deep, I felt drunk and high and on cloud fucking nine as I soaked in the mere presence of her in the bar that night. It was a giddiness usually reserved for a monumental game win.

After a half hour, I stopped caring that every guy in the bar was watching her hungrily, because it wasn't them she was spending her time with.

It was me. At least for tonight, *I* was the one making her laugh. A bubbly, infectious sound that trickled out of her, making me act like a fool over and over, if only so I could keep hearing it. Because out of all the men in Boston, *I* was the one responsible for that smile on her face.

And if I had it my way, I was going to make damned sure I'd always be the one filling that role.

One conversation with Maggie Brynn and I was a goner. And a part of me knew, even then, that something had clicked into place irrevocably.

CHAPTER FIVE

Maggie

I had always had a switch in me that I could flick on and off at will.
At home, my life could be falling apart—my emotions a wreck, my heart shattered—but the second I stepped into the office? I had a goal. A purpose. I didn't have time to lose focus, so I learned to just… turn the rest off.

Besides, what my clients had going on in their lives was usually enough to put things into perspective for me.

"I don't know what to do," Mr. Reilly said, appearing in my office more disheveled than the time before. "It's been a month and she won't answer my calls or texts. I'm going out of my mind here."

"I understand," I told him, "but you've been doing everything right. You signed up for therapy, right?"

He nodded in confirmation.

"And I filed a petition for emergency visitation rights—"

"You did?" He leaned forward eagerly. "What does that mean? Can I see my kids?"

"We still have to wait for court approval, but it could come through within the next few days given your clean record."

He nodded, following along.

"And what if they deny me?"

"Then we'll at least get a hearing scheduled, and Mrs. Reilly will be required to show up and explain herself. And trust me, it'll look worse for her that she's denying you visitation without a solid reason."

"But…" He chewed his lip. "What happens when she tells them what I did? Will that affect things because I—because I cheated?"

"It depends on the judge," I said, trying to be as honest as possible, "but most of them try to do what's in the best interest of the children. And I think any reasonable person would agree that having their father around is in their best interest."

He dropped his head in his hands, fingers working to rub out the crease in his forehead.

"They're not going to understand why I haven't been there," he said, voice raspy as he tugged off his Red Sox cap. "They're going to hate me."

"I don't think it's possible for a kid to hate their parent. They just want to be loved." I offered him a smile. "And it sounds like you do pretty good in that category."

He gave me a half-hearted, weary smile.

"When you have kids," he said, "loving them is the easiest thing in the world."

I didn't understand why his words sent a pang through my chest.

Driving through Chestnut Hill always made me nostalgic. It wasn't just the backdrop to where I studied and graduated college, but it was the place I figured out who I was. What I wanted to do with my life.

I went into Boston College as a party girl with an undeclared major, not taking any of it very seriously. But somewhere along drinking at parties and staying up till four a.m. for most of freshman year, I grew up.

It happened gradually.

Something in a class spiked my interest, or a character's coming-of-age arc in a movie stuck with me, and suddenly I was forming all these opinions about the world—uncovering different layers of myself I'd never had the space to think about before.

I thought about my dad a lot that first year of college. Especially when it was mostly fathers helping their kids move into their dorms. It was hard not to be jealous. It hurt more knowing that mine was alive out there.

At least if he were dead, I wouldn't have to carry the weight of him actively choosing not to be part of my life.

Which, as it turned out, was heavier than you might think.

I guess subconsciously he was the reason I chose the career I did. If my family had to be broken up, then I wanted to at least be part of putting others back together.

And maybe I thought I could figure out where ours went wrong along the way.

But even more saccharine than college being the place I quote-on-quote found *myself*—it just so happened to be the place I found something else just as important to my life: Cassie—the girl who I never dreamed would become my sister.

And apparently, she had a soft spot for Chestnut Hill, too, considering it's the neighborhood she and my brother decided to buy their forever home in.

Their words, not mine.

Personally, I thought that whole concept was kind of bizarre. I mean, *forever home*? Who cares if you get sick of it in five years and want to move? Why tie yourself down to one spot?

But, admittedly, the house they picked *was* pretty impressive. Definitely warranted at least a couple decades here at the least.

As I drove into their obscenely long driveway leading up to their brick mansion… ahem, *house,* I realized I probably should've called to make sure she was home.

I hadn't thought. I just knew I needed to see her. Talk to her. She had this magic power of quieting my mind when it felt like it was about to explode.

But, to my dismay, I didn't see her car in the driveway. Only my brother's. And while we'd gotten a lot closer over the last few years, I sure as hell didn't want to tell *him* what was going on in my screwed-up head.

There were some things we just didn't see eye to eye on. And the topic plaguing my thoughts was one of them.

Still, it wouldn't hurt to wait with him instead of sitting on the steps like a stray cat waiting for Cassie to get home.

Climbing out of my car, I made the trek up to their front door, reflecting on how Liam had managed to find the most private fortress in all of Massachusetts to call home.

Their yard was surrounded by trees and huge fences, reminding me that despite being married for a few years, he still had his fair share of stalker fans. While they typically weren't deranged enough to show up at his house, I knew Liam wasn't taking any chances—especially with Lily to think of.

As I got to the door, I closed my knuckles into a fist, preparing to knock. A new habit for me in regard to my brother—but unfortunately, my days of kicking down Liam's door had become a thing of the past. Since he upgraded to a big-boy home, I had to upgrade to a bit of civility. Even if it was less fun.

I raised my hand to knock, but Liam was already opening it before I even got the chance.

"Wow, you're good," I raised my brows. "You have, like, some type of Spidey-sister sense."

"I also have a Ring," he said, gesturing to the phone in his hand, opened to a live camera showing me standing on his doorstep.

I laughed.

"That's such an old-person thing to have," I said with an eye roll, stepping past him into the house.

Despite its overwhelming size, they'd somehow made it homey—a task I thought impossible considering I was quite content in the four walls of my studio apartment.

But maybe it was hard not to feel like you were in a home when there were such signs of life everywhere. Cassie's colorful jackets and scarves on the hooks, Lily's tutus draped across the stair railings. Liam's hockey duffel halfway unzipped in the front hall.

It wasn't messy, but it was definitely lived in.

"Where's Cassie?" I looked around, stepping over a stray ballet slipper.

"She's out with Lily," Liam said, following me as I made my way into the kitchen. "Why?"

"I need her for a few hours."

"Trying to steal my wife?" he asked.

"Actually, I could make the claim that *you* stole her from me."

"Fair enough," he said with a snort. "Not sorry about it though."

"Clearly," I rolled my eyes, not bothering to tell him that I wasn't either.

It made it easier on me having two of my people in the same house. Saved money on gas that way, too.

Plopping down on one of their swivel chairs by the kitchen island, I stared at Liam as he leaned against the stove across from me.

"So?" he said.

"So?" I asked back.

"Anything you want to talk about, or is this just a random visit?"

"Geez," I said in an exaggerated huff. "What happened to 'stop by anytime?'"

"I'm not saying you can't, I'm just asking—"

"Yes?"

"If you wanted to talk about anything."

"I do." I nodded.

"Okay—"

"With Cassie."

He rolled his eyes.

"Happy to know I'm useless to you," he muttered, and I did actually feel a little bad about it.

But like I said, he just wouldn't understand where I was coming from. My issues with my dad were decidedly different than Liam's with the same man. Because even though we had the same circumstances, it's like we viewed the situation through entirely different lenses.

I shifted uncomfortably away from the feeling, not knowing how to tell him that. Instead, I looked around the room, letting my eyes fall on the huge collage of pictures of their family throughout the years.

Liam and Cassie's wedding. Their honeymoon. When Lily was born. The three of them on trips. It was like an all-encompassing testament to their love.

But I knew they were no different than any other family in the early stages of life. How did so many marriages break apart? How did so many families just like Liam and Cassie's shatter? Didn't the parents want to stick it out for their kids' sake?

Would Liam and Cassie, if it got to that point?

"You love Lily a lot, huh?" I asked him, turning my attention away from the photos.

"My daughter?" He shot me an incredulous look. "Yeah, I'd say I like her a pretty good amount."

"You'd be so sad if Cassie wouldn't let you see her," I remarked sadly, thinking of what Mr. Reilly was going through.

I tried to picture it. Cassie taking Lily and leaving. Ignoring Liam's calls. Liam going out of his mind in this big house all by himself while his family was just out of reach.

"*What?*" Liam's eyes widened.

"I just meant that it must be hard on dads when they can't see their kids."

"What the hell, Mags? What's going on?"

"Do you think if you and Cassie got divorced that you'd be able to co-parent peacefully?"

"We wouldn't get divorced," he said with a resolute expression.

"I mean, hypothetically."

"Hypothetically, we wouldn't get divorced."

"Never mind," I swatted him away. "You're no help."

Just as Liam was about to mutter something back, we heard the front door open and the sound of Lily's rambling fill the house.

"I'm sorry we had to leave the store, Mommy, but I really was getting hungry."

"Well, we'll have to get you a snack then, huh?" Cassie said, and I imagined her tickling Lily's stomach by the way she was answered with a fit of giggles.

And just like that, I watched Liam transform from my normal, disinterested-looking brother to this whole other person I'd only gotten used to seeing over the last few years. He was already smiling before Cassie and Lily bounded into the kitchen.

"Daddy!" she yelled, jumping into his already outstretched arms.

"There's my girls," he said, squeezing her tight against him.

Cassie smiled, coming over to his side at once.

"Hi, baby," he leaned over to give her a kiss.

"Hi," she responded, staring into his eyes.

"Hi!" I chirped in, knowing if I waited for them to stop making goo-goo eyes at each other, I'd be sitting here the rest of my life.

"Auntie Maggie!" Lily wriggled free of her father's arms to run toward me.

"Finally," I exhaled dramatically, "someone who will pay attention to me."

Lily giggled, jumping up and down in front of me like a golden retriever.

"What are you doing here?" Cassie chirped happily, unwinding a scarf from her neck.

"Don't start undressing yet," I told her, making her blush as her hand paused. "You're coming with me on an emotional support best friend walk."

"I want to come!" Lily squealed.

"Sorry, Lil. Next time," I told her.

"But next time is far away," she pouted. "I want to go now time."

"Tell you what," I squatted down to her level, "if you let me take Mommy on a walk now, I'll take you to the playground on Saturday."

"When's Saturday?" She squinted her eyes suspiciously at me.

"This many days away," I held up my fingers.

"Okay," she nodded solemnly, "but I want ice cream too."

I laughed at her bargain.

Yeah, I think it was safe to say she did have a bit of me in her, after all.

I held my hand out for her to shake. We'd made enough deals since she figured out how to negotiate that she knew the drill by now. She shook my hand with the utmost severity, and I winked at her before pulling Cassie by the arm.

"Guess it's you and me, kid," Liam said, scooping her back up.

"I'll be back soon," she said over her shoulder, before looking at me with her analytical eyes. "I think."

"Don't ask her any weird questions!" Liam called to us as we left. "I mean it, Maggie!"

Cassie opened her mouth to ask what he meant, but I shot her a look and muttered,

"Don't ask."

I liked taking walks with Cassie when I had a lot on my mind. For one, she was so naturally good-natured that it seemed to keep some of my darker thoughts at bay.

How could I spend time thinking about everything I was upset about when Cassie was next to me smiling over a pair of squirrels?

Another factor was the speed at which she walked, leaving me no room for anything other than focusing on keeping up with her.

"Slow—" I huffed, "down!"

She turned, pausing in surprise to notice I'd fallen several feet behind her.

"Sorry," she said sheepishly. With considerable effort, she slowed her pace. "But look!"

I stared at her. Then at the background behind her. In all my effort to control my breath and match her speed, I hadn't noticed the route she'd taken us.

"You brought us to our old college," I blinked up at the campus of Boston College.

"Ta-da!" She gestured wildly with an all-encompassing smile.

"But why are we here?"

"Because you seemed contemplative lately," she noted, once again freaking me out with her scarily accurate assessment. "And we used to have the best talks here, remember? By the tree?"

"I don't think sitting in the same spot will make me open up anymore." I laughed. "It only worked in college because I was all young and vulnerable, and you were always bugging me about *how I was feeling.*"

"I still bug you about how you're feeling," she pointed out with a tilt of her head.

"Yes, but I'm not twenty anymore. I've built up better Cassie defenses."

"Why do you need defenses against talking about a problem?"

"I wouldn't say it's a problem. It's just that sometimes talking about something doesn't make a difference."

"Well, let's just go sit and see what happens." She didn't even give me a chance to refuse before she was bounding off toward the quad.

"Look, no one's sitting there!" she grinned, looking back at me.

"That's because it's January," I told her, watching her sit at the base of the tree.

"Meaning, it's too cold for people to sit outside and chat," I emphasized pointedly.

"Then we better get started before we freeze," she patted the spot beside her. "Come on."

I sat, recoiling at the thought of the cold, damp earth rubbing against my designer wool coat, but I knew Cassie wouldn't let that slide as an excuse.

I stared at her.

She stared at me.

And I really didn't think it was going to work, but damn it if those freakily earnest eyes of hers didn't get the best of me.

"Ugh," I groaned in frustration, surprised by how fast the feelings came to the surface. "I guess I've just been thinking a lot about my Dad lately."

Cassie didn't say anything—just let me take my time to get the words together. I knew that if I really didn't want to talk, she would understand and she wouldn't push me.

Which is why I felt comfortable enough to continue.

"I don't know," I picked at the dead grass.

"I guess I'm frustrated that everyone seems to treat him like some big supervillain. He's just a person, you know? He made a mistake, but doesn't it mean something that he's trying now? That he's *been* trying?"

My dad reappeared in my life a few years ago. A random phone call I never expected to get, but had hoped for my entire life.

And since then, he'd been consistent. He answered when I called. He met with me when I asked to get lunch. He hadn't disappeared again, the way Liam had expected him to. But still, it hadn't changed my brother's mind about him.

"I know it means something to you," Cassie said with a soft smile. "That's all that matters."

"But what about Liam?" I implored. "Don't you think it's wrong that he refuses to ever speak to him again? He won't even give him a chance."

"I think," Cassie started carefully, mulling her words over, "that the way people feel about their parents is a complicated thing. And I don't think there's necessarily a wrong or right way to do it."

"What about Lily?" I asked. "Do you think it's okay that she'll never meet her grandfather?"

Cassie sighed, as if knowing it pained me but still resolute in her loyalty to Liam.

"It's Liam's call to make."

"But what if he regrets it after it's too late?" I asked helplessly. "What if Dad dies and Liam is wracked with guilt over having never given him another chance?"

Cassie flinched, and I realized I'd hit too close to home without meaning to. She'd made the decision years ago to cut ties with her own mother, and I knew it was the hardest thing she'd ever done. She didn't talk about it much anymore, but I knew it still ate away at her more than she'd ever admit.

"I didn't mean—" I started, but she held up a hand to stop me.

"No, it's okay." She shook her head. "But I think in that case, he probably assumes the cost of what he thinks he's sparing her from now is worth the risk that he might regret it later."

I understood where she was coming from in one sense. And I understood more that she was probably thinking a lot about her own mother when she said it.

"Do you regret it?" I dared to ask. "Walking away from your mom?"

I watched her body stiffen at the mention of her mother, and from an outsider's perspective, I knew it was the only thing she could do for her own sanity. Even now, years later, I had to watch the ripple effects their relationship still wreaked on her.

She thought about it for a long time, staring off at the students crossing the campus in front of us.

"No," she said finally. "It was the right thing to do at the time. But now?"

She looked toward me.

"I'd be lying if I said it's easy to stay firm in that decision for the rest of my life. Like… what if this time I give her a chance and it works out?"

She shook her head, as if shaking the thought away.

"But then I remember all the times she let me down, and I know I can't risk it. Not for me, but because of Lily. How could I let that into her life when I know there's a higher chance of my mom screwing up than there is of her being what we need her to be?"

She blew out a breath.

"I can't speak for him," Cassie shrugged, "but maybe Liam feels the same way. Maybe he's been burned too many times and isn't willing to risk it."

Sometimes I thought I was selfish, because I never thought of things like that. Of having to put someone else's emotional needs before my own.

For Brody, of course I would, but he was so seldom upset about anything. But a child? The thought of it sounded daunting.

Cassie was used to putting people first. It was second nature to her. And for a second, my heart broke because of what she had to go through to get to where she is now. She puts people first because she *wants* to. Because she genuinely cares about everyone she meets.

Maybe it had something to do with her upbringing. Or maybe it's just her. Either way, I was hit with the sensation of feeling so grateful to fate or destiny or whatever it is that was in charge of making our paths cross all those years ago.

"You're a good person, Cass," I told her, wanting her to know it the same way I did. "I'm glad we're family."

"We were always family," she said. "Even before Liam."

I felt myself smile, feeling her words all through my heart.

"I know."

FIRST HEARTBREAK

Maggie

Twenty Years Ago

It was a Tuesday.

A seemingly random day of the week to walk out on your family, I thought later on.

I wondered if he'd planned it in advance. If when he said goodbye to me that morning before I left for fourth grade, he knew it would be the last time.

Or maybe the need to leave just hit him randomly that day, like the tidal waves I myself had been so prone to experiencing.

For me, they came on suddenly. The need to escape. The feeling like I couldn't breathe until I removed myself from a situation. The urge to run.

I guess I got that from him.

"Where do you think Dad is?" I asked Liam as we sat stiffly in uncomfortable chairs in the principal's office.

I picked at the glittery butterfly wing on my backpack nervously. Dad had taken me to pick it out at the store before the school year started.

I hadn't wanted this one. It looked too kiddish to me. I wanted the sparkly one with the silver sequins.

But Dad said it would get ruined going back and forth to school every day anyway, so really, it just made more sense to get the cheaper option.

It did make sense, and I didn't want to make Dad upset by protesting. He was so busy with work that it wasn't often I was able to go out and run errands with him. I didn't want to ruin our time together by arguing.

"He's probably stuck in traffic," Liam said, his hawk-like attention focused on the principal and secretary whispering across the room from us.

"Do you think he's coming?" I whispered, leaning across the armrest to get close to his ear.

For some reason, I was embarrassed that Dad wasn't here yet. That we'd been left behind, or forgotten. No one else's parents forgot to pick them up today.

It gave me a funny feeling.

"Of course," Liam told me, sounding so mature for his age. "We're his kids. What's he going to do? Leave us here?"

The principal looked over at us and Liam stiffened, sitting up straighter in his chair. I was glad he was here with me. Liam always took care of things when Dad wasn't around. I knew he'd handle this for us, too.

"We're going to call your mother," the principal said finally after what felt like an eternity of waiting.

"No," Liam shook his head. "Dad picks us up on Tuesdays because he gets off early."

"I understand that, Liam," the principal said, "but it's a half hour past dismissal time and we haven't been able to get in contact with him."

"He'll be here," Liam said defiantly. "He knows we're waiting for him. I'm sure he's rushing over right now."

It made me feel better to hear him say it.

I trusted Liam because Liam never lied. Not to me, or anyone else. He told the truth, even when people didn't want to hear it.

Some people didn't like that about him, but I thought it was better to know something than to wonder.

Disregarding him, the principal looked over to the secretary, reaching for a piece of paper she'd dug out of a folder that had been tucked away in a filing cabinet.

He stared at the sheet, dialing numbers on the landline before putting it to his ear.

"Mrs. Brynn?" he asked after what could only have been two rings. "This is Principal Heywood from the elementary school. We have Liam and Margaret here—"

"Maggie," I frowned, correcting him.

"—and they haven't been picked up yet. We were just calling to check in and make sure everything's okay."

He paused, listening.

"No, no. That's fine," he assured her. "We just wanted to call and let you know because we couldn't get in touch with your husband."

Another pause. Liam leaned forward in his seat as if he could hear what our mother was saying on the other side of the line.

"Okay, we'll see you soon." He hung up, then turned to look at us. "Your mother's on her way."

Liam huffed a sigh, shaking his head as if this whole ordeal was completely unnecessary.

I inched impossibly closer to him, taking solace in the fact I wasn't sitting here by myself waiting.

"Is everything okay?" I looked up at him.

He was barely two years older than me, but he had an air about him of being much older. He was serious, determined. More mature than any eleven-year-old had a right to be—that's what adults always told him.

"Of course," he said with complete sincerity. "Just wait. We're going to see him at dinner. He'll probably take us out for ice cream or something to make it up to us for being late. Just wait."

He didn't come to dinner that night.

But I waited.

I waited for fifteen years.

CHAPTER SIX

Brody

I was pretty sure Maggie was pissed at me.

Maggie didn't like being wrong, and I didn't necessarily tell her she *was*, but I intervened in a situation she felt was hers to navigate. Hence, Maggie was definitely pissed at me.

Hence again, why I was on Mr. Waterman's steps with a bouquet of roses, waiting for her to get off work.

"You here to take me to the dance?" Mr. Waterman's voice called out from the window.

I looked up, grinning at the white-haired old man sneering at me with disgust.

"I would, but I didn't bring my dancing shoes." I smiled cheekily up at him.

"Then why the hell are you on my steps again, boy?"

"I'm waiting for my girlfriend!" I called back. "I told you. She works over there." I pointed in the direction of Maggie's law office, only to see her crossing the street toward me with a quizzical expression.

"Why are you yelling?" she asked, coming to stand by my side.

"See!" I wrapped an arm around her, gesturing for Mr. Waterman to see. "My girlfriend!"

Mr. Waterman scowled.

"She's too good for ya."

"Right you are, you old rascal," I said before planting a kiss on Maggie's lips. "But don't say it too loud. I was hoping she wouldn't find that out."

Maggie looked between us in concern.

"Brody, are you harassing an old man?" she whispered in horror.

"Yes, he is!" Mr. Waterman yelled back at the same time I denied it. "Keep him off my steps."

Maggie narrowed her eyes on me and I laughed.

"He keeps me company while I wait for you to get off work," I explained, before noticing her eyes on the flowers in my hand.

"For you," I said, holding them out for her.

She peered down at them suspiciously, then looked back up at Mr. Waterman, then back to me.

Then she accepted them, smiling brightly.

"You're really something, you know that?"

But that something didn't seem like such a bad thing, considering the way she had those happy crinkles by her eyes and was pulling me in for a kiss.

I smiled against her lips, feeling balance restored to the universe once more.

When I looked up, Mr. Waterman had left, his window shut—and probably locked—behind him.

Apparently sitting on his steps was off limits, but he was fine with me kissing beautiful girls there.

"So," I said, rubbing a hand down her arm, "we have guests."

Maggie's brows furrowed for a moment before clearing into an expression of realization. Maggie always figured things out before I gave her any clues.

"Are your sisters here?" she asked, lighting up.

I nodded, amused at how thrilled she was by the prospect of seeing my family.

"Not only that," I said, "but Mom and Dad, too."

"SHARON AND TOM ARE HERE?" she practically shrieked, grabbing onto my wrist with an intensity I didn't think possible for someone her size.

"Yup," I nodded. "The whole Callahan gang has hit Boston."

"Where are they?" she asked. "Are they staying with us?"

"You think my three sisters and both my parents can fit in our shoebox?" I rolled my eyes. "I got them hotel rooms."

"We could've squeezed," she said half-heartedly.

"*Or* we could upgrade our living quarters."

"Never," she said, affronted. "I've been in that apartment for eight years and it's the perfect proximity to everything in Boston."

"Fine," I held my hands up in defeat. "We'll put that conversation on the back burner. Again."

She rolled her eyes.

"But we have to get going because we have a dinner reservation with them," I glanced down at my watch, "now."

Maggie let out a yelp and took off down the sidewalk to the spot where I always parked my car, her heels clicking against the pavement as she scurried along. I had to laugh when she turned around with frantic expectation on her face.

"Come on," she beckoned, "I don't want to be late."

Not for the first time in my life, I chased after Maggie Brynn. Somehow, it never got old.

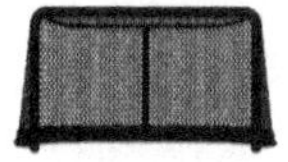

It wasn't easy getting the whole Callahan gang together. We'd all ventured a long way from the tiny town in Michigan we grew up in.

Our parents were still there, but all three of my sisters had spread out to other parts of the country, because as Leah liked to say, "*nothing exciting ever happens in Michigan.*"

But we were still close, despite the distance. I guess that happens when you grow up in a small house where six people have to share one bathroom.

Stuff like that bonds you.

And even though my sisters had only known Maggie the past few years, they'd taken to her as if she had grown up in the sticks of Michigan right along with us.

Sometimes I think they preferred her over me, but honestly, I wouldn't have it any other way.

"—and I showed everyone that article of you being in Boston's *30 Under 30,*" Leah bragged, as if she were the one who had achieved it. "They couldn't believe I have such a smart sister-in-law."

"We have it framed in our kitchen," Mom smiled at Maggie while Dad nodded along. "We are *so* proud of you."

"It really is amazing," Tara agreed, while Megan nodded along with her.

"If only you already had our last name, then it would be like a whole family achievement," Leah lamented with a heavy sigh.

Maggie squirmed under everyone's attention. She was funny like that. Being the center of attention was where she was most comfortable—except when it came to other people acknowledging how incredible she was.

I rubbed Maggie's knee under the table.

"Great way to make it all about you, Lee," I laughed.

"It really wasn't that big of a deal," Maggie said. "It's easy to achieve that when it's the *only* thing I've been working toward. And honestly, I couldn't have done it without Brody."

She gazed up at me with a shy smile.

"You *cannot* seriously be crediting me with this." I shook my head in disbelief.

"I wouldn't be able to do what I do if you weren't taking care of everything else in our lives," she said.

"Cooking a few meals won't get me featured in any magazines," I told her. "Come on, Mags. You're a rockstar. Own it."

She smiled, but for some reason, it was like she still couldn't believe it. That she did it on her own.

My family was about to back me up on that, if it weren't for the waitress coming over to take our order.

"You guys talk so funny here," Tara scrunched her nose after the waitress left.

"Do not!" Maggie said, feigning insult.

"Uh, you do."

I laughed when Maggie looked to me for backup.

"Sorry, babe," I laughed, "but no one in any other part of the country says 'cawfee.'"

"And neither do I!" She turned her nose up at me.

"Then say it," Megan dared her.

"No." Maggie refused.

"Why not?" I asked, poking her side.

"Because I know my speech patterns better than anyone," she said, meeting everyone's smug gaze, "and I know perfectly well that I know how to say 'coffee.'"

The table erupted in a fit of laughter.

"There it is!" Leah pointed.

"Girls, leave her alone," my dad ordered, but even he was biting back a laugh.

"Maggie, dear," my mom reached out to grab her hand from across the table, "your accent is perfectly charming."

Maggie sat back in her seat, defeated, but with a smile tugging at her lips anyway.

"At least I don't call soda 'pop' like I'm in some fifty's movie."

"It's okay, babe. You're still the most beautiful woman in Boston." I kissed her cheek. "Even if you do talk funny."

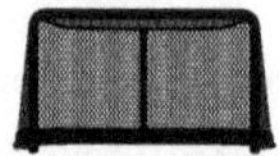

Boston Common was still lit with Christmas lights, even though it was nearing the end of January.

I didn't mind. It made the bleak winter feel more cozy, somehow. I could handle the cold, but the constant cover of gray skies and muddied mounds of snow made something in me die a little each time the season came around.

"That was nice," Maggie said, taking a long inhale of the winter air. "It's always so *nice*. How do you guys do that?"

"Do what?" I asked, looking over to where she walked on the path beside me.

"You all talk the whole time without any undermining or bashing each other or making each other feel like they're not doing enough with their lives—"

"Uh, excuse me," I interrupted with a laugh, "but did you miss the entire portion of dinner where everyone came at Leah for trying to make a career out of being a part-time meditation coach?"

"But even then," Maggie said, "it was just teasing. She could still feel that you guys would support her no matter what."

"That's just family," I shrugged.

"Not all," she said. "Actually, not even most."

I thought about it. I guess on one hand I knew she was right, but I'd never known anything different. My family genuinely loved each other *and* liked each other.

I didn't stop to think that I might've taken it for granted all these years.

"I guess I am pretty lucky," I admitted, feeling self-conscious about it somehow.

Maggie looked off into the distance, feeling like she was a million miles away from me.

"Hey," I nudged her, "what's wrong?"

"Nothing," she said.

"Bull."

"I guess I just wish I could be part of something like that," she admitted, refusing to meet my eyes. "I mean, I have both my parents and a brother—but they're all so separate, you know? I hate that we're so broken up from each other."

"You already are part of something like that," I told her. "You're a Callahan already, through and through."

She smiled, but it didn't quite reach her eyes.

I frowned.

"All we have to do is make it official," I grinned.

I joked about it a lot with Maggie, mostly as a way to see where she was at. I knew going into this thing that she was more independent than most. But I also knew she felt forced into that role in a way.

I'd let us move things at her pace. On her terms. She wanted to build her career first, get established. I couldn't fault her for that. But lately, I'd had the itch to start moving things along.

And with all this mention of family lately, I was starting to think Maggie was dropping hints that she was ready for that too. For all of it.

She paused, looking over at me with wide eyes.

Was she nervous?

"Don't worry, Mags." I laughed at her bewildered expression. "I won't pop the question here next to the Make Way for Ducklings statue."

She laughed, but it came out strained, and I realized my mistake.

Tara, my oldest sister, always said girls liked surprises. I forgot that a proposal was probably the biggest surprise in their life—which meant talking about even the potential of it should be strictly off limits until the actual moment, right?

I cleared my throat, moving on from the topic swiftly, but it didn't escape my notice that the tension in Maggie's shoulders didn't quite seem to settle.

Maggie

Five Years Ago

UNKNOWN: Have I already been ghosted?

MAGGIE: Who is this?

UNKNOWN: OUCH 💔

UNKNOWN: After everything we've been through?

MAGGIE: Gonna need more details, babe. Your number isn't saved in my phone.

UNKNOWN: Aww, pet names already? I guess I'm doing better than I thought. 💀

> **UNKNOWN:** I'll forgive you for ditching me last night, if you let me take you to dinner tonight. I nearly dropped my phone, remembering the boy I'd drunkenly humiliated myself in front of the night before.

Brody.

Oh, God.

Liam's cute friend and *teammate*, Brody Callahan.

How was it possible that this man saw me nearly tumble over myself while drunkenly singing ABBA songs, and he *still* wanted to see me again?

It didn't make sense.

In my defense, I knew last night hadn't been a good look, but I had been as powerless to stop it as anyone.

I'd gotten a message from my dad. An email, if we were being specific. For the first time in fifteen years. Said he saw me on LinkedIn and wanted to reconnect, if I was willing.

Fucking LinkedIn.

The message took the breath out of my lungs in a way I'd only felt once, when I got hit by a softball flying straight at my chest in high school.

Hearing from my father honestly rattled me to such a degree that I stormed Liam's apartment immediately and dragged Cassie out, because I just needed her for moral support.

She made me feel lighter. Less chaotic. Like the world wasn't caving in on itself just because something unexpected and somewhat painful happened.

I think it was because she dealt with so much shit with a smile on her face that it made my problems seem so insignificant in comparison.

Not that *she* ever made me feel like that. And I knew she'd listen if I told her about the email, but how could I do that when Cassie had so many bigger things to deal with? Especially at the present moment. *Especially* when I stuck her into an apartment with my moody, temperamental brother who had already made her cry.

And I *knew* I couldn't tell Liam, because he'd been suffering from chronic emotional constipation for the last decade and would offer me zero support when it came to figuring out what to do about our father.

So, I did what I always did.

I chose the escape route. Don't think about it. Don't dwell on it. Just drink and escape. At least for one night.

I hadn't been counting on Brody, though.

He reminded me of Cassie in the way he was all sunshine and smiles. Being near him felt like basking in the sun on a summer day.

I chased that feeling. Craved it.

And that had scared me, even when I'd been too drunk to remember why that was dangerous.

So, dinner?

It definitely didn't sound like a good idea.

> **UNKNOWN:** I know you're ignoring me. But I promise if you give me a chance, I'll make you laugh even harder than you did last night.

> **MAGGIE:** You didn't make me laugh. It was the alcohol.

> **UNKNOWN:** Then, I'll have to accomplish that feat before you get any alcohol in you tonight. I'll see you at seven.

> **MAGGIE:** Nope.

UNKNOWN: Yes.

UNKNOWN: plsssssss

MAGGIE: ….

UNKNOWN: I'll be there at seven.

MAGGIE: If you can find out where I live, then I'll go with you. (without asking my brother.)

UNKNOWN: pfftt, as if HE would tell me. But challenge accepted. See you 2night.

UNKNOWN: babe ☺

I held in the laugh that threatened to come out at his last message. I wasn't going to let him win that bet of making me laugh *that* early, even if it was in the privacy of my own home.

Still, I saved his number in my phone for reasons I couldn't quite admit and pocketed it away.

CHAPTER SEVEN

Maggie

M r. Reilly had given up the pretense of formality and now showed up at our appointments in his tattered Red Sox hat and worn-out jeans that I would bet money he'd had since the early 2000s. Maybe longer.

With bags under his eyes and a fidgety energy in his step, it was clear he was worse for the wear.

"I showed up at the house and she wouldn't let me in," his voice was agonized as he wrung his hands over and over again.

"You *what?*" I asked, frowning at his words. "We already talked about that. You cannot show up before the emergency visitation comes through."

"I can't wait any longer!" he bellowed. "They're my kids! They need their father."

"I understand, I do—"

"I'm sure you do." He nodded. "And *I* understand your legality standpoints, but *them?* They *don't* understand why their dad wasn't at their birthday last week. Or why I'm not tucking them into bed every night anymore. My little one, he starts t-ball next week. Am I supposed to miss that? His first practice? First game? I can't. I *won't*."

"She could use it against you," I said quietly, not knowing how to advise this man against the very thing his instincts were screaming at him to do.

"I don't care if she sues me for everything I have," he said in a burst of exasperation. "She can take it all. As long as I get to see them."

I watched him, letting him have a moment with his thoughts. I couldn't say anything to make it better for him. I could only *do*. And I swore to him—and to myself—that I was going to do everything in my power to help this man put his family back together.

One way or the other.

"I haven't done anything to deserve this," he muttered into his hands after a minute.

"I know you haven't," I told him. "And I want you to know I am doing everything I possibly can, because I'm fighting on your side. Children deserve to grow up with their father."

He looked up at me wearily, but underneath the exhaustion and the despair, there was a flicker of something else. A speck of something that would serve to propel me forward. To work this case until it came to the conclusion I needed it to.

Hope.

Sometimes, it was hard to stop working.

Controversial statement, I know. Most people couldn't wait to clock out at the end of the day and go home to spend a leisurely night binge-watching some obscure reality TV show that probably rotted their brains.

But me? I physically had to be dragged away from my desk at times. It was hard to stop when the work never seemed to end. There was always a task to do, something I could be working on.

And what made it worse was that the longer I put something off, the longer a custody battle could go on for. It forced me to put time into perspective.

Mine was worth so little in the grand scheme of things. What did I really have to do that was more important than reuniting families?

Hang out with my own? It hurt to do that when I was thinking about the cases I was working on. Go on a date with my boyfriend? I would see him when I went to bed at the end of the day.

My clients *needed* me, and I wasn't going to be the one to delay an already excruciatingly long process.

But—a promise is a promise, and that meant a great deal to a toddler.

Which is why, as I solemnly swore, I picked Lily up promptly at ten a.m. on Saturday morning and brought her to her favorite playground.

It wasn't so bad, really. Lily was an easy kid. Especially when she was with her Aunt Maggie.

Maybe it was because I gave her all the stuff I knew Cassie and Liam were depriving her of, because honestly, how else would I live up to my reputation as the cool, laid-back aunt I strove to be?

I grinned down at her chocolate-streaked face, proud to be the enabler of such joy.

Liam and Cassie thought they were treating her when they gave her whatever organic, clean-ingredient, fruit-based dessert they'd picked up from God knows where, but I knew that the real joy came in the form of Dunkin Donuts chocolate-sprinkled donuts.

Hey, it's what we were raised on, and we turned out just fine.

"You know," I said, "you're very lucky that you have me as your aunt, Lil. Not only do I give you the good snacks, but I'm also basically the reason you're here right now."

She looked at the playground, as if that's what I was referring to. That too, but I meant more in terms of her existence.

"Why?"

"Well, your mommy and daddy didn't know each other until I introduced them."

She shot me a side-eye as she took another bite of her donut. Her hands were covered with glaze that I knew I'd have to scrub off before I dropped her back off at home.

"How you know Daddy?"

"Your daddy is my brother," I told her.

"Why?" she asked.

Her question made me pause.

"Um," I said, thinking. "Because me and your daddy have the same mommy."

"Why?" she asked again.

"I don't really know how to answer that, Lil." I laughed at my niece's round, chocolate-covered face.

Yeah, I definitely needed to give her a good wipe-down before returning her to her parents.

"I don't have a brother," she remarked thoughtfully after a while.

I snorted, knowing that with the way Liam and Cassie were all over each other, Lily's status as an only child was most definitely temporary.

"You probably will soon," I told her, and she beamed.

"Then he can play dolls with me."

"Maybe," I said. "But sometimes brothers aren't as accommodating as we hope they'll be."

"What is acco-acco-accum-a-dating?"

"It means sometimes they'll say, 'tough luck, kid,' and make you play on your own anyway."

Lily didn't like that answer, but I figured it was better to break the news to her early.

"Maybe I want a sister then," she said, with a look of disappointment.

"Smart girl," I nodded in agreement.

But until then, she had her Aunt Maggie to play with. And really, it wasn't so bad a thing to leave work for at all.

"Mommy! Daddy!" Lily yelled, running full speed ahead of me into the kitchen toward Liam's legs. "Aunt Maggie says I get brother soon!"

Jeez.

I watched in real time as Liam froze, turned to Cassie with exuberant bewilderment on his face, and beamed up at her. "Cass?"

"No!" She shook her head, blushing furiously before staring at me in accusation. "Maggie!"

"I was joking!" I held my hands up in defense.

Liam's face fell.

"Weird joke to tell a three-year-old," he muttered, shooting daggers at me.

"Hey," Lily pouted, holding up multiple fingers. "I three and a half."

"That's right, baby," Cassie cooed, picking her up, "you are. And you need a bath, don't you?"

"Nooooo," Lily pouted.

"Yessssss," Cassie countered, kissing her cheek. "Say thank you to Aunt Maggie."

She did, waving goodbye as Cassie carried her out of the room, leaving me alone with my brother.

The truth was, I missed him.

I loved that he had a new family with my best friend and niece, I really did. But sometimes it was hard not to feel like I was being left behind. Replaced.

It was normal, of course. He had somehow pieced together a new family of his very own—he had a wife and daughter. I had a Brody and a job. We both had bigger priorities now.

But sometimes, I missed the way it was. When we were a unit. It was the two of us growing up against the world. Now, he had moved on, leaving me behind with nothing to do but contemplate the past.

I didn't think I could take it anymore.

"I want you to come to dinner with me." The words spilled out of my mouth as I formulated the idea in my head. "This week."

Liam thought about it, and I hated that. That I needed to be considered.

"I have games throughout the week," he said, already planning his excuse for why he couldn't come.

"There are a few nights you'll be free," I said, irritation rising.

"You know, I like to spend those nights with my family," he said, scratching his head awkwardly.

"*I'm* your family, too." I hated that I had to point it out to him.

And it broke something in me when it was met with silence. I fought the urge to turn away from him as if I'd been hit.

After a moment, he softened, rolling his eyes in a teasing manner.

"Of course you are, Mags. You know what I meant."

I stared at him blankly, willing him to continue.

"It's just—I lose so many nights with the girls because of hockey."

"It's one damn night, Liam." I scoffed. "You can't seriously tell me you won't give up *one* of your nights for me."

He exhaled deeply, shaking his head.

"You're right," he said apologetically. "I'm sorry. Of course we can go to dinner."

But his words didn't make me feel any better. I hated that it had to be coerced. I hated that I could never have what came so naturally to everyone else in the world.

A family who *wanted* to spend time with them.

A family who valued them as someone important in their life.

Brody had that. My coworkers had it. Cassie had to work like hell to get it, but now she had it with my brother.

I was the spare. Left out. I didn't have anyone. Not really.

"Mags," he said, tilting his head to stare at me from across the kitchen island. "Just tell me where to go and I'll be there. Okay?"

"Okay." I nodded.

But his confirmation didn't do anything to dull the hollowness I felt.

Maggie

Five Years Ago

Liam wasn't there to see it—the aftermath of Dad leaving.

Not the way I was.

He had friends and he had hockey. And Mom had been too much for him, the same way she'd been too much for Dad.

That left me, feeling too guilty to leave her alone when everyone else already had.

So I'd been with her. To see her cry, watch her break, and listen to her call a phone number over and over and over again with the same depressing result.

She didn't try to pretend with me. Not the way she did with Liam. Because I was a strong girl, she said. And someday I would have my heart broken too.

She said it was normal. A part of life. Something she would help me with when I was older.

But how could I trust her to help me with it when she was barely helping herself?

The more I saw of this supposed heartbreak she warned me of, the more I realized I could never let that happen. Not to me.

I didn't want to be crying in my bed over someone who wasn't there to dry my tears. I didn't want to be so broken that I crumbled to the floor at the sight of someone's shirt hanging in the closet.

But it would happen if I wasn't careful.

Because that's what boys did to girls who loved them too intensely. They left. They left because it was too much to be needed. Too much to be loved that much.

And even though I didn't want to admit it, I was capable of loving just as messily and recklessly as my mother.

But that wasn't safe. It wouldn't protect me from the wreckage my mother was living in. And more than anything, I wanted to be the type of girl who didn't crumble.

Like Liam. He had picked up and moved on. He never uttered our father's name. He threw himself into sports. He excelled in school. He made new friends and stayed out late.

How was it so easy for him to move on when I felt frozen in the moment, still waiting for life to turn back to normal?

I wanted to be strong like Liam. I wanted to not hurt, the way he seemed to.

So, I hardened myself. It took time, but I did it.

The only way to do that was to never care at all. Never get used to someone's presence being permanent.

I had friends, sure. A lot of them, even. But none of them mattered to me. Not really.

That was the secret: to only let people into my life whose presence I could bear to lose. I had friends to shop with and people to talk about celebrity gossip with. I even had a few classmates who would let me borrow their notes without a thought. But I didn't have any friends to tell my secrets to. Certainly no one I trusted enough to do the whole sleepover thing with.

And when it came to boys? Well, I was lucky I learned that lesson early, before I could clumsily let myself get broken by them. But the other girls? They didn't know any better. I watched it over and over again—my friends crying over boys who had already moved on to the next girl before the tears had dried.

Well, it wouldn't be me.

No. I vowed. *I wasn't giving my heart to anyone without a fight.*

I locked it up and kept the key tucked safely away from anyone who might try to snatch it out from under me.

Because I already knew what it felt like to love and be left anyway. And I didn't like the way a heart felt when it bled.

CHAPTER EIGHT

Brody

I fucking loved hockey.

Where else could I watch from the goalie net as a guy I hated got absolutely pummeled by my best friend?

Nowhere.

Unless I joined some type of backstreet alley fighter gang—which I'd thought about, but ultimately decided wouldn't be a good fit for me. I'd spent too many years in braces to take the risk of someone knocking out any of my teeth at this stage.

The best friend in question was currently slamming a rival team member against the plexiglass, no doubt seriously provoked, because Liam tried not to get into fights anymore. Especially when he knew his kid was watching.

"Get him, Liam!" I called from across the ice.

I watched as he sucker-punched Stevenson into submission, and I laughed. The guy was a jerk. Always playing offensive. Always trying to go for low blows.

He was well overdue for everything Liam was dishing out to him.

It took a minute before the refs stepped in, allowing Liam the chance to finish it on his terms. He'd already decided it was over by the time they officially broke it up.

Stevenson was a little bloody, Liam was royally pissed, and they stuck both of them in the penalty box to cool off.

Liam's scowling face lit up on the Jumbotron as the crowd roared behind me. When it panned to Stevenson's face, already swelling, the volume of the arena grew even louder.

Boston was metal as hell—I'd give them that. There was nothing they loved quite as much as a good hockey fight.

And we really hadn't been serving on that front in a while.

The rest of the game passed by in a blur, and when it came time for post-game interviews, Liam was still carrying the chip on his shoulder that had been there all night.

"How do you feel after the win tonight?" a young interviewer asked, shoving the microphone up in Liam's face.

They were either too naïve or too arrogant to be testing Liam's patience when he was already in a mood. Hell, maybe *they* wanted to get their own bruise courtesy of the notorious Harbor Wolves captain.

Like I always said, hockey fans were weird.

"Tired," Liam responded in a clipped tone, leaving little room for the newbie to work with.

The interviewer shuffled on their feet, laughing off the comment before continuing.

"You and Stevenson really got into it earlier. Bad blood there, or just the adrenaline of the game?"

"Does it matter?" Liam retorted, eyebrows raised at the kid, daring him to ask another question.

I shot Liam a look, confused by the irritation bleeding through his words. It was a side of him I hadn't seen in a few years but had been slipping through the cracks more often lately.

These Brynns of mine—they could be testy when they wanted to.

Leaping into the frame of the camera, I made a joke about how our temperamental captain needed to go take a shower and swiftly took over the rest of his questions in a seamless transition.

Liam didn't deserve any bad press just because he was in a shitty mood, and besides, I was much funnier than he was anyway.

At least according to the TikTok edits. Liam had me beat with thirst traps, sure, but when it came to comedic edits, I'd gotten everyone beat by miles.

The interviewer relaxed a bit as I leaned forward into the mic, apparently knowing I was going to give him what he was looking for.

"Crazy shit out there, right?" I commented, knowing everyone wanted to hear the scoop of the fight. "Stevenson's not a bad guy, but he's been a bit too clumsy on the ice, if you know what I mean."

"Clumsy?"

"Oh yeah. I mean, *I* can't think of any other reason why he'd be body-checking our captain the last few games we saw him. Can you?" I smirked. "*I* certainly would know better than to get in Brynn's way, so it's either clumsiness or stupidity. Giving him the benefit of the doubt, I'll stick with clumsiness."

The media team laughed.

"I guess we'll see next time we're against the Jets, though." I clicked my tongue. "If it's a repeat event, then I might have to change my answer."

We bantered back and forth for a few minutes until the conversation came to a natural close. The media team gathered up their equipment and left, satisfied and with plenty of content. I shook my head, blowing a breath of relief once they were gone. Liam was still fuming somewhere, but at least I'd taken care of his media obligations.

Putting one fire out at a time—that's all I could do.

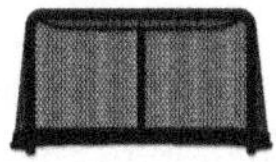

It was worse than I expected.

Liam was sitting on the edge of his hotel bed, staring out the window as if the city lights held the answers to all the horrendous contemplations I imagined were swirling through his head.

"Don't you knock?" Liam growled as I strode into his space.

"That's the beauty of connecting rooms," I smirked. "I don't need to."

He rolled his eyes before grabbing the television remote and clicking it on.

Nevertheless, I persisted.

"Do you want to go out with the team?" I asked.

"No."

"Why?"

"Because I'm thirty-two and want to go to sleep."

"But we're in Vegas!" I exclaimed, taking the liberty of throwing a light punch at his shoulder.

He turned to shoot me an incredulous look.

"We've been in Vegas before. About a hundred times."

"And every time, you choose to stay in your room," I pointed out.

He said nothing, just continued to click through the stations.

I moved in front of the screen, making myself unavoidable.

He sighed before flicking his attention back to me.

"What's going on, dude?" I asked, scanning him head to toe as if I could diagnose whatever was going on inside of him.

"I told you. I want to go to bed."

"No—what's going on with you?" I asked. "You're in a shit mood. And not your usual one either. This is worse."

He was silent for a minute, eyes practically glazed over with detachment until he finally heaved a sigh and shrugged.

"I just think I'm getting too old for this."

"This meaning…?"

"All of this—" he gestured toward the hotel room. "The traveling. The staying in hotel rooms. The being on the opposite end of the country from my family."

I frowned.

"Are you telling me you think you're too old for hockey?"

"Aren't you getting to that point too?" he asked. "Look at our team. We're playing with kids in their early twenties who have nothing else going on but the game."

"Don't shit on them for that," I said defensively. "That was you not very long ago."

"I remember," he said. "It's nothing against them. It's just me. I'm not there anymore. This doesn't mean as much to me the way it used to."

"What are you saying?" I asked cautiously.

He exhaled—the weary sigh of a man already resigned to his decision.

"I just want to be home."

I understood where he was coming from. I really did. Did he think I didn't have a hard time going to sleep in a strange city, leaving my girlfriend alone at home? At least Cassie had Lily with her while Liam was traveling for work.

"I miss Maggie just as much as you miss Cassie."

"Doubtful," he countered.

"Do you think I like going to sleep in a strange bed without Maggie beside me?"

"Ugh," he groaned. "Don't talk to me about you and my sister in bed. It's weird."

"That's not fair. I have to know about you and Cassie in bed, and she's like a little sister to *me*."

"When the hell have I ever talked about me and Cassie in bed?" Liam growled furiously.

"You don't have to talk about it," I countered. "You have a *child*. I already know."

"Jesus Christ, Brody." Liam muttered, running a hand over his face. "You're really something."

"Thanks, Cap."

"That's not a compliment."

"Please don't leave, Liam," I said, feeling a sudden apprehension in my chest. "I don't want to do this without you. It would be too weird."

The thought of flying across the country, warming up on the ice, playing the game without Liam? I couldn't fathom going through any of it without him. He was the piece of home I got to take with me wherever we went. He kept me grounded.

"Nothing's decided yet, Brody," he said, looking wearier than I'd seen him in a long time. "I think I'm just tired."

I sighed, knowing by the look on his face that was all the talking I'd get out of him tonight.

"I guess I'll see you in the morning then," I said, and showed myself out of his room, not knowing where exactly that left us.

I loved my job. I loved hockey—for the sport, yes, but the team most of all. Every day was like hanging out with friends. Cracking jokes. Getting energy out. Feeling important. Included.

And I'd still have that, even if he decided to retire… but the Harbor Wolves without Liam? I'd never experienced that in my whole career. And some selfish part of me didn't want to. We were supposed to retire *together*. And yeah, technically I knew that the clock started ticking on your hockey career once you hit your thirties—but I still felt like the fresh-faced rookie who got drafted all those years ago.

Time was a hell of a thing.

I didn't really notice it passing until I was left with nothing left to do but face the changes.

I knew better than to argue with Liam on his decision. Once his mind was set on something, that was all there was to it. Maggie was the same way.

I shook my head, pushing the thought away. Liam hadn't made up his mind yet. Not officially. Maybe he was right—maybe he was just tired. If I gave him space, he'd realize he was being ridiculous and stick it out—for me, if not for himself.

I left him in his room to sulk, taking my phone out of my pocket to dial Maggie the second I got in the hallway.

Even if one Brynn was abandoning me, I knew with certainty that the other never would.

She answered on the second ring.

Brody

Five Years Ago

"I miss you," I said, whispering into the phone.

We were in Seattle for an away game, and I hadn't seen Maggie since our date the night before. I was pretty sure I was going through withdrawals.

Liam was sleeping in the bed beside me, so I made sure to keep my voice low, because I sure as hell wasn't going to let him wake up to me murmuring softly over the phone to his sister.

"You saw me last night." I heard the eye roll, even through the phone.

I was getting good at reading her. I could practically see her face now, imagine her expressions from just the sound of her voice.

"But that was yesterday," I said. "I need to see you at least once a day for proper functioning."

"Poor baby," she cooed sarcastically. "I think you'll survive."

But I heard her smile, and I knew what that meant.

She missed me too.

Otherwise, she wouldn't even be entertaining this conversation.

I noticed that about her. If she wasn't interested in someone, it was as if they weren't even there. She wouldn't grant them a fraction of her attention, even when they begged.

And oh, how they begged.

Not verbally, usually. But with their eyes, their flirtatious grins, their pleas for attention.

I couldn't blame them. Maggie was the most beautiful girl in any room. The most beautiful girl in Boston, as far as I was concerned. And I'd been one of those helpless guys once, just desperate for her to look my way even for a moment.

I didn't know if it was only me being friends with Liam that gave me the upper hand, but I didn't even care—even if that was cheating.

She picked me.

I was the guy, out of all of them, who she was having midnight phone calls with.

And I was the one making her smile on the other end of the line, even if she'd rather die than admit it.

"When I come home, we're going to a Red Sox game before the season ends."

"How did you know I like the Red Sox?" she asked suspiciously.

"Because you're a girl who grew up in Boston?" I offered bashfully.

"Or?" she said, calling me out on my bullshit.

"Or I may have asked Liam for a few ways to win some brownie points with you," I admitted, grateful that no one was around to see the way my face reddened in the darkness of the hotel room.

"How sneaky of you, asking my brother what I like so you can weasel your way into my heart."

"Is it working?"

"Maybe," she said.

My heart soared.

"But only if you buy me a hot dog."

"I'll buy you anything you want," I told her.

"And sing 'Sweet Caroline' when it plays," she added.

"That's a given."

"And you have to promise you'll say hi to Wally if we see him."

"The Green Monster himself?" I laughed, louder than I should've considering my sleeping roommate. "It would be an honor."

"Fine," she agreed. "Then it's a date."

"It's a date," I confirmed.

I fell asleep that night with the image of Maggie on my mind and a smile on my lips, only because of her.

The future was bright.

CHAPTER NINE

Maggie

Brody didn't know it, but I watched every single Harbor Wolves game he played in.

It didn't matter where I was.

Working late in the office. In the gym. Eating takeout on the couch. I made sure to always have the game playing somehow.

I would never tell him. I think it would go to his head that I was obsessing over him like a high schooler with a crush. The same way I obsessed over tracking his flight each time he was flying home from an away game.

Truly pathetic.

But despite my long-running tendency at playing nonchalant, I could never stop myself from throwing myself at him the second that door opened.

Every damn time.

"Hi, Mags." I felt him smile against my cheek, broad arms encircling me in warmth. "Did you miss me?"

"No." I grinned, pulling away to look up at him.

"No?" He laughed.

"Well," I hesitated, pretending to think about it. "I missed you keeping me warm at night. I get cold without you."

"Oh, is that all I am? A personal heater for Maggie Brynn?"

I nodded.

If only he knew how right he was. Not just at night, but every moment—just the thought of him was enough to make my days feel like sunshine.

When he was gone, it was like a winter day. Cold, barren, bearable—but only just.

"Well, if that's all I'm good for, you better put me to work," he said, picking me up in a swift motion before leading us to the bedroom.

I squirmed, trying to break free from his arms before he tossed me onto the bed. I covered my eyes, knowing what was going to happen next. I couldn't see it, but I felt the mattress sag under his weight when he leaped onto the bed beside me, wrapping me in an ironclad embrace.

I didn't know I was giggling until he pulled my face toward him and laughed.

"I love that sound," he said, before leaning forward to kiss me.

I rolled on top of him, planting kisses all along his cheek and neck and finally his lips—to show him what I wasn't saying in words.

Yes, I missed you.

Yes, I'm happy you're home.

Yes, yes, yes, I love you.

He sighed contentedly, brushing the hair behind my ears as I hovered on top of him.

"I missed you, Mags," he told me, with that casual sincerity that always took me aback.

I didn't know how he could do that. Just say what he felt all the time, without worrying what the response would be.

I didn't say anything, just nuzzled down beside him and waited for him to tell me about his time.

"Recap?" Brody asked, and I smiled.

It was our ritual every time he got home. Our time to share what we'd missed while we'd been apart.

I nodded, waiting for him to start.

"Your brother hurt my feelings." He fake-pouted. "And I won a hundred bucks in the casino."

"How much did you lose?"

He winced.

"Six hundred."

"Brody!" I slapped his chest.

"Hey!" He held his hands up to brace himself from attack. "Those little slot games are addicting. Plus, don't they pump the air full of oxygen in those places so you don't get tired?"

"How would that even work?" I shifted onto my side until I was leaning on his chest to look up at him.

"I don't know, it's just what I've always heard."

"Poor, naïve little boy," I teased.

"At least I have you to teach me the ways of the world, huh?"

"It's a good thing," I agreed.

"And I have you?" He asked, unusually earnest. "For always?"

I nodded, frowning at whatever worries I heard in his voice.

"What's wrong?" I shifted to look at him more intently.

He paused, eyes drifting off to stare at the wall behind me.

"I think Liam wants to quit the team."

"What?"

"Not quit, I guess," he amended. "But retire."

"He's only thirty-two," I said, finding it hard to reconcile my young, active brother and the word *retirement*.

"Most professional athletes retire before they hit thirty," Brody countered.

"But what would he *do*?"

I couldn't imagine it. Not waking up with a purpose. Not having anywhere to be or tasks to complete.

I think it would make me feel empty. Lost. I probably wouldn't last a week.

"Probably continue adding to the Brynn brood."

I laughed.

"Which he could totally do and hold a job at the same time." He paused for a beat. "Just like we could."

"Brody," I groaned, rolling off of him.

"What?" He sat up. "Don't you want a little guy to hang out with you?"

"I have you," I said, grabbing some clothes off the floor and stuffing them into the hamper.

I didn't even know if they were dirty; I just needed a task to do.

"I mean a kid, Mags."

"I know what you meant," I said, moving around the room. "I was deflecting."

Brody frowned.

"Don't you think we're getting to that point?"

"What point?" I asked. "Having kids? Just because I turned thirty?"

"It has nothing to do with age. I just feel like we're ready."

"How could you possibly think we're ready?" I looked at him aghast. "You're away multiple nights a week for hockey, and I'm working seventy hours a week."

"You could cut back at work." Brody shrugged. I made a noise of protest, but he continued. "Go part-time. It's not like we're pressed for money."

"I *like* working," I countered.

"I know you do, but you hardly have a life outside of it lately," he said. "It wouldn't hurt to have something else to focus on."

"So what—you think the solution to me working too much is keeping me home with a baby that I have to take care of for the next *eighteen years?*"

"Why are you making it sound like having a kid is the worst thing in the world?" He drew back. "We always said it was in the plan for us."

"Yeah, but when we talked about that, it was always more of a hypothetical, like in the distant future."

And really, it was more Brody and all his comments like,

When we have a kid I can't wait to teach them how to skate.

When we have a kid I can't wait to get them a baby-sized jersey.

When we have a kid I can't wait for all of us to go to the park on the weekends.

Always these minuscule scenarios with no regard to the practicality of what that life would actually entail for us.

"I mean, this is the future from when we talked about it."

"Brody, stop," I told him. "It's not the right time. Do you get that?"

His face transformed, as if he were in the midst of some great epiphany.

"You're totally right, Mags," he said, taking a step toward me. I stilled, cautious. "I'm sorry, I just got excited. We're not even married yet."

"Right," I sighed in relief, clutching at the excuse for why the timing wasn't right. "That definitely has to come first."

"I know," he said as I let him wrap me in a hug. "Trust me, I'm on the same page as you there."

I tried to relax, I really did. Tried to lean into him in the way that usually felt so safe.

But no matter how hard I tried to tell myself that he was right. We were on the same page. Nothing was going to change.

I couldn't help but feel like I was on the edge of a precipice.

Maggie

It was the night of the father-daughter dance when I finally lost it. It had been a month and a half since Dad left, but I'd been holding out hope that tonight would be the night he came home.

He knew about the dance. He agreed to take me when the slip came back at the start of the year. We signed up. I had a dress—purple with navy blue flowers embroidered on.

I had daydreamed about him remembering the date of the dance and showing up on our doorstep with a corsage for me and open arms ready to twirl me around before we went to the elementary school.

It was just in the gymnasium. It wasn't anything special. But I had been so excited to spend a night alone with my Dad. I thought I could impress him, if I finally had him to myself.

I could recite all the math facts I'd learned. I would *wow* him with how mature I spoke, so he could be proud of me like he was of Liam. I even practiced dancing alone in my room so I wouldn't step on his feet during the dance.

It was going to be a good night.

And even though he'd been gone and we hadn't heard from him, I got ready anyway. He wouldn't let me down. I knew he wouldn't.

But the clock ticked, and even though my eyes were glued to the window, my Dad's car never pulled up.

I waited. And I waited. And I waited.

And then my mom came out, her own eyes still red from crying.

I turned away from her, angry at the very sight.

It was *her* fault Dad was gone. She was the one he left.

Not me. Not Liam. It couldn't be us.

I couldn't stomach the idea of it being us.

"What are you doing, Maggie?" she said, watching me as I stood by the window.

"I'm waiting for Dad to take me to the dance," I told her, feeling stupid as I said it. "He knows it's tonight."

"Oh, baby," my mom said, drying her eyes on the sleeve of her ratty sweatshirt. "I'll take you to the dance. Let me get ready."

"No!" I shouted, furious with her. "I want to go with Dad!"

Why would I want to go to the dance with my mother? What would I say when my friends asked why I brought her instead of my Dad? How would I feel seeing everyone with their fathers when I didn't even know where mine was?

No. If my Dad wasn't taking me, I wouldn't go at all.

"Maggie, your hair," my mother said, coming to touch my fresh curls, still smelling half fried from the heat. "Did you use the curling iron all by yourself?"

I nodded.

"You look so pretty, baby," my mom said, reaching out to hug me.

I pushed her away. I didn't want her touch. I didn't want anyone's.

Everyone disappointed me.

Dad left. Liam was never home. Mom had retreated to her room.

Everyone left me, and I hated them all for it.

I heard the sound of a car pulling up, and my heart pounded with anticipation as I turned my attention away from my mother and back out the window.

Then, it broke all over again, because I'd been foolish enough to hope.

It wasn't him. It was just Liam, getting dropped off by his friend's mom. I watched him walk up the path, hockey bag in tow as he took each step with a heavy foot.

He never wanted to be home anymore.

I didn't either, but I had nowhere to go.

And I had to be home, in case Dad showed up. I had to be here to tell him we needed him to stay.

I started to sob. I couldn't help it.

Everything was wrong, and I had a feeling it was never going to get better.

And worse than the realization of that was the loss of hope that had kept me going. I had only survived this long because of it. Now, that was shattered, too.

The door opened and Liam walked in, staring between me and our mother in alarm as the two of us cried.

"What's going on?" he asked warily, looking like he wanted to take a step back out the door and get as far away from us as possible.

"Maggie's father-daughter dance was tonight," Mom told him. She sounded sorry for me.

I didn't want Liam to feel sorry for me, too, so I forced myself to wipe away the tears and put on a brave face.

"Why'd you dress up?" Liam asked, eyebrows furrowing in confusion. "It's not like he's here to take you."

I wanted to scream.

Why had I dressed up?

Because Liam told me that Dad would come back. In the principal's office that day, he said that dads didn't leave their kids behind. And I had believed him.

I told him as much, and Liam scoffed at my words. He hated when we were crying. I don't think he knew what to do with it.

It made him shut down instantly. Or get angry.

And then I got angry that he couldn't just make me feel better.

"He's gone, Maggie," Liam said harshly. "Face it."

"No!" I yelled. "He's coming back!"

"He's not!"

"His boat is still in the driveway," the tears streamed down my face as my voice grew hoarse from screaming. "He has to come back for his boat!"

"If he doesn't care about his kids, then he doesn't care about a fucking boat, Maggie!" Liam yelled back, matching my volume.

"Language!" Mom interjected, but it was a weak attempt.

It didn't make a difference now, the same way it didn't the hundred other times she'd said it over the last month.

Liam had been swearing a lot lately. He'd been angry, too. All the time.

I wished I had been, too, instead of drowning in the sorrow.

At least then it wouldn't hurt as much.

"But you told me he was coming back," I said again, desperate as I tried to regain control of myself.

"Well, I was wrong!" he said, and I could swear I saw that flicker of pain I felt mirrored in his eyes.

But it didn't feel like he was wrong. It felt like he lied.

Like a betrayal.

And if Liam could lie to me about something, it meant anyone could. And anyone *would*.

Even if they didn't mean to. Even if they thought they meant it in the moment. Things could always change. I had to know that. To be prepared for it.

People changed their minds.

Liam went upstairs and slammed his door.

I ran to mine and slammed mine.

I didn't have to wish to be angry anymore—now I felt it, too. It burned. My chest, my stomach, my eyes.

Pain wasn't just in my head. It was a tangible force, threatening to overtake me.

It was overwhelming as I felt it course through me in waves. Anger. Rage. Fury.

I scribbled on paper and ripped it up. I slammed doors whenever I could. I started getting sent to the principal's office. And I only cried at night when I knew everyone was asleep.

Yes, the anger was overwhelming.

But it was better than the sadness.

CHAPTER TEN

Brody

I had a plan.

The logistics were a little hazy, but I felt secure in the fact that I knew what my next step was.

I needed to do three things.

Propose to Maggie.

Convince Liam not to abandon the team.

Somehow figure out the best way to go about both of those things.

I could only think of one solution.

Cassie.

My favorite little blonde was my go-to person for emotional talks about our mutual Brynns. Shockingly, my girlfriend and best friend weren't always the best at opening up. Especially when it came to their feelings.

But Cassie? She seemed to have this superhuman ability to clock their emotional states with freakish accuracy, giving me insight that I never would've considered.

In a way, she was like my own personal psychic. Only she didn't charge me for her services.

"Where's Liam tonight?" I asked, looking around the living room as if he might pop out any moment and yell at me for going behind his back to talk to his wife about his potential career-ending choices.

"He's at dinner with Maggie," she said, sitting down in the armchair across from me. "Didn't she tell you?"

Huh. I thought she had dinner with her dad tonight.

"I guess I mixed up the details." I scratched the back of my head. Or forgot to listen to them.

That tended to happen sometimes. Especially when I had life-altering plans on my mind.

"I—" I started, hesitating on which aspect of my crisis to dive into before getting distracted by whatever she was pouring into the mug in front of me.

"What is that? It smells amazing."

"Lavender tea," she said. "It's good for stress."

"Do you think I'm stressed?" I laughed.

She didn't say anything, just looked pointedly at my rapidly bobbing knee.

I paused mid-motion, clearing my throat before I reached forward for the cup.

"You're good, Cass," I shook my head with a smile. "I'll give you that. And that's actually why I came here to see you."

"You came here to see *me*?" she said, lighting up a little at the notion. "I thought you came for Liam, realized he wasn't home, and felt bad leaving."

"What?" I drew back. "No, of course not. Cassie, we're friends, too."

She nodded, as if pleased by the words that I thought should be common knowledge by now.

"So, spill." She leaned forward eagerly. "What can I do for you?"

"I'm here about our SOs."

She arched a brow in question.

"Sorry," I amended, realizing I probably spent too much time on Reddit. "Our significant others. Partners. Loves of our little delicate lives."

Cassie smiled warmly, as if basking in the very thought of Liam. I grinned at her reaction.

"What about them?" she asked.

"Oh," I sighed, "where to start? Well, for one, can you tell me why Liam's been so pissy lately?"

Cassie's face fell.

"You noticed, huh?" She chewed her lip, setting her tea down on the coffee table.

"He hasn't been very subtle about it," I admitted.

"I think he's upset about missing so many nights with Lily," she explained. "It's hard on him, being away as much as he is."

"But he *loves* hockey," I emphasized. "I know the away games can suck, but we can't let him quit the team—"

"He told you he's quitting?" she asked, eyes widening.

"Insinuated it."

"I didn't know he was thinking about doing that," she admitted.

"It would be a huge mistake," I emphasized. "You know Liam. He'd go insane after just a week off the ice. I don't want him to do something major that he'd regret the rest of his life. He still has plenty of years left in him."

Cassie nodded, considering.

"Plus…" I hesitated.

She met my eyes expectantly.

"Plus?"

To hell with it. I could be vulnerable with Cassie. She wouldn't judge me.

"Plus, I need him," I admitted honestly. "I don't want to spend the next few years without him."

I thought of practice without Liam, games without him. No one to put me in my place when I was being over-the-top obnoxious. We balanced each other out in a way that was crucial for my sanity.

I knew how the score went. If he left, he'd say nothing would change—that we'd still see each other all the time. But that would be a lie.

People grew apart, no matter their best intentions.

And I wasn't ready for that.

"I agree with you," she surprised me by saying. "Liam needs hockey in his life. I don't think he would know how much he would miss it until it was gone."

"So, you'll talk to him about it?"

She nodded.

"I'll give him my honest opinion, but that's all I can do. I can't change his mind if he's set on it."

I doubted that.

Liam would jump off a cliff if she asked him to, though I understood the position she was coming from.

"Thanks, Cass," I sighed in relief. "Now, about Maggie—"

She looked up at me nervously, apparently expecting the worst. I fought a laugh, glad that I saved the Maggie news for last. I was pretty sure that would be a more uplifting note to end the night with.

"I'm going to propose," I dropped the bomb, and before I even finished uttering the sentiment, Cassie was jumping to her feet and squealing.

"Shhhh," I grabbed her lightly by the wrist, pulling her back down to her seat. "You're going to wake Lily up."

"Good!" she exclaimed. "We should all celebrate!"

"Not yet," I told her. "It's still a secret."

"How are you going to do it?" she asked. "When are you going to do it? Can I be there when you do it?"

"I haven't figured out the details yet. The idea sort of just hit me earlier and I just knew it was the right thing to do."

I shook my head, clarifying.

"I mean, I know Maggie still has a few more things she wants to accomplish, and I know I'm still traveling a lot for work and it's hard for her to travel with me," I said, listing off a few of the reasons why Maggie had wanted to wait in the past. "But I realized, I don't care."

"You don't?"

"I mean, I care. But I don't think it's a reason to wait anymore. There's always going to be a million reasons why the timing isn't exactly perfect, but sometimes you just have to jump anyway. Right?"

Cassie responded with a face-encompassing grin that let me know she was on the same page as me.

"So," I smirked at her, "do you want to help me plan out the most epic proposal, or what?"

Her answer came in the form of another ear-piercing squeal.

Brody

Five Years Ago

"So, what's going on with you and blondie?" I asked Liam in the locker room after a game.

He stared at me, face ridden with disapproval.

A lesser man might've withered under his gaze, but I knew Liam too well to be anything but amused at his overt display of irritation.

"You rush home to get to her. You're always texting her when we're away. You're always thinking about her when you aren't with her—"

"How the hell would you know what I'm thinking about?"

"And don't think I haven't noticed the way that scowl disappears whenever she's in a fifty-foot radius."

He shook his head, muttering a curse under his breath.

"So, I ask again, what's going on with you and blondie?"

"What's going on with you and my sister?" he retorted, arching a brow as if that would deter me.

"Hopefully a lot." I grinned cheekily.

He rolled his eyes. "Well, that backfired."

"It did," I agreed. "Because unlike you, I don't have any issue admitting how crazy I am about the girl I'm seeing."

"I'm not seeing Cassie," he said. "She's my roommate."

"But you are crazy about her." I grinned, noting how he didn't deny it.

Liam couldn't lie, so he just looked down at his skates, pulling them off with a shake of his head.

I had never seen him like this before. So hung up on a girl. I didn't think he had it in him to care about anything but hockey.

It was endearing.

His stalker fans were going to be *pissed.*

But I wasn't going to push him on it too much.

It was enough that Cassie was getting him to open up with her. He just needed one person to be that outlet for him. One person he could let his defenses down with.

I hadn't really met the girl, but I was super fucking grateful for her entrance into his life.

Liam didn't realize it, but he probably owed it all to Maggie.

I cleared my throat, remembering the urgent matter I needed to discuss with him.

"So," I started, "speaking of your sister."

"I'd rather not."

"As you can tell, I like her a lot," I said.

Understatement of the century.

"Like *a lot,* a lot."

"Nice." He said. "We don't need to keep talking about it."

"I just wanted to check in and see if…" I started, almost hesitant to finish. "To see if you're cool with it?"

There was a pause, and I felt anxiety bubble up in my chest.

If he said no, would I stop seeing her?

Probably not, I realized, but I'd much prefer to have his blessing. He was my best friend, after all. And even though he was elusive and grumpy—I knew I was his, too.

I didn't need the validation of hearing him admit it.

"I don't care what you guys do in your free time," he said.

"So, I have your blessing?"

"Whatever."

"No, you need to say it, because I want to invite her to be my date to the gala and I'm not going to do it if you'll make her feel uncomfortable all night."

"Invite her," he bit out. "I don't care."

"No, you have to be clear so there's no confusion. Say, 'Brody, you have my blessing to date my beautiful and intelligent sister.'"

"Fucking yes, Brody. You have my blessing. Okay?"

I grinned.

"Thanks."

Maggie

I was jittery, as if I'd just downed three Red Bulls in consecutive order. A feat I'd only done a handful of times in my career—and only for *very* important cases.

But tonight? The energy thrumming through me had nothing to do with caffeine. Only the nerves of the scene I'd set up and what it would mean for the future of my family.

Liam got there first.

I didn't know if that was preferable. But I didn't have time to mentally debate it because he was already sliding down into the chair across from me, side-eyeing the chair to the right of me.

"Is Brody coming?" he asked.

"No," I started, voice feeling caught in my throat.

I didn't know what I was doing. It was possible I was in over my head, but I knew I had to try or I would regret it forever.

I needed a backup plan—the way everyone else had.

People had their relationships of their choosing—boyfriends, best friends, spouses… but you couldn't *really* rely on them. Not the way you could family.

I knew Brody loved me. I did.

But there was always the possibility something could go wrong. A crack could appear that he might not feel like patching up. If that were the case, he would have his entire family to turn to. He'd never be really alone.

But me?

My family was scattered. Broken.

I couldn't stand the idea of it. Not if I knew I had the chance to repair it.

We were adults now. We could do it. Put aside the past and move forward together. Right?

"Weird spot for dinner, Mags." Liam arched a brow, looking around the dimly lit restaurant. "I figured we'd just get pizza or something."

I scrunched the napkin in my lap, feeling like my heart was pounding out of my chest.

"Liam, I have to tell you something—" I started, but my words evaporated into the air at the sound of Liam sucking in a sharp breath.

"What the hell is he doing here?" Liam glared in the direction of the door.

I turned, following his gaze to watch as our father walked in, handing his coat to the doorman.

"I invited him." I looked Liam dead in the eye.

I couldn't back down now.

"What the f—"

"And before you say anything, or storm out, I want you to *try*. For me. Give him a chance."

Liam's eyes radiated hatred. Rage. And even though I knew it was directed more toward our father than me, I still shifted uncomfortably under the weight of it.

"How many times have I told you—" he said, standing from his seat, nearly sending the chair toppling behind him.

"Liam," I said through gritted teeth. "Sit down."

Our father arrived at the table, staring at Liam with an awestruck look on his face, as if he were in the presence of some celebrity rather than his own son.

"Liam," he breathed.

Liam responded with a clenched jaw, sitting down in an almost slow-motion movement.

He didn't say anything at all, just kept his eyes on our father like he were a threat that might need to be dealt with at any moment.

"Dad," I said, shifting the energy away from Liam and his death glare. "So glad you could make it."

Sometimes I felt like I talked to him as if he were a supervisor. A boss of some kind. I shook that energy off.

He was just my dad. I didn't need to be this stressed about dinner with him.

It took him a minute before he tore his gaze away from Liam and turned to me.

"Margaret," he nodded simply, before sitting down.

Liam scoffed, and our father's energy was once again directed at him, body angled toward him in anticipation.

"Thanks for coming, son," he said wearily. "It—it means a lot to me."

"I didn't know you were going to be here." Liam shook his head, a look of disgust clouding his features.

Dad looked taken aback, turning to me with a curious look.

Didn't he know I did this for him? I gave him what he'd been asking for for years—to see Liam. To have a chance to explain things to him.

"Regardless," Dad shook his head clear of any thoughts, "I'm so happy to see you."

"Can't say the same on my end." Liam bristled.

The waitress came over at that opportune moment, starting her spiel about drink orders, before her head whipped back to look at Liam.

"Oh my gosh, are you—" She narrowed her eyes at him. "Are you Liam Brynn?"

Dad beamed.

"He sure is."

Liam shot him a sideways glare and I sank lower into my chair.

This wasn't how it was supposed to go. Liam was supposed to let his defenses down a bit. He was supposed to be open to conversation. For me.

The waitress, sensing the hostility running rampant at our table, assured us she'd be back with waters and bread, then scurried off as far as possible.

Hell, I was thinking of going in the back to offer help washing dishes, if only to get away from the suffocating resentment pouring off Liam.

I got him here. That was as far as the plan went in my head. I figured the rest would work itself out. Like dominoes falling in line and whatnot.

I should've known my brother would have the willpower of steel when it came to being oppositional.

"Son, I've been wanting to talk to you for so long—"

"*Don't* call me that," Liam spat.

"For God's sake, Liam," I interjected, "give it a rest. He's just trying to have a conversation with you."

"And I already made it clear, I don't *want* to have a conversation with him." Liam scowled at me. "I mean, really Maggie, what the hell were you thinking?"

"He wants to explain." I pleaded.

"Fine." Liam said, turning to face our father with full attention. "Explain. Tell me why you did it. No—tell me *how* you did it without remorse. Or guilt. Or giving a single damn about us until fifteen years passed by and you, what—woke up and remembered we existed in the world?"

"It was complicated, Liam." Dad said firmly. "Your mother is a difficult woman. She was going to make the whole process impossible. I needed a clean break."

"A clean break from your children?" Liam countered, furious.

"It doesn't mean I didn't love you. Relationships are complicated."

"Life is complicated. You stick it out because that's just life. You don't get to quit halfway through."

"I was still young. I had an opportunity to make something of myself. I wouldn't have been able to do that if your mother dragged me to court, putting me through the ringer with custody battles. You two have no idea how ugly those can get."

I froze. He *knew* that's what I did for a living, didn't he? I brought it up every time I saw him. Hadn't he paid attention?

"Real nice guy, isn't he, Mags?" Liam turned to me with a bitter shake of his head.

"What?" Dad said, completely lost. "Son, listen—you have no idea what it's like until you get into the situation for yourself—"

"I will *never* get in that situation," Liam said furiously.

"You're young," Dad continued as if Liam hadn't spoken. "You have an amazing career. If your wife tried to tie you down with child support payments and the threat of facing years in courtrooms, you might start to understand a little more what I was trying to get away from."

Liam shook his head, furious at the words pouring out of his mouth.

I had to agree with Liam. I knew the point Dad was trying to make, but he was going about it entirely the wrong way—especially where Liam was concerned.

"If you chose to just walk away from it all, it wouldn't mean you didn't love Lily—"

"How the hell do you know about Lily?" Liam's voice thundered.

"Maggie's mentioned her over the years," Dad shifted in his seat, before Liam shot a glare in my direction.

Jesus Christ. If looks could kill, I'd be dead where I sat.

"Liam," I said pleadingly, but he was already standing up from his seat. "Don't make a scene."

"I'm not making a scene." Liam said. "I'm just done."

"Liam," I called, standing to my feet to chase after him.

Liam and his damned long legs were already out the door by the time I caught up with him. Rain drizzled down on us, sending a chill through me.

January nights in Boston were frigid, but Liam looked like he was burning from within. I was sure that if I got close enough I would feel it radiating off him in scorching waves.

"Liam," I pleaded desperately. "Please, wait!"

"You don't get to keep doing this, Maggie!" He spun to face me, radiating fury. "I'm a *person*."

"I know that," I said, scrambling for some defense, while the sinking realization crept in that I might be entirely in the wrong.

God, what had I done?

"People don't just exist for your amusement, Maggie!" he yelled, loud enough to draw attention. "I'm not a puppet. I'm not here to revolve around your own soap opera plot line."

I whirled back, feeling the sting of his words like a slap to the face. But he wasn't done.

"I told you how I felt," he said. "I told you a million times. And you just didn't care, because it didn't fit into the plan *you* wanted for yourself."

I hadn't meant to hurt him. I really hadn't. I thought it would make things better. I thought enough time had passed. I thought this was what he wanted but was too scared to say himself.

I thought I knew best—and it bit me in the ass.

"I'm sorry, Liam," I whispered meekly, tears stinging my eyes. "I just thought you would regret it. Regret not giving him another chance. Now that you're a dad, I thought you'd realize how much it hurts when your kid cuts you out of their life."

"Becoming a dad has made me realize *he* never was one." Liam retorted. "He made his own choices in life. And I get to make mine to hold him to them."

"You're just bitter," I said. "Someone screws you over once and you write them off forever. It's not healthy."

He grabbed his face in his hands, eyes clenching shut as if he couldn't believe what I was saying.

A part of me wanted to apologize, to take it all back. He was right that he got to make his own choices, even if I didn't think they were the right ones.

But admitting I was wrong had never been easy for me. It was easier to dig my feet in and die on the hill of my choosing than apologize and face rejection anyway.

I looked to Liam, praying that he would relent first. That he would tell me he forgave me and we could leave this whole mess in the past, never to be brought up again.

But he didn't.

"I can't keep doing this, Maggie." He shook his head sadly. "I can't. I get emotional whiplash from all these grand ideas you force me and everyone else into."

"What are you saying?"

"I'm done. I don't want to be involved anymore. I can't take it."

And then he started to walk away, rain beginning to pour down from the sky as he got farther down the sidewalk.

"So, what?" I yelled shrilly, as the rain plastered my hair against my forehead. "Are you going to cut me out now, too?"

He paused, only turning halfway as he dealt the deathblow to our relationship.

"I love you, Mags," he said, "but you need to learn how to figure your shit out without dragging me into it."

And then he was gone.

Maggie

Five Years Ago

The first time I pulled away from Brody, it was out of pure jealousy.

I hadn't consciously known I was doing it, or even why. It was just an instinct. A knee-jerk reaction that I hadn't quite wanted to analyze too deeply.

All I knew was that I *had* to.

To stay safe, the voice in my head told me I needed some distance.

It had taken a few months before I realized what caused me to spiral the way I did after seeing Brody beside his family.

I was scared of being left.

He'd had this perfect family with corny jokes and easy smiles and a miraculously stable upbringing. And what did I have? A brother who didn't really need me? A mother whose emotions dictated her life?

A father who had just made contact for the first time in fifteen years?

No, I would never be good for someone like Brody. He needed someone normal. A girl who wasn't dragging around an elephant's weight of emotional baggage wherever she went.

And sooner or later, I knew he would realize it.

He had people to fall back on when times got tough, so what did he need me for?

Me with my broken brain and messy life and temper that rose up in the most bizarre of situations, without me even really knowing why.

I'd been quiet that night when I met his family, certain that they would see right through me, spot all the things I was trying to hide.

Would they tell Brody he could do better? Would they encourage him to find some other girl?

It wasn't until we were leaving dinner that I realized he'd be okay without me. He already had a family. A job he loved. A personality that made everyone love him at first sight.

He didn't need the girl with the fucked-up head dragging him down.

So, I pulled back. It was for the best, I told myself. I'd initiate the soft breakup—if we were even at that point—and that way it would hurt less when he realized what everyone else probably already knew.

He could do better.

But Brody noticed.

When I started putting the distance between us, he saw it right away and he gave me hell for it.

"Margaret Brynn," Brody's voice filled my ears the second I'd walked out of the office.

There he was, sitting on the steps across the street, looking absolutely enraged at me.

Oh God, I'd thought, stomach sinking.

I'd been avoiding him. Ignoring his calls. I didn't tell him why, because it sounded crazy even to my own ears.

I thought he'd just let me fade out, the way most people did. I thought he'd move on.

But here he was, storming across the street without a care in the world for traffic—even as they honked at him, rolling down their windows to shout obscenities at him.

"Where the hell have you been?"

"At work," I pointed a thumb to the building behind me, suddenly feeling ashamed.

He didn't deserve this. He didn't deserve to be treated like this. I didn't know why I did it. But I always did. Over and over again.

Brody was just the first person to fight me on it.

"Not now." He exhaled, almost in relief at finally seeing me in the flesh. "The last *three* days."

"I've been busy," I shifted awkwardly on my feet.

I didn't like to lie to him, but what else could I say?

"I almost got fined a fuck-ton of money because I was about to get on a plane and fly back here to find you."

He was going to skip a game for me? I thought, finding it oddly romantic.

"What stopped you?" I asked.

"Your brother told me you do this sometimes. When you need space." He said, pain swirling in his big brown eyes. "But guess what? Three days is plenty of space, so I'm not leaving you alone any longer. You got it?"

Good. I didn't want space. I never did.

I wanted him to care. I wanted to see if he missed me.

Then came the realization of how utterly screwed up I was.

I hadn't been trying to ghost him. I'd only wanted to see if he cared. I had unknowingly tested him. Tested his loyalty. Tested the strength of his love.

And he had passed.

For now.

"I got it." I nodded at him.

And he stared at me, blinking. As if he didn't expect it to be so easy. As if he thought I would put up a fight.

But I didn't want to. I just wanted to love him. And be loved by him back.

He was good at it.

In fact, I didn't think there was anyone better at loving me than Brody Callahan.

CHAPTER TWELVE

Brody

Maggie may or may not have been trying to kill me.

Not only did she wake me up at five in the morning to jog, but she was also hellbent on leaving me in the dust behind her.

"*Babe*," I huffed, forcing my legs to pump even faster. "Are we training for the Boston Marathon or something?"

She hadn't mentioned it, but given the fact that it was *Maggie,* I wouldn't put it past her to sign us up without telling me.

She didn't even pause—just kept running straight ahead. The scariest part? She wasn't even wearing headphones. Nope, she was absolutely rawdogging this run without any type of assistance.

And worse—she inflicted it on me, too.

"*Margaret Brynn,*" I stopped, feeling on the verge of passing out where I stood. "You come back here right now."

Hands on my hips, I sucked in a breath of frigid winter air, trying to regulate my body back to a normal, human rhythm.

She turned, noticing that I'd fallen several paces behind her, and she began to make her descent back to me.

"What's wrong?" she asked, still jogging in place.

"What's wrong is I'm jogging around Boston at five thirty in the morning in *January*." I held my arms out for emphasis. "You know what type of people do that, Maggie?" I narrowed my eyes at her. "Psychos."

She scoffed.

"You gotta tell me what's going on, babe," I said, giving her an examining look.

Her eyes were puffy as if she hadn't slept, and traces of eyeliner were still visible on her eyelids from the night before. Considering Maggie was the type of girl to have organic, biodegradable, makeup-removing cloths from Turkey paired with some insane micellar water cleanser, both of those things struck me as a bit of a red flag.

"We're running," she said. "You didn't have to come."

It was my turn to scoff.

"You think I'd let you run around Boston before the sun rose by yourself?" I gave her an incredulous look. "Let me repeat: only psychos are out at this hour."

She rolled her eyes.

It was times like this when she felt a million miles away. I couldn't get inside her head, no matter what I tried. And until she was ready to talk to me, there was nothing I could do but wait.

Patience was a virtue I had in multitudes.

But, unfortunately, digging her heels in was something Maggie had just as much experience with.

I sighed, gesturing to the path in front of us.

"After you," I said, letting her begin her sprint once more.

I looked up at the sky once, a silent plea to whoever was listening to end both my misery and this hellish jog in a timely manner.

After another twenty minutes of chasing after Maggie, I realized that request would go unanswered.

She cracked sooner than I expected.

But, I guess she had no choice, considering the topic came up by way of text.

I frowned down at Maggie's phone lighting up on the table. She left it there while she showered, always leaving it in my care to make sure it wasn't someone work-related trying to contact her.

There had been times when she had insisted that I bring the phone in, jet stream and all, so she could continue conducting business even when bathing.

But this?

I'd say it definitely warranted a conversation.

"Mags?" I asked, walking into the bathroom, carrying her phone in my hand like a bomb.

"Mhm?" she responded, voice muffled by the sound of the water stream.

"Did something happen at dinner last night?"

She pulled the curtain back rapidly, her heart-shaped face poking out with wide eyes.

"Why?" she started to ask, before her gaze went to the phone in my hand.

"What happened," she reached for it, "did Liam text?"

"No," I said, handing it to her. "Cassie."

Maggie deflated, before clicking on the text thread with Liam, apparently dismayed at the lack of notifications from it.

Green eyes met mine and she whispered,

"I think I screwed everything up."

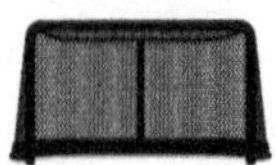

"Maggie," I groaned, rubbing my temples with such intensity as if I could erase myself from existence.

At least then I wouldn't be caught between my two favorite people having the family feud of a lifetime.

"I know," she groaned in return. "It's bad, isn't it?"

"I don't understand what you were hoping to achieve by bombarding him with the guy he's proclaimed to hate for as long as I've known him."

"I thought it was a cover-up!" Maggie said. "I didn't think he actually meant it that literally."

"It's just not your place to make that call for him, though, Mags," I said as gently as I could. "If he didn't want to see the guy, you should've respected that."

"Well aware, thank you," Maggie fumed, never liking to be told she was in the wrong about anything. "But this is Liam. It's not like he's going to hate me forever, right?"

I didn't think so.

But like she said, this was *Liam*. The guy who loved and hated with equal intensity. There never seemed to be much middle ground as far as anyone else was concerned.

You either existed in one of those two categories or you simply didn't exist at all to him. At least, not in any way that he'd acknowledge.

"I think it'll be fine," I told her after thinking about it for a minute. "But I think you really have to make it up to him somehow."

"He was so mad, Brody," she groaned, eyes getting watery. "I'd never seen him look at me like that."

"It'll be okay," I told her. "We'll fix it."

"Yeah?" she asked hopefully, wiping her eyes.

"Yeah, everything will be fine."

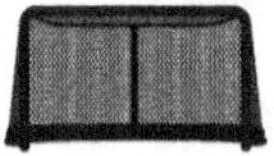

Everything was not fine.

The air inside the arena was frigid, having nothing to do with the ice and everything to do with a one Mr. Liam Brynn, who was apparently extending the cold shoulder not only to his sister, but also to me by association.

"Liam," I urged, watching as he skated right past me for the thousandth time that practice. "Please stop ignoring me, it makes me feel neglected."

Fragments of ice kicked up behind him as he skated past me without a glance.

"Have a fight with your boyfriend, Callahan?" Coach raised an eyebrow, having seen the whole encounter.

I rolled my eyes.

"Looks like it," I agreed, attempting to skate after him once more.

"Liam, please," I said. "I know you're upset, but it didn't have anything to do with me. I had no idea Maggie planned that."

He answered back with a snort.

"You have to believe me—"

He turned to face me, finally.

"I do believe you, Brody. I know Maggie is more than capable of coming up with diabolical schemes entirely on her own."

I frowned.

"I'd use the word mischievous over *diabolical*—"

"You let it happen though."

"What?" My head jerked back in shock. "I didn't—I told you, I had no idea."

"Not that." He shook his head. "I meant in general. Life. You let her think that every day is *The Maggie Show*, where she can do whatever she wants while screwing people over in the process."

"She doesn't screw people over, jackass." I countered, protectiveness rising in my chest. "Believe it or not, she usually thinks she's helping when she interferes."

"But that's what it is. Interfering. And she needs to learn to mind her goddamn business, which she never will since you go around enabling every shitty decision she makes."

"That's *not* true." I shook my head. "You just expect people to be perfect all the time."

"I expect people to know enough to have *boundaries*. Especially when they're fully grown adults."

"I get why you're upset, I do," I told him. "But she knows she messed up. She's not going to do it again."

"That's what I thought last time."

"Listen, Liam. You've got to get over whatever this is, because I have to talk to you about something important—"

"Save the lovers' spat for after hours," Coach bellowed from the sidelines.

I panicked. I felt like I was losing Liam and knew I might not get another chance to talk to him if I let him leave now.

Him and Maggie both were flighty like that. If I let them go, there was no telling when I'd get them back. The only answer was to act fast.

"Liam, wait." My voice was a plea.

He turned to look, face impassive but expectant.

"I wanted to ask your permission," I started, wondering if it was going to sound corny as hell. "I mean, I wanted to talk to you about—"

He raised a brow.

Inside my gloves, my palms were moist with anxiety. Was I really about to gamble the future of my relationship on a guy who was running high on emotions?

But I had to. I couldn't afford to wait the excruciatingly long cool-down process that Liam would need to get over his issue with his sister. It was now or possibly never.

"Spit it out, Brody," he urged, irritation rising as Coach glared at us once more.

My mouth opened, then shut. Liam sighed before turning to skate away, and then I let it all tumble out at once.

"I want to marry Maggie."

His green eyes widened, pausing at the revelation.

I stared at him anxiously. "So, what do you think?"

"Why are you telling me?" he asked with furrowed brows. "Isn't this a conversation to have with her?"

"Well, yeah. But you're supposed to ask permission," I rambled. "Usually to the father, I know. But the guy's a jerk, so—"

Liam huffed a laugh. "Damn right he is."

"So, I'm asking you."

"For permission to marry my sister?"

"Yes, for permission to marry your sister." I nodded. "You're the only consistent man that's ever been in her life. It's only right I should ask you."

He looked taken aback for a second, as if he'd never paid much thought to the role he played in Maggie's development. Despite their spat now, I knew that growing up he'd done everything for her that a father would do.

He took care of her car. He drove her to and from school. He looked out for her in more ways than a normal older brother would usually have to.

He meant the world to Maggie, even if he wouldn't admit it to himself. His approval *mattered*.

"Well, you have my permission." He said it without reservations. "But, along with that, I'm giving you a piece of advice."

I waited, knowing he wasn't the type to throw his two cents in often. Not unless the situation was in dire need of being fixed.

So when he opened his mouth to speak, I listened intently.

"You can ask her to marry you, Brody. But Maggie has always and will always make her own decisions." He paused, looking at me with sympathy, as if he were about to throw a blow he didn't really want to throw. "And going by her record, she's never been one for making the right decisions. Just something to think about."

And then he skated away.

THE BEACH

Brody

Five Years Ago

"**D**amn it, Maggie. Would you just let me catch you already?"

The beach was empty, save for the two of us. Thank God, because from an outsider's perspective, we must've looked like a pair of children running circles around each other on the shore.

Maggie laughed as she ran, sand kicking up under her bare feet the farther she got from me. She taunted me with a look thrown over her shoulder, watching as I struggled to catch up with her.

"You're an athlete, you should be able to keep up."

"I'm a hockey player," I huffed under my breath. "Not a track star. If we were on the ice, it would be a different story."

"Come on," she laughed, filling the October air with the most melodic sound I'd ever heard. Crashing waves and Maggie's laugh and the pounding of my heart in my ears. "Don't boys like the chase?"

"No," I said, inches away from her now as I reached out to pull her in.

Got you, I thought as my hand wrapped around her arm. She let me draw her close to me and I sighed in relief.

This girl sure as hell didn't make it easy on me, but I was willing to put in the work if that's what it took to keep her.

"No?" She arched a dark brow at me, suspicious and disbelieving all at once.

"I don't want the chase," I told her. "I want the girl I'm running after."

She closed her eyes, every inch of her illuminated by the moonlight. I stared at her, amazed at how someone so beautiful was standing right there in front of me.

Like a painting or a line of poetry. Something that should be reserved for better men than myself, but I'd be damned if I'd give her back now.

"You might change your mind," she said, barely audible compared with the sound of water crashing against sand.

"I won't," I told her.

She said nothing, but leaned in closer, and the scent of her filled in the gaps of everything I hadn't known I'd been missing.

"Is it too soon to say—" I started, not even knowing where I was going with it.

I want you. I love you. I already know that you've ruined everyone else for me for good.

But she stopped me, with a quick finger to my lips to silence me with a shake of her head.

"Yes."

That was fine. For now. We had time. Plenty of it, as far as I was concerned.

And she wasn't going to run from me forever. I knew that when I saw the way she looked up at me, with that look in her eyes brimming just below the surface. The one I could see she was trying her damned hardest to contain. It was the look that told me she hadn't been running to get away.

She'd only been waiting for me to catch her.

CHAPTER THIRTEEN

Maggie

I was *not* going to cry.

Not only was it unprofessional, it was also highly embarrassing.

I wasn't the type of girl to cry. Hardly ever. Unless you stuck me in front of the television screen and held me down while you forcibly played *The Notebook*.

At least then, there'd be a little more honor in the tears. I mean, who *doesn't* cry during that movie?

But ten o'clock on a Monday morning definitely didn't warrant sobbing. Even if Mr. Reilly was pulling on every single one of my heartstrings as he blubbered in front of me.

"I saw them," he said, wiping his eyes as if he could play off the fact that water was leaking out from the sides. "They look bigger somehow. Could they be bigger? It's only been a few weeks."

I mustered up enough energy to smile.

"I'm glad you got to see them. I bet they were, too."

"They didn't understand why I had to leave." He jerked his Red Sox hat off, fiddling with the strap as he spoke. "They didn't know why I couldn't go back home with them."

My chest tightened. I remembered that feeling all too well. The days following my dad leaving, when no one had been able to explain his absence.

But it was felt.

In every missing article of clothing, and collection of CDs that had been taken away with him.

I felt it—maybe not more intensely than my mother and brother, but definitely more loudly.

"But his boat is still in the driveway," I had sobbed to my mom. "He has to come back for his boat."

I kept telling everyone that he would be back. He had to come home soon. I didn't know when, but something inside of me had been so certain that he wouldn't stay away for long.

I'd been wrong.

Liam had spent a lot of time in his room, door shut to the world.

I had spent a lot of time trailing after my mother, asking question after question about what happened, or if they had a fight, or why I couldn't call him.

No one had any answers that satisfied me. And those empty questions just left more of a hole inside of me.

I flinched away from the memories, bringing my attention back to the client in front of me. I didn't have time to linger in the past. It didn't matter anymore.

My father was in my life again—no harm, no foul.

And if a part of me still felt like that little girl, wondering why he left her without a word, well, I didn't have time for her either.

Brody was good about knowing love languages.

Like, today when I came home from work with a certain look on my face and a weariness in my step, he knew exactly what I needed. Even before I did.

"Do you want to get all-you-can-eat tacos and margaritas?" The words were out of his mouth before I even dropped my bag down.

"Say less."

Within minutes, I was in his car, brain blissfully shut off from the shitstorm that was my life as we listened to some 80s hits.

I wasn't going to think about my family, I wasn't going to think about work. And I *especially* wasn't going to think about why the two seemed so interconnected lately, each reminding me of the other in annoyingly upfront ways.

My focus was only on the bottomless chips and salsa sitting in front of me while Brody ordered the rest of our food.

I could turn my brain off with him, knowing he had it covered. It was a weird feeling—good, but foreign in a lot of ways. Even after all these years.

It was the feeling of being taken care of. Being safe. Knowing that I didn't have to handle everything on my own, because someone was by my side to pick up whatever I couldn't carry.

I stared at him with a pathetically lovesick gaze I was mortifyingly aware of without even seeing my own face. I couldn't help it. He was the most handsome man I'd ever known, not to mention the kindest.

It was almost endearing how he pretended not to notice when every waitress, cashier, or pedestrian hit on him whenever he left the house.

"—you're my favorite player," I caught the end of whatever sentence the server was babbling at him.

"Really?" He said with a grin. "Thanks."

"Can I get a picture with you?" she asked, sheepishly.

I smirked into the basket of chips, knowing before he said it what his next words would be.

"Sure," he nodded predictably. "As long as my girlfriend can be in it, too."

The waitress looked over to me, as if noticing for the first time I was there.

"Oh yeah, of course. Thanks." She was pleasant enough, but her smile had definitely dampened.

The last few years, I'd learned a thing or two about girls who hit on Harbor Wolves players. Most of them were banking on the fact that most hockey players had a string of casual dates, so they figured it didn't hurt to disregard the girl they were currently sitting with, since it was bound to be someone else within a week, anyway.

It just showed they couldn't have been *that* big a fan of Brody, because I'd been plastered all over his Instagram for years.

He was comforting in that way. I didn't have to wonder where I stood with him. I didn't have to worry.

He was solid. Consistent. Everything I needed.

And when the waitress left, after getting her selfie with our table, I smiled at him. Warmly and genuinely, the feeling of it erasing whatever lingering negativity had built up from the last few days.

"What?" he said, noticing the way I stared at him.

"I love you," I told him.

I didn't say it a lot. Maybe sometimes I even forgot to show it as much as I felt it. But I needed him to know.

A smile overtook his face, as if it were the first time I said it.

"I love you, too, Mags." He reached across the table to squeeze my hand.

"No, really." I emphasized, needing him to understand how important he was to me. "You're my favorite person. Like in the whole world. And I'm so happy to be with you."

He blinked a few times.

"I know you'd make fun of me for saying something corny," he responded, "and you'd punch me for saying 'back atcha,' so I'm weighing my options."

I rolled my eyes at him, but kept his hand securely in mine.

"I'm kidding, I'm kidding." He laughed. "But you know you're everything to me, too. Don't you?"

"Yes," I answered, secure in that knowledge above all else in the world.

The sun would rise. There would be traffic on the I-93. And Brody loves me.

It was one of those facts that I knew couldn't be changed or helped. And in moments like these, when it felt like everything else was unraveling around me, I was desperate to cling onto things that wouldn't change.

CHAPTER FOURTEEN

Brody

I needed things to change.

First of all because it was time.

Second, because everything was all wrong.

Liam was shutting me out. Maggie was pretending to not be bothered by the fact that he was ignoring her. Cassie had been texting me frowny faces every day because she hated the disharmony just as much as I did.

I didn't like the silence. Not from Liam. Not from Maggie. Not from the group chat the four of us had that usually kept my phone buzzing with texts all day.

Usually, it was just me and Cassie talking in it anyway, but it was nice to have the occasional reactions from the elusive Brynn siblings.

Now, nothing. The group had broken apart, and I knew Maggie was reeling from it far more than she'd let on.

But I was going to fix it.

I was going to propose. Secure me and Maggie's future once and for all, and everything else would fall into place after.

Liam couldn't stay mad when he had to celebrate the engagement

124

of his best friend and his sister, and Maggie wouldn't be as down in the dumps when she got to do one of her favorite things in the world: plan a party.

I took a breath, feeling the weight of the mission on my shoulders as I stared down at the rings beneath the glass case.

There were *so* many. And they all looked identical. How was I supposed to know which one to choose when asking the biggest question of my life?

"Can I help you?" A woman's voice sent my head snapping up.

"Oh, um, yes." I stared helplessly at the worker. "I'm going to propose to my girlfriend."

She nodded kindly, even though there wouldn't be any other possible reason I'd be standing there, looking at engagement rings.

"Do you know what style ring you're looking for?" she asked, same polite smile on her face.

"Style?" I panicked.

"Solitaire? Diamond cut? Princess cut?"

I stared at her blankly.

"One stone? Multiple stones? Lab-grown or natural?"

"Uh, can I phone a friend?"

"What?"

Oops. I forgot not everyone watched Who Wants to Be a Millionaire reruns with their families growing up.

"Give me a second, I'll be right back." I muttered, rushing out of the jewelry store faster than I would've if I'd stolen something.

Scrambling for the phone in my pocket, my fingers typed frantically, dialing the number of the one person I knew I could call in this situation.

"Hello?" The answering voice replied.

I didn't have time for small talk, so I jumped straight to the point.

"I'm sending you my location," I said quickly, sounding more panicked than the situation probably called for. "Get here as fast as you can."

Cassie got to the storefront in record time, only looking as out of breath as she did the time Maggie dared us all to run a 5k with her.

All in all, not bad.

Still, I couldn't help but feel a little guilty when I saw her reddened cheeks puff in and out as she took in oxygen.

"What," she gasped, "happened? Are you okay?"

"Sorry," I winced, "I guess I should've clarified that it wasn't life or death."

The corners of her mouth twitched down in a frown. Probably the extent of a negative reaction I'd get from her.

"You could've," she agreed.

"*But*," I grinned sheepishly, hoping the real reason would make up for whatever irritation Cassie was trying to hide, "it's technically an emergency, because as Maggie's best friend, I thought you should be here to give me input on her engagement ring."

Color and vitality returned to Cassie's face at once as she bounced on her heels. After letting out a squeal and begging for me to show her, I had to tell her that I hadn't *actually* picked it out yet.

She crossed her arms over her chest smugly, looking at the storefront behind me.

"Oh, I see. You called me here because you're scared to buy the wrong ring and have Maggie give you hell for it the rest of your lives."

"*No.*" I denied. "Maggie would appreciate anything that came from the heart."

We both stared at each other for a few seconds before bursting into laughter at the same time.

"No, she wouldn't." We shook our heads in unison.

"So, you see why I need your help, then?" I asked anxiously. "I just need it to be perfect."

Cassie gestured to the door. "Lead the way."

With more confidence now that I had Cassie, I ventured back into the store with the intensely illuminating lights and the hundreds of diamonds that taunted me with their relentless sparkles.

It's like even *they* knew I'd pick the wrong one.

"Oh, good," the woman who had been assisting me earlier greeted us with a smile. "You brought your partner."

"What?" Cassie giggled.

"No, no, no." I shook my head, praying that Liam didn't hear that from wherever in the city he was. "This is my—well, this is my girlfriend's—"

"I'm his soon-to-be sister-in-law," Cassie smirked.

"Is that how it works?" I asked.

Cassie frowned, thinking about it.

"I think so." Then she faltered. "It should be?"

I laughed while Cassie turned to the worker and said,

"I'm married to his soon-to-be fiancée's brother. Who also happens to be my best friend." Cassie rambled. "Best friend to his fiancée, that is. Not my husband. But I'd consider him to be my best friend, too."

"Cass," I put a hand on her shoulder.

"Yeah?"

"I think she got it." I turned to the worker. "You got that, right?"

The worker, looking flustered, gave us a polite, albeit confused, smile.

"Anyway," I broke through the awkwardness, "can you ask me those questions again about princesses and stones and all that? It'll be easier now that Cassie's here."

And just like a magic interpreter, Cassie spoke the language of this woman in a way that ended up saving my ass.

Maggie

Five Years Ago

"Say you'll be my girlfriend, Maggie." Brody pleaded over dinner about a month into whatever it was we'd been doing. "I think I'll die if you say no."

"I don't know." I looked down at my plate to avoid his gaze. "I've never been a girlfriend before." I paused, feeling stupid. "I mean, I have, but—"

Not in the way it would be with him, I could already tell.

"We'll figure it out together," he said.

I liked that. We. Together. I wanted it. And it scared me, because if I wanted it, it meant it could be taken away. And I didn't want to hurt. I wanted the path that guaranteed I could avoid it ending badly.

"What about you?" I deflected. "Have any serious girlfriends?"

"Serious?" he mused. "A few here and there, but I guess the longest was Abbey."

I felt rigid at another girl's name on his lips.

That wasn't right. He was mine. How could there have been a time when he wasn't? When he was some other girl's Brody?

It was ridiculous, but I couldn't help it.

"Abbey?" I asked casually, inviting him to tell me more.

Even though I didn't think I really wanted to know.

"My high school girlfriend. Dated for two years. Broke up when we went away to college but, uh"—he scratched his head, looking embarrassed—"we were sort of on and off during breaks."

Tense, I nodded.

"What was she like? Did you love her?"

"I don't want to talk about her," he said. "I want to talk about you and me."

But I needed to know. I didn't want to, but I had to learn every last detail, so if he ever referenced her in the future it wouldn't feel like a sting of jealousy each time I encountered a new memory from his life that I hadn't been a part of. That some other, faceless girl had with him.

Abbey, I frowned.

Why did his past feel like some sort of betrayal? He was twenty-five years old; of course he'd had girlfriends before. I could hardly expect to be the first.

But I wanted to be the most important. I knew it with a certainty above all else. Because I'd had lots of boys before. Some who even claimed to love me.

But none of them had been Brody.

So, when he asked again if we were together, really and truly—I didn't hesitate this time when I told him yes.

Maggie

I caved.

I told myself I wasn't going to be the one to contact Liam first. I told myself I was going to give him space. I told myself that I would let him come to me in his own time.

But it had been two weeks of silence on his end, and I knew the longer I let him keep his distance, the easier it would be to maintain it.

So, I decided, after the game was over I'd follow Cassie right down to the family lounge where we'd wait for Liam to meet her. He wouldn't yell at me in front of Lily, even if he wanted to. And he couldn't kick me out, considering I could be there for Brody just as much as I was there for him.

And I was done with letting him shut me out.

At least Cassie had no such qualms with me.

"Why are you smiling at me like that?" I asked her, suspicious by the freakishly ecstatic way she kept glancing over at me.

Instantly, she reddened.

"I'm not."

"You're not?" I scoffed. "Are you telling me that look on your face right now isn't a smile?"

"I always smile," she retorted, using her high-pitched lying voice.

"You do always smile," I agreed, "but you don't always look like the clown from *It* when you do."

She gasped, looking horrified while Lily giggled in the seat beside her.

"You agree with me," I leaned across Cassie to coo in my niece's face, "don't you, Lily?"

Lily covered her mouth, rosy-cheeked and giggling as she looked up at Cassie's pouting face and then back to me.

"Tell your Auntie that I look perfectly normal," Cassie urged her, tickling her stomach.

Her little body squirmed under her mother's fingers as her eruptive laughter filled the air, garnering the attention of other people seated nearby.

"You can't resort to tickle threats to get the answer you want, Cass," I sighed dramatically.

"You're funny, Auntie Maggie," Lily said, blonde hair matted down by the pink noise-canceling headphones sitting on top of her head. "I was sad 'cause you didn't come to my house anymore."

Welp, that was enough to drain the energy out of the entire arena.

It was true—Brody and I would stop over a few times a week to have dinner with them, or hang out or *something,* but since the fight with Liam, we'd gone from one hundred to nothing overnight.

I didn't stop to think that Lily might be wondering why.

My heart clenched.

"Aw," I grabbed her hand across Cassie, giving her hand a squeeze. "I'm sorry I've been so busy, Lil. I promise, everything will be back to normal soon. Auntie just had a lot of work to do that was keeping her away."

"I think Daddy's sad you've been gone, too," Lily said gravely.

I doubted that. Liam didn't need me. He'd never needed anyone. And now that he had his family, it would be all too easy to let me fade out of his life. To be one of those siblings you only saw at holidays.

Well, I wasn't going to make it that easy for him.

He was my brother, goddamn it, and that was a role you couldn't just walk away from.

Or could he? Would he? Did he want to?

For the first time in my life, I wondered if the damage I'd done had been too great to undo. If Liam and I were at a point that we couldn't turn back from.

He didn't need me. I knew that. The problem was, *I* still needed *him.*

My sweaty boyfriend was trying to suffocate me.

Forcibly stuffed into the crook of his neck, I tried to push Brody off to no avail. It was hard to escape when your boyfriend had more than a few inches and about a hundred pounds on you.

"Get off," I shoved his arm, even though the scent of him post-game wasn't nearly as bad as I'd have him believe.

"Not until I get a kiss." He puckered his lips at me threateningly.

"I can't kiss you when you're covered in sweat," I protested, pushing his face away, even though I knew and he knew that I always relented.

Sometimes I just wanted him to work a little for it.

"You guys are adorable," Cassie cooed, standing beside us in the family lounge. "The most beautiful couple I've ever seen."

"Are you tearing up?" I squinted at her, knowing her well enough to notice the telltale sign.

While I was distracted examining Cassie's tear ducts, Brody took the plunge forward to plant a kiss on my lips. I shot him a look when I saw the smug satisfaction written on his face.

"*No,*" Cassie lied, dabbing at her eyes.

"Yes, you are." I frowned. "You're being weird again, Cass. What's going on?"

Brody stiffened, and I turned to look at him in question when I saw he was silently shaking his head at Cassie.

Also weird.

Why was everyone being so *weird?*

"Is there something I should know about?" I crossed my arms across my chest.

"I was just about to ask the same question," Liam's voice sounded behind us.

"Mommy's crying," Lily offered up.

"I can see that," Liam answered, moving over to her side instantly. "What happened?"

In one fell swoop, he scooped Lily up in one arm and draped his other around Cassie's shoulders in a protective gesture, shooting me a scathing look as if *I* might be the one responsible for making his notoriously emotional wife cry.

And to be fair, I guess I *was,* though I still couldn't figure out why.

Brody clocked the look at once and tightened his own hold on me—a show of solidarity that I was enormously grateful for.

I knew I could fight my own battles—especially with my *brother*—but knowing Brody was right there beside me gave me the courage to do anything.

"Liam, I was hoping we could talk—"

"Can't." Liam said shortly, eyes apathetic and distant.

It made me want to scream.

"I really think we should."

"Not now, Maggie."

How was it possible that I was a thirty-year-old woman, that I was a *lawyer* who literally excelled at verbal debates, and yet I couldn't form a single sentence under the weight of his detachment?

"*Please,*" I felt myself tremble.

"Liam," Cassie looked up at him, frowning.

He looked down at her, and then back at me and let out a measured, controlled breath.

"Maggie, I get that you want to talk, but I'm telling you if we have this conversation now, it's not going to work out the way you want it to."

"Why can't you just forgive me?" I asked.

"Why can't you give a shit about what I want for once?"

"Bad word, Daddy." Lily frowned, looking impossibly like Liam as she did.

"Shit." He repeated, then winced. "*Shoot.* Sorry. Shoot."

He kissed the top of Lily's head and handed her off to Cassie.

"You guys go wait in the car, I'll be right there."

"Take your time, we can wait," Cassie urged, hopefully. I loved her for that.

"No," he shook his head. "I'll be out in a minute."

He kissed her cheek, sending her off with such gentleness so he could turn his attention back toward annihilating me.

As soon as his family left, Liam's face turned to stone once more, the only emotion radiating through him being the rage lurking in his eyes.

"Liam, man," Brody said on my behalf, "you gotta give her a chance."

"No, I don't have to." Liam retorted coldly. "Why do I have to give her a chance when she thinks she can create messes in my life and fix them all by a half-assed apology?"

"I'm right here," I said, furious when I felt my own eyes starting to water.

"Why would I talk to you when it's clear you don't listen to a damn thing I have to say?"

"Why are you so mad? I made a mistake, but no harm was done. You don't have to see him again if you don't want to."

"I didn't want to see him *ever,* but you forced me into a situation I didn't want to be in. Do you know how shitty that is to do to someone, Maggie?"

"I know," I gritted out.

And I did. But this couldn't be the mistake that ruined us. I couldn't lose him because of what I was trying to gain—because I was trying to fix our family.

"It was stupid," I admitted. "I get that now. I understand that things can't be what I wanted them to be."

"No, that's the problem, Maggie." Liam countered. "You *don't* get that. You think you can have a hand in every situation, but that's not how life works. You can't expect everyone to do what you want all of the time."

"Liam—"

"You're selfish, Maggie," Liam said. "You always have been. You've always only cared about what you want."

"Watch it, Liam." Brody's voice spat out harsher than I'd ever heard it.

But even though he was holding me up, I felt myself shrinking from Liam's words.

Was he right? I hadn't been trying to be selfish. I just… thought I knew what would be good for him.

"You keep dumping shit into my life that I didn't ask for, and until you learn to stop, then I can't have a relationship with you."

"What? Shit like Cassie?"

"Don't talk about Cassie."

"Because that's one of the problems I dumped into your life, isn't it? And that turned out okay—"

"This is the shit I'm talking about," he bellowed. "You never know when to stop! You need to learn to stop crossing fucking boundaries."

"All right, enough!" Brody shoved Liam's chest, standing between the two of us as if we might charge each other at any moment. "Clearly, the two of you need to take some space."

"Thank you," Liam sneered sarcastically.

"Stop being a dick, Liam." Brody shook his head, tone heavy with disappointment. "She's your sister."

"Yeah?" Liam said. "Well, you can deal with her now. I have to go home with my family."

The words pierced me sharper than an arrow. What was he doing? Disowning me as his sister? Confirming my fears of being replaced by the family he chose?

It wasn't fair. I wanted to scream. I wanted to punch him.

I let out a sigh so desperate it nearly turned to a gasp as I watched Liam turn on his heel and leave, door shutting behind him with a thud that felt permanent.

Brody pulled me into a hug, holding me against his chest with an intensity that I was sure was the only thing holding my broken pieces together.

Liam was gone. Cassie had been *mine,* my person, my best friend— and I knew she still was, but now even she belonged more to Liam than she did to me. Another loss that I couldn't come to terms with.

Brody was the only one left on my side. I felt it in the way he held me, and the careful way he wiped the tears from my face. I felt it in the way he drove me home, holding my hand the entire ride as we sat in the silence of my mistakes.

He was here. He was real. He loved me.

But some part of me wondered if maybe it wouldn't be long before he got tired of it all, too.

GALA

Maggie

Five Years Ago

"So, what's going on with those two?" Brody leaned over his chair to whisper to me.

We were official now. Boyfriend and girlfriend. And that meant we didn't have to hide anything anymore.

I didn't have to hide anymore. Not how I felt about him, or anything else.

Because, shockingly, miraculously—he seemed to like me, too. Maybe just as much. It made me feel safe. But more than that, it made me feel *happy*.

It was hard to tear my gaze off of him, but he was still staring across the table, and if I remembered correctly, he'd just asked me a question.

I followed his line of vision to where he was looking at Cassie draped over Liam's arm as she talked to the Harbor Wolves coach.

"Oh, them?" I said distractedly. "They're pretending to be a couple to get Liam excused from the auction."

"Right," Brody laughed. "Bullshit."

137

I arched a brow at him.

"Are you seriously looking at them and telling me you think any of that is fake?" he asked. "I mean, come on. It's *Liam*. You think he could pull off a stunt like that? He can't even pretend to listen to me tell a story, never mind pretend to be that infatuated by someone."

I examined them closely. Brody had a point. Liam didn't go the extra mile for anything unless he meant it and he wanted to.

So, if he was putting all this effort into the whole facade, well, Brody was right—the whole thing was bullshit.

Which meant…

"Oh my god!" I gasped, watching him lean *into* her touch rather than stiffen and shrug away. "He loves her."

"Duh." Brody rolled his eyes. "I've known it all along. I can't believe you haven't noticed. Here I thought you were going to give me the inside scoop."

I guess I'd been too wrapped up in Brody lately to notice anything else going on around me.

Plus, the weird-as-hell lunch I had with my dad that still had my head spinning every time I thought about it.

It had been everything I ever wanted since I was a girl, but finally getting it? It felt strangely hollow.

I hadn't done enough in my career yet. I lacked the accomplishments I wanted so desperately to show him, to prove that I was a daughter he could be proud of. The same way he was still proud of Liam.

But I didn't want to talk about that now. I didn't even want to think about it.

I just wanted to dance with the boy who made me feel all the things I never thought I'd let myself feel.

When I tugged him to the dance floor, he came with me willingly. Despite the protests from his teammates, sullen at the thought of losing their comic relief, he stared only at me.

We swayed on the dance floor, while Elvis Presley sang about the humiliating experience I was currently going through without my consent.

I really *couldn't* help falling in love with Brody.

It just happened. He encompassed me entirely, not in a way that felt scary, but in a way that felt safe.

CHAPTER SIXTEEN

Brody

I drove to Rhode Island.

I didn't really know what else to do, I just knew I needed time to clear my head and figure out the next step. Driving usually helped.

Maggie had gone to work earlier than usual, eyes still red from crying the night before. Liam hadn't answered any of the numerous texts I sent him, telling him off about being a jerk to my girlfriend. And with all the tension running rampant in our group, I really felt like imaginary walls were closing in around me with each breath I took.

So, I got in my car and I took off south. I thought maybe the ocean might bring me some peace of mind. I mean, didn't Ernest Hemingway write a novel about that very thing?

I don't know. I never actually read it. All I knew was that the sea was supposed to take away the stress of life. Or at least make you forget about it for a little while.

Coach didn't love that I was blowing off morning practice, but I guess even he could tell that I was unraveling a bit at the seams. Plus, after years of not missing a single game, practice, or event, he probably figured he owed it to me.

I could've stopped at any of the beaches along the way, but all of the local ones felt too close, and I had plenty of angsty songs left on my playlist that I wanted to listen to. Besides, I needed space from the problem, which led me all the way out of state.

It only took about an hour and a half before I got to the Rhode Island shore. Partially because I left after rush hour, but probably mostly because I was speeding.

And it took me about three solid minutes of staring out at the vast majestic stretch of blue before I realized it wasn't going to do shit for me.

But I knew what would.

Some of those deep-fried clamcakes I smelled coming from the shack down the road.

My hands in my pockets, I treaded down the sidewalk, trying to figure out what the hell to do about Liam and Maggie.

It was weird, but I felt all disheveled because of it, like it was *my* life being wrecked by their rift. I knew on some level that it was their shit to deal with and it went far beyond what I was capable of fixing, but it felt like I couldn't relax until I had at least *tried*.

If I couldn't help the people in my life, what good was I to anyone?

After ordering some clamcakes and chowder, I made my way back to the seawall with my emotional support snack in tow, resorting to the only thing I could think to do in that moment.

Pulling my phone out of my pocket, I shot out a text to the one other person who might be capable of helping me fix this mess.

BRODY: Care to take part in operation reunite the Brynn siblings?? 👀

CASSIE: I'm in!!! Just tell me what to do.

BRODY: You work on Broody Brynn. Try to get him to calm down and see reason. I'll take Beauty Brynn.

CASSIE: I've been trying, but I think he's really hurt.

BRODY: Come on, Cass. Don't be a quitter.

CASSIE: I'll keep trying.

CASSIE: BTW, Liam is not broody.

BRODY: Keep telling yourself that.

CASSIE:

I pocketed my phone, feeling the slightest relief that I was at least making an attempt. I wasn't sitting back doing nothing, letting my people be miserable.

Plus, I still had a plan to execute after all.

The plan would fix everything.

CASSIE

Brody

Five Years Ago

It was hard to get her alone, considering the way Liam circled her like she was the President and he was the sole member of Secret Service, but at last I got her.

I was surprised that he'd left her side for even a second, but at this gala he had responsibilities. There were teammates who wanted to talk to him, probably knowing it might be another ten years before anyone could get him to show up at a social function again.

Everyone always wanted to talk to Liam, and the fact that he didn't want to talk to anyone didn't seem to deter them.

Well, I didn't want to talk to anyone except the little blonde I was about to ambush.

I slid over into the seat beside her, noticing the way she flinched in surprise when I cleared my throat.

She'd been so totally lost staring off at Liam, who was talking to some of the guys a few feet away, that she hadn't heard me approach.

143

Liam, razor-sharp instincts and all, clocked me the second I appeared next to his girl and shot me a warning look.

"Hey, blondie," I said, "we haven't gotten the chance to officially have a conversation yet, so I figured it was time to rectify that considering we're going to be in-laws and all."

"W-what?" she sputtered, face reddening in seconds. "What does that mean?"

"Oh, because I'm marrying Maggie," I told her. "And since you clearly stole my friend's heart, it looks like you two won't be that far behind us."

I didn't think it was possible for her face to turn even pinker, yet somehow she exceeded my expectations for the shade a human complexion could turn when faced with embarrassment.

I laughed. She *was* pretty adorable. I could see what Liam saw in her. And honestly, she was the perfect girl for him—someone sunny to balance out his broodiness.

"I thought you knew that we were just pretending," she whispered, but I heard the bullshit in the pitch of her voice.

"Pretending, huh?" I grinned. "If you say so. But just so you know, Liam already promised me a spot in the wedding party."

Cassie's head snapped over to where he stood so fast I thought she was going to break her neck. And I'd be responsible. And Liam would kill me. And then I'd never get to marry Maggie.

So basically, I had to wrap this up.

Cassie and Liam needed to figure it out on their own and I was content to let them do that, because I knew they would.

I had a knack for things like that. Knowing when a couple had what it took to go the distance or not.

That's why I knew right away Maggie was the one for me. *I* felt it. And my instincts had never led me astray before.

"Anyway," I said, knowing I only had a few seconds left before Liam stormed over demanding what I said to make Cassie have that scared-shitless look on her face, "I just wanted to let you know that if you ever need anything I'll be your go-to guy, because like I said—we're practically family now."

"Go-to for what?"

"I don't know. If you need to rant about Liam and his scowling problem—"

She laughed.

"—or anything else." I shrugged. "I'm here. Part of your team now."

"Why?" she asked, completely dumbfounded.

"Because you're Liam's girl—"

"I'm not," she shook her head hastily.

"And because you're Maggie's, too. And those two are the best people in my life. So, I've got your back. Okay?"

I stood up, content with our conversation and having finally gotten an official feel on the girl that was important to both my best friend and my girlfriend.

She had my stamp of approval.

Hell, she probably had everyone's.

I was glad that Liam and Maggie had someone like her in their corner.

"Hey, Brody," she called, as I started to walk back off into the crowd to find my girl.

"Yeah?" I turned back.

"I've got yours, too."

CHAPTER SEVENTEEN

Maggie

Sometimes, under duress, I had a tendency to act out.

It wasn't healthy, but it was what I did. My lovely and expensive therapist, Linda, thought it was my way of avoiding pain. I tried to get angry instead. Or make other people angry at me.

Considering I'd already done both of those things and achieved zero results, I resorted to my other coping mechanism. One that might actually be useful to someone.

I threw myself into work, day and night.

I had other clients, but Mr. Reilly's case took the forefront of my mind at all times. I couldn't explain the compulsive need I had to reunite him with his children, but it kept me in the office long after everyone else had cleared out.

I just felt that if I could be the reason his family got put back together, it would fix things. Fix me.

He deserved it. And he would be so grateful to me. If I could just accomplish this one good thing, I could prove to myself that Liam was *wrong*. I wasn't inherently selfish.

At least, I didn't try to be.

Brody had been walking on eggshells around me lately, which I felt bad about, so I just sort of stopped going home. At least until I knew he was asleep.

It was better that way. I couldn't burden him with all these ugly emotions fighting for the forefront of my mind. I couldn't unload even more family trauma on him than he'd already seen. He just wouldn't understand.

Besides, if I became the girl who went to him crying all the time, how long would it be before he got sick of it and left me?

No. I needed to get a handle on myself before I could self-sabotage the last good thing I had in my life. And for his sake, it was better that I was keeping my distance. At least until I could get back into a clear headspace.

"Are you nervous?" Mr. Reilly's voice asked me, his eyes trailing down to my knee.

I placed a hand to steady it, plastering a smile as I looked over to him.

"Not at all," I lied. "And you shouldn't be, either."

He gave an uneasy, half-hearted smile.

Some great lawyer I was. If the client could sense my nerves from a mile away, what would the judge think of me?

I stared off down the corridor, fixing my gaze on something in the distance to calm myself.

"You know," Mr. Reilly cleared his throat. "This is where me and Pattie got married."

"The courthouse?" I asked, slightly surprised. "You eloped?"

"Yeah," he smiled, eyes glazing over in memory. "We hadn't been together that long, but we just knew." Then, as if forcibly pulled from his reverie, his eyes refocused to the present surroundings. "Seems funny to be here now, all things considered."

His hands reached to tug for his Red Sox cap, and when they found it missing from its usual home atop his head, he wrung them relentlessly instead.

I fought the urge to sigh. So many stories just like his. People who thought they were going to be together forever, rushing into marriage without a second thought for what might be down the road.

I knew I couldn't make that mistake. It's why Brody and I were taking our time. People change. Things happen. I wasn't going to risk ruining both our lives by doing something too hastily.

I had the strangest urge to bite my nails. It was something I hadn't done since I was a kid, but now I felt an overwhelming desire to nip at the white-lined French tip on my index finger.

But before I could break the air of professionalism I was maintaining by resorting to a childhood habit, the court officer strode into the hallway, looking to us with disinterest.

"Reilly vs. Reilly?" he asked with an air of indifference that came from seeing a string of broken families all day long.

Mr. Reilly nodded, while I was already getting to my feet.

"We're ready for you."

I brushed my hands against my slacks, grateful that the clamminess from my palms wouldn't show against the black fabric.

I wasn't sure why I felt so nervous. I'd been in court hundreds of times. But this case felt different. Personal. And I was all too aware of how this might go down.

Courts didn't often side with the fathers. Not in the way Mr. Reilly was hoping.

Here he'd been, in therapy programs and respecting his ex's unreasonable requests of distance—and all he wanted in exchange was the chance to be in his kids' lives the way he was before.

I knew he wasn't going to get that. But if we were lucky, he might get more time than the sparse visits here and there he was getting on his ex's whims.

It wouldn't appease him. I knew that. How could it? How could a judge expect any father to go from spending every day with their children, tucking them into bed every night, bringing them to school each morning—to only getting to see them every other weekend?

It was cruel. It was unfair.

And if I had any say in it, it wouldn't be the case for Mr. Reilly.

He wanted split custody. And if Mrs. Reilly was hellbent on kicking him to the curb forever, then the least she could do is give him equal rights to time with their children.

Sucking in a silent breath, I braced myself for the battlefield that was court and walked in with my head held high.

I heard Mr. Reilly suck in a breath at the sight of Mrs. Reilly at the opposite podium.

She looked normal enough. Her mousy brown hair was up in a clip and she wore a neutral expression, not even sparing so much as a glance in our direction.

Did she know she was being selfish, I wondered? Did she know she was tearing a family apart because of a mistake?

She looked like my mom, a little bit.

Not for the first time, I wondered why my mom couldn't just hold it together, be what my Dad needed her to be for our sake. Why did she have to force him away when he had kids at home who needed him? Why couldn't she just be a little… *less?*

Less emotional. Less needy. Less overwhelming to him. Then he might've stayed.

I turned away, locking my attention on the judge in front of me. I didn't know why I was panicking, or why this moment felt so much bigger than myself when I'd done this countless times, but I found myself slipping in and out of focus as thoughts pulsed through my head.

I was grateful for all the years I'd already spent in a courtroom, because muscle memory became my saving grace in getting me through the formality of the opening while I unraveled internally.

The judge peered down at the papers in front of him, then glanced between our two podiums before stating,

"As I understand it, this is a preliminary hearing to determine temporary custody arrangements pending final divorce proceedings. Is that correct?"

His statement was met with murmurs of agreement before we were invited to share our case.

"Given Mr. Reilly's demonstrated stability and cooperation, we believe joint custody is both fair and in the best interest of the children."

I heard the words coming out of my mouth, going by the professional script of the courthouse rules even when I felt like screaming the words out instead.

I reminded the judge of Mr. Reilly's consistent history of employment, his attendance of parenting classes the last few weeks, how he's kept away from the children per his ex's unreasonable demands, despite the fact I knew it was tearing him apart to do so.

But it didn't seem to matter.

Mrs. Reilly's lawyer was flipping the script. Claiming that the kids were too young, the situation too fresh to have their time split up. He proposed postponing the hearing until further notice.

Which meant, indefinitely. Divorces could drag on for years. I wasn't going to let Mr. Reilly wait that long, miss significant moments in his kids' lives while the whole ordeal played out.

"It's in the best interest of the children to have the stability of remaining in their own home without the constant back and forth."

"Objection," I cried. "Your honor, it's in the best interest of the children to see their father. Mrs. Reilly has placed significant restrictions on Mr. Reilly's contact with his children."

"Objection," her lawyer interjected. "Your honor, Mrs. Reilly is navigating a difficult situation and is doing her best to keep as stable a home environment for her children as possible during this time of upheaval in their lives. I think we can all agree it's not in the best interest of the children to be shipped back and forth like luggage."

"Enough," the judge interjected, tone full of authority earned from years at the head of a courtroom. "This matter is not up for the defenses to determine. It's up to me, and I've made a decision."

I held my breath.

"Mr. Reilly," the judge turned his attention toward us. "With the separation being so recent, and due to the matter of your unstable living situation—"

"Your honor, my client *has* a stable living situation."

"I'm staying with my brother," he added quickly, and then, forgetting himself, hurried to add, "your honor."

"And this is your permanent residency now?"

"Well, no." Mr. Reilly shuffled on his feet. "It's just until I can find a place of my own. But the housing market is a wreck, 'specially in Boston. But you don't have to worry—my brother would never kick me out until I got on my feet. And the kids love their uncle."

"I'm sorry, Mr. Reilly, but you must know that without a permanent residency, there cannot be any granting of equal custody."

"Your honor," I faltered, desperately. "His home life is stable. He's proven time and again to be reliable. The children have made their desire to see him evident—"

"And would you have those two young ones sleeping on their uncle's floor half of the week?" He tilted his head at me in question.

"I got air mattresses," Mr. Reilly's voice cracked beside me. "We could turn it into a fort. We make them all the time. They'd love it."

My heart shattered. He wanted this so bad. I had promised, foolishly, that I could make it happen.

Why had I done it? Wishful thinking? Because I thought myself more capable than I had any right to believe I was?

"My decision is final. We will reconvene at a later date. Mr. Reilly will be granted his temporary visitations, but until he has a residency of his own, those children will stay where they are. Court adjourned."

I lost my breath. My mind scrambled as I thought of what else I could've done. A different method. A more impassioned argument. I should've played dirtier. Found more against Mrs. Reilly.

But I hadn't. I had wanted to keep it civil, and some foolish part of me believed that people would see the sense in letting a father be present in his kids' lives.

Mr. Reilly dropped to the bench, head in hands as he cried. Mrs. Reilly left, a smug look on her lawyer's face as he led them out of the room.

I didn't know how I looked exactly, but I knew how I felt.

Like a failure.

Because *I had failed.*

Failed. Failed. Failed.

Because of me, Mr. Reilly's children would be wondering why they only saw their father on weekends. Because of me, two children wouldn't be getting tucked into bed by their daddy. Because of me, a little girl would grow up and not know how to trust in love.

Because of *me.*

I didn't know what to do. I felt unraveled. Desperate.

I had failed. I had failed miserably at something I'd let myself want. It was enough to set me over the precarious edge I'd been balancing on.

I needed something real to hold onto. To stabilize me back to reality. I needed answers.

I drove to my father's house, feeling ashamed even as I sped all the way there.

He had never told me where he lived, and I had never felt comfortable enough to ask, but I'd looked it up in the public records, just to have an idea in my head of the type of place he called home.

I pulled up to the address, not knowing if it was still accurate, or if it ever had been in the first place. But I had to try.

I needed to see him. To ask him the questions that were bubbling over inside of me. The ones I'd kept at bay for so long for the sake of not wanting to disrupt the carefully constructed peace we'd managed to build over the last few years.

I'd been too scared of making a wrong move and losing him again. Afraid that any pushback might result in losing him for good.

But tonight, it didn't matter.

Tonight, I was ready to know.

"Dad," I banged my fist against the door, hearing a trace of mania slip into my voice.

I let out a shaky breath, knowing I had to collect myself before he answered. I had to stay calm. He didn't like emotional women. It was why he and my mother never stood a chance.

"Dad," I repeated, banging again, this time more collected.

It took a minute, but I heard the footsteps. Heard the sound of the deadbolt unscrewing and then the creak of the door.

"Margaret," he opened the door just a crack, peering out with suspicious eyes. *My* eyes. "What are you doing here? Do you know what time it is?"

"Can I come in?"

Why did I have to ask? Why did I have to be afraid of showing up uninvited? It wasn't fair.

It wasn't fair that some girls had fathers who changed their oil and taught them how to drive and intimidated their boyfriends into treating their daughters nicely and I had a father who was peering at me through a crack in his door asking why I dared show up on his doorstep.

"Dad, please," I begged, hating myself for it.

I looked a wreck. My hair was plastered down against my head from the downpour and I was sure my makeup was probably running down my face in ugly streaks.

He sighed, opening the door a few inches to let me inside. I breathed in relief, walking into his condo before he had the chance to change his mind.

It was spacious. Open. Filled with the types of flashy things I figured he might have. State-of-the-art television. Pristine marble-top counters. An enviable record collection that part of me longed to sit and sort through with him.

But there wasn't a trace of me anywhere. No pictures. No framed articles of my magazine features. Not even a childhood drawing or card—the kind I imagined he'd always been secretly hiding away somewhere, a trinket he might pine over when he revisited his regrets about leaving us.

Guess it was nothing but a pipe dream, after all.

"Care to tell me what you're doing here, Margaret?" he asked, narrowing his eyes on me in suspicion.

As if I were here to raid his house or ask for money—or worse, emotional support.

"It's Maggie," I said, for the first time in years. "I don't go by Margaret."

He scrunched his face as if he'd smelled something sour.

"Margaret sounds much more professional. You want to be taken seriously, don't you?"

"Is this a business meeting?" I asked, eyes widening in what I tried not to be accusation. "Why do I have to be professional?"

"It was just a bit of friendly advice, Margaret. What's going on?"

"I was just—" I looked around, trying to gather my thoughts. "I wanted to know—" I paused again. How could I phrase it without sounding pathetic? "I—"

"What is it, Margaret?" he asked, and the irritation in his words was enough of a trigger to let it explode out of me.

"Why didn't you fight for us?"

His eyes widened, as if it were the last thing in the world he'd been expecting.

Maybe it was. Maybe he thought he'd trained me well enough not to ask those types of questions. After all, he'd successfully dodged any real discussions about the past in all our meetups over the years.

And I'd let him.

I let us both avoid it. Pretend it never happened.

But I couldn't anymore.

"I just need to know," I sighed. "I need to know why you didn't come back for us. Not once."

"It's complicated," he said, averting his gaze. "You wouldn't understand."

"Try," I begged. "Help me understand."

It wasn't sarcasm. I wanted nothing more than for him to take the unrelenting weight off my chest. To give me a feasible reason why he couldn't come back for me. I was ready to listen. To understand what could make a father turn away from his family like that and not think twice about it.

"We've talked about this before." He shook his head, squeezing his brow as he stared down at the floor. "Your mother can be difficult. It would've been too much—"

"So, you were fine with never seeing your kids again because it would've been too *hard*?"

"I see you now!" he retorted, irritated at me for neglecting that piece of information. "Quite regularly, might I add."

"You were gone for fifteen years," I emphasized, fighting the tears that were threatening to drown me.

"I wasn't meant to be a father to young children. Not every man is. Children aren't for everyone. I couldn't handle it all. The two of you. Your mother. The perfect family life she wanted."

"Then you shouldn't have had them!" I yelled. "But you did, so you're supposed to *learn* how to handle it. You just figure it out. Even if it's hard. Even if it takes a little bit of work. You figure it out!"

"Margaret," he scolded as loud as he dared. "Be sensible."

"It's Maggie!" I yelled, infuriated at his pretense of calm while I was boiling over with years of half-buried emotion.

"Lower your voice!" he ordered. "I have neighbors."

"I'm your *daughter*," I said even louder. "Do you know that? Do you understand?"

"What is your point?" he asked, and the way he refused to confirm it was almost too much to bear.

"Don't you love me?" I asked, feeling my heart break in my chest as the words escaped in a pitiful whisper.

He stared down at me, shaking his head in disgust.

"You're just like your mother. I thought you were smarter than that, but clearly you're every bit as emotional. It's a shame. You might've done great things otherwise."

I felt the breath leave my lungs, along with every bit of fight left in me.

I didn't want to tell him I had already done great things. I wanted him to already have known. I wanted him to be proud of me.

I didn't want a father, I wanted a *Dad*. And it took every ounce of courage in me to admit to myself what I hadn't dared even think.

He wasn't ever going to be who I wanted.

And I couldn't change the past.

And, maybe worst of all, my brother had been right.

"I have to go," I said in a whisper, still only steps away from the door I came through.

When I reached for the knob, he didn't try to stop me. For some reason, I didn't even care.

Brody

"Brody," Maggie's voice spoke into the darkness.

The bed rustled, and then she was beside me. I reached for her before I even opened my eyes, relieved she was finally home.

"Hi, Mags," I mumbled sleepily, trying to pull her down beside me. I squinted through bleary eyes when I felt her resistance to my tug.

"Get up," she whispered, pulling at my arm. "Let's go on a ride."

That got my attention. I moved to a sitting position, feeling half delusional in my state of exhaustion as I stared at her, still dressed in court clothes.

"What time is it?"

"I don't know," she admitted. "Past midnight."

"Where have you been?" I asked, highly aware of the manic energy she was vibrating with.

"I was at work, then I was out driving."

"Driving?" I asked. "Where? Why?"

"It doesn't matter." She shook her head. "Come on, let's go."

"Mags," I said, grabbing her hand as if she might slip away if I weren't anchoring her down. "You gotta tell me what's going on because I'm not going to lie, you're kind of making me nervous lately."

She frowned, pulling back.

"Why?" she asked.

"You've been off lately. And I know you've been upset about Liam, but this feels bigger than that. You haven't been talking about it. You've been out all the time. You're constantly in motion. I'm worried, Maggie. And I miss you."

"Then come hang out with me," she pleaded. "Please."

I stared at her, imagining the stormy green shade of her eyes, despite the darkness of the bedroom.

Maggie had been known to drag me into her adventures whenever the whim took her, but this felt different. This felt like she was trying to escape something. And I was scared that if I didn't go with her, she might escape without me.

I had practice early the next morning, but it didn't matter. What mattered was Maggie, and she needed me. I liked being needed by her. *Needed* to be needed by her, in fact.

So, I didn't give her the opportunity to ask me again, because I knew she wouldn't.

That was the thing about Maggie. She only asked for something once, and if you were too slow to act on it, then you lost it for good.

I wasn't going to lose Maggie.

Not now, not ever.

So before she had the chance to slip away, I was already getting out of bed and putting clothes on. I didn't need to ask where we were going or what we'd do when we got there.

Being with Maggie was enough. It had always been enough.

"Okay," I told her, understanding that she just needed me to go along with this without question, for the sake of whatever storm was brewing inside of her. "Let's go."

As it turned out, Maggie didn't know what she wanted.

A common occurrence with her—knowing she wanted *something*, but unable to figure out what exactly that might be.

That's where I usually came in, content to fill in the blanks.

I knew Maggie. I knew her better than I knew anyone else in the world. I could understand her, even if she sometimes seemed like an unsolvable puzzle to everyone else around her.

She was simple when it came down to it. Her actions, seemingly impulsive, were usually triggered by something bigger.

That was usually the biggest mystery to figure out. Not trying to rationalize what she was doing, but trying to figure out the *why*.

Right now, Maggie wanted fresh air, freedom, to feel the expanse of the world around us without feeling like the walls were closing in on her.

I could tell that by the way she was crawling out of her skin, hell-bent on escaping whatever feelings were bottled up inside of her.

I couldn't push her, not until she was ready to talk. I knew that. I could be patient. I always was, and she always came around.

I think it made her comfortable, knowing I was there to listen, that I never pressured her into analyzing her feelings before she was ready to come to the conclusion herself. Sometimes, like Liam, she just needed a little space to sort herself out.

"Where are we going?" she asked me expectantly, knowing I had already taken over the matter of deciding our destination, even though the whole midnight adventure had been her idea.

"I know a place," I told her.

"I don't want to go—"

I interjected, knowing she was going to list off a myriad of places I wouldn't bring her, anyway.

"Babe, trust me." Reaching out my right hand to place on her knee, I felt her relax. "I know everything about you. I'm not going to take you anywhere you don't want to be."

She settled, contenting herself to stare out the window as I drove to a spot I'd been waiting to take her to. A spot that might look even more beautiful in the darkness.

Plus, there was a weight in my pocket consisting of all my dreams of the future that I was desperate to make known.

And a girl sitting beside me that I was aching to make mine. Permanently. For good. Forever.

Now seemed as good a time as any.

Piers Park always felt like the edge of the world. When you stood at the overlook, staring out at the harbor and the skyline, it was easy to feel like you were finally outside the hustle and bustle of it all—far enough away to just breathe it in.

You could admire Boston from a distance without being swallowed by its noise. Just for a moment.

And tonight, under the cover of the black winter sky, the city lights in the distance and wide space around us seemed like the perfect place to bring Maggie.

"This okay?" I asked, pulling into a parking spot.

She exhaled a sigh of relief.

"Perfect."

I jumped out of the car, digging for a coat from the backseat.

I held it out to Maggie, rolling my eyes when she shook her head in refusal.

"I don't need it."

I frowned.

My stubborn, obstinate girl.

"Babe," I fixed her with a look. "I don't care how hot you are physically, it's February and I'm not letting you outside without a coat on."

"Fine," she wrinkled her nose at me, accepting the offering. "But only because I like getting compliments."

"Good thing I like giving them."

"To everyone?" She faked a frown.

"To you," I told her. "Only ever to you."

She smiled, contented so easily.

Some people thought Maggie was complicated. Hard to understand. She wasn't. She just wanted to be loved, and reminded of it often.

It was easier than breathing to give that to her.

She slipped the coat on, swallowed by the enormity of it. I knew it wasn't the fashion statement she hoped to make, but God, she looked gorgeous in it regardless.

"This is the perfect spot," she sighed contentedly, looking out at the skyline. "You know why?"

"Why?" I smiled at her, following as she led me to the railing.

"Because I don't feel as lonely here."

"Do you feel lonely, Mags?" I asked her.

"All of the time," she admitted, staring out at the black water of the harbor. "But here, seeing the lights from the city, it reminds me that there's life out there. People are still awake somewhere, driving, working, loving. Even when I feel all alone, someone is awake somewhere."

No. That was wrong. That meant I wasn't doing enough. I wasn't being there for her enough. How could I let Maggie feel lonely? How could I have let her feel that way and not have fixed it?

I let her work too much. I let her get too caught up in the shit with Dad and her brother. And I hadn't been there to pull her back from the edge.

I felt the pressure on my chest—a need to assure her that I would fix it. Whatever she needed, I would do it for her. She wasn't alone.

I would never let her be alone.

"I know you've been upset, Mags, but it's going to be okay," I told her. "I talked to Cassie and she's going to try to talk to Liam—"

"You talked to Cassie about me?" She whipped her head around. "Why would you do that?"

"Because you're upset. I'm trying to fix it—"

"I don't need you to fix it," she countered. "If my brother doesn't want to ever speak to me again then that's fine. I don't care."

Lies.

"And besides," she added, trying so hard to keep her voice light. "Cassie is his person now, anyway. You shouldn't have involved her."

What?

"Cassie's your best friend," I stared at her dumbstruck. "You're not going to lose her because of what's going on between you and Liam. It won't matter to her."

"Oh, it's not?" she retorted. "Just like you and Liam are fine since him and I got into all this?"

I stared at her, not quite knowing what to say. Her emotions were running high and more than anything I just wanted to be whatever she needed me to be. I didn't want to make things worse for her. Just remind her of what she seemed to be forgetting.

"Cassie loves you, Mags."

"They're *married,* Brody. We can all pretend there aren't sides, but you know that Cassie's going to stand by him over me if it came down to it."

"I think you underestimate her loyalty to you. Why do you think she can't be there for you both?"

"Never mind," Maggie shook her head, ripping her gaze from mine. "It doesn't matter."

She started walking and I panicked.

"Maggie, stop. Please."

She didn't. She was trying to outrun something, but I couldn't figure out the whole picture. I kept feeling like there were pieces I was missing. Things she wasn't telling me.

"I'm fine," she said, and the words pierced me.

Lies. Lies. Lies.

Why wasn't she trusting me anymore? What was happening?

The feeling of being unable to reach her made me want to crawl out of my skin. She was hurting, and I couldn't fix it. Not without knowing what I was up against.

"I feel like I'm losing you," I breathed out, reaching out for her arm as I tugged her close to me. "Why do you keep pulling away?"

"I'm not," she said, feeling stiff in my grasp. "I'm sorry. I'm just overwhelmed and—"

I could pick apart in the silence the word that she was too afraid to speak.

Scared.

"I know," I told her, cupping her face.

She was scared. Of losing Liam. Of losing Cassie. Maybe even of losing me.

And that was something that would never happen. I had to prove it to her, now more than ever.

That *I* was going to stand by her side, no matter who or what we faced. I needed to show her that she could finally let herself relax because I wasn't going anywhere.

It had to be now. I couldn't afford to wait for the perfect moment. Not when Maggie was already retreating into her shell, trying to hide somewhere I couldn't find her.

For both of our peace of minds, it had to be now.

I slid my hand into my pocket, reassuring myself of the ring that I knew I'd find there.

My hands were sweating. What if I grabbed it and dropped it and ruined the whole moment? What if it slipped right out from my hands and into the harbor?

I pulled Maggie an inch back from the railing, just in case.

"What are you doing?" she asked, staring down at our feet, watching my hand that still had a grip on her arm.

"I, uh—" I started.

How did people do this?

How did *Liam* do this?

I felt like I was on the verge of blacking out.

"Brody, what's wrong?" Her voice turned anxious. "You don't look so good."

"Thanks, Mags," I attempted to joke, but my breath was quickening.

She watched me cautiously, and I figured the best way to go about it was to just start.

"You know I love you," I said, pathetic as hell.

"I do," she smirked, the night wind blowing back her dark hair.

Damn it, why'd she have to be so pretty?

It made me nervous. I could never think straight when I was looking at her.

"And I know you love me," I told her, "which is why this sort of feels like it's been a long time coming."

She stilled. "What is?"

"But you were so busy before. We both were. And the timing just never seemed right for us."

"What timing?"

"But you know what I realized?" I continued, before I could lose my nerve. "The timing is *never* going to be right. You have to *make it* right."

"Brody." Her face was pale as the moonlight, but that was normal, wasn't it? Girls got just as nervous about this moment as guys did.

Right?

"Maggie," I said, dropping to one knee, pulling the ring out of my pocket with a death grip around the box. "Will you marry me?"

Her breath caught. I could see it in the air in front of her. Her dark hair streaming down around her shoulders, huge black oversized coat coming down to her knees. Green eyes wide and terrified as they glanced frantically between me, the ring, and our surroundings.

I knew what she was doing. Maggie was always looking for an escape strategy. No matter where she was, she needed to know where the exit was.

But it had never been me she'd been trying to escape from.

What was happening?

Maggie and a clear February night and Boston Harbor and diamond rings and the city lights. This was supposed to be our moment. It was supposed to be the start of our forever.

I thought it was.

But Maggie wasn't responding, just staring down at the ring in my hands as if it were a bomb about to detonate instead of a promise of forever.

And because I could read her like a fucking book, I knew before her mouth even opened that her answer was about to tear my world apart.

CHAPTER NINETEEN

Maggie

"Maggie," he said, kneeling before me.

Oh.

"Will you marry me?"

Oh no.

His eyes were so earnest, so hopeful.

Mine were wide and panicked.

I couldn't breathe. Couldn't think. I felt myself seizing up as I stared down at the love of my life offering me the thing every girl dreamed of.

But I had to think, because he was watching me, face deflating at the deafening silence.

"Maggie," he pleaded.

I looked around for an exit, for a way to escape this situation. A way to hit pause on this moment.

"Maggie, say something."

He was statue-still in the proposal stance, save for the slight tremble of his hand—the one offering me a life with him.

"Oh, I—" I faltered. "But *why?*"

"Why?" he asked, looking as if I'd burned him. "Because I love you,

Mags. Because I thought you loved me—"

"I *do.*"

I did. More than anything. That would never change.

"—because when we talk about our life, we talk about being together forever."

"We will be." I emphasized, grabbing his hands as he rose to his feet.

"Then why does it feel like you're rejecting me?" he asked. "That's what you're doing, isn't it?"

"No," I shook my head. "I just don't understand why anything has to change. I thought you were happy with the way things are."

"It's because I'm happy that I want us to move forward. I want us to have a life together."

"What do we have now?" I asked, affronted.

We spent every day together. Most nights. He was the person I wanted to call before anyone else. The one I wanted beside me for all my big moments. I loved him, in every sense of the word.

But marriage? I couldn't picture it. Not to anyone.

"What's even happening right now?" He shook his head, as if in a daze. "I thought we were on the same page here."

So had I.

"Brody, I love you. Isn't that enough?"

"If you love me, why can't you marry me, Mags?" His voice sounded agonized.

"I need time," I scrambled for an excuse. "You can't just spring this on me like this."

"Time," he muttered to himself, pulling himself to his feet with considerable effort. "More time than the past five years?"

"That's not fair," I shook my head. "We've been busy all this time. I've been working. Making a name for myself—"

"And now you have one. You've won every award you can possibly win. You've dedicated all of your twenties to being the best damn lawyer in Boston and you've done it—"

"And you're upset about it?" I asked, knowing he wasn't but feeling the ugly instinct rise up in me. The urge to fight. To deflect. To cause chaos instead of dealing with the problem in front of me.

I'd rather him be mad at me than see that look of devastation on his face. I couldn't bear to see him sad. I'd rather have him hate me than watch his heart break.

"You know I'm not," he countered. "I'm more proud of you than I've ever been of anything. You're the smartest person I've ever known."

"So, what's the issue?"

"I don't see why your career has to get in the way of us getting married. Do you think you can't be successful and my wife at the same time?"

"Things would change." I crossed my arms against my chest.

"No, they really wouldn't. That's the point. We already live together. We're already committed to each other. All we'd be doing is making it permanent."

"It's just paperwork!" I countered.

"You *love* paperwork!" He matched my volume.

"And what about the kids?"

"What kids?"

"You want to get married and have kids, don't you? You can't honestly think *that* won't change our lives."

"Getting married doesn't automatically put a baby in you, Mags," he said adamantly. "It's not just something that *happens* to you. You get to choose it, when you want it."

"I can't do this," I said, grabbing my head as though it might implode. "It's too much. I can't think."

Weddings. Changes. Promises.

I hated making promises. They made me feel boxed in and claustrophobic. The idea of never being able to change my mind. To take something back.

And people lied. They didn't take marriage seriously. People got divorced after *vowing* to spend their whole life with someone.

I saw it every day. More than most people.

I saw what it did to families. What it did to *my* family.

How could I continue that cycle when I already knew I wasn't stable enough to handle it?

Sure, I loved Brody. With all my heart, I did. And sure, maybe he thought he loved me too. But how long would it be before I messed up and he took off?

Being married would be like skating on thin ice for the rest of my life, never knowing when you might fall through. People left every day. There was no predicting why or when. There was no predicting the emptiness I'd feel if I had to experience that.

So I wouldn't. I refused to. I couldn't live my life in that fear. And I especially couldn't put any hypothetical kids through that.

"Maggie," he said again. "Say you'll marry me. I know you're scared, but we can do this. Together. I *know* we can. You have to trust me."

I stared at him.

My beautiful boy who had the perfect family and the sunshine smile and the words to make anyone laugh at the tip of his tongue.

How could I saddle him with *me?* The girl who couldn't even keep other families together, let alone one of her own making.

I didn't trust myself. Not in relationships, especially not with kids.

My dad was right. I was like my mom. I tried to repress it and run from it, but when I felt—I felt *everything.*

My emotions would cloud my judgment. I'd get desperate. I would beg and cry and plead with him. I know I'd cause fights because of how much I loved him. How much I cared. I'd cause fights to test if he matched that enough to fight back.

It was wrong, but I couldn't help it. I couldn't lower myself to that, not when it wouldn't make a lick of a difference if he ever actually decided to leave.

You couldn't make people stay for you if they didn't want to. And

I wasn't about to wait for the inevitable exit, fearing for that moment every day until it happened.

"I can't," I whispered, taking a step back as if putting distance between us would fix the hole in my chest that felt like it'd been clawed out.

Brody sucked in a sharp breath.

I didn't know I was crying until I felt the wetness against my cheeks.

It hurt. Everything hurt. My heart. My chest. My stomach.

His face. God, I'd never forget it for as long as I lived.

Liam was right. I was a selfish bitch for causing Brody pain for the sake of protecting myself from my own.

That's how I knew it was the right decision.

Brody was good and kind and perfect.

And me? I ruined things. Especially things that were good. I couldn't help it. It was my nature.

And if I loved Brody, I needed to let him go. To get him as far away from me as he could, because I refused to be something he'd regret for the rest of his life.

Instead, I'd be something he lost.

I'd rather have him hate me than regret me.

So, when he handed me the keys to his car and told me to leave, I went.

CHAPTER TWENTY

Brody

When I was eight, I almost died.

I'd been skating at the local pond by myself and fell through a patch of thin ice. Ironic for a hockey player, I know, but that's how it happened.

I'd loved the ice in a way that none of my family did, and sometimes I just went out there to be on my own. The house could get hectic with a bunch of sisters and two loud and bold parents filling up all that space.

With a house that full, it was easy for me to just slip away unnoticed. And I needed the quiet sometimes. To think about my own thoughts and figure shit out.

When I was around too many people, it was too easy to let myself get swept away. I was the kid who made people laugh. The one who lightened the mood when life got too heavy. And I was good at it.

But sometimes, it just felt like a role I played. When I came to skate, I sort of got to figure out who I was. What I loved to do. Without pressure from anyone to be anything different than what I was.

If I'd told my mom where I was going, it wouldn't be mine anymore. It would be another thing I had to share with my sisters.

171

I wanted this time for *me,* so I never told my mom where I was going. But when I fell through that patch of ice, I regretted not sharing it more than anything. Not telling anyone about my dreams.

It was cold, but that wasn't even the worst part. No, the frigid temperature numbed me until it nearly burned.

What was worse was the panic. The helplessness. When you fall through the ice, no one tells you about how the current moves you until you're so far from where you fell in, you can't even find the opening above you anymore.

I was flailing under the water, losing my goddamn mind as I slammed against a layer of ice thicker than concrete, and I remember thinking, *No one knows I'm here. I'm all alone. No one is coming to save me.*

But, you know what?

I'd been a goddamn idiot, because it turned out they knew the whole time. That's what they told me after.

Because my dad came out running just a minute after I fell through. He shoved a branch through the hole I'd made, and I latched onto it with the last of the life I had in me.

My sister Tara had been there too, standing behind him, crying. I guess someone always came to watch me skate, but no one ever told me.

They thought I was embarrassed about it or something. Said they didn't want to discourage me from something I loved.

After that, I never lied to my family again. Sure, they could be annoying and overbearing. Sometimes they were loud. Sometimes I could get lost in the role of brother or son or jokester. But they loved me. And I loved them.

I could put aside the rest.

But the pain, the terror from falling through the ice that day? I never forgot that moment. And I never thought I'd ever feel a bone-deep ache like that again.

But I'd been wrong.

Because this? It was a thousand times worse.

"She said *no?*" Cassie asked, covering her mouth to stifle a gasp. "Are you sure?"

"Pretty damn sure," I muttered, letting my head drop into my arms as I leaned over their countertop. "I think I'm going to be sick."

"Maybe we should move this conversation to the bathroom, then?" Liam muttered, flipping a pancake.

"Be more sensitive, Liam," Cassie scolded.

"Yeah," I said, head still down on the counter. "Listen to your wife."

"What?" I heard Liam say. "I'm just saying better be sick there than the place our daughter is eating breakfast."

I turned my head sideways on the smooth countertop to peek at Lily sitting beside me.

"Want some pancakes, Uncle Brody?" she smiled, face streaked with syrup as she held a forkful up to my mouth.

I groaned and turned my head back face-down.

"It's okay, Lil," Cassie said. "Uncle Brody's not feeling well right now."

"Maybe 'cause he's hungry," she suggested.

"I'm not hungry," I answered.

"His heart is a little hurt right now, Lil. But he'll be okay," Cassie said.

"Why's his heart hurt, Mommy?"

"Because he didn't get something he really wanted," Cassie said carefully. "Remember how we talked about that big word disappointed?"

"Mhm," Lily said. "Uncle Brody's feeling disa-diss-ponted and now his heart is hurting?"

"Right," Cassie agreed.

"Maybe we can put a Princess band-aid on it?" she suggested.

"We can try," Cassie said, and I heard Lily jump off the stool while she and Cass went in search of an adhesive cure for my heartbreak.

"This is a new brand of misery," I groaned, lifting my head to look at Liam, who was putting the rest of the pancakes on a plate.

"What?"

"Having to listen to my suffering be dissected to a three-year-old."

"That's what you get when you show up on our doorstep at six thirty in the morning."

"Hey," I protested weakly. "I was here at five, but at least I had the decency to wait until the sun came up."

I didn't have it in me to crack a joke, even though I knew that I'd be expected to smile in spite of my heart shattering. Because that's what I did, wasn't it? I picked up and carried on, no matter what.

But this was different. This was life-altering. Earth-shattering. I didn't know how I'd ever be able to carry on again.

Not without Maggie.

"I'm sorry, Brody," Liam said, staring at me with a rare expression of sincerity. "Really, I am."

"Don't be sorry," I said. "It's not *your* fault."

"What happened?" he asked. "It doesn't make sense."

I didn't want to talk about it, because talking about it would make it feel real. I just wanted to close my eyes and keep it all out, and hope that maybe I'd wake up in bed beside Maggie with the whole thing having been a warning, prophetic dream.

"I don't know," I admitted, groaning into my hands.

And that was the worst part. I really didn't.

"Did she never love me?" I asked.

"She loves you," Liam confirmed.

I thought she did. I *knew* she did.

Just maybe not enough.

"Then why did she say no?"

"You know her as well as I do." Liam shrugged. "Maggie's... complicated. Unpredictable. She doesn't like to be boxed into a corner, and I think maybe she's just running scared."

"So, maybe she just needs time?" I asked hopefully. "A little bit of space? I mean, once she thinks it over, she'll realize that it was a mistake, right?"

Liam grimaced, pain written all over his expression as he stared at me with what felt like pity.

I hated pity. I didn't want it. It meant he wasn't going to give me that spark of hope I was so desperate for.

One thing about Liam was, he would never let me live in delusion. Even when I wished he would.

"Listen, man," he said carefully. "She's my sister, and I love her." He paused. "But you're my best friend, and if I'm being honest, I can't tell you to wait around for a train that might never come."

And there it was. My hope deflated, chest aching at the realization of his words.

Maggie always knew what she wanted and went like hell to go after it. But this time, what she wanted—it just wasn't me.

"Fuck," I said, tears finally escaping my eyes.

This was real. There was no undoing it. No going back.

The door swung open, and Lily bounded back into the kitchen, holding up a band-aid with a sense of urgency as she rushed toward me.

Cassie followed behind, eyes looking red and puffy as she trailed behind her daughter. I watched Liam clock her mood and maneuver around the counter to be by her side in an instant.

If anyone had asked me five years ago who out of the two of us would be married first, I would've bet every last dollar in my bank account that it would be me.

I actually wanted it. A wife. A family. Liam couldn't have cared less about it. Not until Cassie.

I had a strange pang of jealousy seeing him live the life I envisioned having with his sister. A dream that had been ripped away from me before I even had a chance to see it slipping away.

"Here, Uncle Brody," Lily said, staring up at me with wide, innocent eyes. "I got this to make you better."

"Thanks, kiddo," I said, forcing myself to smile down at her.

"I'm gonna put it right here, okay?" she said, before placing the band-aid on my chest, right on the fabric of my shirt. "Because your heart is in here and this will make it better."

My throat felt hollow, stomach twisted. Everything hurt. I had a feeling everything would always hurt now. I better get used to it.

"Thanks, Lil," I said, but she interrupted me with a kiss on top of the band-aid.

"You'll be better now, because when someone who loves you kisses your boo-boo, it makes it all better. Right, Mommy?" She turned, and I followed her gaze to see a sniffling Cassie, as Liam stood with his arm around her.

"Right, baby," Cassie nodded.

"And I love you, Uncle Brody," Lily confirmed, turning her green eyes back to me. Green eyes like Maggie's.

"I love you, too, Lil," I told her. "Thanks for fixing my heart."

I lied for her sake. I knew there was nothing left to fix.

CHAPTER TWENTY-ONE

Maggie

Sometimes, I avoided going to therapy.

Especially during the times when I needed it most.

I just… didn't want to feel like I was broken and needed to be fixed. I knew I had problems. Everyone did. But I didn't see what dumping them on another person would really do for me in the long run.

The thing about Linda was, she never made me feel like that. Instead of being a person I ranted at, she was like a mirror being held up to me, giving me the tools to cut through my own bullshit. And she wasn't afraid to tell me when I was being a pain in the ass, which was honestly pretty refreshing. Her words weren't usually as colorful as that, but I appreciated the sentiment nonetheless.

I liked people who were genuine. They were all too rare to come by, and I had a knack for seeing through facades.

The double-edged sword was that—so did Linda.

"How are you?" she asked, trying to open the conversation.

I should let her. I should just talk. It's why I came to therapy after all. But blabbering about my problems felt too vulnerable. Even though by law my pathetic feelings would never leave the privacy of this room, it still felt too embarrassing to share. Too personal.

"I'm fine," I told her, bobbing my head in a nod.

"You're fine?" she asked, narrowing her eyes.

"Yes," I lied. "I'm good."

If she really wanted to know, she'd keep asking, and eventually I'd give in and tell her. But it would be too pathetic of me to just lay it all out there after a simple How are you?

"I know that you're not," she tsked, as if my refusal amused her. "And do you want to know why?"

"I *am* fine," I countered, "but for curiosity's sake, I'll bite. Why?"

"Because I know for a fact the receptionist told you the joke of the day, and you didn't so much as crack a smile when you walked in here."

"Maybe it wasn't funny."

In fact, I had been so zoned out checking in that I hadn't heard a word the secretary said.

"It *was* funny, and I know if you were fine you would've thought so too. Especially since you laugh at everything," she said easily.

I liked that about her. She knew how to break the ice with easy banter. It made me feel at ease. Comfortable. Linda was older, but she never made the sessions feel stuffy or dated. She was relatable. She could meet me at my level. It's probably why she was my longest-standing relationship to date.

"I do not laugh at everything." I fought the urge to smile.

"You do," she said in a sing-song voice, seeing the start of it forming on my lips.

"Most people aren't smart enough to make me laugh," I countered, just for the thrill of arguing.

"Hey," she protested. "I've been known to get a laugh from you on occasion."

"*You* have a doctorate," I told her, scanning over to her plaque on the wall for emphasis.

She snorted.

"Glad to know my credentials are approved by you."

Linda was good. She made therapy comfortable. Breathable. It was like talking to a friend rather than someone I was paying an inordinate amount of money to fix my brain.

If that were even possible.

"So, what brings you here today, after all this time?"

"Oh, Linda," I groaned. "Where do I even begin?"

"And then he just… proposed!"

Linda blinked, as if waiting for the punchline.

"Did you hear me?" I repeated. "Brody proposed to me! Just sprung it out of nowhere."

She shifted in her seat, choosing her words carefully.

"Are you telling me the two of you never talked about it?" she asked carefully.

"I mean, he's brought it up, but I thought that I'd steered him off the topic well enough to discourage him from actually doing it."

She stared at me intently in a way that made me squirm.

"Do you not imagine a future with him?"

Her words were like an ax to my heart. I couldn't imagine a future *without* him.

"Of course I do," I told her.

"But you're running from intimacy with him."

"Trust me," I muttered, "intimacy is *not* the problem here."

"I'm not talking about sexual intimacy, Maggie. I'm talking about emotionally."

"But I—"

"You have a pattern of running away or shutting down when things start to get too—what's the word—real?"

"That's not true."

"As your therapist of ten years, I can say with confidence that it is."

"So, are you saying my five-year relationship is invalid because I don't want to get married?"

"Not at all," she said. "In fact, I think your relationship with Brody is one of the realest things in your life. And I think that's why you're so scared."

"Scared?" I asked. "Of what?"

"You tell me, Maggie."

"I just don't want to lose what we have. I don't want things to change."

"Why?"

"Because marriage changes things. It ruins them. You get too comfortable. And then bored. And then resentful. And then someone leaves."

"*All* the marriages you've witnessed follow this pattern?" she narrowed her eyes at me.

"Besides Liam and Cassie," I said. "But they're the exception to the rule. They're practically soulmates, and I don't even believe in that concept."

"I've been married for twenty-five years, you know," she told me.

"You're a therapist," I said. "You practically have a cheat sheet to relationships. *I* don't. I'd screw it up. He'd end up hating me, and I wouldn't know how to fix it."

"I think you need to be more honest with yourself about what you're afraid of."

I pulled back. "I'm not afraid. I'm realistically cautious of screwing up the best thing in my life."

"If it's the best thing in your life, I'd think you should have more faith in it."

"Everyone starts out with faith until it blows up in their faces," I countered. "No one goes into marriage expecting divorce."

"And which divorce particularly gave you all these reservations?" she asked pointedly.

"What do you mean?"

"I think, Maggie, that you're afraid of repeating your parents' mistakes."

"I won't make their mistakes," I said vehemently.

"Right, because you're closing yourself off to the possibility of that ever happening. It's self-preservation."

I frowned.

Sometimes, talking with Linda felt like a mental chess game.

"What am I trying to preserve myself from?"

"The same thing everyone is trying to," she said. "Pain."

I stared at her, wagging a finger. "You're good, I'll give you that. But so what if I don't want to feel pain. Is that so wrong?"

"Pain is part of life. And if you spend all your energy trying to protect yourself from it, you're going to miss out on the good parts. The parts that make it worth living."

I exhaled, cradling my head in my hands.

The agony of Brody's face washed over me, a perfect mirror of what I felt inside my chest when I forced myself to walk away from him.

Sometimes I didn't understand why I acted the way I did. Why I ran from things I wanted. I was the master of self-sabotage, telling myself that if someone really loved me, they'd find a way to stick through it all.

It wasn't until the aftermath of one of my episodes that I could see clearly. See reason. I couldn't put people I loved through that just to test them—just to see if they cared.

But, despite that knowledge, I did it again and again and again.

And now? Now I had no one left.

"Now, listen, I'm not saying you should get married," she said, holding her hands up in defense. "In fact, if you have any doubts, I'd actually say exploring that is the smart thing to do before making that type of commitment. So, what do you say we get into that? Figure out the root of some of those fears?"

I started speaking before I even knew where I was going with it. Like word vomit, I just spoke as the thoughts entered my mind.

"Dating feels different to me than marriage because now, when he's with me, I know it's because he wants to be with me. There's no legally binding law forcing him with me until death. He doesn't have to worry about legal fees and paying half of his assets to an ex-wife if he wants to leave. But if we're married… how would I ever know if he's staying because he still loves me, or if he's only there because of a legally binding contract? I just can't become an obligation to him. I won't."

"You make marriage sound so technical, Maggie," Linda said softly.

"Isn't it?" I asked.

"It might be to you. But what is it to Brody? Why do you think he wants to get married?"

"Because he loves me," I said, certain of that truth. "And he thinks he wants to be with me forever."

"And you don't think he does?"

"I think people change their minds," I said carefully, biting my lip to keep back any words that might give me away. "And I think losing a husband, after I thought in my head that he was my forever… well, that would hurt a lot more than losing a boyfriend."

"I don't think the label makes a difference. Men and women get married every day without the love that you seem to have for your Brody."

My Brody, I thought.

Was he still?

Or had this final rejection been too much? Pushed him too far away?

"You do love him. Don't you, Maggie?"

"Of course I love him," I breathed out. "More than anything in the world. That's why I'm so scared."

"Have you talked to him?" she asked. "Since this all happened?"

"Of course not."

"Well, what about your brother?"

"He's still not speaking to me."

"What about Cassie?"

"I can't talk to her. She's going to be on Liam's side."

"Maggie," Linda took a breath. "It sounds like you self-isolated from every single person in your life."

"If they loved me, they would reach out. Wouldn't they?"

"You tell people you want space, and they're going to give it to you."

"I didn't say I wanted space," I said, irritated.

"Actions can speak just as loud as words, Maggie. I think your loved ones know you well enough to understand when you need some time."

But I didn't want time. I didn't want space.

I just wanted to be loved.

But somehow, whenever I tried to ask for it, all I did was make the people around me hurt.

"I need—" I said, sucking in a breath as I felt tears sting my eyes. "I just need—"

"What do you need, Maggie?" Linda asked, as if she actually cared.

Not just because I was her client. But because I was a person.

I exhaled, letting out a shaky breath as I admitted the one recurring thought that screamed louder than the rest.

"I just need to be fixed."

CHAPTER TWENTY-TWO

Brody

I hoped I wouldn't get thrown in jail for this.

But honestly, a night in a cell might be the exact thing I needed to clear my head. Get some peace of mind.

I couldn't stand spending another night in Liam and Cassie's guest room. Not when I knew I was supposed to be home with Maggie.

In fact, I'd been pathetically chained to my phone waiting for the text to come in from her telling me to come home.

What I got instead was a whole lot of silence.

And coming from Maggie, silence was a very, very bad thing.

Which led me to my last desperate attempt at reconciliation with her. A face-to-face conversation.

I wasn't going to bombard her before work, and I definitely wasn't going to show up at our apartment.

So, I contented myself with trying to catch her when she was leaving the office. Trying to avoid the risk of looking like a creepy stalker ex-boyfriend, I found myself knocking on the door of the man whose shit list I was already on.

Hence why I was contemplating the very real possibility of jail time.

"I'm coming, I'm coming." The old man's voice called from behind the closed door as the thuds of his footsteps drew closer.

I shifted on my feet, suddenly nervous.

The door opened, revealing Mr. Waterman in all his elderly glory, and I looked him up and down as I took in the sight of him up close.

"You're taller than I imagined," I said, staring at the cardigan-clad man.

"How the hell did you find my apartment?" he practically growled.

"I counted the levels of windows and did the math. It wasn't hard. Can I come in?"

"Why would I let you in?" His eyes bugged out.

I smiled. I liked Mr. Waterman. Found him endearing in a way. He was the only person as grumpy as Liam, and it was a comfort to play off of his crankiness.

"Because I'm heartbroken and need advice from a wise, old man."

"What makes you think I'm qualified to give a punk like you advice?" he scowled. "And what makes you think it's okay to show up *at my door?*"

"You've been alive a long time. You pick stuff up over the years." I peered into the apartment. "So, can I come in?"

"If I say no, are you going to leave me alone?"

"I don't have anywhere to go, so probably not."

He groaned, turning on his heel to wobble back into his apartment. The lack of door slamming in my face gave me enough encouragement to follow him inside.

Shutting the door behind me, I peeked around at his place. Simply decorated, sparse furniture, but pictures on every wall I looked.

The smell of cigarette smoke filled my nose, and I turned to see him lighting one up as he stared out the window. The same window he so often had looked down at me from.

"You're going to kill yourself with that habit," I told him, moving awkwardly around his apartment.

"Good," he muttered.

Sarcastic old man, I shook my head.

"Now, tell me, now that you're here *in* my house instead of on my steps—what do you propose we do?"

"Ugh, don't say propose." I groaned.

He narrowed his eyes in irritation.

"I don't know," I exclaimed helplessly when he kept looking at me expectantly, "should we trim bonsai trees or something?"

"What the hell is wrong with you?"

"Lots, I guess," I muttered, sliding down into an armchair across from him. "But that was a movie reference."

"Tell me why you're here," he grumbled. "Or I'm sending you back out the door."

"I proposed to my girlfriend," I started with a sigh. "You know, the one that I'm usually on your steps waiting for?"

"And that leads you to me *because*—?"

"She said no," I finished flatly, turning my attention out his window where the sight of her law office taunted me.

"Hm," he muttered, putting the cigarette out.

"Well, aren't you going to tell me that was a stupid thing to do? Proposing?"

"No," he said. "But I'll tell you it's not the end of the world that it didn't work out."

"Then you don't know Maggie." I shook my head. "Because it quite actually is."

The end of *my* world, at least.

"Don't be dramatic, kid."

"I'm thirty," I responded. "Not a kid."

"Yeah, well, I was your age almost fifty years ago, so to me—you're a kid."

His words fell on deaf ears because I was leaping to my feet and barging toward the window.

There was Maggie, walking out of the law office with some *man*.

"That's her," I gestured wildly, looking back to Mr. Waterman to confirm he was seeing what I was seeing.

He rose to his feet, making his way to stand beside me as my eyes widened in a way that probably made me look like some disturbed insect.

"Who is she walking in with?" I asked frantically. "Who the hell is that?"

"Relax, boy," he responded, staring out with equal intrigue. "Maybe it's her coworker."

"Well, why is she talking to him like that?"

"Like what?"

"Like with so many words!" I groaned, unable to tear my eyes away from the sight of my beautiful Maggie in her black pantsuit and tidy updo walking beside a man who wasn't me.

"Maybe it's her boss and she has to talk to him," Mr. Waterman offered.

"I don't care if he's the patron saint of *law*, if he doesn't stop talking to my girlfriend I'm going to—" I deflated.

"You're going to what?" Mr. Waterman snorted as I tore my gaze away from the window.

Stepping aside, I paced in the center of his living room trying to get my head straight.

"Well, I guess there's nothing I can do, is there? Because Maggie isn't my girlfriend anymore." The words tasted like poison to get out.

"Is that so?"

"Isn't it?" I asked. "Isn't that what happens when someone says they don't want to marry you?"

"Well, I suppose usually, but that depends on whether you and your Maggie are made out of the real stuff or not."

"Who have you known to survive a rejected proposal and still have a happy relationship?"

"My wife and I."

"What?" I asked, dumbfounded. "Your wife?"

He nodded, and suddenly I took notice of the woman's face featured in so many of the pictures on the wall.

From what looked like her twenties up until what seemed to be a few years ago by the quality of the photographs.

Looking around, it was clear that there was no Mrs. Waterman living here, and I knew enough to connect the dots of what must've happened. Apparently, Mr. Waterman was no stranger to heartache.

I couldn't imagine losing a partner to something as permanent as death. The thought of it made me sick to even think of.

I was sure he didn't want my condolences, or to tell the tale of heartbreak of losing her, so instead I settled on a more uplifting topic, asking about the start of their story, rather than the end.

"Did she really reject you at first?" I asked.

A soft smile touched his lips as his eyes glazed over in memory.

"She certainly did," he said. "I chased after that girl for years; she never as much agreed to a date with me."

"So what changed?"

"I pursued her relentlessly. She rejected me relentlessly. I went off to Vietnam. She thought I died. When I got back, she was mine."

He shrugged, as if it was simple as that.

"She said losing me nearly killed her. Made her realize there wasn't another man around she wanted to waste her breath on." He chuckled, staring at a picture of the two of them on the wall, directly across from his chair.

"Well, I can't fake my death to win Maggie back."

"Are you an idiot, son?" He glared at me, snapping out of his reverie. "That's not what I was suggesting at all."

"So what—"

"She just needs to feel what it's like to lose you. Then, if the love is real, she might come around to her senses."

"So, to get Maggie back? I need to… stay away from her?"

"Let her come to you," Mr. Waterman corrected. "If she really loves you, she will."

I chewed my lip.

"Will she?"

"Maybe not." He stood up, gesturing me toward the door.

"Hey!" I protested, sending him a frown over my shoulder as I made my way toward the exit.

"Haven't you heard that saying… if you love something, set it free. If it comes back, it's yours. If not, it was never meant to be."

"I hate that saying." I frowned. "And we *are* meant to be."

"Then just trust her," Mr. Waterman offered. "And in the meantime, live your life. It's not like you can do anything else, anyway."

Live my life, huh?

How could I do that when she was it?

"Thanks for the advice, Mr. Miyagi," I said with a humorless laugh, walking out of his apartment.

Mr. Waterman muttered, shaking his head as he reached for the door.

"Goddamn kid shows up at my doorstep and doesn't even know my name," he muttered before shutting the door and locking it behind him.

CHAPTER TWENTY-THREE

Maggie

"**M**aggie Brynn, you open the door right now!"

Oh, shit.

I sat up with a jolt from my position on the couch, nearly sending my laptop toppling to the floor as I jerked upright. I was in Brody's hoodie, surrounded by takeout containers and half-drunk wine glasses.

"Just a second," I shouted, looking around at the disarray that had become my life.

Shit. Shit. Shit.

I couldn't let Cassie walk in and see me like this and still try to convince her I was fine. One look at the place and she'd know just how bad off I really was.

She'd tell Liam. Liam would tell Brody. And Brody would realize how pathetic I was. How better off he was without me.

I brushed crumbs off my lap, folded the blanket, and tried to make it look like I *hadn't* been camping out in the living room the last few days because sleeping in our bed suddenly seemed wrong.

"Maggie," Cassie called again, refusing to be ignored.

I'd done plenty of that the last few days. Her calls had gone unanswered. Texts unresponded to. Hell, I was pretty sure she'd tried showing up here before, but I'd been working weird hours at the office to avoid having to be at home.

"Damn it," I muttered under my breath, knowing that the mission was a lost cause.

Cassie would see that my life was in shambles and in usual Cassie fashion, would try to save me from it. But there was nothing she could do unless she had a time machine—or maybe a miracle up her tiny, colorful sleeve—so really, what was the point in even getting into it?

I sighed, walking over to the door with dread in my step.

"Look, Cassie, I—" I opened the door, ready to over-explain a myriad of reasons why she *didn't* have to worry about me when I felt the wind knocked from me.

Cassie barreled toward me, wrapping me in her arms with the strength of someone much bigger than her tiny frame seemed capable of.

"Maggie," she said, patting my hair down. "I'm here."

My lip quivered. Tears sprang to my eyes. And suddenly I was holding her back, crying into my best friend's arms.

For the first time since that night, I let myself feel it all. Every mistake. Every wrong move. Everything *I'd* done to get me to this point washed over me at once.

"I ruined everything," I sobbed into Cassie's hair, holding onto her like a lifeline. "I always ruin everything."

"You don't," I felt her shake her head as she held me tighter. "And you didn't."

"Everyone's gone now," I said, realization sinking in. "I made everyone leave me."

"I'm here," she told me, giving me a reprieve from the flood of pain that I'd been drowning in. "And I'm not going anywhere."

I guess my plan of insisting I was fine went out the window the second I cried in Cassie's arms like a newborn baby.

Cassie was a lot of things, but stupid wasn't one of them, and I doubted that I could convince her everything was fine and dandy while I had mascara stains under my eyes and hair that quite obviously hadn't come out of its bun for four days.

Cassie, saint that she was, pretended not to notice my dishevelment. Instead, she got right to work.

"What are you doing?" I asked her, watching her move around my apartment like a tornado.

"I'm cleaning up," she said, holding a broom, a container of paper towels, and disinfectant spray.

"Cassie, you don't have to—" I started, but she fixed me with a stern look that she had recently perfected during motherhood that silenced me at once.

I watched as she cleared the living room of debris, carrying my dirty dishes to the sink and swatting my hand away each time I tried to intervene.

"Just sit down and relax, okay?" Cassie said. "Let me help you."

Sit down and relax.

I'd done nothing but sit down lately, and it had done nothing for me. My mind had been a constant buzz since everything imploded on itself.

Or rather, since I set off the bomb.

Still, I listened to her, feeling too numb to do anything else. When she finished tidying up the space, she sat down next to me on the couch, not saying anything at all.

"I really missed you, Cass," I told her, after a few minutes had passed.

"You didn't have to," she said, laughing softly. "I've been right here waiting for you the whole time."

"I know," I said.

"Liam misses you, too."

I snorted. "I doubt that."

"It's true," she said. "You're his baby sister."

"Did he tell you this?" I shot her a look of doubt.

"No," she admitted, "but that's just because he can be as stubborn as you sometimes."

"Must be a Brynn thing," I laughed, using the sleeve of my sweatshirt to wipe my nose.

"Oh, for sure," she agreed with a grin.

Another pause.

"Have you seen Brody?" she asked carefully.

"Not since that night." I tugged at his hoodie. "I think I saw him outside of work yesterday, but I got scared and bolted."

"Why?"

"I don't know." I shrugged. "I mean, what could he have to say? The damage has already been done."

And I couldn't stand to face him after what I'd done. I couldn't stand to talk to him and know he wasn't mine anymore.

"Okay…" Cassie said, moving onto the next topic. "How's work been?"

"Fine," I said through a barely contained grimace.

"Maggie." She stared me down, strangely intimidating as her blue eyes locked on mine.

I squirmed. I knew she could smell my bullshit from a mile away, so I sighed and gave in. She would figure it out anyway with that emotional radar of hers.

"I let down a client. Someone I had wanted to help more than anything," I admitted guiltily. "It sort of did a number on me."

Cassie looked at me thoughtfully, carefully processing what I was saying.

"When was that?"

"I don't know." I shrugged. "A few days ago."

"When?"

"Friday."

"Friday," she said. "As in, the night Brody proposed to you?"

"I guess," I said. "Earlier in the day."

"So, you had a bad day at work and then came home and he proposed?" Cassie asked. "That doesn't sound like him, to do that when you were in a bad state of mind."

"Well, I didn't go home right after that," I told her, looking away. "I couldn't."

"Where'd you go?"

"To my dad's," I said guiltily. "And, uh, it didn't go well."

Stupid, pathetic tears wet my eyes again, and I hated it. I was so sick of crying over a man who never cared about me. A man who I had tried over and over again to please, just to end up here, having pushed everyone away who actually cared.

"Oh, Maggie," Cassie said, reading between the lines of everything I wasn't saying. "What happened?"

"I basically came to the realization that everyone else beat me to a million years ago. He doesn't care, and he never did."

Cassie deflated, as if my pain hurt her too. I guess that's how it worked having a best friend. You felt their heartbreaks with them. But you also felt their triumphs too. It seemed like a fair trade-off, in the end.

She dropped her head in her hands, shaking her head as she muttered, "No, no, no."

I arched a brow at her.

"Why would Brody propose when you were in such a bad headspace?" She threw her arms up in exclamation. "I just don't understand what that boy was thinking. I mean, of course you weren't going to say yes when you felt like your entire world was crumbling around you!"

"Well, I didn't exactly tell him."

"About your dad? Or about work?"

"About any of it."

"*What?*" she asked, bewildered. "Why?"

I knew it was hard for her to understand, considering she and Liam told each other *everything*. But I knew to be more guarded, especially when telling someone meant getting feedback I didn't want to hear.

"Because it wouldn't have made a difference! What would he have said? 'I told you so?' Because believe me, I know that everyone tried to warn me about my dad. I just…" I exhaled, "I thought I could make him care. I guess I'm as much of an idiot as everyone thought."

"You're not an idiot for wanting your parent to show you love," she said, reaching out to grab my hand.

Cassie was the only friend who really knew me, and I guess that was my fault for never letting people all the way in, but I didn't choose it with Cassie either.

No, that was all her. She came in with that wide-eyed innocence and sunshine-y smile and took her emotional pickaxe to my walls.

I was forever grateful to her for being the first to do it.

"Well, I guess I'm an idiot for thinking he was capable of it," I huffed out a breath.

"Screw him," she said, so uncharacteristically it made me giggle. "What?"

"Yeah! Screw him. You're brilliant and funny and the most amazing daughter he could ever hope to have and he doesn't even see it. That's *his* loss. Everyone else in the world sees you for who you are, Maggie. You don't have to prove anything to him."

Maybe not, but I had something to prove to myself *because* of him.

Because of how I felt when I was around him. Because of the little girl I'd been who had just needed her dad.

But I wasn't the only one left burned by Timothy Brynn. And instead of being someone to lean on, I'd struck up the match and held it where it hurt to the one person who'd always been there for me.

I hurt Liam, and even though he acted tough and above it all, I knew him.

He hurt and he felt as deeply as anyone. And when he shut people out? That's how I knew I'd really done damage. By trying to bandage up my own wounds, I poked at my brother's that had never even had a chance to heal over.

I hated myself for it.

"How's Liam?" I dared to ask.

Cassie sighed.

"He has a lot on his mind, I think." Then she deflated. "Honestly, I don't know what to do for him to make him feel better. It makes me feel useless."

"Cassie, I know you absorb everyone else's emotions like a sponge—"

"Hey—" she opened her mouth to protest.

"You do," I stopped her. "But you don't have to feel responsible for other people's feelings."

"I can't help it; I just love you guys so much."

"And we love you, Cass." I wrapped an arm around her shoulder. "That's why we don't want you taking on all of our problems."

"That's your problem, Maggie." She frowned at me. "You think you have to do everything alone. Well, I won't let you."

She smiled smugly, settling back against the couch in contentment.

"At the end of the day, we're all on our own, aren't we? Isn't it easier to just get used to figuring shit out by ourselves? Instead of expecting people to swoop in to fix it and get disappointed when no one does?"

"That's…" Cassie frowned. "An incredibly sad way to think about life."

"Well, lucky for you, you don't have to. Liam thinks he's your emotional shield whose sole duty is to keep you from harm."

She blushed. "He does not."

"He does," I confirmed. "It's not a bad thing. He's head over heels for you, Cass. Honestly, I should be sickened by it on account of him being my brother and you being my best friend, but really I'm glad you have each other."

"Were you mad at Liam?" she asked suddenly. "For dating me when I was your friend?"

"Oh yeah," I laughed jokingly. "But I got back at him by getting with *his*."

Then I sighed, remembering everything.

"Maggie, can you honestly tell me you don't want to be with Brody?" She fixed me with a look. "And tell me the truth because I'll know if you're lying."

"Honestly, Cass. My head is so screwed up I don't know *what* I want," I told her honestly. "But I know I don't want to do this without him."

"Do what?"

"Life," I said. "He makes it easier. Better. He makes it all feel bearable. But I don't want to be selfish. I can't keep dragging him down into my problems."

"You're not dragging him down. He loves you."

"He has the perfect family. A job he loves. A correctly functioning brain," I emphasized. "How is it fair to crash into his life and constantly pull him into my own emotional turmoil? I've done nothing but make life harder for him."

"I doubt he sees it that way, Maggie," she said. "You don't know how he looks at you. Liam's always said that since the moment Brody saw you, he had his sights set on you."

"I know," I told her. "But he deserves better."

"No," Cassie said adamantly. "You deserve each other. You know why? Because you love each other, and people who love each other should be together."

"Is it that simple?" A corner of my lip quirked up.

"It should be," she said. "It can be."

She shifted until she was on her knees facing me, a pleading look on her face as if she were about to ask for the world and was already expecting I wouldn't give it.

The thing about Cassie, though—you couldn't help but want to give her whatever she asked for. She was just so sincere.

"Maggie, you just have to go to him and apologize. You have to tell him everything that you've been dealing with in that pretty head of yours and let him help you."

Help me?

But if I showed him how much I needed him, how much I would always need him, that would just send him running.

But I didn't want to get stuck in this cycle of wreaking havoc and then living in the fallout of my own chaos. I couldn't bear it. It was unsustainable. I needed to change.

For Brody's sake. For Liam's sake. And for my own.

So I heaved a deep breath, readying myself for the challenge of a lifetime, and looked into her eyes.

"Okay."

Brody

How was I supposed to think about *hockey* when my heart was shattered in more pieces than a jigsaw puzzle?

And not the kid version. Hell no.

I'm talking those 1,000-piece expert-level puzzles that gave me hives just *thinking* about. I mean, who sat there and did shit like that for *fun?*

The only reason I felt somewhat decent as I skated onto the ice for the home game that night was because I had hope.

I had to, didn't I? In order to keep functioning in any semblance of the word, I had to believe that the love of my life really wasn't gone from me forever.

No way.

Maggie and I were meant to be. I knew it the first time I saw her and felt that certainty deepen each time I was with her.

We were going to be just fine. It was only a matter of time.

And doing what Mr. Waterman suggested—letting her miss me. Letting her come to me.

Giving her space? I could do that, right?

It was sort of easy, having Liam around. He was like a walking reminder of Maggie. A way to be closer to her.

"Stop staring into my eyes like that," Liam snapped, shifting to skate away from me. "It's creepy as hell."

"Sorry," I muttered, skating over to the net.

I had to focus. Get into game mode.

Especially because my sister Tara was somewhere in the stands tonight.

I'd texted her about the... *incident* with Maggie, and even though I certainly wasn't labeling it a breakup, that's exactly how Tara was treating it.

Full of sympathy and a dire need to tend to my emotional wounds, she booked a flight to Boston, telling me we could go out to dinner after the game.

I wasn't really up for it, but I guessed dinner with my sister beat yet another tea party with Lily. I couldn't watch her cry again when the rubber bands of the fairy wings she tried to force onto my back snapped.

The rush of the crowd filled TD Garden. I felt that pre-game electricity as the screams and thud of the music surrounded me.

I shook my head and blew out a breath, getting into game mode.

I could get through this. I could get through this because I had to, so really there was no other choice. The team was depending on me and I couldn't let them down.

Liam skated by, not looking me in the eyes when he dropped the news.

"Just so you know, Maggie's here," he said. "And Cassie said she wants to talk to you after the game."

My heart pounded.

"Cassie wants to talk to me after the game? Or Maggie does?"

"Maggie, obviously."

"Well, I just had to be clear."

He muttered something and skated away, getting ready for the start of the game.

But all I could think about was that my beautiful girl was somewhere in the stands, waiting for me at the end of all this.

Had Mr. Waterman been right? Did she just need some time and space to think it out? I saw light at the end of the tunnel.

Everything was going to be okay.

Maggie was here. She was here for *me*.

With that knowledge tucked securely in my heart, I played the best I'd ever played in my life.

CHAPTER TWENTY-FIVE

Maggie

How did you apologize to the love of your life after telling them you didn't want to marry them?

"Psych?"

"Sorry I broke your heart, but I didn't mean it?"

"No, I really do want to marry you, I just have some inner shit to work through first?"

Somehow, every line I worked through in my head fell flat. I was well aware that it might not even make a difference, anyway. Maybe I already had my shot with Brody and blew it. Maybe that was the only chance at happiness I would get.

Because I knew with a certainty deep in my bones that no one would ever love me the way Brody did. And even if someone could, I wouldn't want them.

Which left me with one option: trying.

"Just relax," Cassie said, sitting beside me. "I already told you it's going to be fine."

"How do you know?" I asked, desperate for reassurance.

Because even though the idea of laying it all out there, offering up my heart with all its imperfections at Brody's feet, the fear of it getting trampled on haunted me.

"Because he's been with us for the last week since it happened and he's been miserable the entire time."

"Maybe it's the effect of being in Liam's company." I shrugged sarcastically.

Because Brody sure as hell didn't look miserable on the ice tonight. No, every time I caught a glimpse of his face on the jumbotron, he looked exuberant. Like nothing could touch him. As if nothing ever happened at all.

Maybe he'd realized he was better off without me.

"*Stop,*" Cassie said, reaching out to hold my hand. "I see all of that going on in your head and you need to breathe. Everything is going to be okay in the end, you'll see."

Gosh, I forgot what it was like to have her unwavering attention focused only on me. With my mom babysitting Lily, I had become Cassie's emotional project for the night.

Flattering, but at times uncomfortable. There was nowhere to hide under her knowing stares. And what's worse, when she looked at you, you didn't even *want* to hide. You wanted to tell her every little dark secret of your heart and let her tell you that it would all work out.

She was like one of those carnival psychics wrapped in sunshine-and-rainbow packaging.

I just hoped she was right.

The game ended on a Harbor Wolves win, which I hoped would be a good omen for how the night would go.

But even as Cassie and I made our way down to wait in the family room, my hands shook by my sides as if I were getting ready for a first date.

As if this weren't *my* Brody I was about to go see for the first time in over a week.

It felt longer. Unbearable. I was crawling out of my skin with the sting of his absence, and I realized—maybe too late—how vital he was to my very being.

I wasn't dramatic. I knew that *technically*, I could live without him. But God, I didn't want to.

Liam came in first, eyes locking instantly with Cassie's, smiling. And then his gaze looked at me with detachment. There he went, building his walls like he was some freaking carpenter instead of my big brother.

But I understood. Not only was I the sister who screwed him over by throwing our father at him unexpectedly, but now I was the jerk who broke his friend's heart, too.

If I hadn't been standing next to Cassie, I was sure he would've turned on his heels the second he saw me. But as it was, being best friends with the love of his life had its perks.

Namely, the chance to make it up to him.

"Liam," I said as he pulled Cassie to his side.

"Maggie." He answered, staring at me blankly.

It hurt. Being ignored hurt.

"I wanted to say I'm sorry." I told him shakily. "About—"

"It's fine." He said, decidedly *not* fine.

"No, it's not." I said, determined to smash down those walls the same way Cassie had. "Liam, I was wrong."

He shrugged. "Not a big deal."

"Stop pretending you're not upset with me."

"I'm not upset," he said. "I'm just not putting myself in a position where I'll let you do that again."

"I won't do it again." I promised him. "And I know those are just words right now and the only way I can prove it to you is by following through," I rambled, "so forgive me and let me show you that I can do it."

He shrugged, casually breaking my heart.

"Like I said, not a big deal. Let's forget about it."

"When you say 'forget about it,' you really mean, 'let's let it fester and be this weird wedge between us for the rest of our lives,' and that's not what I want."

"Well, you don't get everything you want all the time, Maggie. Contrary to popular belief."

"Liam," Cassie said, pleading.

I didn't know for what. I don't think she did either other than wanting the conflict to be over.

"Both of you, stop." Cassie said. "We're all family."

"We're all good, Cass." He said, his hold on her tightening before pressing a kiss to her temple. "I promise. Right, Maggie?"

His gaze on me was intentional. There was a right answer to this, and even though I knew we weren't okay yet, I had hope we would be.

I couldn't force him to forgive me and I didn't want to. I wanted to show him that I could do better. Be better.

"Right."

The door burst open and I turned, anxiously expecting Brody to be there, ready for the moment of truth.

But instead, it was a face I hadn't been expecting to see at all.

"Tara?" I asked, and then the words died in my mouth as a small brunette appeared behind her.

I didn't know why, but the sight of her made my stomach plummet about a thousand feet. She didn't look familiar—at least, not a face I'd ever seen in person—but she felt like someone I should know.

"Maggie?" Tara frowned, face paling at the sight of me.

Nervously. Guiltily.

Odd, because she'd never been anything but thrilled to see me.

Then I realized, she must know. About what I'd done—what happened. She must not have been expecting me to be here.

I made a step toward her, to go clear up the whole scenario. To tell her, no, it was all a mistake. I love your brother. I'm going to tell him the second he comes in.

And then he was there.

Golden and brilliant and perfect.

"Brody," I said, but the words died on my lips before I was even sure he'd heard them.

Because even though his eyes were locked on mine, and even though I had already taken a step toward him—ready to put this entire mess behind us—I was too late.

That girl—the beautiful one who'd walked in with Tara—was calling out his name, drowning my voice out until it was nothing but white noise.

And before he even looked down at her, she flung herself into his arms and pressed her lips to his.

CHAPTER TWENTY-SIX

Brody

I t didn't make any sense.

One minute, Maggie was on the other side of the room, staring at me with rare vulnerability and wide, hopeful eyes.

This is it, I thought. *Everything is going to be okay.*

I had taken a step toward her, needing to be beside her. Needing everything to be fixed once and for all.

With everything happening at once, all I knew was a fluff of brown hair and a body colliding against mine.

Instinctively, I reached out to grab whatever had made impact with me, mind whirling as it tried to process how Maggie could've gotten over to me so quickly.

And then, lips were on mine—light and airy.

My stomach hardened like lead because they felt *wrong*. It took one second to realize these weren't Maggie's lips, soft and tasting like cocoa butter. And this wasn't the way she felt against my chest.

The whole moment had lasted two seconds, maybe three, and then I was opening my eyes, trying to figure out what the hell was going on when I saw her.

My Maggie—not in my arms, but still several feet away where I'd last spotted her. Her green eyes frozen in heartbreak that I already knew would haunt me the rest of my life.

"Maggie?" I said, not sure if it was loud enough. Not sure if it even came out at all.

But she had already turned on her heel and ran.

"Maggie, wait!" Cassie said, running after her.

Needing to understand what was happening, I finally looked down at the imposter next to me, freezing when my brain finally made sense of the situation.

"Abbey?" I reeled back, dumbstruck and furious all at once.

"Hey." She smiled up at me, as if she hadn't just made the overstep of a lifetime. "I've missed you."

In a daze, I stepped around her trying to get to Maggie, but she was already gone.

"What's the matter?" Abbey frowned, her familiar voice sounding wildly out of place in its current setting. "Aren't you happy to see me?"

"Why are you here?" I asked, probably more harshly than she deserved, but I couldn't find it in me to care.

I'd known the girl since kindergarten, dated her all through high school and then some. She was as familiar to me as a memory from childhood, or a room in my parents' house—but right now, I couldn't see her as anything other than the obstacle standing between me and my girl.

"Tara invited me," she said, brows furrowing in confusion. "She thought you might want to catch up."

I spun toward my sister, finally registering what the hell was actually happening.

My sister was here. For the dinner we agreed on. Just like she told me she'd be. What she didn't mention was the fact that she was dragging my ex-girlfriend across state lines to pay me a visit.

I didn't blame Tara. Abbey and I had never been on bad terms, which

I guess was why we'd always toed the line between friends and friends plus a little more, even after the breakup.

It had worked for us, for a while. It had been easy. I'd just been a kid, going off to college, taking comfort in what was familiar to me whenever the opportunity arose.

But we hadn't been that way in a very long time, and damn if it wasn't inconvenient timing for her to pop up *now*.

"I don't have time—" I said, frantic with each passing moment. "I have to go get Maggie—"

"Maggie?" Abbey shot a look at Tara. "I thought you said they—"

"Broke up?" Tara finished. "They did."

"First of all, we never clarified that," I said. "Second, why are you spreading my business around to random people from high school?"

"Hey," Abbey said, affronted.

"I'm *not*," Tara countered. "I just wanted to cheer you up with some familiar faces."

"Faces?" I asked. "As in, plural?"

"It was supposed to be a surprise." Tara bit her lip. "But everyone's here… Sean, Aiden, Matt."

"Matt T. or Matt C.?" I asked, slightly interested.

"Both," she said. "They're all meeting us at the restaurant. They can't wait to see you. I thought you'd be excited."

Damn. My entire high school friend group. Tara had really pulled out the big guns, which led me to think my situation was more dire than I'd been willing to admit.

"What? Is this like an intervention?"

"No. It's me bringing your friends to you because you can't be bothered to visit home anymore."

"I'm busy," I told her.

And I was. It wasn't an excuse. I had a life here, in Boston. I always made time for my family, but between hockey and media events and overall *life*, it wasn't easy to just slip away to Michigan on a whim.

But I didn't have time to defend any of that to her. I needed to find Maggie.

"I gotta—" I pointed vaguely toward the door she'd escaped through before stepping around my sister and Abbey to head toward it.

Before I even touched the handle, the door was opening and Liam was stepping through it, scowling down at me.

"I have to see Maggie," I said, trying to step around him when he blocked my exit.

"Don't bother," he said. "She's with Cassie. She won't want to talk to you."

"But—"

"Seriously, Brody, what the hell were you thinking? I know she caused this mess, but kissing a girl right in front of her? That's shitty."

"I *did not* kiss another girl," I said, replaying the moment.

I hadn't even known what was happening. All I'd been focused on was Maggie. She couldn't seriously believe that had meant anything, could she?

She knew what she was to me. She knew what *we* were.

"Whatever." He shrugged, halfway pissed at me but trying not to show it. "Let her cool off. You don't know what she's like when she gets like this."

"No. Screw that," I said. "Everyone keeps saying to give her space, but all that's doing is pushing us farther apart. Maggie doesn't need space. She needs me to be there."

"Do what you want." Liam held his hands up in defense. "I'm not getting involved."

"Glad to hear it," I said, pushing past him.

But when I got out of the family lounge and down the hallway that led to the rest of the Garden, I realized that I'd never find Maggie in this crowd. If she was even still in it.

I took my phone out, dialing her number frantically.

Went straight to voicemail. I called again, on the off chance it was an error. By the third attempt, I realized that Liam was right—there was no way Maggie was going to speak to me tonight.

Maybe it was for the best. She could have time to cool off. See the situation more clearly after the emotions died down. She knew I'd never touch another girl. She'd realize that.

Plus, I'd be an absolute asshole to blow off my friends after they'd come all this way to see me.

With a sigh, I walked back into the lounge with tail between my legs. Liam stared at me, eyes fixed on me with a look of *I told you so.*

"Don't worry about her," Liam said. "Cassie's with her. Just go—hang out with your sister. The two of you can talk later."

"Fine," I bit out, storming over to him. "But when you see her, make sure she knows we're having a conversation later. I'm not going anywhere."

"Trust me, Brody." He shook his head. "Everyone knows that."

CHAPTER TWENTY-SEVEN

Maggie

"I'm going to vomit," Cassie muttered, head between her knees as we sped down the road.

"Since when do you have such a weak stomach?"

I glanced over to where she sat in my passenger seat, pale and slightly sweaty.

"Since when do *you* drive ninety in a thirty-five?" Her head popped up, barely long enough to glare at me. "Oh, nope. Head's going back down."

I laughed as she resumed position and slowed down to an easy 70 mph.

"Where are we going, Maggie?" Cassie groaned, staring down at the floor mats. "And how are we not already there yet at this speed?"

"I have some business to take care of," I told her.

And a lot to say before I lost my nerve.

Running high on emotion, adrenaline, and the horrific memory of Brody's lips on another girl permanently branded against my eyelids, I pressed my foot harder against the gas and accelerated once more.

Cassie groaned, and I reached one hand in the backseat to grab an empty takeout bag.

"Here," I shoved it at her. "In case you get sick."

My fist pounded against the door, eager to do something with the anger practically radiating from it.

"Maggie!" Cassie yanked on my arm to whisper-hiss. "Whose house is this? I don't think you're on close enough terms with any of your clients to show up at their home in the middle of the night!"

"It's not a client." I banged again. "It's my dad."

"What!" she yelled, before clasping a hand over her mouth to stifle the sound that had already escaped. "You said it was for work."

"No," I said slowly. "I said it was business. As in, the *unfinished* variety."

And I had to do it now or I never would.

"I can't meet Liam's *dad* like this." She gestured to herself, hair wild from the windows she'd rolled down for the sake of 'fresh air,' and the huge Harbor Wolves jersey that fell down to her mid-thigh.

"You don't need to impress him, Cass," I told her. "He's nothing but an arrogant, waste-of-space, sorry excuse for a father, ass—"

The door opened, and there he stood, in all his glory.

"Making a habit of this, are we, Margaret?" he asked, looking an infuriating mixture of bored and indifferent.

Then, he peered to where Cassie was shrinking behind me, eyeing her up and down.

"Are you girls coming from a high school game?" he asked sarcastically, taking note of our jerseys.

Asshole, I thought.

He was just bitter that he was too ashamed to show his face at the Garden after Liam told him off five years ago.

"Hi," Cassie said uncertainly. "I'm—"

"Don't tell him who you are," I told her. "Because we're never going to see him again."

He rolled his eyes and sighed, as if I were nothing more than the child I was acting like.

But then, his eyes widened, and I realized he was noticing the details of Cassie's jersey.

Number twenty-six branded on the arm. The fact that it wasn't a knockoff fan jersey, but a real, genuine Harbor Wolves one.

"Are you—" he stared at her, slightly speechless. "Is she Liam's—?"

"Wife?" I filled in the blanks. "Yes. And she doesn't want anything to do with you, either."

And even after everything—even after knowing what he was and even after claiming that this was the end, the last time I'd bother with him—it still hurt that even an extension of Liam was of more interest to him than his daughter standing in front of him.

"I didn't know you were so closely acquainted with Liam's wife to be making late-night ambushes with her," he said, still staring at her instead of me.

"That's because you don't know *me*," I said, feeling myself breaking. "And you don't even want to, do you?"

Disregarding me, he stepped out of the doorway, staring at Cassie intently as he slipped into the role of charming father-in-law.

"It's so nice to finally meet you," he held out a hand, which she felt obligated to take. "Unfortunate that it's taken this long."

I scoffed, shaking my head at his audacity.

Cassie, ever fearful of being impolite, said nothing, even as she squirmed to put some distance between the two of them.

"My son's been stubborn—takes after me in that way." He chuckled. "But Maggie's told me about you. He'd do anything for you. *You* can get him to talk to me, to give me another chance—"

"Oh, no, I—" she stumbled over her words, freezing on the spot.

I stepped in front of her, shielding her from the slimy man in front of us. I didn't want my father anywhere near her. I didn't want him to even look at her.

Not because he was a creep or anything. He was, but not in *that* way. But because he was an exploiter who would prey on someone's weakness to get what he wanted from them.

And Cassie, pathological people pleaser as she was, would be trapped and defenseless when up against a guy like him.

"You just can't give it a rest, can you?" I laughed bitterly. "Liam wants nothing to do with you. Cassie wants nothing to do with you. Hell, anyone with a properly functioning brain would want nothing to do with you. But you know who did? *Me.* I wanted a relationship with you, and you didn't care. I'm your *daughter*, and you still didn't care."

"What's all this about, Margaret? Between this and the showing up at my doorstep the other evening, you're starting to raise some concerns."

I was starting to raise some concerns?

No. I think I was finally acting like a normal person.

It was like everything that had happened, everything he'd done had finally clicked in my head. The rose-colored glasses were off, the wool had been pulled from my eyes.

He wasn't the man I'd put on a pedestal. He wasn't the father I dreamed that maybe he could be, with more patience, more effort on my part.

He was just exactly who he was.

And it wasn't enough.

"I just wanted to tell you that I don't need anything from you any-more. I don't need you to validate my successes, which you never did anyway, by the way—"

"Margaret—"

"I don't need you to view me in the same light you see Liam. And I really don't need to keep doing these father-daughter luncheons at shitty, overpriced restaurants where you pay more attention to my boyfriend or the bottle of scotch you order than you do to me."

"Yeah!" Cassie said behind me.

"Where is this coming from?" he scowled. "Is this your mother talking?"

"No," I said, outraged. "Because I barely speak to my mother, since for so long I blamed *her* for *you* leaving. Can you believe that? I actually blamed the only parent who stuck around for me. She wasn't perfect, but she tried. And you know what? She did a good job."

"If this is the type of woman she raised, then that's debatable."

"Screw you," I told him. "And you know who else stayed? My brother. And after years of him being distant and all screwed up over you, we *finally* broke down all these walls that had always been between us. And for the last few years, we've had a *good* relationship. He wasn't just my brother, but my friend. And I screwed that up too! For you! I hurt Liam because I wanted *you* to be happy. And proud of me. And finally see me for once in my life."

I think I ended on a whimper, but it felt good to get it all out there, the ugly truth swirling in the frigid air like bombs that had lived precariously inside of me for years.

"Stop it, Margaret," he said with a look of disgust. "You're being too emotional. You're embarrassing yourself."

"For the last time, it's *Maggie,* you absolute sociopath!" I yelled, his words blowing the lid off my carefully contained temper. "And there's nothing wrong with having emotions! Maybe if you had a few of them yourself, you wouldn't have abandoned your family and I wouldn't be so screwed up!"

Instead of sympathy, or guilt, or any of the myriad of human emotions I expected to see cross his face when I finally confronted him with all the pain he'd left me with, I only found irritation.

Not even anger. No, that was too strong a feeling for someone like him to have. I wasn't even worth his rage. Before, it might've made me feel pathetic and small and inconsequential, but now it just solidified my belief that he was nothing but a monumental waste of my time.

"And maybe if I didn't let myself get screwed up by you, I wouldn't have pushed away the only man I've ever loved. And now, it's too late."

He snorted.

"And you wonder why," he stared down at me disapprovingly. "You think any man wants to deal with such a basket case for a partner?"

His words coiled inside of me, filling me with dread. Filling me with anger.

He should've stopped. He should've shut his mouth. If he'd stuck around, he would've known that I had a temper on me I couldn't contain even if I tried.

But he didn't know me, so he kept going anyway, throwing one final blow at me that might've knocked me clear off my feet any other day, but tonight only fueled the storm that was already inside of me.

"If you didn't push him away," my father said as he looked me in the eye, "he would've left on his own."

And then I lunged at him.

CHAPTER TWENTY-EIGHT

Brody

"**W**hat about that time when Brody unleashed like a thousand crickets into the school for senior prank?"

"That was good, but it wasn't better than the time he prank-called Mrs. Thornton and convinced her that her husband was lost in Walmart."

"He made the call from the back of the classroom! While she was in the room! How did she not figure it out?"

My friends' voices were the loudest in the entire restaurant, and I couldn't be sure if all the attention we were getting was because more than a few customers had recognized me (which they had), or if my friends were just *that* obnoxious.

Somehow, the night had turned into recapping Brody's Biggest Hits, which ordinarily I would've been fine with, but tonight I was too exhausted to play the role required of me.

Still, I found myself slipping into it anyway, because what else could I do? Drag everyone else down? Put a damper on the first evening I'd had with my old friends in years?

"You know how it goes," I shrugged with a trademark grin.

218

All of that stuff I'd only done to get my friends to laugh, because that's why people kept me around.

I was the comic relief. The one to keep everyone in good spirits. The one to fill the awkward silences with a quippy remark.

It had been exhausting back in the day, but now? It was honestly unbearable.

I didn't know what was the matter with me. These were my friends. My best friends since childhood. This is what we'd always done. Got together, cracked jokes, blew off steam.

But tonight? It felt so empty.

I didn't want to talk about bullshit pranks I pulled in eleventh grade. Or recap the way we got drunk at our senior prom and spray-painted the side of the school. Those were fun times, and I'd enjoyed them. But this wasn't my life anymore. And all I wanted was to run like hell back to it.

I wanted Cassie talking so fast through a story that I could barely figure out the punch line. I wanted Liam making everyone who approached us for autographs uncomfortable with his dismissive stares and broody silence.

And most of all, I wanted Maggie.

To sit beside me, with her hand on my thigh under the table. To ask me what we had for snacks when we got home. To whisper something in my ear that had even me blushing. To just be here, with me.

Instead, I shifted in my seat, mentally rehearsing a list of clever comments to pull out later when everyone looked to me expectantly.

"Hey," Tara leaned over, "are you okay?"

"I'm great," I said. "Thanks for getting the crew together."

She stared at me.

"I'm sorry if this isn't what you wanted. You just seemed so sad and I just thought—well, you always seemed so happy around your friends."

I always did seem to be happy around my friends, because they wouldn't have wanted to be around me if I wasn't. But why the hell was it so much harder now to keep that smile on my face that I thought I'd already perfected?

Because now you know what it's like to have people you don't have to pretend around.

"I just thought it would cheer you up," Tara continued. "I didn't mean to overstep."

"You didn't."

Abbey might have. But I didn't blame Tara for that.

"Really, it's nice to see everyone. Thank you for bringing them here."

"You're my little brother," she half-shrugged. "I just want you to be happy. You know that, right?"

"Yeah, Tara." I nodded. "I know."

So that's what I did for the night.

I was happy.

At least, I pretended to be.

Maggie

"**I** can't believe your dad really let the cops take you," Cassie said, sitting next to me behind metal bars.

"You can't?" I asked. "I'd say it's right on par with the father-of-the-year status he's been working toward."

She let out a laugh.

"That was a pretty good hit though. You looked kind of like Liam when he gets mad."

"How would you know?" I said, eager to get my mind off the whole horrid night. "He never gets mad at you."

"I've seen it from afar." She shrugged. "Hockey and stuff. You guys both scrunch your nose up right before you hit someone. It's cute."

The clerk who'd been handling us for the evening moved in front of the bars, fixing us with a bored expression.

"Either of you want to make a call?" she asked.

I didn't know who I would call. The only girl who'd come get me was already sitting beside me. And I wasn't desperate enough to call my mother to bail me out of jail.

"Nope," I said, at the same time Cassie jumped to her feet.

"I do!"

"Great." The clerk unlocked the flimsy gate holding us in the cell and led Cassie to a payphone in the corner of the room.

"I'll call Liam," she said, smiling as if she'd just solved all of our problems.

"You can't call my brother." I stared at her open-mouthed. "He'll kill me!"

"He's my husband!" she protested, hand still hovering over the payphone.

"Which means he'll doubly kill me for dragging you into this!" I exclaimed. "And then, knowing him, he'll probably ban you from planning me the extravagant funeral I deserve!"

"You didn't drag me," she frowned. "I came willingly."

I snorted. "Good luck getting him to believe that."

"Fine," she said, holding the phone out toward my cell. "Then you call Brody."

"Thanks, Cass, but I'd rather die in jail."

She shrugged. "Then, back to Plan A."

And before the protest could even leave my mouth, she was dialing numbers on the payphone and holding it to her ear.

He answered almost immediately.

"Liam?" she said, tucking a strand of blonde hair behind her ear. "Hi, I'm—no, I'm okay. I know I didn't come home when I said I'd be home. I'm still with Maggie. We got a little held up."

I laughed. That was an understatement.

"Uh, yeah." Cassie said, turning to look at where I sat on the bench. "Maggie's okay, too."

I arched my brows at her, mouthing, really?

"Yes, I'd love if you could pick me up." She said, eyes shutting in relief at her white knight swooping in to her rescue. "That's actually why I was calling you. Maggie and I both need a ride home because we're kind of…" She paused, biting her lip. "Well, we're sort of in jail right now."

She held the phone away from her ear and winced, before dragging it back reluctantly. I groaned out loud as the clerk watched us with amusement.

"No!" Cassie protested. "It's not all Maggie's fault. Look, I'll tell you the story when you get here. But everything is fine, I promise."

I rolled my eyes, because of course he would assume that I was the one responsible for landing us in jail.

He was right. But still, the assumption hurt.

"No, Liam!" she squealed, and then cradled the phone a little tighter to her ear before lowering her voice. "We aren't next to any murderers. I don't think they even keep them here." She looked around. "We're in some sort of holding cell, I think."

She stared at me with sympathy, and I could already tell my brother was giving her an earful about how she never should mix her sweet, innocent self with the likes of me.

But honestly, he was probably right.

"Okay. I'll see you soon. Thank you. I love you, too."

She hung the phone up, turning to me with a look of guilt.

"Liam's coming," she said, almost apologetically.

"Great," I exhaled, and collapsed backward onto the bench. I shut my eyes, content to block out the rest of the world for as long as possible.

"Liam Brynn?" the clerk said, interrupting my solitude. "As in… the hockey player? Do you think he'll give me an autograph?"

I groaned.

Maybe it wouldn't be so bad if Liam killed me, after all.

CHAPTER THIRTY

Brody

Despite her best attempts at longing glances and suggestive comments, I'd managed to dodge Abbey for most of the night. Luck ran out around the same time the alcohol did, when everyone decided it was about time to be getting back to their respective hotel rooms.

It wasn't lost on me that more than a few of them made their excuses to let Abbey and I "catch *up*" before they took off.

It wasn't their fault. This was the way it had always been. As long as I've known them, my name was always said in relation to Abbey.

Brody and Abbey. The one consistent pairing of the friend group for all those years.

While the rest of them tended to trade off partners on a quarterly basis, Abbey and I had always sort of stuck together.

Because we got along, yeah. But mostly because it was easy. Low stress. Low drama. She made me laugh. I didn't really know what more to ask for.

It had been the perfect first relationship, and the fact that it never ended on any dramatic cliffhanger didn't hurt.

But tonight, Abbey seemed determined to remind me of just how good it had been.

We were standing outside the restaurant when everyone left—Tara included—but Abbey, persistent as ever, stayed firmly glued to my side.

I couldn't be an ass and take off in the opposite direction, so I just sort of lingered beside her, listening to her make small talk.

We walked down the sidewalk, Abbey asking questions about hockey or making comments about how lucky I was to live in a city like this.

More than anything, I wanted to go home and go to bed with Maggie beside me, but I couldn't. The next best thing would be escaping to Liam's guest room, where I could sleep this whole night away and hopefully see Maggie in the morning.

But something about Abbey was so tinged with sadness that I couldn't just leave her. She was tipsy on wine and lost in her feelings, and I couldn't stomach letting her navigate the streets of Boston alone.

Besides, she *was* technically the oldest friend I had. And if I'd been in a better mood, it would've been nice to see her. Catch up a little.

"I have a hotel room nearby," she said, looking up at me expectantly.

"I'll walk you there," I offered.

"Thanks," she said, slipping her hand in mine.

As naturally as I could muster, I pulled it from her grasp, tucking it safely away in my pocket.

"What?" she laughed. "I'm not allowed to hold your hand anymore?"

"Not really. No."

"I thought you'd be happy to see me after all this time." Her face fell in defeat. "I've missed you, Brody. You never come home anymore."

"I *am* happy to see you, Abbey," I said gently.

"But you won't hold my hand or kiss me. Even though that's what we do."

"What we *did*," I told her. "Abbey, I've had a girlfriend for the last *five* years. I haven't even seen you in six. We can't just pick up right where we left off. Things change."

"You didn't," she told me. "And I didn't."

There she went again, with that sad look in her eyes. Somehow, I didn't think it was entirely about me.

"Don't you remember our pact?" she said suddenly, stopping mid-sidewalk.

Traffic blurred past us, people passed by—a comfort making me feel a little less alone in the moment.

"Our pact?" I repeated slowly, while she looked at me expectantly. "What do you—"

Shit, I thought, when it finally clicked.

That joke we had made when we were sixteen. If neither of us were married by thirty, we'd just marry each other.

"Abbey, we were kids when we made that," I told her. "That was back when we thought thirty was old as hell."

"Doesn't it feel like it sometimes?" she asked quietly, voice barely audible against the sound of traffic around us. "Like life is just passing by too quickly to catch up with?"

"Sometimes," I admitted, thinking of how it felt like yesterday I was a fresh-faced rookie in the first year of his career and today I was at an age where people had started asking me about my retirement plans.

"It does for me," she said, walking under a streetlamp. "It feels like everyone we know is married, with kids and houses and... I have—"

"A cat and an overdraft checking account?" I offered with a smirk.

She let out a laugh, breaking through the barrier of melancholy she'd cloaked herself in.

"Low blow, Callahan." She punched my shoulder lightly. "But glad to see you still know me. That's a comfort."

It was, I realized. A comfort. To have someone who had known you for that long. Who had seen you in every phase of life and had stayed through them all.

"I know what you mean, though." I thought of Liam and Cassie. And all my old friends who had started to settle down and start real life. It was hard not to feel left behind in comparison. "I've been thinking about it a lot, too. It seems like everyone else is hitting all these milestones and I'm struggling to catch up."

"Tara told me what happened," Abbey said. "With your ex."

"Don't call her that," I said, flinching.

"Why?"

"Just feels wrong."

Abbey shrugged. "Well, for what it's worth, I'm sorry. I never would've done that to you."

I didn't know what to say, so I didn't say anything. We just meandered the streets of Boston in a comfortable silence. I didn't have to try to figure out what she was thinking or worry about how she was feeling.

It was nice. Almost as if I could turn my brain off for a little while in the companionship of a friend.

When we reached the lobby of her hotel, I was almost sad that the night had come to an end. Sad to have to go back to Liam's guest room and face the reality of my situation.

Sad that nothing had worked out the way I'd planned.

"Goodnight," I told her. "Thanks for coming. It means a lot."

"No problem." She shrugged. "I needed to get away for a little bit, anyway."

I nodded, understanding.

I wondered what my life would've been like if I stayed back in Michigan instead of coming here. I probably would've gotten a job where my dad worked.

And if I were being honest, I probably would've been married to Abbey now.

As if reading my thoughts, she started to speak, a little uneasily.

"I know the pact was a joke," she admitted softly. "But I always thought you and I would sort of find our way back to each other. Didn't you?"

I thought about it.

Back then, I didn't know what I had thought about the future. I remember thinking Abbey was as good a person as any.

"I guess I did."

"We're friends still. Right, Brody?" she asked, hopefully.

"We'll always be friends. You know that."

"Then can I ask you something?"

I nodded.

"Will you come hang out with me for a little while? Because I really don't want to be alone right now."

I don't know if it was because I was feeling as empty as she was, or if the thought of going back to a house that wasn't home felt as uncomfortable as any other option I had, but when she stared up at me waiting for an answer, all I did was shrug and say, "Sure."

CHAPTER THIRTY-ONE

Brody

"**M**aggie's in *what?*" I exclaimed into the phone, blinking in the darkness of the hotel room.

"In jail," Liam said, an anxiety to his voice that I'd never quite heard. "And not just Maggie. Cassie's with her. So, can you watch Lily or not?"

"No, I fucking can't." I laughed incredulously. "You think I have time to babysit when my girlfriends in fucking jail?"

"She's not your girlfriend. You just kissed someone else in front of her a few hours ago." He said, sticking a pin into my heart. "And my *wife* is there, so I need to go get her, *now.*"

Liam's silence on the other end of the line alerted me to the fact that he might set me on fire if I refused, but I couldn't do anything but.

"Sorry," I bit out. "But I'm coming with you. You have to pick me up."

"You think I have time for that?" I could tell Liam wanted to curse me out, but I also knew that his mind was probably already whirring with thoughts of what to do with his daughter.

"I'll call your mom, have her go there and watch Lily. You know she will."

"I can't wait that long," he said, and I pictured him glaring daggers at me.

"Too bad. You're going to have to."

"Where are you, anyway?" he asked, irritated.

"At a hotel."

"Why?"

"I was catching up with an old friend," I said, feeling guilty.

Abbey was sleeping in her bed. I had fallen asleep in the armchair across the room. We'd talked about old memories for an hour until we both had fallen asleep, probably mid-sentence. It had been totally innocent, but some part of me felt like it was wrong, even still.

"Catching up with the old friend who kissed you earlier?"

"It's not like that—" I started to protest, but he cut me off.

"Not my business," he said. "You do what you want. But I need to get Cassie, so you better be waiting outside in fifteen minutes."

"I will," I told him adamantly.

"I mean it. You're not there, I'm not waiting for you."

"Yeah, Liam. I got it," I said, irritated.

But I couldn't blame him for being panicked, because it was the same for me. I understood his desperate need to get to his lady, because no matter how much he thought Cassie meant to him—

Maggie meant just as much to me.

And I was going to go get her.

Liam burst into the jail like a bull in a china shop, ready to demolish anyone standing in the way of his goal.

I knew we had to be more sensible, unless we wanted to get thrown in there right beside them for unruly behavior or whatever type of crap they tried to pin on us if we made trouble tonight.

Smiling politely, I tried to greet the clerk by telling them who we were there for, but Liam had other plans.

"Cassie Brynn," he said, leaning forward intently. "I'm here for my wife."

"And Maggie Brynn." I shoved him out of the way with a frown.

The officer at the front desk peered at us with interest, eyes widening as realization struck.

"You boys play for the Harbor Wolves, don't you?" The man was a little older, voice thick with the Boston accent that Maggie denied existed but anyone not raised in the city could hear from a mile away. "You look bigger in person, somehow."

He paused to laugh, probably chuckling at the irony of the players he'd just watched on the small television screen in the corner of his desk now standing in front of him, here to bail out their partners.

"You wouldn't mind if I get a picture, would you?" he said, already standing and coming around the desk. "My son will never believe it."

Oh, great.

We didn't have time for this. Not when Maggie was probably hungry and cold in the holding cell.

But I knew well enough that people were more likely to help out an agreeable person than one with a stick up their ass, which is why Liam was pissing me off so much.

"No," he gritted out.

"Shut up," I mouthed at him, sending him a glare.

He threw his head back, blinking rapidly as he tried to maintain his composure before looking back at the man in charge of Maggie and Cassie's fates.

"Fine. But we have to make it quick."

"Yes, sir," he said, wobbling over to us. "Hey, Steve. Get off your ass and come take a picture of me."

"What?" a voice called from the back office. "Why the hell do I want to take a picture of you?"

Steve, in all his near elderly glory, appeared with an expression of irritation that instantly transformed into one of awe at the sight of us.

"Holy smokes," he let out a whistle. "There's something you don't expect to see on a Tuesday evening."

"Right," the first man said, handing over his cellphone before making his way to stand with us, "so take my phone and snap the picture, would you?"

He was tall himself. Almost as tall as me, and just a few inches shorter than Liam. He stood between us, wrapping his arms around us both as if we were his sons and he was posing for the family Christmas card.

Liam muttered something under his breath, and I wanted to pinch his arm at the way he deadpanned the camera.

His lack of enthusiasm when meeting fans wouldn't do him any favors if the photo leaked, but then again, neither would the picture of us standing in jail, so I guess it was a wash either way.

"Let me see here," the elderly man said, hand shaking as he held the camera. With a wobbly finger he pressed the button and smiled. "Got it!"

I was sure it was about to be the blurriest fucking photo anyone had ever seen, but I was hoping they wouldn't take the time to look it over.

"Great, now bring me to my wife," Liam said, leaving little room for debate.

"And mine," I said, not bothering to get into the specifics of our current relationship status at the moment.

"Ah, you two like the troublemakers, huh?" the first officer said with a wink. "If it's those two pretty ladies I saw earlier, then I don't blame you. Follow me."

He led us to a back room where a woman sat at a desk in front of a small holding area with ugly gray bars—the kind you saw on sitcoms where the main characters got into some rambunctious debacle and had to spend a night in the cell.

But there was nothing funny about the way Maggie looked laying down on the bench, eyes fixed blankly at the ceiling.

Something had broken her.

Had it been me?

Surely she must know how I felt about her. That the kiss hadn't been anything on my end at all.

"Liam!" Cassie, who was sitting on the floor with her back against the wall, gasped at the same time Liam's anguished voice called out, "Cassie!"

"What's the bail?" I asked, trying to keep my head straight at the sight of Maggie's look of crumbled dejection.

Her eyes panned to mine, but I couldn't read them. Or maybe I just didn't trust myself to anymore, after all the misunderstandings between us lately.

"Who cares? You can take my whole fucking wallet," Liam interjected, actually dropping it down on the desk. "Just get my wife out of there."

"Your wife isn't being held," the clerk fixed him with a look. "She chose to be in there with the other one."

Liam's head snapped toward Cassie and he groaned.

"Why, baby," he said, eyes closed as he attempted to rub out the crease between his brows. "Why are you trying to kill me?"

The clerk, acutely aware of the dire situation, got to her feet and unlocked the holding cell.

The second the bars slid away, Cassie was out and into Liam's arms as if they hadn't seen each other in days.

And I would've been judging them if I didn't take the opportunity to head straight into the cell and crouch in front of Maggie, who for some reason wasn't jumping at the chance to get the hell out.

"Maggie, babe," I stared at her painfully expressionless face. "What happened?"

She sat up, flinching away from me when I tried to reach out for her.

Running headfirst into barbed wire would've hurt less.

"Yeah, Maggie, what the hell happened?" Liam said, still holding Cassie tucked under his chin.

"It's complicated," Cassie squirmed, peering over to Maggie, who sat statue-still on the bench in front of me.

"Margaret here was brought in for charges of assault," the clerk said.

"*What?*" Liam and I gasped at the same time.

"Maggie?" I asked, eyes widening as I looked at her, waiting for an explanation.

She didn't say a single word to defend herself. She was so completely and utterly lifeless, so un-Maggie-like, that I felt fear coiling inside me and didn't have a single clue how to reach her.

"No!" Cassie said from behind me. "It wasn't like that! It was just her dad."

I turned in shock, eyes focused on Cassie, who I hoped was clear-headed enough to tell me every detail.

Maggie had seen her dad? Without me?

No wonder she was such a shell right now. That guy screwed with her head like nobody's business. My hands balled into fists at my side at the knowledge I hadn't been there beside her during whatever happened.

"Assaulting a parent is still considered assault, Mrs. Brynn," the clerk's voice countered.

"She didn't *assault* him," Cassie emphasized. "She threw a punch at him. Just one. And trust me, it was well deserved."

"Why didn't you just come home, Cass?" Liam groaned. "Or call me?"

"You think I'd let Maggie sit in jail alone all night?" Cassie asked, affronted at the insinuation.

Hell yeah, Cass, I thought. Maggie needed someone by her side.

If she wouldn't let it be me, I was grateful it was Cassie, at least.

"Maggie, what the hell were you thinking? I told you that guy was no good. I told you to stay away from him, but you think everyone in the world is wrong except you—"

"Hey!" Cassie raised her voice, turning her angry eyes onto Liam. "That's my friend you're talking to. And she already had a hard night, so leave her alone."

Then, in predictable Cassie fashion, she still leaned up on her tiptoes and kissed his cheek. "But thank you for coming."

Liam sighed, draping an arm around Cassie's shoulder.

"Look," he said, "we're all tired. We can all talk about this in the morning. Let's just go home, okay?"

"Maggie?" My voice nearly cracked, and finally—*finally*—she rewarded me with her gaze.

It was a look of exhaustion from fighting battles unbeknownst to me, and it hurt me just as much to know I wasn't able to fix whatever it was haunting her.

"Yeah," she said, standing. "Let's go."

CHAPTER THIRTY-TWO

Maggie

Brody breaking me out of jail took the top slot for the most humiliating things to ever happen to me in my entire life.

I had started the night with the hope of swooping in, winning him back, and showing him how much better I could be than I'd been. How ready I was to grow and change.

And what had I done? Given him more proof of the exact reason why he deserved better.

I was a loose cannon, unpredictable, and easily led astray by her emotions time and again.

All I could do was stare out Liam's car window, fighting to suck in a breath each time Brody's knee brushed against mine in the backseat.

After the fourth time, I started to think it was intentional, which just seemed cruel after his lips had been locked with some random girl from his past mere hours ago.

I forcibly turned my body to look out the window, scooting as far to the left as I could possibly get.

Ha. There was no way he could accidentally bump me now. Even with those outrageously long legs of his.

Part of me knew that I was responsible for all of this.

But the part of me running the show right now was the emotional, high-strung girl my father accused me of being, and even though she understood the logic of it all, it didn't stop the pain from scorching her.

"Maggie," he said through a wince. "Maggie, talk to me."

Here I was, hurting him again.

I couldn't do it anymore. I couldn't be selfish with him.

I turned to him and forced, if not a smile, then at least a neutral expression.

Liam and Cassie were dead silent in the front seat, making the whole situation all the more awkward. I needed to hold onto a shred of my dignity after everything.

"You can have the apartment for a while," I told him in what I thought would be a selfless offering. "You've stayed with Liam and Cassie long enough. I'll take a shift with them now."

"What?" Brody shook his head. "No, Maggie, that's not what I—"

"It's okay," I stopped him. "It's what I want."

And really, I did. I couldn't bear to be alone in the apartment anymore. Not where every corner held a memory of him, and I was ninety percent sure I had turned into my mother, bursting into tears at the sight of his dirty laundry on the floor.

But I didn't deserve to cry, because it was my fault.

"Well, I'm not doing that," he said blankly.

"Well, I'm not going back to the apartment," I said resolutely.

"Fine, then neither am I," he said, matching my snark and crossing his arms across his chest.

"So," Liam cleared his throat, "where am I driving to right now?"

"I'm going to your house," I met his gaze in the rearview mirror while he stared at me in a way that said, *stop being a stubborn pain in the ass.* "Like I said."

"Brody?" He turned, exhaling the weariest of sighs.

"As am I."

I turned, frowning at my smug-looking not-boyfriend sitting next to me in what looked like victory.

Whatever, I thought. Liam and Cassie's mini mansion was big enough for both of us, but I sure as hell wasn't going to lock myself in the tomb of memories that was the apartment. I just couldn't.

"Fine," I bit out, daring him to back out first.

"Fine." He smiled at me, tauntingly.

Liam groaned, taking a sharp left instead of continuing straight toward mine and Brody's apartment.

"Yay," Cassie let out an anxious giggle, looking at Liam with a nervous smile. "Sleepover."

CHAPTER THIRTY-THREE

Brody

Being near Maggie again felt like being on a roller coaster. The air filled with anticipation, the nerves rolling around in the pit of my stomach. The thrill that you feel right before the drop.

Look at me. I pleaded wordlessly. *Look at me and let me know that everything is going to be fine.*

But she didn't. Not even once.

It was past midnight when we stumbled into the foyer of Liam and Cassie's house, and while the latter tried her best to linger—ready to extinguish any fires that might arise between Maggie and me—Liam was quick to usher her up the stairs, telling her she needed rest.

"Well," I said, as Maggie and I lingered in the darkness. "He's been extra broody lately."

Maggie was silent, doing anything and everything except meeting my eyes.

She looked so small with her arms crossed over her chest. So helpless. It took everything in me not to step forward and reach for her. To ask her what I could do to erase everything that happened lately and go back to normal.

"Maggie?" I said into the darkness.

Nothing.

"Come on, Maggie." I sighed. "Let's just go home."

At that, her eyes snapped up, fury boiling beneath the surface as she glared at me. My heart accelerated. At least she was *looking* at me.

"Why would I go anywhere with a guy who spent the night making out with another girl?"

"Hold on, I did *not* make out—"

"Who was she anyway?" she asked. "Some hockey fan or stalker or something?"

"Her name is Abbey. She's my—"

"Your ex-girlfriend Abbey?" Her eyes narrowed into terrifying slits.

I fought the urge to gulp. I'd never actually been on the receiving end of one of Maggie's death stares. It was uncomfortable, to say the least.

"Uh," I scratched my head guiltily. "Yeah… but—"

"Oh, that's great!" She clapped her hands in mock cheerfulness. "Well, I'm *so* happy I got to be there for your long-awaited reunion."

"Maggie," I groaned, rubbing a hand over my face. "It's not like that and you know it."

"So, where'd you go after?" she asked, deadpanning.

"What?"

"If it's not like that, then I'm sure you just went home after, right?"

I said nothing.

"Right?" she asked again.

"No." I gritted out. "We all went to dinner with some old friends from high school."

"We, meaning you and Abbey?"

"Abbey was there… yes."

"How perfect," she laughed. "Another high school sweethearts success story. You'd make the perfect Hallmark movie!"

"Maggie, stop." I grabbed her shoulders. "Listen to me. It's nothing like what you're thinking."

"I don't care what it's like," she lied. "Because it's none of my business."

"*I'm* your business," I told her, and then made the idiotic motion to lean forward and kiss her.

For one, because half of me thought it would make everything better—show her that there wasn't anyone else for me. And another because it had been a week and I honestly thought I might die if I had to wait any longer.

For half a second, it worked. She relaxed under my touch, lips moving against mine. For half a second, we were just us again, and everything made sense once more.

And then, because she's Maggie—stubborn, beautiful, obstinate Maggie—she remembered she was pissed at me and shoved me off of her with the strength that no female her size should have.

After making a dramatic show of wiping the kiss off on her sleeve, she turned her furious expression back toward me.

"I know *you're* obsessed with kissing ex-girlfriends," she said, already headed to make a dramatic exit up the staircase, "but I'm not interested in that."

I stared after her, watching as she stormed up each step with the fury of a woman scorned.

"And *I'm* taking the guest room." She threw one last remark over her shoulder before disappearing from my sight.

I let out a sigh, slumping down on the bottom of the stairs, alone in the dark.

But something bubbled in my chest. An excitement accompanying the knowledge that it wasn't over. Not entirely. I still had a chance.

Because no matter how pissed she was at me, no matter how much anger she had inside of her—I *knew* her, and her anger gave me hope.

Because Maggie Brynn didn't fight over things she didn't care about.

CHAPTER THIRTY-FOUR

Maggie

I wasn't very in touch with my inner child. I didn't like being a little girl even when I *was* one, so it made it a bit hard to get into character when I tried to play with Lily.

I sat criss-cross in the center of her bedroom, watching as she dragged a bucket of toys into the middle of the room before plopping down across from me.

In one swift motion, she turned the bucket upside down, dumping the entirety of its contents onto the rug between us.

"You have a lot of toys, Lil." I remarked. "Your dad just buys you whatever you want, huh?"

"Yup," she said, popping the "p." "'Cause he loves me."

I laughed, watching her pudgy hands shift through the Barbies on the floor.

"Here," she held one up to me. "You can be this one 'cause your hair is brown."

"Okay," I took the doll between my fingers, pushing her plastic arm this way and that.

I'd never been much of a doll kid. Growing up as Liam's shadow, I

242

sort of just went along with whatever he was doing. My girlhood was spent trying, and usually failing, to perfect the hobbies that seemed to garner him so much attention and praise from the adults in our lives.

As a result, I was far more comfortable with a basketball or a skateboard than I was with Barbie's Dream House or stuffed-animal tea parties.

But for Lily's sake, I tried.

It was confusing to follow the chain of events she'd set up for us as we rapidly switched between playing family, then mermaids, then under-the-sea explorers. But stiff as I felt, I forced myself to follow the script she laid out for us.

"What are you girls doing?" Brody stuck his head in about fifteen minutes into our playdate.

My traitorous stomach did a somersault at the sight of him—his hair tousled from sleep and brown eyes feigning innocence.

"Playing dolls." Lily answered. "Wanna play?"

I opened my mouth to protest, but he was already gliding into the room with a smile on his face.

"Sure do!" he chirped, forming the third point of our triangle as he lowered himself to a sitting position.

"You can be him," she said, handing him a Ken doll. "'Cause he's the only boy I got. And you can pretend you have an ice cream store."

"Got it," he nodded, instantly getting into character.

I'd always been jealous of how he was able to interact so naturally with Lily in a way that I never could manage. He just understood her better—understood the illogical rules of children in a way I never would.

"How can I help you today, Miss?" Brody said, forcing his Ken doll to talk to Lily's Barbie.

"Uhhhhhh," she drawled, smiling up at his attentive expression. "I want some chocolate ice cream."

"Chocolate ice cream?" He floated his doll over a few feet, as if pretending to fetch it. "You got it. That'll be a zillion dollars."

Lily erupted into a fit of giggles. I rolled my eyes.

"Your turn, Auntie Maggie." Lily turned to me.

I didn't feel particularly thrilled about interacting with Brody through the means of dolls, especially after I was still feeling the pang of rejection—not to mention the humiliation of the events the night before.

But before I opened my mouth to even try, Brody beat me to it.

"Oh, I know what Aunt Maggie wants." Brown eyes taunted teasingly. I huffed a scoff.

How dare he sit here playing dolls with me when less than twenty-four hours ago he was kissing another girl!

I knew I had no leg to stand on, considering I was the one who made a mess of our relationship, but still. It hurt. He knew it would hurt. And sitting here with him just exacerbated the guilt I had over the entire thing being my fault.

"Oh, I don't think you do." I said, trying to preserve whatever dignity I had left.

"You get the same thing every time."

"Sometimes our preferences change." I shook the doll in my hand, as if it were the one talking. "Like ice cream flavors. Or girls we want to kiss."

"Ew." Lily scrunched her nose.

"Well, *my* preferences don't change." He countered, still wiggling the doll in conversation. "I still like Rocky Road, like I always have. And I still like all the other things I always have."

He shot me a look that felt too intimate for eight in the morning while we played with toys.

"You know what?" I said through the doll. "I think I'm going to go to a different establishment. Is there a pizza shop around here?"

"No, you gotta order the ice cream." Lily groaned. "You didn't pick out the toppings."

"Just take your pistachio ice cream, Mags." Brody made the doll push a minuscule plastic toy bowl across the rug. "Because I know you like the same things you've always liked, too. Even if you won't admit it."

"Yeah," Lily chirped, "get the 'stacio."

"If Uncle Brody wanted me to buy ice cream from him, he shouldn't have been giving out free samples to other Barbies." I sniffed.

"Uncle Brody," Lily said, "can I—"

"Well, maybe you shouldn't have let your ice cream melt while I was waiting for you to eat it." He sat back, irritation growing in his voice.

Good. Arguing. I knew how to do that. It was safer than feeling hurt. Safer than feeling rejected or sad or alone.

"How was I supposed to know it was melting if you never told me?"

"Ice cream doesn't last forever! It melts! It's a delicacy!"

"Auntie Maggie," I was vaguely aware of Lily tugging on my sleeve.

"Just a second, Lily." I told her, never breaking eye contact with Brody.

"Why don't you just admit that you don't like Rocky Road anymore?" I asked. "That you want to venture out to new flavors?"

"Oh, come on!" he said. "You're being stubborn and you know it. I have spent the last five years only eating Rocky Road and literally proposed to never eat any other ice cream flavor again."

"Uncle Brod—"

"And if Rocky Road had agreed, would you have still been taking a bite out of lemon sherbet after the hockey game the other night?"

"Why are you guys—"

"If Rocky Road had agreed, then I doubt my sister would've ever tried to bring any other flavor here." He said, irritated.

I was vaguely aware of Lily huffing and running out of her bedroom, but I was too impassioned to take any real notice.

"Well, your sister wouldn't have brought her here if she didn't think you wanted her!"

"I *didn't*!" Brody countered.

"You did—" I argued.

And then the door opened, and there stood Cassie with a look of utter disappointment on her face while Lily hid behind her legs.

Brody and I dropped the dolls guiltily.

"Brody and Maggie, you need to let Lily play with you." Cassie spoke in a voice that had been perfected over years of disciplining unruly children in a classroom. "If you can't share with your niece, then the dolls will be all done."

Then Brody looked to me, whispering conspiratorially as he said, "If she's the teacher, I *really* hope Liam's not the principal, because I have a feeling we're getting sent to his office next."

CHAPTER THIRTY-FIVE

Brody

As much fun as it was arguing with Maggie, I had a feeling that nothing conducive to rebuilding our relationship would come out of snarky banter exchanged while the rest of the Brynn family pretended not to notice the tension we were filling their house with.

And I said as much to her, suggesting that we try talking back at *our* place, but the only thing that came out of it was her smacking me on the arm and saying, "Since when do you use the word conducive?"

Since you forced me into this position, that's when, Margaret.

The entire morning had consisted of Maggie trying to avoid me but being unable to help herself and throwing out sassy comments, all while my phone blew up with messages from my old high school group chat that had been largely dormant for years.

"Who's that?" Maggie asked over my shoulder as I stared down at the phone.

"My friends," I said, largely aware of her proximity to me. "They want me to hang out again before they leave."

"Well, you should go," she said. "Obviously."

Should I? It was hard to leave when things weren't fixed yet and Maggie was still feeling crappy about everything. When *I* was still feeling crappy about everything.

"I don't see how it's any of your business," I said, playing her game, eyes locked on her as she moved to sit beside me. "Seeing as you're hellbent on ignoring me."

"I'm not ignoring you." She said, arms crossing on the kitchen island as she feigned innocence. "I'm telling you it'll be good for you to see your friends."

"But you're only saying that because you're doing your weird self-sabotage thing, and you think if I go, I'm going to spend time with Abbey."

The very mention of her name had Maggie stiffening, lips curling slightly in irritation.

"Nope." She said, scooting her stool an inch or two away. "You just haven't seen them in a while and I—"

"You what, Mags?"

You're scared you're not going to be able to put up a fight for much longer before you let yourself feel sad?

"I'll go if we can go back to being normal," I said, when it became clear she had no response.

"This is normal," she said far too casually to be believable. "We're friends."

"Friends?" I laughed. "We've never been friends, Maggie."

"Well, we are now," she said. "And as your friend, I'm allowed to give you advice."

The word *friend* felt toxic on my tongue when regarding the two of us, but I figured I'd use it to my advantage.

"So, as my friend," I leaned into her, "you can come hang out with me and my other friends, then?" I raised my eyebrows in challenge.

"Absolutely not." She frowned.

"Why?"

"There's no way in hell I'm having another front-row seat to watch you and your ex-girlfriend snogging all over Boston."

"We're not—" I said, but my phone started ringing, cutting me off.

"Answer it," she gestured toward the phone currently flashing a face of Matt T.'s crappy senior photo.

I sighed and reached for the phone.

"Hello?"

"Dude," Matt said, "we're on our way to pick you up because you weren't answering the phone."

"Most people would take that as a hint," I grimaced.

"A hint of what?" His voice transported me back to my teen years, reminding me of the calls we'd had when I was sixteen and had nothing better to do than ride around our neighborhood with him.

"That I'm occupied, Matt." I said, but couldn't help but laugh. There was a comfort in the way he hadn't really changed at all over the years.

A sort of sadness, too.

"Dude," he blew out a breath, "you sound way more uptight than you used to be. I thought money and fame were supposed to mellow a person out."

I laughed.

"We're only kidnapping you for a little bit, then you can get back to your regularly scheduled drama or whatever it is you're up to lately."

I opened my mouth to respond, but Maggie was already reaching over to grab the phone from my hands.

"He'll come," she said, darting around the kitchen island with my phone pressed to her ear.

"Maggie," I said, maneuvering around to chase her.

Her arm flailed out, phone extended just out of my reach as we did what probably looked like some type of badly choreographed dance around the kitchen.

"Give me the phone, Mags," I told her, fingers reaching out to grab it. I could vaguely hear Matt's muffled voice from the phone until

Maggie pressed the speakerphone button and the room was filled with the sound of my childhood best friend.

"—must be the hot ex, right?" he said with interest.

"Shut up, Matt," I called out, trapping Maggie in my arms while we fought over my cellphone.

Maggie laughed.

"Because you're *more* than welcome to join us," he said with insinuation.

"Oh, I don't think—"

"You know what?" I said, "she'd love to. Pick us both up."

"Sweet!" he said, like it was a victory on his part. "Be there in twenty."

"We'll be ready."

CHAPTER THIRTY-SIX

Maggie

Was I being a little territorial? Maybe.

Logically, there was no good reason why I should've agreed to go out with Brody's high school friends considering the current relationship between us—or the lack of one, I should say.

But I usually made decisions based on the vibe rather than the logic, and well, morbid curiosity won out. I wanted to scope the scene out. Get a glimpse into who Brody was before I ever knew him. And even if it was some form of masochism, I *wanted* to be near him.

Even if I had to fight him tooth and nail on everything to keep my feelings at bay while we navigated this weird new relationship we found ourselves in.

I already knew it was going to be painful. Abbey would be there. Stupid Abbey with her stupid beautiful hair and stupid history with Brody.

Guys never got over their first loves. Wasn't that the oldest story in the world? And she swept in just in time, right in the wake of our breaking up, so she could get her probably unmanicured claws into him again.

Stupid. Stupid. Stupid.

"Uh," Liam's voice stopped me in my tracks. "Are you okay?"

I ceased my movements, pulling my head off of the fridge I'd been banging my head against.

"Yup," I said, slightly mortified.

"You sure? Because it looked like you were trying to leave a Maggie-sized dent in my refrigerator door."

"I was trying to get the bad thoughts out of my head," I admitted.

"Yeah. I know," he said. "I haven't seen you do that since we were kids."

"Sometimes I feel like there's too much frustration being kept in my body," I said. "Do you ever feel like that?"

"Not anymore," Liam said. "But I remember what it was like."

"How did you get rid of it?"

"I had to just let it go." Liam shrugged.

"I don't know how to do that." I bit my lip.

"I didn't either. Or maybe I wasn't ready to back then. I think you and I are the type of people who like to torture ourselves a little bit." He let out a humorless laugh.

"I definitely like to torture myself," I agreed, thinking of how I'd successfully pushed away everyone that mattered. The way they were in pain, too, because of me. "And apparently, I like to torture everyone around me, too."

I stared up at my brother, feeling exposed by the sincerity I was trying—and probably failing—to express.

"I really didn't mean to. And I'm sorry."

Liam shrugged. "Forget about it."

"I won't," I promised. "I'll remember it, and remember how much it hurt you to remind myself of why I need to think things through before I do them."

"I appreciate it, Mags," Liam said. "I do."

"Sometimes I think I like to cause chaos before I can let chaos happen to me," I said. "Stupid, isn't it?"

"A little unhinged, maybe," Liam agreed. "But not stupid. It's not like we had anyone around us to teach us any better."

"How did you end up so perfect and I became the emotional train wreck?"

"To be fair, I don't think I'd ever been considered the model for a healthily adapted adult, either." He cocked his head.

"True." I laughed, thinking about how guarded and closed off he'd been for most of his life. "But you pulled it together, didn't you?"

"Yeah," he said, looking around his house at the life he's built. "Because I let people help me."

His words held meaning. I knew what he was trying to say. Cassie had helped heal a part of him. Or maybe that was wrong. Maybe another person couldn't heal you. But maybe they could make you want to heal yourself.

I had Brody. And if anyone was worth overcoming my screwed up, toxic patterns for, it was him. I just didn't even know where to start.

"So," I started, "hypothetically, of course."

"Of course." He nodded, waiting for me to continue.

"If someone *were* to ask for help on how to put their life back together, what would you tell them?"

"Coming from someone who knows you, I would say, hypothetically"—he rolled his eyes—"that you need to slow down and catch your breath. You never give your wounds a chance to heal. You just pick up and start running again. And you know what happens?"

"I get away from the mess faster?" I added cheekily.

"No. You never find your balance, and end up falling right back down again not long after."

I scoffed.

"I'm your brother, Mags. I taught you how to ride a bike, remember? When you fell down and scraped both your knees, you didn't even bother to cry. You just got back up because you wanted to succeed."

I remembered, I thought with a pang. I remembered how I had been practicing with Liam so when Dad took me out, I could impress him with how well I already rode. I imagined him praising me, telling me what a natural I was, the way I sometimes heard him say to Liam. But he never took me. Not even once. I'd been pissed about it. Or hurt, I guess. But Liam had been there. He'd been there and I hadn't cared. I'd been so focused on the things I didn't have, I never stopped to appreciate the things I *did*.

"You know, I used to be mad at you that Dad gave you all his attention," I admitted hesitantly.

"I used to be mad about it, too," he agreed. "I wish it wasn't the case."

"It was never your fault. I understand that now. Actually, I think I understand a lot of things now that I never let myself really see before," I said. "Like how you and I both turned out fine without him."

"And we'll continue to be fine without him. Right?" Liam asked, almost pleading with me to agree that we'd be done with that guy forever.

Finally, I was ready.

To let him go. To deal with my shit surrounding him. To put the pieces back together of my life, because even if he had broken them, I was the only one responsible for putting them back together.

"Right," I said, and meant it with all my heart.

Liam breathed out a sigh of relief and took a few steps to pull me into a hug.

"Proud of you, Mags. You don't need him. You never did."

"I do need you though. Is that okay?"

"That's okay," he laughed. "I'll always be here."

But there was someone else I needed too, and if anyone could help me figure out how to get him back, it was Liam.

"Hypothetically," I pulled away from the hug to look up at my brother, "if you were going to give someone advice about how to fix things with their boyfriend..." I trailed off, waiting for him to save me from the misery of asking.

"The truth?" he said, with a look as if I might not be able to handle it.

But I was becoming a better version of myself. The type of girl who could hear hard truths without erupting. So I nodded in confirmation.

"You need more trust in people. You can't keep pushing people away just to test if they'll stay, Mags," he said carefully. "Because eventually, they're going to get tired of chasing after someone who they don't even know wants to be caught."

Damn, I thought, taken aback.

If Liam was serious about retiring from hockey, he'd make a hell of a therapist.

CHAPTER THIRTY-SEVEN

Brody

aggie was staring at Abbey the way she sometimes did when questioning someone on the stand.

I was preparing for her to at any moment start a sentence with, "Please state your name for the record," before questioning her about that stupid kiss.

Abbey, for her part, didn't seem to notice. Or pretended not to. In the crowd of us, it was easy to focus on anyone else. Unfortunately, that anyone else happened to be me, only serving to infuriate Maggie further.

I shifted uncomfortably in my seat. Maggie next to me, Abbey across from me, and the rest of my friends scattered around the table of the pizza parlor around us, the air was thick with tension that only I seemed to be aware of.

"So, what's the deal with you two, then?" Matt C. asked, gesturing between Maggie and me with a fry between his fingers.

I didn't say anything, figuring I'd let Maggie explain it for herself. She was the one sitting here jealous over my ex-girlfriend.

Her attention snapped to him, body rigid.

The table seemed to pause, everyone apparently interested in her answer. I relaxed back in my chair, hoping to take the pressure off, even slightly. To act as if my entire existence didn't depend on her answer.

"The deal?" she asked carefully, narrowing her eyes on him as if she might intimidate him into retracting his question.

"Are you together?" he asked, matching her gaze confrontationally.

"Why? Are you jealous?" she asked, in a way I knew was meant to buy time.

I leaned back in my seat, ready to let her take charge of the conversation, because Matt wasn't the only one eager to hear her answer.

I had a lot riding on it. Because I knew Maggie, and if she was as threatened by Abbey as she seemed to be, I knew she'd make some type of public claim, even if she wasn't ready to get back together now.

That was fine, though. If I had hope for our future, then I could wait. But if she still denied it… if she opened up the door for someone else to swoop in… well, I didn't want to think about what that meant for us.

"Actually, a little," Matt said with a laugh. "Brody hasn't been back home in years and the only reason for that is probably you."

He didn't say it in any harsh way, on the contrary, it sounded more like a joke than anything else. But I still felt irritation prickle against me at the insinuation.

"Hey," I said, "that's not true. I've been home."

"Like twice." He scoffed.

"We've been more than that," Maggie looked to me with concern in her eyes.

I could see what she was thinking. Wondering if it was her fault that I hadn't been home. But it wasn't. I hadn't wanted to go home because, well, I was content where I was. I missed my family, yeah. But we'd found ways to see each other over the years.

"I play hockey," I countered. "I don't exactly have the most flexible schedule to work with."

"We're getting off topic," he waved my comment off, shaking his head.

I rolled my eyes.

"Basically, I'm just asking if you're together or not."

Maggie was silent. My hands felt jittery.

"You're really invested in my dating life, Matt," I said, trying to lighten the atmosphere.

"I think we're all just a little confused," Tara said gently. "We all thought you broke up, but now you're here together…"

I sighed. Everyone was nosey as hell and the last thing I needed was my relationship under a microscope while we were still trying to figure it out ourselves.

"But you're here, so you guys must be *something*, then, right?" The question was a dagger aimed directly at Maggie.

She looked up at me, eyes scanning the entirety of my face as if it were the first time.

"He's my best friend," she answered them, never tearing her eyes off mine.

I stilled, fighting the urge to suck in a breath, because I could've sworn she was looking at me with something. And for half a second, I felt like I was on the verge of reaching her again.

"Mags—" I started, but Abbey spoke at the same time, her voice louder than my own.

"So, you're not together?"

"We're—" I started.

Working through it? Getting there? Going to be fine?

I'm not even sure what would've come out of my mouth because I never got the chance to say it.

"No," Maggie answered flatly. "We're not."

And there it went. My heart deflated like a balloon in my chest. My last shred of hope gone.

If Maggie, my territorial, means-business Maggie, was admitting we were over in front of someone she viewed as a threat, then I guess that meant we really were.

It wasn't enough to hope that someday she might change her mind. To linger in her life and wait for her to be ready, while consoling myself that she didn't *really* mean it.

Because all that would do was hurt me more, giving me a front row seat to watch her find someone she actually wanted. Someone she didn't hesitate to say yes to.

I slumped back in my chair, feeling the finality wash over me.

Everything in my life had fallen apart in a matter of weeks and I felt like I'd been trying to tie it back together with threads of cobweb.

Maggie's phone rang, and her fingers darted toward her purse, desperate to reach it.

"Excuse me," she said, looking at the name on the screen. "This is for work, I have to take it."

And then she took off toward the door, phone pressed to her ear, apparently as eager to escape the table as I was.

My heart shattered into pieces and we hadn't even gotten our entrées yet. Perfect.

"So," Matt clapped his hands together. "Now that that's settled, what's the move?"

"The move?" I responded dumbly, rubbing a hand over my face in utter exhaustion.

"You've got nothing keeping you here anymore. You're free."

"Free?" I asked.

I was never trapped.

"You and your girl are dead and buried—" Aiden cut in.

I groaned, taking a long chug of beer. "So not in the mood to recap that right now."

"No, no, dude. This is a good thing," Aiden responded, while the rest of the guys nodded their agreement.

I snorted. "I'm failing to see how my life falling apart is a good thing. Every plan for the future I had revolved around that girl being in it." I gestured toward the door she left from.

"You're looking at it from the wrong angle." Matt shook his head. "You have to view it as an *opportunity*."

"Just tell him what you mean," Abbey rolled her eyes.

"We think you should come home," Tara interjected, beating them all to the punch.

"What?" I nearly choked out a laugh. "I can't go hang out in Michigan for a week. I have a job."

"We don't mean a vacation," Matt said. "We mean, like, come home."

"Again, I have a job," I repeated incredulously.

"Your contract's almost up," Tara defended.

"And don't all you hockey guys retire in your thirties, anyway?"

"Well, yeah, but—"

"So what are you going to do? You don't have a life here anymore," Tara said.

"That's not true," I argued. Even though, now I guess it kind of was.

I was staying on the couch of my ex-girlfriend's brother. And yeah, technically he was my best friend, but how would that dynamic change now that Maggie and I were over?

She wouldn't want her ex-boyfriend lurking in the shadows, and I wouldn't want to make her uncomfortable by lingering in the background of her life.

I had the hockey team, I guess. But they were all young guys just starting out in their careers, and I was past the point of wanting to spend my free time bar hopping.

Liam already had retirement on his mind, and stubborn bastard he was, it was only a matter of time before he finalized that decision.

And Cassie—sweet, nervous Cassie—would be wracked with guilt trying to navigate maintaining a friendship with her best friend's ex-boyfriend.

Tara, harsh as she was, was right.

There was nothing left for me in Boston but loneliness and heartbreak and reminders of the life I almost had.

But Michigan? I hadn't consistently lived there since I was in high school. It was nostalgic. And comfortable. But was it my future?

"What would I even do there?" I asked, wondering if I was insane to even be considering the possibility of going back.

"The same thing you'd do here." Tara shrugged. "Take some time. Regroup, figure stuff out."

"Only this time," Matt said, "you'd be surrounded by your friends."

"So, what?" I asked, leaning back in my chair. "Is this something all of you have talked about?"

"Pretty much, yeah," he said as they all nodded their agreement.

"I can't believe I'm pathetic enough that I needed an intervention." I rolled my eyes.

I looked to my sister, hoping to find some answer in her eyes directing me toward the right path. Just like that day at the lake when I'd fallen in the frigid water, it seemed like she was here to pull me out of the life I was drowning in.

"Look," she said, reading the pain in my expression. "I know you loved Maggie. I did too. But you can't make someone want to be with you. You just have to stick with the people who do." She finished with a shrug, and a sad smile that only made my heartbreak more.

"We want you to come home, Brody," Abbey said suddenly. "I want you to come home."

I looked at her and saw the girl I'd grown up beside. She didn't look that different, really. Same freckles on her cheeks. Same eyes that looked at me in a way that hadn't changed despite the years or time between us.

It would be so easy, to step back into my old life. Apparently, it was still waiting for me. An option I hadn't even known I'd had.

I had enough money to get my own place. I could work for my Dad, give him a chance to take the back seat a little bit now that he was getting up there in age. I could be surrounded by places and people I'd known my entire life. It would be comfortable. Familiar. Safe.

Just when everything had fallen apart, my friends were here to hand over the pieces and the opportunity to put them back into place. If I wanted to.

I opened my mouth to respond, but stopped when the scent of Maggie's perfume filled the air. Dolce & Gabbana Light Blue. I let myself breathe it in one last time.

Maggie didn't need me anymore. Maybe she never did. But back in Michigan? I could be useful there. I could be needed.

"What did I miss?" Maggie asked, sliding down into the chair.

"Not much," I said. "Just making some plans."

CHAPTER THIRTY-EIGHT

Maggie

I'd spent most of my life in delusion.

I thought if I acted confident enough, or pretended I didn't need anyone, it would make it true. Over the years, I'd gotten so good at pretending that sometimes I even managed to fool myself.

The thing about pretending, though, was sometimes you could trick other people when really the only one you wanted to convince was yourself.

Brody thought I didn't need him. Brody thought I was fine on my own. And I would let him think that, rather than let him see how broken I was without him. I couldn't tell him he was the only piece I needed to complete the puzzle of my life. Not when I'm the one who broke everything apart in the first place.

I was done with dragging Brody through my ups and downs. I needed to stabilize myself first before I could even think of trying to get him back.

And if he moved on in the meantime, well, he deserved happiness more than anyone else I knew.

Standing in the wreckage of my life, I was finally seeing things clearly. I knew what I had to do—and for now, that was putting some distance between me and everyone I cared about while I sorted through my own baggage.

And unfortunately, that happened to be the one client I'd wanted to help more than anyone. I'd already proven I couldn't be what he needed. I'd already failed him.

"Mr. Reilly," I said into the phone, pacing outside of the restaurant. "Hi."

"Maggie," Mr. Reilly said, and I couldn't help but smile at the fact that he'd taken me up on the offer of using my first name. "Sorry I'm calling out of the blue. Do you have a minute?"

I blew out a breath, staring behind me through the glass window where I still had the perfect view of the table.

Brody was surrounded by his friends. A life I'd never been part of. I felt foreign and uncomfortable in my own skin sitting there, knowing everyone was aware of how I'd broken his heart.

Little did they know, I'd broken mine, too.

"Yeah, I do," I answered, wanting a few minutes' reprieve from the lunch.

"You haven't answered my last email, so I got worried. I know we only just had the court hearing last week, but I need to know what our next step is."

"Our next step... right," I said, clenching my eyes shut, because the thing was—even thinking about his case *hurt.* It was the catalyst that forced me to finally open my eyes to my own life. The reason I unraveled it all.

How could I help this man when I'd let my emotions get in the way of the facts? I'd spent so long trying to repress everything, to keep my personal feelings at bay—and now they had opened up like a dam, drowning out every rational part of my brain.

"You see, the thing is, Mr. Reilly, I just don't know if..." I paused, gritting my teeth. He was another person I was going to disappoint. But if I wanted to help him, the best thing to do was just remove myself from the picture. "I don't think I'm the right person for this case anymore. I can refer you to someone great—"

"*What?*" His voice on the other side of the line was filled with betrayal. "No, no, no. Absolutely not. *You've* been working on this with me. You're the only person I trust with this!"

"How can you still want to work with me after the mess I made at court?" I said, fighting the urge to cry. "I got emotional and—"

"That's *why* I trust you. You care about me. My kids. I see it and I feel it when we work together. This is more than a job to you, isn't it? Your work matters to you, and that's something I can't say the same for any of the other lawyers I've spoken to before."

I sighed. He was right, I did care. But could it be that he was right? Was it something to be proud of, an asset, even—instead of something I had to shy away from?

My entire life I'd guarded myself from my feelings. I left before they got the better of me. If I cared about something too much, it meant I was already too invested and that's when I knew I had to pull the trigger on it.

Caring too much could hurt you.

But running away might be even more detrimental than I'd ever realized.

"Please don't give up on me, Ms. Brynn." His voice was a desperate plea. "If anyone can help me, it's you."

I could do this, emotional entanglement and all. And if I could do this and *succeed?* Well, it might even prove that I was capable of more than I knew. It might prove that I didn't have to suppress who I was and what I felt to be a good lawyer, or sister, or partner.

Because the thing about burying everything deep down is… it always finds a way to bleed through the cracks. Maybe it was time to stop patching the surface—and start rebuilding what was underneath instead.

"You've got yourself a lawyer, Mr. Reilly," I confirmed to him, newly energized with a purpose to drive me forward. "And I'm not going anywhere until we get you what you need."

It was strange that Brody had an entire life I'd never really seen before.

I mean, it made sense. Everyone had a past. But these guys, they weren't just casual acquaintances or teammates he used to play with in high school years ago.

They treated him like a brother.

Brody was *loved*. Of course he was. He was brilliant and wonderful and made everyone who spoke to him feel like they were being bathed in sunlight. And even though he hadn't seen these friends in probably years, they still embraced him as if no time at all had passed.

We were in the backseat of his friend Aiden's car, with a guy named Sean riding shotgun. The entirety of the car ride had been spent half in tears over stories from high school.

"And then," Aiden laughed, doubling over the steering wheel, face red and breathless from lack of oxygen, "the vice-principal chased us down the hallway with the bird flying out of his office after him."

"Yeah, I remember." Brody laughed, eyes locked with Aiden's through the rearview mirror.

"Brody," I gasped. "I had no idea you were such a little menace!"

"Retired menace," he corrected, all the while reveling in the memories of his glory days.

I stared at him, appreciating the way his face lit up when he was happy. I hadn't seen him laugh in a while and hated myself for how much I'd put him through lately.

Without thinking, he dropped a hand down to my knee and squeezed, my body freezing under a touch that used to be the most natural thing in the world to me.

I missed it. I wanted to lean into it. I wanted everything to go back to normal.

But then he remembered and ripped his hand away as if it had touched a stovetop rather than my thigh.

"Sorry," he winced, barely looking at me as he said it.

"It's okay," I told him.

I watched as he shifted in his seat, pretending to fall back into the conversation, but I knew him well enough to see the tension locked in his jaw.

With his body angled away from mine, he felt farther away than ever as he sat right beside me.

The rest of the car ride passed in a blur, and when we pulled back up to Liam's house, I was more than ready to get out of the stifling atmosphere of the tension-filled backseat.

"Don't forget what we talked about," Aiden said, giving him a dab handshake through the driver's side window.

"Yeah," Brody said, sparing a quick glance at me. "Will do."

"It was nice to meet you guys," I said, even though I had the oddest sensation of jealousy toward them that I couldn't explain.

I guess if I tried, it would be simplified down to one thing: when you're dating someone, you're the most important person in their life. But once you break up, you're out of it, as if you never existed at all.

But his friends? They would be able to talk to him, see him, hear him laugh long after I was a blip in his memories.

I even resented them for the conversations I was sure he'd have about me someday. I'd probably go down in their group lore as the stupid girl who let Brody get away.

Not that I didn't deserve it.

"Yeah, you too," Aiden called out, and I wasn't sure if I was imagining the judgment radiating off his gaze. Sean offered a nod and a wave, and then we watched their car disappear down Liam and Cassie's driveway.

"That was fun," I said, trying to break the ice as Brody and I made our way into the foyer. "Thanks for bringing me."

"Fun?" He raised his brows. "You mean the part where they interrogated you at lunch, or the Family Guy impressions over dessert?"

"They weren't interrogating me," I huffed out a laugh. "They're just… protective of you. It's nice to see."

"Yeah," he mused. "I guess they are. But I'm sorry if it made you uncomfortable."

"It didn't," I told him.

The only thing that made me uncomfortable was the truth I had to admit out loud about our relationship, but that wasn't anyone's fault but my own.

"Well, good." He said, and we lingered in the silence for a few moments. Brody looked as if he wanted to disappear, and I was so worried that if I let him walk away, we might lose any chance at repairing the damage.

If nothing else, I at least wanted to bridge the gap between us a little. Show him he could talk to me like a normal person, despite the erratic behavior I'd been displaying of late.

"Well, I should—" He pointed a thumb upstairs, and I just knew he was going to say something about getting his stuff and leaving, and I couldn't bear for it to be all the way over yet.

"It is weird though," I said, cutting him off.

"What is?"

"That you had this whole other life before you came here. Before we ever met."

"Well, yeah, Mags." He let out a chuckle. "Isn't that true for most people?"

"I guess," I shrugged. "But you're so immersed in every part of my world. You've been to my childhood home, you know my family, you've met everyone I've ever cared about. I don't know, it just feels like—well, it just feels like I've known you my entire life."

And somehow it still feels like I'll know him for the rest of it, too.

"Yeah," he exhaled a breath. "Yeah, I know what you mean."

"You do?"

"Yeah." He nodded. "I mean, you've never walked through the halls of my high school, or maybe you haven't met the guys I used to hang out with growing up before today, but—you know the story behind every scar on my body. You know how I cried like hell when my aunt died and the only thing that made me feel better was watching Golden *Girls* reruns. And you know about how I had to drive myself to the ER after I split my head open playing hockey because I was too worried my mom would pass out at the sight of the blood I was covered in."

I was still, listening to him. To these stories I'd memorized until they'd become part of my own. Brody was ingrained in my very DNA and I didn't know how I was supposed to part with him. How was I supposed to spend a Christmas without remembering the time he was eight and caught his dad dressing up as Santa and he ruined it for his siblings by waking them up to tell them all? How could I pass an Italian bakery without thinking about the little cannolis he loved so much? How could I do anything without the memory of him lingering over me for the rest of my life?

I couldn't. I wouldn't. I didn't want to.

"You might not have been there for any of my earliest core memories, Mags," he said, staring me dead in the eye. "But it feels like you might as well have been."

Oh, Brody. I thought with a pang to my heart, not knowing how I could miss someone so desperately who was standing right in front of me.

I know I broke everything, but I'm going to fix it. I swear.

"I—" I started, not knowing what I could possibly say in that moment besides *I love you.*

But that would be selfish of me. Just like with Liam, I couldn't rely on empty words anymore. I had to show him I meant it with actions and follow-through.

And before I could do that, I needed to get a grip on my life. I needed to follow through on my promises.

"I have to go to practice soon," Brody said, offering me a sad smile at all the things unsaid between the two of us. "I'll see you later, okay?"

"Yeah, okay," I said, but he was already walking up the stairs.

I waited till he rounded the corner before breathing out, "I'll be seeing you."

CHAPTER THIRTY-NINE

Brody

"Can you keep a secret?" I asked Liam early the next morning, watching as his hands worked to brew a pot of coffee.

It was a rare moment of calm before the rest of the house woke up and might be the only chance I got to talk to him without listening ears.

"Can I?" Liam asked, his back still turned to me as he moved through the kitchen. "Or do I want to? Because those are two different answers."

"Actually, I think they're the same," I grumbled, sitting at the counter.

He turned with a glare. "You think I can't keep a secret?"

"Not anymore," I agreed. "You tell Cassie everything."

"Cassie doesn't count," he said.

"Why not?"

"Because wives are excluded from vows of secrecy. It's just a given that you share everything with them."

"Even if your best friend asks you *not* to?"

Liam paused, granting me his full attention.

"Just tell me what the deal is, Brody."

"I'm thinking about moving."

"Okay—" he said in confusion.

"Back to Michigan," I clarified.

"Oh." He said, eyes widening. "Wow."

"Yeah."

"Because of Maggie?" he asked, backing up until he was leaning against the sink.

I shrugged. "I just… don't know what else I'd be here for. I only have a couple good years left in me for hockey, and then what?"

"Have you talked to Maggie about this?" he asked, seemingly skeptical about the entire idea.

"I don't see why I would," I said dejectedly. "My life plans don't really concern her anymore, do they?"

Liam stared, lips tight in the way I knew meant he was holding something back.

"You don't think it's a good idea?" I asked him, because at the end of the day, I really did value his opinion—more than almost anyone's.

Or maybe I was just looking for someone to tell me to stay.

"Look," Liam sighed, "you need to do what's best for you. If you think that looks like going back to Michigan and trying out something new there, then you should do it."

"But—?" I asked, knowing it was coming.

He stared at me, seemingly at war with himself over words unsaid. But I knew I couldn't force him to say whatever was on his mind unless he absolutely wanted to say it. And apparently, he didn't.

"But nothing," he said finally. "I think this is something you have to decide on your own."

"Gee, thanks," I scoffed, as he poured two mugs of coffee, pushing one across the counter toward me. "Glad to know my best friend doesn't care if I stay or go."

"So dramatic." He rolled his eyes. "Of course I don't want you to go. But because you *are* my best friend, I want you to do what's right for you more than I want you to do what's comfortable for me."

A shit-eating grin encompassed the lower half of my face at his words.

"Are you finally admitting out loud that I'm your best friend?"

"You've always known it."

"Yeah, but my love language is words of affirmation, and it's nice to hear it out loud every once in a while." I batted my eyes at him dramatically, much to his disdain.

"Brody?" he said, fixing me with a glare.

"Yeah, bestie?"

"Don't push it."

"Got it." I nodded, sobering up quickly with a sip of black coffee. "But anyway, since we're on the topic of following my heart and what-not... I sort of agree with you. Problem is, I don't really know how I'm going to feel about being in Michigan until I'm back there."

Liam waited for me to continue.

"So, I booked a flight and I'm leaving in an hour," I said, watching with amusement as his face transformed to one of utter shock.

"You're leaving for Michigan *today?*"

"Don't start planning my farewell party just yet," I hurried to add. "I'm just going there to check out some apartments. See what the job scene is like. Feel out the vibes." I shrugged. "Basically, I'm just hoping I'll have a strong gut reaction either way telling me if I'm making the right choice or not."

Liam shook his head in disbelief.

"I can't believe you're changing the course of your life based on 'the vibes.'"

"I already told you, I'm not changing anything. It's more like a trial run." I shook my head. "And anyway, I'm asking if you'll keep it quiet because I don't want Maggie to know."

"Why can't Maggie know?" he asked. "I mean, I get not going out of your way to tell her, but why are you trying to swear me to secrecy over it?"

"Because I just don't want her to think she's, like, running me out of town or something. I mean, really it has nothing to do with her."

It has everything to do with her.

"You know what this reminds me of?" Liam said.

"What?"

"That episode of The Office where Jim moves away to some branch in Stamford after Pam breaks his heart."

My jaw dropped. Whatever I'd been expecting him to say, it wasn't that.

"Since when do *you* watch *The Office?*" I cackled, nearly spitting out the sip of coffee I'd been drinking.

"Cassie and I watch sometimes after Lily goes to bed." He shrugged, clearly not seeing the big deal.

"Oh, how much you've changed over the years." I shook my head slowly.

"And you haven't at all," he responded, and I was struck with the realization that he was completely right.

How long had it been, ten years since I've known him? And in that time, he got married, had a kid, bought a house, became Captain of the Harbor Wolves… and what have I done except stand still?

It was depressing as hell the more I thought about it. Especially since I had hoped and planned and truly believed I'd be at a similar stage of life as him by now.

But I wasn't. Not even close.

"Hey, Brody," Liam started, sensing my deflation.

"I gotta get ready to head out," I said, standing from my seat. "Thanks for the coffee and the chats and everything."

"Brody," he called again, but I was already out of the room.

I didn't need Liam to comfort me, to tell me that it didn't matter how "behind" I was in life because everyone moved at different paces. But the thing was, this wasn't the pace I wanted to be moving at.

And if I stayed here in Boston, then I knew I'd spend the rest of my life pining after Maggie Brynn forever.

Yeah, I thought, *maybe Michigan wasn't looking so bad after all.*

CHAPTER FORTY

Maggie

"Have you seen Brody?" I said, walking into the darkness of the living room where my brother and his family were settled on the couch having a movie night.

It was such a mundane, normal night, but I felt the strangest feeling wash over me that I was intruding on something private.

"Oh, never mind," I said quickly, taking in the scene in front of me, the three of them cozied up on the couch as the flickering light of the TV illuminated their faces. "Sorry for interrupting—"

"No, stay," Cassie urged, shifting to sit up and pat the space beside her on the couch. "We're having movie night."

It was one of Liam's few nights off, and I knew how much he prioritized spending time with his family. I'd made a promise to him to show him with actions rather than empty words how much I respected him, and worried that barging in on his night might be selfish.

But when I looked to him for an answer, I found nothing but openness.

"Yeah, come hang out," he agreed. "You've been working all day."

It was true. My mind was fried after having done a deep dive into Mr. Reilly's case and overanalyzing every possible next step we could make. After exhausting every avenue and formulating a new plan going forward, all I wanted was to mindlessly watch something to distract myself. Even if it was some animated children's film.

Plus, I really didn't want to be alone. Especially after I'd come to the realization that I hadn't seen Brody around at all the entire day.

Had he found somewhere else to stay? Was he back at the apartment? Was he taking space away from me?

All valid scenarios. Still, none felt particularly pleasant.

"If you're sure," I said, plopping down on the farthest end of their three-section couch.

Liam stretched an arm behind him—the one not being used to cradle his family—and tossed over a throw blanket in my direction.

I grabbed it midair and laid it over me, settling back into the couch, feeling waves of tension ease off me for the first time in a while.

It was nice—the life Cassie and Liam had built for themselves here. It wasn't just because they had a big house or a lot of money. It was because they had a lot of love. And with that, they'd turned this place into a home.

It was almost tangible, the feeling of peace and calm that existed here. There wasn't room for uncertainty or fear. Only the love the three of them had for each other.

I'd pushed Brody away for so long because he had wanted exactly this.

Was this everything I'd been scared of? I thought suddenly.

But then I thought, no. This was exactly what I was scared of losing. And the part of my brain that had led all my decisions the last few years had somehow convinced me that it was better to never have it at all than to have it and lose it.

Now, I wasn't so sure.

I shook my head, distracting myself from thoughts that wouldn't serve me. Right now, I just needed to work my way through Mr. Reilly's case and go from there. That was all I had the energy for at the moment.

But a night of *Moana* wouldn't hurt to take the edge off.

Cassie and Lily's feet poked out from under their blanket, and I laughed at the colorful fuzzy socks they both wore. I panned my gaze to Liam's, noting the stark difference in his generic Nike socks.

"What? No matching pajamas?" I joked.

"Oh, we have them." Liam widened his eyes as he nodded.

"But Liam hates wearing them," Cassie pouted.

"I do not," he said, staring down at her. "They're just a little… tight."

Cassie scoffed. I giggled, raising my brows at him, as if to say, *really? Matching jammies?*

"Let's just say Cassie and Lily look a hell of a lot cuter in them than I can pull off."

"I believe that," I said with a laugh.

"Shhhh," Lily said finally, never tearing her gaze off the screen. "Too loud."

"Oh, I'm sorry, missy." Cassie poked her. "Are we interrupting your movie?"

"Yes, you are, Mommy. Movies are for listening, not for talking."

"Ouch," Cassie placed a hand atop her heart. "My own daughter using my own words against me." Then Cassie turned to me in explanation. "It's what I taught her before we went to the movie theater for the first time. I guess she really took it to heart."

"Shhh," Lily said again, and this time Cassie stared at her with a grin, miming a zipper coming across her lips.

The movie played for a while, and I'd gotten so into it that I hadn't realized Lily had fallen asleep until Liam was standing up and scooping her in his arms.

"I'm going to put this one to bed," he whispered. "I'll be right back."

Cassie and I watched Liam leave, carrying a sleeping Lily out of the living room, leaving us alone in the flickering light.

"So," I said, twisting my body so I could look over at her on the other side of the couch, "have you seen Brody at all today?"

"No," Cassie admitted. "I don't think he's been around today."

"But where would he go?" I asked, heart breaking at the thought that I might have driven him away.

We were his friends. His family here. Where else could he be but with us? Nowhere that made any sense.

"I honestly don't know," Cassie shrugged. "Liam didn't offer up any details, and I didn't really want to pry into it. I've sort of just been trying to stay out of everyone's way as much as I can while you work through this."

I laughed. "We're in *your* house and you're trying to stay out of *our* way?" I shook my head with a smile. "Typical Cassie. I bet all this disharmony is killing you."

"So much." She agreed with a wince. "I just want you guys to be happy, and I know you won't be until everything is right between you."

I knew I definitely wouldn't feel okay until everything was right either, but a realization had struck me recently that I shared with Cassie.

"I want everything to go back to normal more than anyone, but I'm starting to think it's selfish of me to even try."

"What do you mean?" she asked.

"I mean, I broke his heart and told him I wasn't ready for a future with him. I can't just tell him that it was a mistake and I actually *do* want to be with him. He'll feel like I'm playing a game of tug-of-war with him or something."

I sighed, staring at the television screen instead of Cassie's unwavering eyes.

"Maybe if I really love him," I started, blowing out a breath with the words that hurt so badly to utter, "I need to just… let him go."

"What! Why would you do that?" she screeched, sitting upright.

"I don't know! Isn't that what the poets say?"

"Screw the poets! Show me one romance novel that ended with the heroine 'letting him go.' No way." She shook her head, adamant in her stance.

"Well, we're not in a romance novel, Cass. This is real life. And I can't go screwing with his life for the sake of my own happiness."

"It's his happiness too, though. Look, you've seen The Notebook. It never does any good when you let the person you're in love with 'move on' because you think it's better for them. Then, it's just two people with broken hearts missing each other and not saying anything about it!"

"So what do you want me to do? Build Brody his dream house and wait around for him to see me in some newspaper article and come back to me?"

"Interesting that you cast yourself as Noah," Cass quirked a brow. "But, no. That's not really the scenario I was going for. I'm telling you, skip the whole decade-long separation and reconcile *now*, before you have to lose any time."

I thought about it, but couldn't come up with any clear answer. I just needed to talk to Brody. To apologize to him, and maybe help him see the position I'd been coming from. I wouldn't beg him to forgive me, if that wasn't what he wanted. But I could see where he was at, and we could go from there.

"Do you think I'm stupid?" I asked her. "I was so afraid of being alone, of being left, that I pushed him away before he had the chance to do it. I mean, that's objectively insane, right?"

"I think it gave you a sense of control that a younger version of you might've been desperate for. It's not crazy. It's understandable. Don't you remember how I almost ruined everything by running away from Liam back then?"

I smirked at the memory of her showing up at my apartment, terrified and red-rimmed eyes because she'd just kissed Liam and was afraid of what happened next.

I guess Cassie and I were two sides of the same coin, in our own messed-up way.

"Yeah, Cass. I remember," I told her with a laugh. "Difference is, you thought you were running away, but my brother wouldn't have let you get far."

She snorted.

"I'm serious. That man would've followed you to the ends of the earth hoping you might change your mind."

Cassie blushed, waving away my comment as she continued on her spiel.

"The point is, if I hadn't pulled it together and started dealing with my crap, I would've missed out on all this." She gestured around her, and I knew she wasn't referring to the house itself, but the home she'd made with the help of the two people upstairs.

I understood what she was saying, because the thought had been haunting me terribly lately. I wasn't only mourning the life I'd had with Brody, but the future I might never get to see now.

But I guess that's just where the cards fell after I played a shitty hand. Once you make your move, you can't take it back.

"Let's just watch The Notebook," I muttered, shifting onto my side again. "I'd rather be depressed about fictional people than my own real, and very pathetic, life."

"Whatever you want, Mags," Cassie said, though I could hear the disappointment in her voice as she said it.

She thought I was giving up.

She thought I was throwing in the towel and ruining my life. And maybe I was. But at least I wasn't ruining Brody's.

Because the truth was, I knew I wanted to marry Brody. I knew I'd be happy with him and have the life of my dreams.

But what I didn't know for sure is that it wouldn't be a mistake for *him*. I couldn't be responsible for ruining his life. I wouldn't. Not when he could have any number of women who could probably guarantee him more happiness than me.

I loved Brody with my whole, entire heart.

And that was almost the cruelest part of it all.

CHAPTER FORTY-ONE

Brody

It was almost midnight by the time I landed back at Logan Airport, and I couldn't fathom how I'd been to Michigan and back in the last twelve hours.

My mind was exhausted. My body was cramped from travel. And all I wanted to do was go home and dive into bed.

But that wasn't even an option anymore.

The only comfort I had waiting for me was the admittedly soft cushioning of Liam's couch.

I didn't know if Maggie had chosen to go back to the apartment, or if she was still at Liam's. Honestly, I didn't know which would be worse.

I couldn't be near her, but I couldn't be away from her either. It was a hell of a place to be.

My car was waiting in the lot where I left it, and I drove to Liam's house in a near delirious state, still trying to mentally weigh the pros and cons of uprooting my entire life to go back to Michigan.

I'd looked at a handful of apartments while I was there, but it didn't matter to me where I lived. It could be a box for all I cared. I always thought it wasn't the house that made a home but the family you had beside you.

And considering I was going to be entirely by myself, I guess I might as well have chosen a sturdy box to settle down in. It wasn't like I had any pets, or kids, or even furniture for that matter.

Fuck.

I wiped a hand over my face, willing myself to stay awake. The only Dunkin' that was open at this hour was the one attached to the gas station, so I pulled in to the drive-thru and ordered a small, hot regular.

It probably wasn't good to be drinking caffeine this late, but despite the physical exhaustion I felt, I had a lot of shit in my mind to sort through, and I knew I wouldn't be getting much sleep regardless.

"Can I have a plain donut, too?" I stuck my head out the window, listing off my order to the intercom.

"Yup," an indifferent voice drawled, apparently not thrilled to be working the Dunkin' drive-thru at this hour. "Will that be all?"

"Yeah, thanks."

"You can pull forward."

I got my order, giving the kid with the half-dead expression a ten-dollar bill tip in the hopes of cheering him up. It might've worked, but his expression didn't really change, so I couldn't know for sure.

I resumed the route to Liam's house, sipping the coffee, and shitty as it was, there was something about Dunkin' that brought comfort to the heart.

Dunkin' Donuts. Yeah. I needed to put that on the pro column for staying in Boston.

But my family, I thought while driving. They were so happy to see me today. I hadn't told them I was coming, just surprised my dad at his shop and dropped the bomb that I was thinking about moving home.

Damn, if his eyes didn't light up with joy at the mere possibility.

When I was a kid, before I got serious about hockey, when I thought about the future, I guess I always pictured following in my dad's foot-steps, taking over the business for him when he got too old for it.

And I guess that time would've been around now. There were wrinkles around his eyes that had never been there before. And his hair, once a dark brown, was now starting to gray.

How did that happen?

And did I really want to miss out on these years with my parents?

It was as good a life as any. I had friends back in Michigan. I had family. I could find purpose. And most of all, I wouldn't be reminded every single day of Maggie fucking Brynn. The almost love of my life.

Because I had to believe she couldn't be the actual love of my life, because that would be depressing as hell. You were supposed to *end* up with the love of your life. Not have a brief stint with them in your twenties. Right?

I killed the engine when I pulled into Liam's driveway, using the spare key he'd given me to let myself in as quietly as I could. At nearly 12:45 a.m., I was expecting the house to be blanketed in darkness when I walked in. Not the glow of the television coming from the living room that *I'd* taken up residency in as of lately.

And I certainly wasn't expecting to see the couch almost entirely occupied.

"Well, this is cozy," I said in a whisper to Liam, who was the only one of the three still awake.

Cassie's head was in his lap as he played with her hair absentmindedly, and Maggie—God, Maggie was beautiful as ever—looking the most relaxed I'd seen her in weeks as she slept soundly, her body curled underneath a throw blanket.

I stared at her, probably with more creepy longing than an ex-boyfriend was entitled to. Damn, was it weird as hell to miss watching someone sleep?

"They fell asleep a half hour ago watching a movie," Liam said. "I haven't gotten around to waking them up yet."

Speaking of sleep, my body was too exhausted to stand up for another minute, so I let myself slip down onto the couch next to Maggie.

"What movie?" I asked, to make conversation.

"The Notebook."

Liam huffed a laugh.

"Oof," I winced. "They Notebooked you?"

"It wasn't so bad," Liam shrugged. "But it was sort of depressing as hell."

"Tell me about it. I've watched that with Mags like a dozen times."

That's what worried me. It was her go-to film when she was at her lowest of lows. But during all those times, *I* had never been the reason for it. It gave me a bad feeling in the pit of my stomach.

One look down at Maggie, and I could tell she was in one of her deepest sleeps. I knew that girl better than I knew anyone else, and over the years I'd seen her when she hit lows like this. It always worried me. She worked so many hours, tried so hard in every aspect of her life. I couldn't imagine the strain that it put on her mind. She was probably exhausted every moment of the day. And I knew that the last few weeks had taken their toll on her, too.

With my arms stretched across the back of the sofa, I tilted my head back and let out a groan of frustration, letting the pent-up energy leave my body all at once.

"Should I even ask how it went today?" Liam asked, keeping his voice low.

Maggie slept like the dead, but I wasn't sure how light of a sleeper Cassie was, so I matched his volume when I responded.

"Shit."

"Michigan's shit? Or the day was shit?"

"Both. Everything's shit. I don't know what the hell I'm going to do."

"What do you *want* to do?" he asked.

"What I want is irrelevant because it exists on an alternate plane of existence where none of this ever happened in the first place."

"I'm sorry," Liam said honestly. "You're right. It's a shitty situation either way. How did it feel to be back there, though? Is it something you could live with?"

I blew out a breath.

"I mean, honestly?" I asked. "Yeah. It did. That's why I feel so torn right now. Half of me was thinking I'd go there, think, this fucking *blows,* and know immediately that I couldn't move back there. But it didn't."

"It didn't?"

"No. It felt normal. Not right, I guess, but familiar. Like it could be right again someday. I could make it my new normal." I felt like I was rambling, but I didn't care. I needed to bounce my ideas off of someone, and I knew Liam was the last person in the world to tell me what I wanted to hear. I knew I could count on him to give his full, uncensored opinion.

"So my dad, he owns this hardware shop in town. I practically grew up in it. Did my homework on the counter. Worked the cash register on weekends. I know the ins and outs of that place like the back of my hand. My plan was always to take over for him when I was old enough. I think now he's sort of scrambling to figure out what to do with the place now that he's getting up there in age," I said, trying to piece my feelings about it together. "I mean, he doesn't *need* to keep working. I've got them covered for life and they know it, but—Liam, it would *kill* him to sell it. It's been in the family for years. His grandad opened it and passed it to his father, who passed it to him, and now here I am, ruining the family legacy by playing some stupid game."

"I doubt your dad sees it that way, Brody," Liam said. "He's probably just happy you're following your dream."

"But that dream has an expiration date," I exhaled again, "and it's really fucking soon."

"I get it, man," he said. "I've been in your spot. And you know what Cassie told me when I was freaking the fuck out the way you are right now?"

I raised my brows, waiting for him to continue.

"She told me that I should think of it as an opportunity to… what did she say? Find a new dream?" He laughed to himself, staring down at her sleeping form with a fondness he reserved solely for her.

I looked away, giving him that privacy, and jerked my gaze when I found myself staring down at Maggie. She was beautiful, dark hair fanned out on the couch, face relaxed—for once not on guard or ready for the next battle she might have to face.

That was the thing about Maggie. She always had her armor on. Sword at the ready. Sometimes I think she was so braced for attack, she forgot some of us were on *her* team.

Find a new dream.

Maggie had been my dream for so long. Or at least, she was always at the forefront of the picture. Everything else could take the back burner as long as I could have her. But it was too late for that now.

I cleared my throat, trying to bite down the thick swell of emotion to no avail.

"Cassie's pretty wise sometimes, huh?"

"She's wise all the time," Liam rolled his eyes affectionately. "She's just so bubbly that people sometimes overlook it."

"So, what do you think Maggie's plan of action is now?"

"You know Maggie," Liam said. "She does whatever occurs to her that moment. Kinda plays it minute by minute."

"That's a hard way to live," I said, looking down at her again. I couldn't help but look at her. Always.

"Her choice," Liam said. "She's always been that way."

But I didn't think it was a choice at all.

I think it was the result of trauma. Of the fear of everything being taken away from her eventually, until she learned to just be content with what was in front of her at that present moment and let go of the rest.

"I'm gonna take Cass up to bed. You can take the guest room if you want, since Mags is out here," Liam said.

I moved to stand up, but Maggie shifted, and I froze, terrified to wake her up and see those sleepy green eyes look up at me the way they used to every morning.

But they didn't flutter. Instead, she just moved closer, as if sensing my presence even in sleep. And then, before I knew what was even happening, she curled up against me and exhaled a contented sigh.

I looked down at her, holding my breath in fear of breaking the moment.

Do I wake her up? Do I let her sleep? Do I wait a few minutes and see if she moves on her own?

I looked to Liam for guidance, but he just smirked at me and shook his head.

"On second thought, you look pretty cozy here. Good night, Brody," Liam said over his shoulder, carrying Cassie out of the room.

"Good night," I said.

And before I could overthink it, I sunk back into the couch, letting myself feel the warmth of Maggie's body so close to mine again. I could have this, just once.

Because in all likelihood, this would probably be the last time.

CHAPTER FORTY-TWO

Maggie

Brody was haunting me.

Literally and figuratively.

Not only did I see life-sized images of him every corner I turned in Boston—*thank you, Harbor Wolves marketing team*—but I woke up with the feeling of being in his arms again.

It was a dream, of course. It couldn't be anything else but my subconscious trying to transport me back to the time when I'd been happy, so I clenched my eyes tighter, urging sleep to keep me subdued so I could hold onto the feeling for a little longer.

When I awoke on the couch exactly where I'd been the night before, I'd been alone. But even still, it had allowed me to sleep more restfully than I had in weeks.

Fine by me. I had a busy day, and I would take the newfound spring in my step awarded to me thanks to phantom Brody of my dreams.

I went back into the office with a fresh perspective and newfound motivation driving me forward.

First thing was first: documenting a paper trail of Mr. Reilly's stability. I had letters attesting to his character by his employer and co-workers. I had consistent pay stubs documenting his proof of employment.

Mr. Reilly had been on the ball with providing it all, further proof of his competency. If that wasn't enough, I knew he'd been out day and night viewing apartments.

There'd been a few that were suitable, he said. But he didn't want suitable. He wanted perfection. He said it wouldn't look good to get the first available apartment only to move in a few months when he found something bigger and better fitting the needs of his family.

No, he wanted to do this the right way. He wanted to go all in. And honestly, I admired him all the more for it. How many fathers had I worked with who had tried to take the easiest possible route? How many fathers had fought for custody, not because of any real desire to have equal time with their children, but as a way to get revenge against their ex-partner?

Sometimes, that was the hardest part of the job. Watching kids get stuck in a game of monkey-in-the-middle while their parents used them as weapons to get back at each other.

Mr. Reilly was different, and it showed. And because of that, I was going above and beyond to secure the best outcome for this case for him and those kids.

I met him in my office that morning, after a week of communicating via emails and calls. I didn't know what type of meeting I'd be walking into—if I'd have to reconvince him of my faith in his case or bring hope back to him that I would do everything I could—but it turned out, I didn't need to.

"I got an apartment!" Mr. Reilly exclaimed the second he opened the door to my office.

"Wow," I said, eyes widening.

"And it's perfect! Two bedrooms. Nice neighborhood. Close to the kids' school. And he said I could move in immediately!"

I arched a brow. "Are you sure? You don't have to rush into anything."

"No, this place is perfect. I mean, the lease said it wouldn't be available till April 1st, but that's still weeks away. I told him the situation, and it was vacant anyway. He just needs a few days to do a professional clean, but I can be in at the end of the week!"

"That's great—" I told him, but he was too excited to register it, continuing on in a frenzy of passion.

"And, I didn't even tell you the best part." He finally slid into the chair across from my desk, face red with glee as he braced both his hands on top of his cap, as if he were the only thing keeping it on his head.

I stared at him with a smile, waiting for the news he was nearly bursting at the seams with.

"Pattie told me as soon as the place is set up, I can have the kids for a weekend!"

"She did?" I forced my jaw to remain firmly in place, despite the shock of his words. "That's amazing. I'm so glad to hear that."

And really, I was. But it was in my nature to be skeptical. People's minds change like the weather, and that's why it was better to get everything in writing and legalized so the other party couldn't take anything back later.

People did that. Tried to rewrite the story. Change the facts. And if no one was around to witness it, his ex-wife could just as easily claim she never promised such a thing.

"I still can't believe everything is working out." He sighed contentedly. "What changed?"

"I guess the initial shock of everything died down," he said in a daze. "She said the kids have been missing me, and she apologized for how she'd been acting. She said she wanted to make this situation work. Learn how to co-parent, for their sake."

I forced a smile that didn't meet my eyes, but thankfully Mr. Reilly was too overjoyed to pay me much notice. I couldn't help the sinking feeling in my stomach. I wanted to say, *don't get excited yet. The other shoe might still drop. It always does.*

After all, hadn't my own father told my mother they could work things out right before he left?

My mind instantly came up with a million scenarios. Mrs. Reilly might take it back. It might be a passing moment of selflessness. Or maybe it was a bold-faced lie as she continued to build a case against him. I didn't know. I didn't know this woman's character, so I had to suspect the worst. I had to be prepared for anything.

But, for now, I let him have his moment. He was doing everything right on his end. He secured housing. He had been consistent in working.

The rest was on my end. I had to finish drafting the parenting agreement—something stating, in permanent terms, the days and times he would have his children. I wouldn't breathe easy until we took it to court and had it declared fair and legal by a judge, so no one could take it away from him.

Because in my experience, every time you felt something was just in your reach… that's when it usually got ripped violently away.

CHAPTER FORTY-THREE

Brody

Was I a traitor?

Or a liar? Or just an overall shitty person?

There had to be a word for a guy who kept playing with his teammates every day without even mentioning the possibility he might not be renewing his contract at the end of the season.

Logically, I knew guys did this all the time. It made no sense to bring the topic up to anyone when I wasn't even set on it myself. But still, I'd never been the type to keep secrets. I'd never been the type to do anything except tell people whatever the hell was on my mind at any given moment.

It was an issue, actually. So maybe I could just view this whole thing as an experiment in practicing my own self-control.

"What's up with you?" my teammate Ryan said, skating up next to me during warmups. "Do you have something to tell us?"

I jerked my head in his direction fast enough to hurt. "What do you mean?" I asked, feeling my eyes go wide and buggy.

Play it cool. Play it cool.

He narrowed his eyes suspiciously.

"This." He gestured a hand up and down the length of me. "You're acting twitchy as hell lately. The guys sent me over to ask if you're on something."

I blinked. Okay, I guess he wasn't as on to me as I thought he was.

"What the hell? No." I said, affronted. "Why would you even think that? We get drug-tested."

He shrugged. "Didn't know if you just didn't care, since you and your girl split or whatever."

Yeah, I thought wryly, *I guess I need to work on my nervous* tics.

"Well, I'm *not* on drugs." I said. "And even if I was, do you think I'd tell you?"

"Sounds incriminating." He looked at me skeptically. "So, are you saying there's a chance you might be?"

"No, I'm just pointing out the error in your methods," I said, mostly because I was prone to rambling and helplessly trying to deflect from the real reason I'd been a bit on edge lately.

"Whatever, man." he said, not looking entirely convinced. "Just don't screw us over with a shitty performance tonight, okay? We're counting on you."

I scoffed. "When have I ever?"

"Never." Ryan grinned. "That's why we were worried. We can't afford to lose you. You're one of the best we've got."

My eyes widened. It was rare to hear something like that, especially from a guy like Ryan. And look, I knew my stats. I knew that I was a fan favorite. But it was one thing to see social media posts about you made by strangers online, and quite another to be told it by your own teammate.

"I got you," I told him, feeling like a liar. "You know that."

For now.

"Good man," he said, slapping my back. "And whatever's bugging you, try to let it go on the ice. I mean, that's the good thing about this game, right? Perfect way to kill off steam."

"Yeah," I agreed. "I'll do that."

"You're a good guy, Callahan. I'm sorry to hear about you and your girl splitting, but you always have us." He looked behind him to our teammates skating around the ice during warmups. "You know that, right?"

I felt like too much of a fraud to respond in words, so I just gave him a tight nod and skated off, knowing I couldn't promise the same.

But I could promise to give them all I've got while I was still here.

Maggie

I didn't know if I was welcome anymore—or particularly wanted, for that matter—but that didn't stop me from showing up at the Garden that night.

And I mean, Harbor Wolves games were for everyone. As long as you had a ticket you were golden. It didn't matter if you were the ex-girlfriend of the goalie or the black sheep sister of the Captain.

And really, who would I hurt by sitting in the arena? Brody would never even know I was there. I was just one of thousands. That invisibility gave me the courage to go.

Not because I wanted to, but because I *needed* to.

For years, it had been my way of decompressing after a long day of work—to go, sit with Cassie, and watch our boys on the ice.

The blast of cold air, the roar of the crowds, the blaring horn when someone scored a goal. The noise was constant, and I welcomed it gladly.

For some, games could be overwhelming. But for me? It was almost like the external atmosphere grounded me. Kept me from thinking about court cases and documents I had to file and people I had to deal with. When I was in the arena, I focused only on the game.

And, of course, Brody.

It calmed something in me to see him having so much fun in his career. To see him excelling at such a physical role, so different from my own job.

And I guess, despite everything that happened, I still craved that—he was still my safe space. If I was miserable, at least I could go and be comforted by the fact that Brody was still living his life and doing what he loved.

No matter what happened, I could always count on that.

"Hey," I said, sliding down into a seat beside Cassie and Lily.

I came in almost halfway through the game, after struggling with my better nature for a while. There was a good chance Brody wouldn't notice me—a benefit to us sitting behind the goalie net—and for that I was grateful.

"Hey!" Cassie's eyes lit up. "You didn't tell me you were coming."

"I didn't know I was either, until I was already driving here," I admitted.

"Typical Maggie." She laughed, before taking note of my clothes. "Did you come straight from work? You must be hungry. Do you want a snack?"

My stomach growled. I'd forgotten to pay attention to things like that lately: food and nutrition and hydration and whatnot.

Those needs weren't nearly as demanding as the little gremlin in my body that demanded caffeine at regular intervals and seethed cruel words in my ear demanding I get my work done.

But now that I was sitting? It was all catching up to me.

"Depends what you have," I said, eyeing her bag warily. "It's not that trail mix you make, is it?"

She rolled her eyes. "The trail mix is not *that* bad."

"No," I agreed. "But it would be better with some M&M's in it."

"I want M&M's," Lily said, snapping to attention at the mention of chocolate.

"Like Auntie, like niece," Cassie muttered, rifling through her bag. "Lucky for you two, I just so happened to have a craving for something sweet today."

She pulled out a bag of watermelon Sour Patch Kids, followed by a few Almond Joys, some chocolate-covered pretzels, and a bag of Swedish Fish.

"Random selection," I noted suspiciously.

"I just went to CVS and bought whatever looked good in the moment," she responded sheepishly. "I know, I splurged."

"It's okay, Cass. I think you can afford to."

"Yeah, but now I don't even want any of this junk." She said, sounding emotional over it all. "Now, all I really want are some chicken tenders."

"Then go get your chicken tenders, girl." I said, snatching the snacks from her. "Trust me, this 'junk' won't go to waste. In fact," I said, ripping open the bag of Swedish Fish, "it'll sustain me for at least the next three days."

"See, Maggie?" Cassie snorted. "This is why you can never leave us. You need to be under our roof so we can nourish you."

"Nourish me?" I laughed out loud.

"Yeah, Auntie Maggie. You should live with us forever."

"There's a thought," I snorted. "Go on, Cass. Go get your food. We'll be good here."

She smiled gratefully and rushed off to do so, after asking three too many times if I was *sure* I didn't want anything from the concession stand.

As she left, I took a moment to look over and admire my niece. Her hair was in pigtails with blue ribbons and she wore her mini BRYNN jersey, which was like a tiny pickaxe to my cold, impenetrable heart.

"You know," I said, making a point to whisper loudly, "your mom is kind of silly, Lil."

"Yeah." Lily agreed. "She is silly. Like Uncle Brody. He keeps missing all the pucks."

I furrowed my brows, glancing at the scoreboard. Lily was right; the Harbor Wolves weren't doing great.

"Maybe 'cause he's sad about leaving."

"Leaving?" I asked.

"Yeah, he said it to Daddy." she chirped, distracted by each clamoring noise coming from the ice. "He was telling Daddy in the kitchen and I was supposed to be sleeping. But I wasn't sleeping. I was hearing at the door, 'cause I woke up early."

"What did he say, Lil?" I asked her, knowing I was putting too much stock in the words of a three-year-old but unable to help myself for any scraps of information that concerned Brody.

"He said he wanted to go back."

"Back where?"

"I don't know." She shrugged. "Maybe home? People like going homes."

I frowned, wondering what she could've overheard. Did Brody want to go back to the apartment? Probably. The situation we were currently in was unsustainable, to say the least.

But neither of us had even approached the topic yet of going back to the apartment. I guess, technically, it was mine. It was where I lived before I met him. But now, I couldn't associate it with anything except memories of us.

And I'd been holding off on any talk of moving out because that would mean it was really over, which I just couldn't admit.

But I had made a promise not to be selfish anymore, and that meant having hard conversations. I couldn't keep him in a state of limbo, even if it was more comfortable to exist in that than the uncertainty of what came next.

After the game, I thought. *That's when I'll talk to him.*

CHAPTER FORTY-FIVE

Brody

If for some reason, anyone would ever care enough to write a biography about me in the distant future, I knew that I was currently living through one of the most significant chapters.

It would go something like this.

> *In Callahan's tenth year of his career, he was dealt some devastating blows. Not only did he lose the love of his life (a feat which we can see he never truly recovered from) but he lost the love of the game along with it. Around this time, things began to happen quickly, faster than the simple-minded Callahan could keep score of. His game deteriorated, his reputation as one of the NHL's best defenders was in jeopardy, and he was on the verge of running home crying to his childhood home in defeat. A tragic fall from grace for the former golden boy of the NHL who naively believed he almost had it all.*

A real page turner, huh?

Pathetic.

Even though I went out onto that ice and tried like hell to give it my all, I fell short. By a long shot.

The thing was, I'd never been very good at deception. It wasn't in my nature. And it shook me to my core to be out there on the ice with my team and act as if my heart was entirely in something that I'd already mentally checked out of.

How could I care about a game when the entire trajectory of my life was changing course around me? I didn't. Apparently, I couldn't even pretend to.

"It's okay, man," One of my teammates said afterwards in the locker room, "we all have bad nights."

"Bad nights?" Another one called out. "Callahan didn't block a single fucking puck all night. Talk about a waste of a game."

"Hey," Liam boomed, "lay off. You've played like shit more than a few times during your career and we've never given you slack for it."

"No." I told Liam. "He's right. It's my fault."

"No," Liam countered. "He's not. We're a team, and we won't be getting anywhere if we start degrading each other over mistakes we've already made."

"It doesn't matter." I gritted out. "I know I fucked up."

I fucked up with Maggie. I fucked up with the team. I fucked up my head by not knowing what the hell I was doing with my life anymore.

I ran a hand through my hair, feeling utterly exhausted right down to the bone. Everything felt too much. Everything felt out of reach. I couldn't make sense of this bizarre reality I found myself in. One where I played like shit, let everyone down, and didn't have Maggie by my side.

"Fucking damn it," I groaned, throwing my helmet to the floor and sinking down against the lockers.

Nobody said a word as it fell with a thud against the floor, echoing the sound of my misery for all to hear.

I couldn't pretend anymore that I was keeping it together, because the truth was: I wasn't. I forgot what keeping it together even looked like at this point.

"Hey," one of my teammates said, rare tone of concern in his voice. "Callahan. It's okay."

"Yeah, man. Nicholson was just being a dick. Nobody blames you for tonight."

"You should." I said. "You all should. I have one fucking job and it's to protect the net. And I couldn't fucking do that right."

"Woah, man." One of the guy's laughed uneasily. "Easy there. You're starting to sound like Cap. All bitter and cynical like."

"Yeah, Callahan. That's not you. You're like our… golden retriever hype man. You can't go getting all pissy like the rest of us. You're the one who keeps us all going with your annoyingly optimistic bullshit."

I snorted.

"Yeah." I agreed. "What a joke."

"What about you?" I looked up almost confrontationally at Liam who was staring at me from across the locker room. "No pep talk telling me to get my act together and be the 'old Brody' again?"

"Nah, man." Liam shook his head. "I'm not holding you to any bullshit standards. You're allowed to feel whatever the hell you feel. Contrary to what you may believe—it's not your job to keep everyone happy all the time."

And whatever I'd been expecting from him, I realized that nothing else he could've said would've made me feel better than that.

I was the funny guy. The laid-back guy. The comic relief guy. And I loved being that guy. But damn, if it didn't get exhausting after a while.

But after so long of playing that role, it was daunting almost, to let the act drop. To admit to everyone, Hey, I get pissed off too. I want to lose my shit sometimes, too, just like the rest of you. I'm not invincible.

Though if I were being honest, there was only one person in the world who made me feel like I was.

And she was gone.

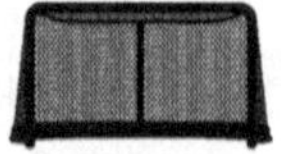

I stormed out of the locker room in a rush, not caring that I hadn't showered. Not caring that I'd freaked out half the team by the newly emerged dark side of my personality. Not caring that the Garden was still swamped with fans lurking around who would probably be less than thrilled to encounter me in the state I was in.

All I wanted was to get the hell out of here.

I exited through the players-only hallway leading to our parking garage. I knew there going to be fans behind the barricades hoping to get a photo or an autograph, and usually, I was the guy to do that.

But tonight? I guess I'd be the asshole in some kid's memory because I fully planned on walking straight to my car, baseball cap pulled low, eyes directed down so I didn't have to see the disappointment in anyone's face when I passed them by.

But sometimes, life throws a wrench in your plans.

Or more specifically, Maggie Brynn did. At least in mine. Because of all the people calling out my last name, voices mixing together until they were indecipherable, I could pick hers out in a heartbeat.

"Brody," she called, arguably softer than any other voice in the parking lot, but because it was her voice, it might as well have been the only thing I heard.

"Maggie." I said, head snapping up to see if my delusional ass had really conjured up some fantasy of her.

But low and behold, there she stood in dim light of the parking garage, looking so slight next to the grown men beside her that it made my heart clench.

With my eyes locked on hers, I took a step in her direction, my body knowing instinctively that if Maggie was near, I had to get to her.

The people around her erupted, shoving and calling out my name as if I were coming to see them personally. In the chaos, Maggie got shuffled toward the back, much daintier than the drunken men who were fighting to get in front of each other.

"Hey," I called out, pulse spiking as I watched Maggie get shoved to the rear. "Everyone back off."

But my approach only made the crowd get rowdier, amping up with each step I took in their direction.

I dropped my duffel bag, hopping the barrier to get to Maggie who nearly took an elbow to the face in the process. Hands reached out to me, shoving paper in my face, or phones to take pictures. It was chaos, especially because I'd planted myself in the midst of it. But I didn't have any other option.

"Everybody calm the fuck down," I roared, "before you crush my girlfriend!"

I pushed through the crowd of people, finding her pushed back in the middle, fierce look on her face as she shoved back against the people who clearly didn't have any fucking common sense as they mindlessly shoved any and every one in their path.

Jesus, I thought. All this for a picture with me?

Despite being in the center of a crowd of rowdy hockey fans, she wasn't scared—though my heart was still threatening to give out—she was pissed as hell.

That's my girl, I thought. A fighter till the end.

"I said, back the hell up." I called, shoving a few out of the way myself until I got to her.

"Maggie," I breathed, stepping in close until my body practically shielded her from the chaos around us. I reached out to grip her waist, steadying her on her feet. "Are you okay?"

She looked up at me in a daze, as if she couldn't believe I was there in front of her.

I know the feeling, baby.

Without thinking, I cupped her face in my hands, giving her the once over for any damage. Finding none, I breathed out a sigh of relief, trying to force my heart to return to its normal rhythm.

"Brody," she said my name again and I closed my eyes to savor the sound.

"You know," I brushed my thumb against her cheek, "there's easier ways of getting my attention besides getting crushed by hockey fans."

"What can I say?" She said, sounding a little breathless herself. "I've always had a flair for the dramatics."

I gave her a lopsided smile. "That you have."

"Besides," she cleared her throat. "You weren't answering your phone and I—" she paused, chewing her lip as if she weren't sure she wanted to finish the sentence.

"You what?" I said, gently, reaching out to tuck a piece of hair behind her hair.

Miraculously, she let me, and I had to pull my hand back before I did something stupid like scoop her up in my arms and put her in my car, away from all these people.

"Callahan," I still heard them call, and I turned swiftly to warn them off.

"I'm not taking any damned pictures tonight on account of my girlfriend almost getting run down by you all, so you can all go home." I scowled, ejaculating my voice as loud as I could manage.

A few drunkenly staggered back, surprised by the vehemence in my tone, whereas some of the others had the decency to look a little ashamed.

Without listening to anything else, I pulled Maggie's hand, taking her with me to the side of the parking garage where we could speak in relative privacy.

Some of the crowd staggered away, realizing I wasn't going to sign their beer belly with permanent marker, while a few others lingered nearby, snapping photos on their phone from a distance.

I didn't care. Let them take all the photos they wanted. But God help them if they got close to my girl again.

Not technically mine anymore, all things considered, but it didn't matter—as far as I was concerned, Maggie Brynn would always be my girl.

Mine to protect. Mine to keep safe.

And I would.

Of course I always would.

But I should probably clear that up to her, so she didn't think I was living in denial by my use of the term 'girlfriend.'

"Sorry about back there. The whole 'girlfriend' thing. I just figured it was the easiest way to get the message across."

"What, 'best-friend's sister slash ex-girlfriend' was too long for you to explain to them?" She gave me that smartass look of hers that always drove me crazy in the most mind-blowing way.

"Something like that," I agreed. "Now are you going to tell me the real reason you came out here to linger with all the groupies instead of talking to me back at Liam's?"

Her face fell.

"I don't know." She said. "I just needed to see you and I was so scared you were going to leave before I found you so I rushed out here and—" she paused, as if trying to catch her breath.

"I just… didn't want you to leave without you saying goodbye." She finished, looking up at me with raw vulnerability.

"I didn't even know you were at the game," I told her, dumbfounded.

"I didn't know I was going to be here, either." She shrugged. "It was sort of a last-minute decision."

"Why did you come?" I asked, my voice sounding pathetically like a plea. "For Liam?"

Or for me? God, please say for me.

She didn't say it in words, but her eyes were all the confirmation I could ever need. Brimming with earnesty, she stared up at me and said, "I really miss you, Brody."

"I miss you, Mags." I said, hand wrapping around the back of her head. "God, you have no idea—"

"Mr. Callahan," a small voice that was either my savior or my demise called out, because fuck, I'd just been about to kiss the shit out of Maggie.

Still might. I thought. After I tell them to screw off.

I opened my mouth to do just that, not even bothering to turn in their direction when Maggie's expression made me pause.

Her eyes narrowed, focusing in on the figure behind me before a look of shock registered on her face.

"Mr. Reilly?" She breathed out. "Is that you?"

I turned, finding a middle-aged man with two kids by his side. A boy and a girl—both under the age of ten. All three wearing Harbor Wolves jerseys.

"Ms. Brynn?" The man said, her own surprise mirrored on his face. "I'm so sorry, we didn't mean to bother you, we just—"

"No, no. It's fine." She said, stepping around me, looking down at his children with an unusual expression. "Are these your kids?"

"They are." He said. "I have them for the night." He beamed at Maggie as if this was particularly wonderful news. And for some reason, Maggie seemed to think it was, too, based on the genuine smile that crossed her features.

"Hi," Maggie said to his kids, who were hiding shyly by their Dad's side, staring up at me in awe. "I'm Maggie. It's really nice to meet you."

"How do you know Daddy?" The younger one asked her.

Maggie looked to the man, and he cleared his throat before responding.

"Uh, we work together, sweetie."

It didn't take a genius to put together that this man was obviously one of Maggie's clients, which meant this man was in some type of custody battle for the children that were right in front of me.

Thank God I didn't tell them to fuck off, I thought.

Even though my first instinct was to do exactly that considering they interrupted the first real moment I'd had with Maggie in who knows how long.

They were cute, I noted, and they looked remarkably like the man Maggie had referred to as Mr. Reilly.

My heart went out for them all. I couldn't imagine what it was like for any of them. My family, cramped as we had been, had stuck together my whole life.

I guess I had taken it for granted. The fact that I got to stay in one home with both my parents, instead of being swapped back and forth like luggage. There was no yelling, no fighting, no slamming of doors or words of anger.

And what I once had thought of as a relatively normal, maybe even boring upbringing—I now saw for what it was: unbelievable luck.

And more so, I couldn't imagine that Maggie had to deal with shit like that every day. The clients and the court cases and every little detail into these people's hellish home lives. It was depressing as hell, if I were being honest. And it explained a lot of the cynicism in Maggie's way of seeing the world.

I'd always known her job, of course. But seeing the real people affected? It wasn't just a blurry image in my head anymore. It was real and tangible proof of the weight that Maggie carried every day. I didn't think it was something I could shake off.

And even though she never admitted it, I know it killed Maggie that her own father had never even made an attempt to get partial custody.

He'd been willing to walk away from it all, her included. And for the first time, I was realizing what that knowledge might do to a person.

If her own father could walk away from her, if her father could not fight for her—why would she ever believe that anyone else might?

"Hey, kids." I said, scooting down in front of them, trying to process the whirlwind of emotions currently taking over. "Did you guys have fun at the game tonight?"

"Yeah!" They both cried in unison.

"I'm sorry I didn't play so well." I winced dramatically. "If I'd have known you two were in the audience, I would've done a lot better."

They giggled.

"But hey, I can promise you next time you come, I'll make sure I don't let any of those pucks into the net, okay?"

They both started babbling, acting as if we were the oldest of friends, while I saw Mr. Reilly watching us from the corner of my eye with something like overwhelming fondness for the kids. And gratitude towards me.

Huh. I thought. Gratitude for simply taking two minutes of my day to talk to some kids.

That was the thing about my job that I never really got. People screamed my name, wanted pictures of me, wore my name on their backs.

And I was just, me.

It never really made any sense to me.

"We're sorry to bother you," Mr. Reilly said, profusely apologetic. "We saw the chaos that happened back there. That wasn't right."

"Don't worry about it." I told him. "Not your fault."

But I knew for sure, I was never going to walk past any kid again who wanted to say to me again. No matter how shitty a day was, what was a minute of my time compared to a moment they might cherish forever.

Just because I played a silly game.

I got it. Believe me I got it. I'd had heroes of my own back as a kid. It wasn't until a few years into my career that I realized—they were just normal people, who happened to make their livelihood off of a game that for some reason was a multi-billion-dollar enterprise.

"I just wanted to give them a great night." I heard him tell Maggie. "They love hockey. And I—well, I just wanted them to have a good night with me."

"Hey, do you guys want to take a picture?" I asked, trying to give them something they might really remember.

"Yes!" They both bounced in unison.

I grinned at their excitement, feeling it wash away the sour mood I'd been in. It was impossible to be upset when there were kids in the world who got so excited over the most mundane of things, even when the circumstances in their lives were undoubtedly shitty.

Maggie and Liam had been just like these two kids, I thought.

"Hey Mags," I called out, "will you take a picture of the four of us?"

"You sure you want an old eyesore like me in the photo?" Mr. Reilly laughed.

"Yes, Daddy!" The little girl said, dragging his hand to come stand beside us.

"Yeah, Dad." The older brother agreed. "You gotta!"

Maggie grinned, staring at the family with a sense of contentment as she slipped her phone out to snap the photo.

"Here," she said, "I'm going to take a few."

She clicked away, calling out, "now do a silly face!"

We all did, the kids giggling as they stuck their tongues out, faces scrunched up in amusement.

"Thank you, Mr. Callahan." The man said, and then turned to Maggie with something akin to admiration in his eyes. I knew because I looked at her like that, myself. "And thank you, Ms. Brynn. For everything you do."

Maggie waved it off, but I saw her eyes getting misty.

This client meant something to her. His case, his kids. They were important. Which meant they were important to me by extension, because there wasn't a thing Maggie Brynn cared about that I didn't.

That's just what happened when you loved someone.

And I knew that these people were lucky, because once Maggie decided to go to bat for someone, there wasn't a force in the world that could stop her.

"I'll see you for our meeting next week?" She said to Mr. Reilly, and he confirmed with a nod.

"Kids, say thank you." He instructed, and once they did, they set off, the kids skipping all the way out.

"Thanks for that." She said, coming to stand beside me.

"For?" I smirked down at her.

"I don't know. Talking to them. Taking a picture. It meant a lot. To them. And to me."

"It was nothing," I told her, knowing I would do so much more, if it earned me even a fraction of the smile she was sharing with me.

"It was something, Brody." She argued. "You give away pieces of yourself to everyone, do you know that? You're so incredibly selfless, even during the times you have every right not to be."

I've given all of myself to you.

"Do you—"

Do you want me?

Do you love me?

Do you—?

"—need a ride?" I finished lamely, a million things unsaid between us.

I stared at her, praying for her to say yes. I just wanted her beside me. Needed it, actually. And because I was a desperate, pathetic man, I wasn't above begging. "Please say yes."

She nodded, smiling shyly.

I exhaled in relief, opening the passenger door. Watching as she climbed inside and buckled herself in, I shut the door behind her.

It was only when I settled myself in the drivers' side, drove us out of the lot and under the city lights of Boston did I finally feel like myself again.

Because that was the thing. Maggie was a part of me. Probably the biggest part.

And I hadn't been me without her.

CHAPTER FORTY-SIX

Maggie

Can he hear my heart pounding?

The car was silent as we drove, save for that. Dark, but I preferred it that way. He couldn't see how nervous I was in the dark.

Then again, maybe he could. Brody always had a way of sensing the most subtle of shifts in me.

Was he thinking about the last time we were alone in this car together, driving through the night just like this?

"What? No audiobooks tonight?" I said, more to distract myself than anything else.

He laughed.

"No, actually. I haven't been listening to any lately."

"You *always* have an audiobook playing." I gaped. "Don't tell me you've been sitting in silence with your thoughts?"

"Nah, I haven't quite turned into Liam just yet." He smirked. "I've actually been listening to music."

"Like what?" I asked, because Brody hardly ever listened to music. I knew audiobooks helped him unwind in a way music didn't. Gave him something to focus on besides his thoughts, he always said.

People thought Brody was all happy-go-lucky and grins and jokes, but the truth was, it took a lot out of him to present that way all the time.

People didn't see the other side of him.

But to me? It was my favorite one. Because it was real. I wanted to reach out and grab his hand, hold it in my own. The urge was so strong I had to stretch out my fingers to shake it off.

"Let me see your playlist," I said, grabbing his phone out of the center console.

He raced me to it, but I got there first, grabbing his phone before he had the chance to—

I stared down at the lock screen. Still a photo of us. One that Cassie had taken of us, with my head leaning on his shoulder, hugging his arm to my body. Him looking down at me, the way he always did.

He stared at me as I looked down at it, neither of us saying a word. I didn't want to hear an explanation or have him hurry to say he would change it soon—and I really didn't want to tell him how the sight of it caused hope to bloom in my chest.

So, I ignored it, going to the home page because his phone still recognized my Face ID and opened up for me. I pressed the Spotify logo, looking at the most recent playlists.

sad boy winter.

I clicked it open, scrolling through—

"*The Scientist. Dancing On My Own. Skinny Love.* Brody, these songs are depressing as hell."

"Don't judge." He pulled the phone from my hands. "Sometimes the deep cuts hit the spot."

"I'm not judging." I said. "I think it's good for you to acknowledge your emotions. Process them."

Even if I'm not processing mine. Even if we're both hiding from our apartment, living in a delusional fantasy land where we've put all our issues on pause in order to just keep living.

"So, let's see what Maggie Brynn has been listening to, huh?" He grabbed my phone from me.

In a similar motion, he looked down at my phone, stunned as if it were a bomb about to go off, when he noticed my screensaver similarly unchanged.

"Mags, what does this—" and then I took the phone, opening up my playlists before tossing it back onto his lap.

"Gracie Abrams?" He said, glancing briefly down at the phone as he drove. "A lot of Gracie Abrams. Oh, look. A playlist with the same song repeated thirty times."

"That's enough of that," I said, grabbing the phone back. "Eyes on the road."

But then I noticed where we actually were at seemingly the same moment he did.

"Shit, sorry." He said as we drove through our neighborhood. "I guess I wasn't thinking about where I was going and—"

Forgot what was happening here? Me too.

"It's okay." I said. "Actually, I need to grab a few more things. Let's go back h—to the apartment."

He smiled and pulled down our street.

How could something feel so wrong and right at the same time?

This place. This is where we were supposed to be. But this wasn't supposed to be how *we* were—with this space between us and words left unsaid.

Maybe if I just laid it all out there, told him how I'd let fear ruin our lives, he'd forgive me. Maybe he'd take me back.

But the thought gnawed at me: how could I have fixed myself in the short amount of time that had passed from then and now?

I wanted to be with him. More than anything. But I also wanted him to know and believe that I wouldn't sabotage it again.

If I tried too early, he might shut me down.

"What are you thinking about, Maggie?" he said, taking a step closer to me.

He reached behind me to pull a lamp string. Beside the faint glow, only what little light streamed in from the city illuminated the space. I felt protected in the darkness.

"What? Nothing."

"That's not true." He tucked a strand of hair behind my ear. "You're lost in thought. I know you."

"I was just thinking…" I started, "it's a dump in here."

He laughed.

I looked around. "Looks like we've been slacking on the cleaning."

I had clothes thrown over the couch, cabinet doors open in the bathroom, a blow dryer discarded on the floor.

"Looks like Hurricane Maggie has been through here."

"I've been coming back to get stuff every now and then." I explained. "I know it's stupid. I might as well just come back for good. I just… didn't want to be alone."

"I get it." He said, looking around the space we've shared for so long. Now a graveyard of memories.

"I've missed it." he admitted.

"I've missed you." I said, despite myself.

"Maggie, I—" But I didn't hear what he was going to say, because I was already pulling his face toward mine.

His body reacted probably before his mind did. Ours knew each other well. In perfect synchronicity we moved together, until his hands were all over me, remembering something he should've never had to forget.

I clawed at the back of his shirt, trying to erase any separation that had ever been between us, while his hands roamed up into my hair, tugging it just enough to angle us into a deeper kiss.

What were we doing? I thought. *We've been so stupid. Being apart, but not really apart. It's like it was all leading back to this—*

"I'm moving to Michigan." he said, his lips still hovering over mine.

"What?" I blinked, trying to pull away. As if predicting my next move, his hands came up to cup the back of my head, holding me in place.

"I decided to go back." he said. "Because—well, I didn't have any other plan."

"Oh." I said shakily. "Oh, okay."

I would *not* cry. That would be selfish. Here was Brody, who had never chosen a thing for himself without consulting other people, now for the first time having the chance to navigate his own life.

If this is what he wanted, I would be happy for him.

"What do you think of that, Maggie?" he asked, pleading for something.

Probably for me to tell him it was okay. That it wouldn't destroy me if he left. That I would manage to survive, somehow.

And for his sake, I would lie.

"I think it's good." I told him, nodding up and down like a bobble-head. "Really."

"What?" he asked, as if he weren't expecting this response. As if he were expecting the selfish answer.

I couldn't blame him. It's the only side of me he'd ever known. I was always selfish when it came to him. Wanting him with me, near me, part of me all of the time.

"If it's what you want—" I started, but he cut off with a furious shake of his head.

"Do you want me?" he asked.

Of course I wanted him. I think it was pretty clear I wanted him, based on the direction we'd been heading just a few moments ago.

But I wasn't going to jump in and derail his life all over again. He'd made a plan. He was leaving. And being with him again, knowing that? It would've hurt too much.

Brody was leaving.

It *hurt*. Like I couldn't take a full breath. Like I'd taken a punch to the gut, and somehow the air would never replenish itself.

"Because Maggie, I want you." he continued, groaning. "God, I want you. So badly I feel like I can't go on without you anymore."

I knew holding him, being with him again, would ease the pain even momentarily, but I couldn't put either of us through that. Brody was determined to move on, and I was determined to not be selfish anymore. No matter how badly I wanted to.

So, I pushed him away and said, "I can't. *We* can't."

He sucked in a breath, shutting his eyes as he nodded along with me. "You're right. Of course."

Slowly, he stepped away. Though it was only a few steps backward, it felt like the earth had cracked between us, leaving me stranded on the other side, never able to reach him again.

"You're too important to me. To lose, I mean." I said, trying to salvage whatever mess I'd just made again. God, what an idiot I'd been to kiss him. Expecting everything could go back to normal.

But Brody was as much of an extension of myself as a limb was, and I knew the only way to keep him in my life was to offer up that root of friendship that had always existed at the heart of our relationship.

"You don't have to lose me, Mags." he said, sounding agonized. "That's not what I want."

"Good," I nodded, cutting him off. I couldn't bear to hear anymore. "So, it's settled then."

"What's settled?"

And though it killed me to say it, I offered up the only solution that let me keep him.

"You and I." I gestured between us, offering a hopeful smile that tore my soul apart. "Friends?"

And he responded, in the flattest of voices, in a way that made me think he didn't mean it at all.

"Friends."

CHAPTER FORTY-SEVEN

Brody

"Yup, this one is great," I told the realtor with what was probably the most bored expression I'd ever worn.

"Great?" Abbey said, pinching my arm.

"Yeah, it'll be fine for what I need it for." I shrugged, looking around at the carpeted apartment floors.

I'd flown back to Michigan for this. To see apartments. Abbey had come along to help, a woman's eye and all that. But honestly, it didn't matter. This place was as good as the next.

Sure, the wallpaper was sort of outdated, and the heating system made an obnoxious noise, and maybe it wasn't the most spacious. But who cared? It was just me, and it didn't matter.

"What you need it for..." Abbey said incredulously. "You mean *a home?*"

But it wasn't going to be a home. I couldn't picture any type of long-term life in this apartment, but the thing was, I couldn't in *any* of the ones I'd seen.

Maybe when the pieces of my life started to click back into place I'd be in the right headspace to find somewhere else.

318

"This isn't going to be a 'forever home'." I air-quoted with a dramatic expression. "Just a for now one."

"Well, actually, there's a real cute condo for sale that might change your mind about that," she said in a sing-song voice.

"I just want to rent."

"Excuse us for a second," she said, tugging me by the arm away from the realtor.

"Look, Brody. Renting doesn't make any sense if you're moving here permanently. And you're clearly not struggling financially," she said. "I think it's best to start setting down roots right away. Find yourself a nice home, somewhere you'll be comfortable in. Somewhere you can picture yourself raising a family."

My stomach lurched. I couldn't even picture that life anymore if it wasn't with Maggie. Honestly, what was I supposed to do? Meet some woman in the grocery store and forget that I'd spent the last five years imagining my future with someone else?

God, why did I tell her I was moving to Michigan?

You know why. It's because you wanted her to ask you not to go.

If she had said she wanted me, it would've changed everything.

But she didn't.

So there I was.

…in Michigan. It fucking sucked.

"I want to leave. I can't be here right now," I said. "Let me go sign the papers so I can fly back to Boston."

I just needed to make the decision and be done with it all. I couldn't be sitting on some hypothetical fence any longer. The damage was done, the decision was made. As soon as it was official, I'd be able to accept it in a way that I couldn't now.

"Brody, take a breath," Abbey said. "You're being hasty. Just let me show you this other place I found and if you hate it, I promise we can come right back here and I'll personally move you into this dump myself."

I would've said no, but honestly, I didn't care either way. It wouldn't be home. No matter what.

Apathetic had never been a term to describe me, but this entire trip, it was all I felt. And it showed.

"Fine." I shrugged. "Let's go check it out."

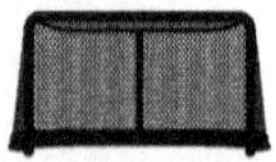

"See?" Abbey said proudly, hands on her hips with smugness written all over her face. "This is much nicer, isn't it?"

It was. Even I had to admit.

"I fell in love with it when I was looking for a new place, but alas, it's out of my price range." She feigned a sigh and sat back down onto the couch.

"It is your style," I had to admit.

"That's the best part. It comes fully furnished!" she squealed. "The woman who lived here is so rich that she just decided she'll buy all new furniture in Europe, which, by the way, is where she's moving. What a dream."

"You should've charmed your way into her life and convinced her to take you with her," I laughed, watching as Abbey examined the golden frames lining the walls of the apartment.

I wasn't much of an art guy. But it was pretty to look at. I'd probably leave it up. Besides, Abbey seemed to like it. And if I was moving back home, my old friends would probably come over a lot.

We could do game nights. Or movie nights.

And basically I'd go back in time about fifteen years, resorting to my teenage self.

I knew logically that a ton of people stayed in the towns they grew up in, made a happy life there and lived happily ever after. Maybe even once, I thought I might do the same. But I couldn't help the sneaking feeling that somehow, I'd outgrown this place.

That I wanted different.

Not just Maggie.

But workouts with Liam. And texting memes to Cassie. And being a part of Lily's life, and whatever other kids the two of them spawned out over the next few years.

I would miss it. All of it.

"So, do you like it?" Abbey asked, with the realtor staring at me with that billboard-looking smile.

What the hell. It was modestly priced. A ten-minute drive from my parents. There wasn't anything particularly offensive screaming out at me. Might as well.

"Yes." I lied. "It's perfect. Exactly what I was looking for."

And then, to ensure I didn't back out of my plan to figure out my life away from the Brynns, I bought the place outright.

The realtor was thrilled. Abbey was thrilled.

I, however, felt like I'd signed my own death certificate. But I figured I'd probably power through that feeling eventually. Hopefully.

We drove back to the airport in relative silence, Michigan passing by in a blur around me.

Shouldn't I feel something? Nostalgia? Excitement for a new journey? Gratitude to be able to buy a condo for myself so close to my family?

But all I felt was sickening dread.

"You're thinking about her again, aren't you?" Abbey asked, more matter-of-factly than any real type of question.

"I'm thinking about a lot of things."

"A lot of things all relating back to her."

She wasn't wrong. But then, Abbey had always known me pretty well.

And while I appreciated all the help she'd given me today—driving me around our old neighborhood, picking me from the airport, coming to all of the apartment showings with me…I had to set her straight on something.

Maybe she wasn't thinking it at all, but either way, it needed to be said.

"Abbey," I said carefully. "I want you to know that even though I'm coming back home… you and I, we're not going to pick up where we left off."

"I sort of figured." She said. "I saw the way you looked at your ex. I've known you a long time… and well, I've never seen you look at anyone like that. Not even me. That sort of thing is hard to get over."

I sucked in a breath. It was harder than she knew.

"Yeah, well. I need to get over it. I think we both need to work on moving forward instead of settling for what's comfortable. Don't you think?"

She looked up hesitantly. "I do love you. I always will. You know that."

I heard the pause in her voice. Not a declaration of love, but a way to brace me for whatever was about to come next.

"But?" I asked.

But, I think you're right. I don't think we were ever *in* love. I mean, not in any real sense of the word." Her face fell. "Not that what we had wasn't *real* for how young we were—"

"No, no, no. Abbey." I stopped her, a wave of relief washing over me. "You don't have to explain. I feel the same exact way."

"You do?" she said, daring to meet my eyes, relief of her own washing over her.

"Yeah. I do." I said, utterly grateful that I didn't have to be responsible for breaking her heart.

"So, it's true, then?" she asked, not hurt or upset. Just curious. "You didn't love me the way you loved her—Maggie. Did you?"

I exhaled, pressing my eyes shut.

"I've never loved anyone the way I loved Maggie." I admitted. "And I probably never will."

"Then you shouldn't let her go." Abbey said, and when I opened my eyes, I found nothing but sincerity there.

"I didn't let her go," I said. "She chose to leave."

"Take it from a girl who's seen the two of you together. It's not over for her."

I stared at her, half wanting to believe what she was saying, while at the same time not daring to hope it might be true. This was exactly why I was leaving. I couldn't live the rest of my life half-starved on hopes that might never come true.

No. I needed a fresh start. A clean slate. I had no choice but to leave.

"What about you?" I deflected. "I don't believe you've actually been pining away for me all these years."

She rolled her eyes, but it didn't escape my notice when an unmistakable blush rose to her cheeks.

"Ah, there's someone, isn't there?" I poked her side.

"No." She said, too quickly. "I mean, maybe." She sighed. "I mean, no. Nothing that'll ever go anywhere."

"And why not?"

She paused, looking as if she were debating holding it in or letting it all fly out. Predictably, Abbey chose the latter. Or rather, it chose her. I laughed to myself. She'd never been any good at keeping her own secrets. She wore her heart on her sleeve, no matter the cost.

"Because it's Matt," she said quickly, "and anytime anything ever got close to happening, he said he couldn't because he didn't want to betray you like that."

"What?" I asked, dumbfounded. "All this time you've been crushing on *Matt*—wait, Matt T. or Matt C.?"

She scrunched up her nose in disgust. "Who do you think?"

I thought about it for a moment, and finally said, "Matt T." simultaneously with Abbey.

We both erupted into laughter, before a look of guilt passed over her features.

"You don't hate me for it, do you? I know he's your friend."

"What? *No.* Of course not. I only hate that the both of you have waited so long on *my* account."

"So, you're really okay with it?" she said hopefully.

"Of course I am. You guys never needed my permission."

"It's just that, well, we care about you, Brody," she said, staring at me. "I know you've been gone for years, but that doesn't mean we love you any less."

"We're getting old as shit, huh?" I said, feeling all those years that came upon far more suddenly than I ever would've thought.

"I guess that means we can't afford to be wasting any more time, huh?"

"And what does that mean?"

"It means," she said pointedly, "if you know who you want to be with… then go get her. Can you really tell me it's over?"

I stared at her, not knowing what to say.

Of course it wasn't over with Maggie. But that was exactly the problem.

I didn't know if it ever could be.

CHAPTER FORTY-EIGHT

Maggie

It didn't make sense to be so nervous. I'd done this hundreds of times—thousands, even, for God's sake. It was my career. My passion.

And Mr. Reilly had everything to back us up. The paystubs, the character references, the proof of secure living arrangements.

And more than that, I was Maggie Brynn—recognized on Boston's 30 Under 30, graduate of Boston College, and one hell of a lawyer, if I do say so myself.

I took a breath, straightened my posture, and walked into my courtroom as if I owned it, ready to accept nothing but the conclusion I wanted. It was the only way. I had a face to those children now. I'd seen the joy that being with their father brought them. And I was here, in this courtroom, in this very profession, to do what was in the best interest of children who couldn't fight for themselves.

So I did it.

With Mr. Reilly behind me, counting on me, I presented an un-flinching case.

And in the end, it didn't matter. Because Mrs. Reilly changed her mind.

When I proposed a 2-2-3 schedule, giving Mr. Reilly as close to equal custody as was possible in a court of law, I'd fully been expecting Mrs. Reilly's counsel to counter with a proposition of weekend visitation.

I thought of every angle they might take it from.

The infidelity: *a person's status as a partner does not define their quality as a* parent.

His egregious work schedule: *he'd already spoken with work to have his hours adjusted to be able to pick the kids up from school on his days with them, choosing to work overtime on the days he* didn't. *Because of his longstanding loyalty to the company, they had formally agreed.*

The kids needing the stability of one household: children of their age are incredibly adaptable, and the stability they get from having regular contact with both parents will be far more valuable to their emotional well-being.

I had every argument lined up, thought out, fire in my pants ready to ignite me into action at any moment, only for Mrs. Reilly's lawyer to say, "My client now concurs. She believes it is in the best interest of the children to have regular visitation with their father. We are in agreement with counsel's proposed schedule."

I know they say gamblers have mastered that famous "poker face" they always talk about, but I think lawyers do it even better. Because despite the shock I felt at the total switch-up, I held it together without a trace of emotion flickering across my face.

It would be two days with parent A, two days with parent B, three days with parent A, and then switching order the following week.

In other words, best-case scenario. I couldn't have asked for any better.

Mr. Reilly sucked in a gasp, looking over to Mrs. Reilly from across the courtroom with raw, unfiltered emotion. And miraculously, gratitude. Humility.

"Thank you," he breathed, barely audible, but she understood the sentiment and nodded back at him.

Maybe the anger had died down. Maybe, despite being hurt by him, she recognized the invaluable force he was in their children's lives. Whatever the reason, when she looked at him I found no animosity, no duplicity. Only a quiet respect of his role as the man whom she'd once shared a life with.

There they were, two people with countless years behind them. No one stands up at the altar assuming one day they'd be here. Many resort to a lesser version of themselves they never would've expected to encounter. Most can never put their anger aside, even for the sake of children.

But these two had recognized that no matter the outcome of their relationship, their lives would always be intertwined. They'd been partners once, and now perhaps would still be, in a different way.

There was still love there, that was certain. How could there not be? They wouldn't stop being a family despite the dynamic looking a bit different. There may still be hurt there, but there was immense love, as well.

Humans were messy and emotional and reckless, and despite it all, we were still drawn to each other like magnets, throwing caution to the wind regardless of the potential for damage.

But almost all of them, when asked if they would do it all over again, always agreed that they would.

And me, foolish as I'd been, had spent so long trying to avoid pain that I in turn had avoided happiness.

Not anymore.

CHAPTER FORTY-NINE

Brody

"So, did you officially tell your agent yet?" Liam asked as we strolled through Boston Common.

It was the kind of gray, drizzly morning that made you realize New England winters held on kicking and screaming before spring reluctantly forced *its* way in.

"I told him," I said, hands shoved in the pocket of my hoodie to keep from freezing. Despite growing up with Michigan winters, I had never quite gotten used to the cold.

I hadn't entirely dressed for the weather when I invited Liam to come walk with me. And infuriatingly enough, despite Liam being dressed similarly in jeans and a hoodie, he looked *unfazed* by the forty-degree weather.

Plus, the fact that it was so early in the morning didn't help matters much. But that was Liam's condition to avoid being approached by fans the way we would if we were out any later in the day.

"And?" Liam pressed for more information.

I grimaced.

"He was less than pleased by the news."

"Meaning, he was completely pissed?"

"To put it lightly."

"Can you blame him?" Liam asked. "You're one of the greats. It'll be a huge loss for Boston to see you go."

"Captain Liam Brynn calling me one of the greats?" I pressed a hand to my heart. "I'm touched. I've truly made it. I can sulk off into retirement in contentment now."

"Shut up."

"But really, it won't be anywhere near as big of a deal as *you* retiring," I said, tugging my beanie closer against my head.

"Why do you always do that?" Liam stopped, turning to face me.

"Do what?"

"Undermine yourself. You're a hell of a goalie. You should know that. Own it."

Him and Maggie—they were so adamant when it came to forcing you to accept validation, even when you didn't want to. It was endearing, really, despite them looking so damned aggressive as they dished it out.

"I do," I said, knowing that I'd put my body through the ringer over the years for the sake of the game. Knowing that objectively my stats were impressive. Knowing that Coach was proud of me. "It just... doesn't feel like enough anymore."

I guess Liam had rubbed off on me, because I couldn't help the way I'd started to think of it not as this epic thing that I used to live and breathe and sweat for, but now as just... a game?

Because without hockey, when I looked around at my life, I was left with nothing. And that didn't sit well with me. Not at all.

"It doesn't erase the fact that you've broken records, played for the Stanley Cup twice, and become *the* fan favorite of Boston."

"That last one is more to do with my sparkling personality than anything I've done on the ice."

"It's both, and don't pretend like it's not."

"Thanks," I told him. "But I'm ready to start building a life outside of it. The way you've done."

I didn't want to be thirty-five, on the last leg of my career, standing in an empty locker room while everyone had gone home to their families.

"I get that. Trust me, I do. I just don't want you to sell yourself short to yourself. Most people will never accomplish half the things you've done in life, and hockey isn't even at the top of that list."

"Who knew you were so sentimental?" I gushed, knowing if I told him how much his words meant to me, he'd shrug it off like it hadn't come from the very pits of that closely guarded heart of his.

He shook his head and picked up the pace, forcing me to take a few big steps to catch up with him again.

"What about you, though? How are you feeling about retirement?" I asked him.

"Honestly, I'm feeling extremely at peace about it all. I'm ready for it."

"Wow, we're really at the end of an era, huh?" I said, feeling the finality of decisions made washing over me.

"It's time for a new set of kids to take our place," Liam said. "Time to pass on the torch."

"It's scary how fast time went by." I shook my head in disbelief. "I still feel like a kid myself. Except my body feels sort of like an old man's."

"Yeah, you look like one, too," Liam said in that dry way of his.

"Take a look in the mirror, buddy. I have the baby-fresh face of an angel." I patted my freshly shaven cheeks. "Whereas you are sporting a few gray hairs."

"I am *not*."

He wasn't. But I made a point of looking, anyway.

"How about you shut up and tell me what your next step is?"

"I guess I'm going to go back to the apartment today, pack up my stuff, and ship it to Michigan."

"Yeah?" he asked, slightly surprised. "And when are you officially leaving?"

"Well, that depends on when we're booted, but probably right after," I said, thinking grimly of our piss-poor performance this year.

"Yeah," Liam grimaced, in turn ashamed. "My heart hasn't been in it. My mind's been occupied with… other things."

"And I've completely dropped the ball. I know that. This might be our worst season in our entire career."

Liam shrugged. "It happens. We're human."

He said that, but I knew he was disappointed in himself. If this was truly his last season, then he deserved to go out with a bang.

I couldn't reconcile the fact of me leaving on such a sour note, for that matter, either. But I didn't see what else could be done about that.

Some things crashed and burned, despite how brightly they started out—whether that be hockey or relationships or life in general. Lucky me, it was all three at once.

"If you want, I can come help you pack everything up now," Liam offered. "We've got a few hours before we're due at the rink."

"Honestly, man? That would be great," I told him.

I couldn't think of anything more depressing than packing up my entire life on my own, with nothing but my thoughts to keep me company.

"Are you going to tell Maggie you're packing up?"

"She won't care," I told him, remembering that word she used, solidifying the nail in our coffin. *Friends.* "Besides, I just want to get it done and over with."

"All right," he said skeptically, remaining firm in his decision to stay out of it. "Let's go do it then."

And as casually as that, we went to go pack up the last decade of my life.

CHAPTER FIFTY

Maggie

"Brody?" I burst through the front door of the house, searching for the man I had a hundred things to say to.

Namely one, more important than the rest, that just might change the trajectory of everything.

"Brody?" I called again, poking my head into various rooms, finding them all disappointingly empty.

I was desperate and frantic and excited all at once with the newfound realization that I had more power than I'd ever given myself credit for.

Brody and I loved each other. I knew we loved each other. Had known all along we had loved each other. I had just never put enough faith in that certainty. But I wasn't afraid to anymore. To bet everything on him. On us.

I heard steps descending the staircase and hurried back into the foyer in the hopes of seeing him, only to be once again disappointed.

"You are not the person I wanted to see."

"Oh, gee, thanks." Cassie rolled her eyes with a good-natured smile.

"No! I'm sorry. I love you!" I assured her while hurrying past her up the stairs. "I'm just looking for Brody. It's kind of urgent."

"He's not here."

I paused, turning back to face her. This really wasn't going according to the plan I formulated in my head fifteen minutes ago on the drive over.

"Did he go to the rink early?" I asked, already digging through my purse for my car keys. I really needed to stop just dropping them in anywhere. I could never find them when I needed them.

I hurried back down the stairs, still searching, and contemplating whether I should get one of those big, absurd fluff-ball keychains Cassie had for this very reason, when her words stopped me in my track again.

"He's not at the rink. He's at your apartment."

"He is?" I said, feeling elated. "That's great!"

He must've been on the same page as me. He must've changed his mind about moving to Michigan. He must've realized what I did—that we can't give up on each other. Not now. Not ever.

"Hey, Mags?" Cassie gripped my forearms. "I need you to relax because your eyes are kind of bugging out and it's making me nervous, okay? Let's take a breath."

I did, nodding along excitedly as I blew out a breath in sync with her. Feeling more grounded, I focused on my friend in front of me. How pale she looked. And the scent radiating off of her.

"You smell kind of pukey, Cass."

"I feel kind of pukey," she answered.

I took a generous step back.

"It's not contagious!" she quickly assured. "Something I ate. Anyway," she waved it off. "Why don't you tell me what's going on in that pretty head of yours?"

"I'm going to pull a Noah!" I told her. "Like you suggested."

"What does that mean?" She shook her head, completely lost.

"'*The Notebook*,' Cass. I'm going to take a page out of Noah's book and give Brody some big romantic speech or gesture or... I don't know, but I'm going to do *something*. Maybe I'll stop and get him flowers?"

"Flowers?" Cassie echoed.

"Yeah, Brody's always getting me flowers and I'm so stupid. I'd never thought to give him any. I mean, guys like flowers too, don't they?"

"Yes, but—*why?*"

"Because I love him, Cass! I love him, and I want to ask him to stay, and after everything I feel like I need to do it in some big way to show him how much he means to me."

Cassie paused. Processed. Then took my hands and squealed, jumping up and down in excitement. For once, I joined her in the absurd display of celebration.

"*Finally.*" She threw her hands up in victory. "I've been waiting for you to figure this out." Then she dragged me toward the front door, opening it for me and practically shoving me out before yelling, "Wait!"

I turned, watched her plunge her hand into the vase by the door and pull out the calla lilies that were still dripping by the stems.

"Here," she shoved them toward me. "Don't waste any time stopping. Take these and go now."

We both laughed at the absurdity of the situation and the thrill of *me*—Maggie Brynn—going to profess my love.

"Good luck," Cassie said, pulling me in for a hug.

"Thanks." I breathed her in, feeling the puzzle pieces of life settling back into place again.

"Now, go get your man."

"Come on," I bit my lip, furiously jamming my finger repeatedly against the elevator button.

I waited a solid eleven, maybe twelve seconds before bolting for the staircase, feeling too much urgency to waste even seconds of time that could be spent reconciling with Brody.

Taking the steps two at a time and thanking my past self for the strict cardio routine I'd endured for the past ten years, I reached our floor in record time.

Turning to the right, I saw our door already wedged open, like a sign from the universe.

I bolted right through the door, into the apartment and smack into a solid chest. I dropped the flowers, trying to brace against the collision.

"Maggie?" Brody's voice was shocked as his hands moved to steady me. "What are you doing here?"

"Brody." I breathed out in relief, allowing myself the pleasure of sinking into his touch. "I was looking for you."

I felt myself burning with all the love I'd been silently carrying around for him, knowing it was finally about to be released one way or another.

I practically felt my eyes shining as I stared up at him, looking like the most beautiful sight I'd ever seen. I must've looked like a lovestruck fool, but I didn't care. I *was*.

I was ready to show him all of me. I didn't need to be scared of vulnerability. I was safe with Brody, I'd always been safe with Brody, I'd always be—

"Wait, why does the apartment look weird?"

I stepped around him, taking in every detail of the space, or rather the glaring absence of detail.

"Your stuff is gone." I turned to him slowly. Numbly. Processing the unfathomable.

I looked around to reconfirm that I wasn't mistaken, but it was true. His stereo was gone. His framed picture of Bobby Orr securing the Stanley Cup. His collection of duffel bags that I always thought cluttered up the doorway area and now realized just left it depressingly empty without them.

"Yeah," he said uncomfortably, slipping his hands into his pockets. "I just finished packing up. Figured I'd get a head start on sending it over to my new place."

"Your new place?" I said numbly. "You already got a new place? In Michigan?"

"Yeah." He shrugged, looking away.

Maybe I was too pitiful to look at, standing there in the ashes of my life, my arms hugging myself as if I could keep myself from crumbling.

"I didn't know it was official. I just thought it was something you were thinking about." I mumbled. "I didn't think it would be this fast."

I thought I had time to change your mind.

But of course it was happening this fast. That was Brody. He made a decision and he stuck with it. He wasn't the one plagued by uncertainty and indecisiveness. He wasn't the one who was so afraid of screwing up that he wouldn't take a step in any one direction. That was me.

I'd been the one holding him back.

"Yeah, well, you know we've played a shit season. It's not like we'll be making the playoffs. So after our last game in a few days, I figure I should just be on my way."

"Is this what you want?" My voice was a weak, feeble thing. I heard the pitiful crack and could only just barely stop myself from crying right then and there.

He hesitated for a beat, staring at me. He opened his mouth, then shut it.

"It's for the best," he said finally.

I nodded. Accepting that. I wanted what was best for him. I didn't want to stand in his way anymore. So even though it killed me, even though it tasted like glass going down, I swallowed all the words I'd come to say.

But I couldn't stop myself from asking—

"You weren't even going to say goodbye?"

"I couldn't." His face contorted into an expression of utter devastation. "I just... couldn't."

I crossed my arms around my body, trying to hold myself upright although the pain threatened to bring me to my knees.

"I left you a letter," he said, nodding toward the coffee table. "You don't have to read it if you don't want to. I just needed to say it."

"Fine." I said, looking away to that thick envelope on the coffee table.

"I just want you to know," he said, gripping the door as though it were the only thing anchoring him in that moment, "I don't regret any of it. Even if this is how it was always going to end, I would do it all over again for the time we had together. I—" he paused, looking away. Blinking. "I just wanted you to know that."

And then he left.

And true to his word, he didn't say goodbye, as if it were truly too hard for him to utter. But honestly, I might not have been able to handle it if he did.

The lump in my throat sat heavy and unmoving, and I wondered if it might be there forever.

Moving toward the coffee table, I grabbed the envelope, tearing it open, desperate to hear the last parting words I'd ever get from Brody Callahan.

Maggie,

I'm not very good with words, but still I couldn't leave without having something said between us. After all these years, a letter seems a pretty shitty way of concluding our story, but I'm too much of a coward to say goodbye in person. I hope you'll forgive me for that. Or at least understand.

Now here comes my second apology. As you'll see, most of what I have to say in this letter aren't my words at all, but I hope you'll forgive me, because our friend Nicholas Sparks managed to perfectly capture how I'm feeling better than I ever could. (I have a feeling you'll recognize the passage I'm including below.)

Now listen Maggie, just because these aren't my words doesn't make them any less true. I mean them. Sincerely. Every last one.

So, I'll stop rambling and get to it.

My Dearest Maggie, "I couldn't sleep last night because I know that it's over between us, I'm not bitter anymore because I know that what we had was real—"

I paused, eyes welling up with tears as I read the paragraph he included.

He'd written Noah's last letter to Allie. That bastard was quoting my favorite movie in his goodbye letter to me, and all I could do was sit here on the floor of the home we once lived in and bawl my eyes out.

Using my blouse sleeve, I rubbed an arm across my eyes, staining the white fabric black with makeup. But I couldn't bear the thought of ruining this letter with tears.

The last piece of Brody I'd ever have.

I sat there, savoring his words, thinking of the beautiful boy who wrote them. The boy who'd only ever wanted me to be happy. The boy who had never done a thing to hurt me in his entire existence. The boy who lived and breathed for the people he loved.

And I wondered how I could have ever been so afraid of that gentle boy hurting me when all along I should've known it was my own hand that would cause my heart to bleed.

Brody

It was an odd thing, to put on my jersey and get ready for what very well might be the last game of my career.

It was the last game of the season, and unless a miracle came through, we already knew we weren't making the playoffs.

Clearly, my life had been pretty void of miracles lately.

Honestly, it was a shitty way to go out. Definitely not the way I used to picture retirement when I was first getting started.

No matter how favorably the media was towards me, there would be no way to sugarcoat my piss-poor performance during my last season. Not that anyone really knew that yet.

The news of my retirement hadn't come out yet, so the fans had no idea that I'd be walking away from the Harbor Wolves at such an all-time career low. They would hope for better next season, not knowing that for me, next season would never come.

My agent was still holding hope that I'd have a last-minute change of heart. The official decision to not re-sign didn't have to be made quite yet, so even though I told him I was leaving. Told him I'd bought a new place. Told him everything was said and done, the guy still wouldn't budge, infuriatingly saying, *"you never know."*

That was true, I guess. You never knew where life might take you. One year ago today, if someone told me I'd be playing the last game of my career today and moving back to Michigan without the love of my life, I would've told them they were crazy. I would've said that's the very last thing in the world I would ever want for my life.

I had a sense of wrongness about it all. Discontentment.

And no matter how much was riding on my performance tonight, I knew it would be almost impossible to give it my all. Because in moments of weakness, when I looked out at the crowd for strength, or encouragement, or a goddamned shred of hope, I knew the one person I needed wasn't going to be there.

Maggie

My desk wasn't the most comfortable place to rest my head, but my head wasn't exactly the most comfortable place to be in at present, so I figured I didn't owe it any comfort anyway.

With my cheek pressed against the dark walnut surface, I stared blankly at the pictures arranged tauntingly on my desk.

The case was over, and while I had plenty of others to focus on, Mr. Reilly's had been special to me. Now that we'd come to a conclusion, I was allowing myself a few minutes to wallow before throwing myself into the next thing to distract myself from how utterly miserable I was.

A coworker appeared at my door, peering at me with either amusement or judgment. I didn't know, or care.

"What do you want, Brian? I'm clearly in the middle of something here," I responded.

"There's someone here for you. Should I tell them to go away?"

"A client?" I said, picking my head up. "Why didn't the secretary call down?"

"Secretary left. Everyone left. It's almost six," he said. "I was on my way out myself. It's the only reason I saw the guy."

I glanced up at the clock, realizing he was right. The game hadn't started yet, but it would soon. Brody was there now, getting ready to play what might be his last game in Boston.

I didn't want to hear a thing about it. I figured it would be better not to know if they qualified or not. If it was truly his last night here or not. Like waiting for disaster to strike, it was better to not know when it might happen.

So, the way I saw it, the longer I lingered in the office, the better.

"Send him in, then."

"I'm not your errand boy, Brynn."

"Well, you're on your way out anyway, aren't you?" I fluttered my lashes dramatically.

He waved a hand dismissively and turned to leave, but a moment later the client in question was standing in my doorway, causing me to stand from my seat in surprise.

"Mr. Reilly? What are you doing here?"

"I'm sorry to come so late," he said. "I just got off of work or I would've been here earlier."

"No, it's fine," I assured him. "Please, sit down."

"Oh, no, I won't be here long. I just wanted to—" He took his hat off, twisting it between his hands. "Well, I'm not very good with words. But I really just wanted to let you know how grateful I am for everything you did for my family."

I blinked my surprise.

"It was nothing," I told him. "It's what any lawyer would've done."

"No." He shook his head adamantly. "You're something special, Ms. Brynn. You better believe that."

"Well, thank you," I told him.

Like him, I was also a woman of few words. And both of us were clearly not wanting to get any more emotional than we already were.

"Anyways," he said, holding out a small gift bag in my direction. "This is for you."

"Oh, you didn't have to—"

He held up a hand in protest.

"It's nothing special. Maybe nothing to you at all. But I just figured, if you ever wanted to know if your work matters, you can take a look at this and remember how you changed my life for the better."

I reached in delicately, pulling out the framed photograph of Mr. Reilly, his children, and Brody.

I stared down, feeling the tears well in my eyes. I held the photo against my chest, touched that he wanted to share this piece of his family with me forever.

"I love it," I said honestly. "Thank you."

He scratched the back of his head awkwardly, shifting on his feet.

"That young man of yours is lucky to have ya," he said. "And trust an old guy like me, he knows it."

I laughed. "He's not—"

"The way he looks at you," Mr. Reilly nodded in confirmation of something only he seemed to know. "That's when it's real for a man."

"It's real for me, too."

"I can tell." He grinned. "Two kids in love are about the least subtle people in the world. Trust me, I've been there."

I offered a half-smile, holding the picture against my chest.

"Anyway, thank you. Again. I'll always remember what you did for me."

And I'll always remember what you did for me.

Inadvertently, but nevertheless, I had to admit a lot of the reflection in my life as of late had been a direct result of working on his case.

He'd shown me what a father's love was supposed to look like. He reminded me what I fought for in my career, why my work was important.

And somehow, after all that, I'd realized how utterly stupid I'd been to have spent so much of my life running.

"Thank *you*, Mr. Reilly," I told him, knowing he would never understand the depths of my gratitude toward him. "It's been the absolute honor of my career working with you."

"Well, I'll be off then." He nodded at me. "You take care of yourself, Ms. Brynn. And take care of that young man of yours."

I couldn't say anything, so I nodded back at him and watched him go.

CHAPTER FIFTY-THREE

Maggie

It was ironic for a girl who feared being alone so much to always end up exactly that, due to her own self-destructive actions.

Hurricane Maggie, a nickname bestowed on me that had more truth than most people probably realized.

I destroyed everything in my path, not because I wanted to, but because some part of me would rather destroy them before they destroyed me.

Trauma responses were a hell of a thing.

I walked out of the office, down the steps, staring only down the block in the spot where Brody used to park his car when he came to pick me up.

It was a nice thing. To look at the clock, knowing my day was almost over and he would be out there waiting for me. Someone to go home to. He had always been the best part of every day.

And in that moment, the thought of never seeing him parked there again made my heart hurt so badly that I shut my eyes tightly so I didn't have to bear witness to his absence.

"You there," a voice called from above.

Startled, I looked up to find that old man Brody used to torment, with his head out the window.

I looked around, searching the street for sign of the person he was calling out to. When I saw no one else around, I pointed a finger at my chest in question.

"Yes, you, young lady. Have you patched things up with that young man of yours yet?"

I felt a little silly hollering up to yell at an elderly man, but the look on his face told me he very clearly expected a response.

"He's moving to Michigan."

"What?" the old man hollered back, so I raised my voice even louder.

"He's moving to Michigan!"

"I heard you! The goddamn boy is an idiot! I told him to be patient, not flee the state!"

He shook his head in what looked to be incredible disgust.

"When did you talk to Brody?" I asked, highly doubting they had an entire conversation about our relationship through the method I was currently engaging in right now.

But I didn't hear whatever he said next, because my phone rang.

The thing about heartbreak is, no matter how unrealistic it is, your mind still hopes for miracles. Even though I knew Brody was on the ice, playing his last game, even though I knew he hadn't dialed my number in months—I still hoped it would be him.

It wasn't.

But it was probably the last person in the world I ever expected to see calling my phone again.

"Tara?"

"Hi, Maggie." Brody's sister's voice was restrained. "I don't know if I should be calling you, but… well, I couldn't live with myself if I didn't try."

I was silent, barely breathing, not knowing if she was going to tell me off or break my heart all over by telling me Brody had always been too good for me and I never deserved him anyway—all would be justified. But she didn't say any of those things.

"Listen, I'm pissed you broke Brody's heart. And I'm pissed at myself for meddling in it. And yes, I'm aware of the irony that I'm still meddling by calling you now, but I'm his sister and I love him—"

"I know that, Tara," I assured her.

"So, I'm just going to come out and say it. I know my brother, and he doesn't want to move to Michigan."

"What?"

"He wants to stay there with you. And your brother, and your friend. And I know you guys are just as much his family as any of us, and it's going to destroy him to leave you."

Was that true? Would it break his heart? I'd been so sure that's what he wanted.

"Now, I know you're your own person, and even though he's like the greatest guy in the universe, you're under no obligation to be with him, but even just to be his friend—"

I shook my head, stupidly.

"No," I told her. "No, that's not what I want."

"You can't even be his friend?" Tara's voice rang through with irritation.

"I don't want to be his friend, I want to be with him," I said. "Forever. Always. As long as he wants me. I don't care. I just want him."

There was silence on the other end of the line. I bit my lip, preparing for the outrage I was certain to face. But then, the silence broke, giving way to laughter on the other end of the line.

"Well, you better get him, then, before he has to waste time on a plane ride only to turn right back around."

I grinned, nodding my head frantically.

"Yes, that's exactly what I'm going to do. And you know what, if he really does want to move to Michigan, I'll move there with him."

"You *what?*"

"You think it'll break his heart to leave? Well, it'll break mine even more to have a life without him in it," I told her, feeling clarity like I'd never felt before. "Wherever he goes, I'll go, too."

"What about your job? Your life?"

"What about Brody?" I told her. "It's time for him to get what he wants for a change."

"Trust me, Maggie. He's only ever wanted one thing. Go talk to him, and I think you'll figure that out."

We hung up quickly, and I spun around in a daze, giddy with renewed energy and hope.

"Well, what was all that about?" the old man, who apparently was more nosy than I'd given him credit for, asked, still waiting in his window.

"Brody's sister," I told him, dizzied and excited. "I have to go."

"Where?"

"I gotta go see about a guy," I threw over my shoulder, already running down the cobblestone to where my car was parked.

The last thing I heard was the old man's laughter swirling through the night air.

"Ah, lucky bastard got off easy!" he called out. "At least he didn't have to go to war to win you back!"

CHAPTER FIFTY-FOUR

Brody

They say hard times make for strong men.

At least, I *think* someone once said that; if not, I'm a fucking genius because it was true.

The game was brutal. Perhaps one of the worst games I'd ever had the honor of playing in.

But something about it changed everything.

I'd come to a lot of realizations during the course of that game. Namely, that I sure as hell couldn't retire on such an absolute shit note.

And I sure as hell couldn't leave Boston.

This was home. I felt it in my bones. And once I realized that, everything else fell away.

Life had a funny way of working itself out. And what was meant to be yours would always come to you. I truly believed that.

So, I'd take life as it came. As long as I was where I was meant to be, I had to have hope that what was meant to be would be. That was all I could do.

I had a feeling, though, that Liam didn't have the change of heart that I experienced when it came to retirement.

He lingered around, long after everyone had left the arena, savoring it. He stood in the middle of the ice, long after the game had finished, taking it all in. Looking around at the place where he'd built a legacy.

I waited behind him, letting him have his moment before telling him the decision I'd landed on somewhere smack in the middle of our piss-poor, history-making game.

When he finally turned back to where Cassie and I waited in the ice box, I saw the finality in his eyes. The acceptance that the game that had been his life for years was now firmly settled in the past. The chapter closed.

"How does it feel?" I walked out onto the ice next to him. "Knowing we've played our last game together?"

"Don't get all emotional, Brody," Liam said. "We'll come to Michigan all the time, and we can kick the puck around on some little pond out there."

I laughed, preparing to tell him the news, when Cassie blinked up at me in tears.

"So, I guess you're leaving now?" Cassie blinked, teary-eyed up at me.

Liam wrapped an arm around her for support.

"Well, actually—" I said, grinning, "I—"

"Brody!"

I spun, and there was Maggie like a figment of my imagination, running toward me breathless and excited.

"Maggie?" I said, but she was already running onto the ice, slowing considerably as she realized that, though she was a mastermind in heels, they weren't exactly ideal for walking on ice.

"Mags, don't you dare break your neck on this ice or I'll kill you."

I ran forward, holding her up as she started to ramble.

"Thank God I'm not too late," she told me, steadying herself with a tight grip on my arms. "I drove like a maniac all the way here—"

"How many times have I told you not to speed?" I scolded. "Jesus, Maggie. You gotta be careful."

"I've never gotten a ticket."

"I'm not worried about a ticket, I'm worried about you crashing your car."

"The car's insured."

"Again, not about the car." I shook my head in disbelief. "About bodily damage to *you*."

"Never mind that!" she said, excitedly. "I had to come see you before you left for Michigan because—"

"About Michigan—" I started.

"No!" she said. "Please, let me go first. Please."

My lips went thin and I nodded at her to continue.

"You can't leave. You can't go to Michigan, and you can't go be with someone else," she started, shocking every last thought out of my head.

"Not even some beautiful ex that you clearly have a ton of history with and is probably a lot more emotionally stable than me."

"Maggie," I shook my head, about to tell her everything, but she kept going. An unstoppable force that never failed to leave me reeling.

"I'm working on everything. I know I have issues. But the thing is, I love you, Brody—*I* love you. And I know I've been crazy lately, and I get caught up with work, and I make messes wherever I go—but I love you so much, and I couldn't let you go without at least trying."

"Maggie," I tried again, but still she wasn't done.

"And if you're dead set on moving to Michigan, then I'm coming with you!" she told me firmly, eyes blazing with that stubbornness I loved so much. "And you know what, even if you don't want me to, I'll still come, and I'll wait until I can prove to you that we should be together. Because I'm willing to wait as long as it takes, because we belong together and that's what you do when you love someone as much as I love you."

"Will you let me go now?"

She nodded, entire body stiffening as if bracing for impact. Slowly, and reluctantly, her arms dropped from around me and she took a step back, forcing herself to meet my gaze.

There was something there. Fear, maybe. Certainly something she'd never let me see before.

"Maggie, listen when I say this. I don't care that you get caught up with work, because I love how you lose track of time when you're determined to see something through. I don't mind cleaning up your messes because I love seeing traces of you in every room I enter. And I don't care about how much history I have with someone else, because the only person I ever wanted a future with is you."

Her breath hitched.

"I love you, Maggie," I said, imploring her to understand it. "Only ever you."

"Me?"

"If it's not you, it's not anyone," I answered with devastating honesty.

And then she flung herself at me once more. I felt my body move of its own accord to catch her, as if it were second nature to have her in my arms. I gripped her so tightly so that she might never slip away from me again.

"Even though I put you through the ringer?" her voice was muffled as she spoke against my chest.

I inhaled the scent of her—argan oil and jasmine—as I laughed into her hair, resting my cheek atop her head.

"I like jumping through your hoops. It kept me in shape."

She sniffled, eyes wetting my shirt as she let out the emotion she'd tried to keep buried for so long.

All I could think was, *finally.*

Finally you're letting me see you.

And I loved her more in that moment than I ever had in my life because I felt the change in her. She was trusting me, lowering her guard. Letting go. Finally and completely giving me her heart in a way I'd never realized she'd been too afraid to do before.

"I know I've been a shitty girlfriend," she said, sniffling, "but I think if you gave me another chance, I could end up being a pretty decent wife."

I stilled. "What are you saying?"

"I want to marry you. I always wanted to marry you, Brody. Always. I was just scared that I was going to be too much for you. And I was afraid of what would happen when you eventually realized it."

"How could you possibly think that, babe?" I let out the softest of laughs, gently tucking a strand of hair behind her ear. I couldn't believe she was here in front of me, saying all this. I couldn't believe I was touching her again.

"I was scared that if I didn't have my life together, you wouldn't see any reason worth staying. That I wouldn't be able to offer you as much as you've always given me."

How could she think that? So little of herself when she had always been *everything* to me from the very first night in the locker room. Since the moment I saw her, I was done for. My hands were tied, fate sealed.

It was Maggie Brynn from that day forward, and I knew then—just like I knew now—that's how it would be forever.

"Don't you get it, Maggie?" I held her face in my hands. "Relationships aren't about keeping score. It's just about loving each other, through whatever shit comes our way."

Her green eyes brimmed with tears and she nodded, as if urging me to continue. To give her the words—the reassurance she never dared ask for before.

"It's you and me, Mags. I'm not going anywhere. If there's a problem you're facing, then guess what? It's *our* problem, because I love you, Maggie. And that's what love is. If you think I'm going to walk away because life gets messy, then I'll be happy to prove you wrong over and over and over again."

"Shut up," she pushed at me playfully, but I held tight. "You're literally the definition of a man written by a woman."

"And you're literally a raccoon," I cooed back, brushing my thumb under her makeup-stained eyes.

"Hey," she swatted at me.

"But hands down the most beautiful raccoon I've ever seen—smudged eyeliner and all."

She opened her mouth, no doubt ready with another smart-ass comment, but I leaned forward to capture her lips with mine. There would be plenty of time for banter later. For now, we had other business to catch up on.

I pulled away from her grasp, watching her eyes widen in confusion as I took a step back from her.

"What are you—" she started, but I was already down on one knee in front of her.

"Let's hope this goes better the second time around. Maggie Brynn, will you—"

"Yes!" she cried, sinking down to her knees in front of me, both hands shooting out to pull my face to hers for a kiss I had no desire to dodge.

"Yes?" I repeated after we broke apart, needing the confirmation in words. "You'll marry me?"

"Yes!" she squealed. "Tomorrow. Tonight. Right now? Name the time and I'll be there."

"I don't even have the ring with me." I laughed, guilty and giddy and drunk on the moment all at the same time.

"I don't care." She shook her head back and forth.

"And our knees are getting wet," I laughed, looking down to where we knelt on the ice.

"Who cares!" she yelled, crying now tears of joy. "We're getting married! Let's go now, to the courthouse."

The only type of tears I ever wanted to see coming from those pretty eyes of hers ever again.

"Babe, babe, babe," I said, as Maggie scrambled to her feet. "Wait. Let's not get ahead of ourselves."

"Why not?" she asked, looking as if it would be fine to head there right now, me in my hoodie and skates, her in her work clothes and makeup-stained face.

"Because if there's one thing Maggie Brynn loves, it's a party. And I sure as hell won't be the one to stand between you and the biggest party of our life."

"Say that again," she said, eyes gleaming.

"What?"

"Our life," she said sincerely. "That's all I want. You and me, always."

"Done." I nodded my agreement. "Easiest yes of my life."

From somewhere behind us, I heard Cassie weeping and finally turned to see Cassie and Liam standing in the bench door, watching us.

"Come here, you guys," Maggie said, gesturing for them to join me on the ice.

"Oh no," Cassie protested. "We can't ruin your moment!"

"Sorry, but Maggie just agreed to marry me! *Nothing* could ruin this moment."

She shoved my arm, though her eyes were radiating love when she looked up at me.

Fuck it. I leaned down and kissed her again.

Because I could. Because I'd missed her. Because I couldn't believe I almost lost her.

And most importantly, because she was going to be my *wife*. We might've taken the long way to get there, but it didn't matter now. It had been worth it.

Cassie wobbled out onto the ice with outstretched arms to keep her balance, her Converse sliding on the ice as she took a few cautious steps.

"Careful," Liam said, practically glued to her side to make sure she didn't fall.

"Oh, right!" Maggie chirped, looking from them to me with humor. "Cassie's pregnant."

"What!" Cassie and I said at the same time.

"Maggie! How did you know?" Cassie pouted.

"Because you've been alternating between crying and throwing up all week."

"Maybe it was the stress of your separation," she defended weakly.

"*Or,*" Maggie emphasized, "maybe it's the hormones."

I laughed, pulling Maggie to my side so I could wrap an arm around her as we watched Cassie try to blubber out an excuse.

"Plus the fact that Liam's been extra glued to your side lately—a seemingly impossible task, but then again, my brother's always been an overachiever."

Liam rolled his eyes, and before Cassie could stammer out a retort, he leaned down to kiss her cheek, instantly setting her at ease.

"It's okay, baby," he said. "We wanted to tell them anyway."

"Yes, but not *now!* We stole their thunder!"

"First of all, you did not steal my thunder, because *I* announced it," Maggie said. "Second, we're all a family. And I don't want there to be any more hiding things from family."

"In that case," I interjected, a little sheepishly. "I should let everyone know that I decided not to move to Michigan."

Everyone stared at me blankly.

"Yeah, babe." Maggie laughed. "I think we figured that since we just got engaged."

"No," I corrected, "I mean before that. I decided not to go."

"When?" Maggie blinked. "Why?"

"When we were skating together," I said to Liam. "I realized the same thing Maggie's saying—we're a family, and, well, families are supposed to stick together, aren't they?"

"Yeah." Maggie nodded, for once no witty comment to be made in response. "They are."

"Don't cry again, Cass." I stared at our friend whose behavior lately suddenly made sense with Maggie's revelation.

"I'm not. I'm not." She waved us away. "I'm just so happy that everything worked out."

"It was always going to," Liam said. "You think Brody's the type to ever give up on things?"

"I guess I wore down both of the Brynn siblings, huh? I infiltrated my way into your heavily guarded hearts, and now, here you are. Stuck with me, forever."

I grinned between them both, as Liam rolled his eyes and Maggie shook her head but gripped my hand all the more tightly.

"Let's get out of here," Liam said, nodding toward the exit. "I'm sure you guys will want to get back to *your own house*."

Maggie and I laughed at his subtle approach of evicting us from his house.

Fine by me. Maggie and I had a life to rebuild together.

"Don't be rude, Liam," Cassie said as they headed toward the exit.

"I'm not being rude, Cass," he said, and then his words were lost to me, my mind too focused on processing the present moment all around.

We walked out of the arena together into the sweet air of a spring evening. The buds were blooming with new beginnings and the city lights twinkled, as if Boston itself were welcoming me home. Or reminding me that it always had been.

Liam and Cassie a few steps ahead of us, their voices filling the air. Maggie's hand in mine, the weight of a promise we'd spent the rest of our lives fulfilling. I ran a finger along her ring finger, where I'd put the engagement ring on as soon as we got home.

This city. These people. This girl beside me who I had given my heart to so long ago.

This was all I'd ever need.

Six months later

I couldn't lie. I did love a good party.

And I wasn't ashamed to admit, I especially loved a party where I was the center of attention.

I loved the reception hall. (The Newbury Boston)

I loved the dress. (Silk A-line gown with a V-neck)

I loved the cake. (Earl Gray cake with vanilla buttercream frosting)

And most of all, I loved the man waiting for me at the end of the aisle. (Brody Andrew Callahan, goalie for the Harbor Wolves and keeper of my heart.)

Yes, Brody had decided to renew his contract. For now, at least. He said the idea of being a hot trophy husband wasn't exactly his cup of tea, and despite my pleas, he signed on for one more season.

He and Liam had already been making plans for future endeavors they might get into after Brody joins him in retirement. Namely, co-coaching a youth hockey team.

I was glad for them, not only because Brody was like a golden retriever

358

that needed to be occupied at all times to get his energy out, but also because I sort of liked the idea of any kids we might have in the future learning to play hockey with their dad and uncle.

Brody had already agreed, or rather, begged to be a stay-at-home dad. And while I agreed, I was also thinking about cutting my hours back at the office when that day came. We weren't in a rush, but the idea of a little family all our own was sounding better and better each day.

It had only been six months since that night at the rink when we officially committed to each other for the rest of our lives, but the time had flown faster than I would've hoped.

It was by the grace of God we planned this whole wedding in that amount of time, though it didn't hurt to name-drop Boston's two favorite Harbor Wolves stars when trying to book wedding-related things. I wasn't above playing a little dirty to get the job done.

Brody made fun of me, saying I was rushing the wedding because I was scared of getting cold feet and backing out.

In reality, I was just so excited to marry him I couldn't imagine waiting any longer.

If I didn't like parties centered around myself so much, I would've considered eloping, but somehow I didn't think it would be as special without our families around us.

Plus, my wedding dress deserved to be seen by the masses.

Lily was our flower girl—a role in which she went above and beyond.

Cassie cried the whole time, and it was hard to tell if it was pregnancy hormones or just simply *Cassie*. Probably both.

And Liam, who apparently had absorbed some of his wife's pregnancy hormones, definitely got emotional during his best man speech. I mean, if you count alternating between a few different facial expressions emotional. And considering it was Liam, I definitely did.

It might not have been visible to anyone who didn't know him super well, but I knew that the hint of emotion on his face was reserved for really special moments like this.

He had walked me down the aisle—a job I wouldn't trust with any other man on Earth. For my whole life, he'd looked out for me, taken care of me in a way most brothers never had to. But Liam had never backed down from the hard parts of life. And I wouldn't either. I learned that from him.

My mom cried through the whole ceremony, and for the first time, I admired how beautiful it was to feel everything so deeply. Wasn't that the point of being alive?

All of our friends were there—even Brody's group from back home. I smiled at Abbey, who was cozied up against one of their friends. She looked radiant and happy. Apparently, Brody had gifted her her dream condo in Michigan. It was easier than trying to sell it, he'd said, but really I knew it was just him being his generous self to an old friend.

The whole day passed in such a blur that I barely got to soak in the present moment with Brody—and that was what I wanted most of all, for the rest of our lives. To appreciate every moment together.

It wasn't until our first dance, when I had him in my arms, that it felt real. This man was mine. My husband. My soulmate. My best friend.

I knew with a bone-deep certainty that we could face whatever life threw our way, as long as we stuck together.

"See?" he said, twirling me around the dance floor while *I Won't Give Up* floated from the speakers. "It's not so scary, right?"

"No," I stared into his eyes, more certain of anything in the world that they were the ones I'd look into every night for the rest of my life, "it's not so scary at all."

Acknowledgements

I can't believe I get to write one of these a second time! I'm so excited to be able to share my gratitude with all of the people who helped me along this amazing, and at times agonizing, journey of writing a sequel.

To Megan Jayne, for creating the cover of my dreams once again. You always understand the assignment. Thank you from the bottom of my heart.

To ALT19 Creative, for creating another gorgeous interior that makes my little story feel like a real book when I flip through the pages.

To all the readers I connected with on Instagram and TikTok who shared the kindest words and made me feel like my story meant something to you. I am eternally grateful for every message I've received.

To Jade, for being the first person to read this story completely through and for encouraging me all the while. This story might have sat half-finished in a Google Doc forever if it weren't for you.

To Katie Weller, for making me feel like this story was worth seeing through to the end.

To Kayla, for all your creativity in helping bring these characters to life with your beautiful art—and for still being a friend all these years later.

To Sierra, for our endless writing days over the years and for always bringing the most beautiful balance to my chaotic energy. Love you!

(Also, to Sierra's mom, for giving my first book a shot by reading it—thank you so much! I hope you like this one, too!)

And lastly, I have to thank Wesley—my most important teammate in life, and the person who has always supported, encouraged, and done everything in his power to make sure I sit down and write, because that's what I've always told him I wanted to do. Without him, I might never have held a book with my name on the cover. I love you, Wesley.

About the Author

Emma O'Dea is a Rhode Island-based author with a wild imagination and a soft spot for fictional characters. When she's not working in a special education preschool, you can find her drinking obscene amounts of iced coffee, running by the ocean, or daydreaming cinematic montages in her head set to the soundtrack of Taylor Swift songs. Though she dreams of living in Ireland one day, for now she's content at home with her partner, Wesley, and their calico kitty, Nala.

Off the Ice is her debut novel.